SHOPPING LIST 2

ANOTHER HORROR ANTHOLOGY

A HellBound Books LLC
Publication

www.hellboundbookspublishing.com

Printed in the United States of America

SHOPPING LIST 2

ANOTHER HORROR ANTHOLOGY

A HORROR ANTHOLOGY COMPILED BY
HELLBOUND BOOKS PUBLISHING LLC

FOREWORD

Well, here we are again, Dear Reader – due to popular demand, our supposed 'one off' anthology has spawned a sequel! I suppose there's something to be said for offering a sly insight into the lives and dark minds of horror authors by means of their shopping lists – much like we all love to take a sneaky peak in the shopping cart ahead of us in the line and try imagining the secret life of its owner…

There are twenty-one superlative authors nestling within these beautifully designed covers, strange bedfellows indeed. We have seasoned writers and rookies, and a whole gamut in between, all with one thing in common – the love of a good horror tale well told.

We do hope that you enjoy Shopping List 2 – maybe even enough for us to consider a third volume…watch this space, as the man said.

We make no apologies – as is our wont – for the British syntax and spelling that creeps in to some of the tales, carried to our anthology in much the same way the Pilgrims brought Britain to the American colonies; to edit the 'u' out of *colour*, or stick a 'z' here and there would be sacrilege to the mother tongue – they don't call it *English* for nothing!

And so, Dear Reader, it is on we go, boldly marching towards what fates mat await us, blindly embracing the sheer horror, the insidiously dark and the nightmare-inducing blackness that this collective of twenty-one of the finest independent horror authors writing today have to offer. It is our wish that you enjoy, and our deepest desire that you experience a sleepless night or two because of this terrifying tome…

HellBound Books Publishing LLC
2017

Contents

SHOPPING LIST 2

ANOTHER HORROR ANTHOLOGY

M.R. Wallace's Shopping List

Carne asada
Key limes
Onions
Cilantro
Tortillas
Tomatillos
Avocados
Bottle of gin
Bread
Milk
Cheese
Coffee
Coffee creamer
Chips
Vegetable oil
Lunchmeat
Mustard

Hyena Country

M.R. Wallace

Sporadic gunfire rattled out of the trees. More fighters from one of the Fronts. Bas had long ago given up trying to remember which ones were which. Their unifying theme seemed to be a love for the words justice, resistance, liberation, and front. His primary interest in them was avoiding being shot. Looking north out of the city of Bol, if you could call it a city given its twelve thousand or so residents, he saw the figures moving back and forth through the foliage. He moved closer to the edge of town, taking cover behind the corner of a house facing his opponents. He pulled a monocular from its pouch on his belt and trained it on the greenery beyond the limits of Bol.

"Oh shit," he said morre to himself than anyone else. The fighters in the distance looked much like all the others, except for their primarily black clothing and headgear. One of the idiots was standing in front of the concealment provided by the tall grasses and plants of the marshland. In his hand he held a large black flag, which he waved boldly back and forth while his comrades continued to fire into the town. The severe black cloth emblazoned with white Arabic lettering and symbols declared the group to be none other than Boko Haram. Bas grimaced. They'd become a real nuisance in recent days, fucking up the normal flow of life around Lake Chad for everyone.

He returned the optic to its place and pulled his rifle around from his back on its tactical sling. The battered old Israeli warhorse was missing bluing in places, mostly corners and controls, but she still ran like clockwork. Peering down the sights, Bas leveled the rifle at the flag-waving insurgent. He doubted that this one would get to receive his virgins in paradise. He pulled the charging handle and flicked the safety onto semi auto.

Down the barrel, standing in the grasses at the edge of the greenery, the Haram color-waving idiot stepped aside. Bas Rademaker cursed and ducked around the corner. He scurried away from the house, crossing an alleyway and slamming himself against a wall. The thunderous roar of a rocket propelled grenade echoed through the streets as it flashed by where he'd been standing. It detonated loudly, a single beat against a titanic bass drum. Dirt rained down around the impact area. Then came the screams. Bas did his best to put them out of his mind. There were always screams, always someone in the kill zone. It didn't seem to matter that these guys couldn't shoot for shit, they always managed to do some damage.

Returning cautiously to his previous post, the tall man trained his Galil back across the terrain to the group of fighters. They were moving now, leaving the concealment of the marshland and approaching the outskirts of Bol. His heart began beating faster. Facing Boko Haram in close quarters would suck. Hard. They reached halfway across the desolate expanse when Bas opened fire. The rifle bucked against his shoulder, producing a loud bark that echoed down the street. Blood spurted from the chest of one of the fighters, sending him tumbling into the dirt as the 7.62 NATO round tore through him. As if a switch had been flipped, everything else went fuzzy around Bas and his rifle. The whole world had shrunk down to encompass him, his Galil, and the Boko insurgents running toward town.

The cracks and pops of return fire reached his ears. It was mostly Kalashnikovs of one type or another. Bas lined up a second shot and squeezed the trigger again. He tagged another of the animals, this one just a glancing blow to the shoulder. He spat in the dirt and aimed for him again. This round hit lower in the torso, but put the fighter onto his face in the sand. Bas Rademaker inhaled, exhaled, fired again. Without conscious reaction he began squeezing the trigger as soon as the sight picture looked right. His heart thudded ominously in his ears; his breathing was fast but deep. Nearby he heard other weapons roar to life. His comrades had joined up with him. Glancing right, he saw Diambu heft his RPK up to his shoulder and depress the trigger.

The machinegun, a longer variant of the AK platform, belched fire out one end and brass out the other as it spat rounds into the oncoming force. Little fountains of dirt spurted up from the ground where the bullets had missed, splashes of wet dark red bloomed where they had not. Following a short burst of fire, the lumbering Nigerian ducked back behind the wall as return fire stitched a path up the road toward him.

Bas leaned out again and fired into the group, now a few members lighter. Heads wrapped in black cloth bobbed around as they ran. Their weapons glinted in the sunlight of late afternoon in Chad. Bas used his scarf to wipe the sweat from his face before reaching up to slick back his sun bleached blond hair. His blue eyes trained on another fighter as he lifted his Galil to his shoulder again and squeezed. Time stretched out, a minute seemingly becoming an hour as he and several of the other city guards repelled the invaders. Bas dropped an empty magazine and slammed a fresh one home. He chambered the first round and fired three quick shots into the last Boko Haram agent he saw. The city went quiet. Their job was almost done.

After the group of mercenaries had gathered together, they dragged Boko Haram bodies out of the streets and across the plain to a place outside the city, but still far from the marsh. Here they piled the bodies, preparing to burn them. Diambu slung his machinegun behind his back and went to retrieve the gas cans. He had almost returned to the base of the corpse stack when the wind kicked up, half blinding them all with sand.

"Well," Diambu announced, "looks like we will burn these scum tomorrow. No need to have a fire out here if it can get away from us. Finish out your shifts and return to your homes, gentlemen. There's no telling what tomorrow will bring." With that, the dark-skinned man trundled off into the town. Bas checked his watch. His shift was already over. He gave his farewells to the others and made his way to the little condo he called home near Bol's center. He climbed the stairs to his second-floor flat and set his equipment down by the door, which he locked with a pair of deadbolts.

Bas slumped onto his bed, kicking his boots off after doing so. His back and shoulders ached as much from the tension of battle as from the weight of his armor vest. He smelled of sweat and gunpowder. But most of all, Bas was tired. His focus eroded, the big Afrikaner man drifting off to the type of sleep one can only get following a firefight. Just before his eyes closed for the night, he heard the distant barking laugh of hyenas.

Pesky mongrels, Bas thought. The pile of Boko Haram men would be short a few limbs by the time they got to it in the morning.

Bas Rademaker slept less soundly than he would have liked, waking early in the morning. The sun was nothing more than a lightened smear of sky in the east. He rubbed his face in front of the grimy bathroom mirror, turning on the cold water to help himself wake up. He drenched his head, sucking in breath before standing again and grabbing a towel.

"Fok," he sighed. Cursing in his mother tongue always made him feel better, even if only slightly. He turned on the shower, an anemic fountain of tepid water arcing into the floor drain as though it couldn't be bothered to act like a proper faucet. Stripping out of his sweaty, dirty clothes from last night, Bas stepped into the grimy tile stall and washed himself quickly. He finished and toweled off, rooting through his rickety dresser for the day's clothing. Not that there was much variety. Antimicrobial socks, moisture wicking t-shirt, and rugged cargo pants. These items were invariably drab colors that blended decently with the town and its surroundings. Today's clothes were gray and tan. Finished off with his daily rig—rifle, pistol, shemagh, and steel-toed boots—he placed his sunglasses on his face and exited his flat.

The streets were in their usual dusty, heat-blasted and sun-dried condition. Bas strode toward the edge of town. His beat up Galil hung across his chest today, ready for immediate deployment should more trouble arise. He was almost positive it would. Boko Haram were a pestilent bunch of *hondenaaiers* and they'd be back for more. Rademaker walked out to where the bodies still sat, a squatting mass of hot, sickly dead flesh buzzing with flies. He walked around it. On the side opposite the city, he found exactly what he'd expected.

The pile had shifted, body parts being pulled toward the tall foliage of the marsh. Those damned hyenas. The Afrikaner mercenary pondered a moment. He'd really only heard one hyena last night, right before he'd fallen asleep. He hadn't thought about it at the time, but now he was. Hyenas were pack scavengers. They rarely traveled alone. So hearing only one was a bit odd.

More than that, the bodies all seemed to be intact, as much as they possibly could be following a firefight. No missing limbs to be found later, stripped to the bones on the lakeshore. There was, however, a trail of disturbed sand leading off toward the glade. That was strange, Bas thought. It wasn't like hyenas to haul away a whole corpse to eat, much less two as the trail indicated. The hot, dry wind blew through the city from the south. Pulling his shemagh up over his mouth and nose, Bas Rademaker walked back to the streets of Bol. Hot and dry. They probably wouldn't dispose of these fuckers tonight either. He grimaced. One or more of the bodies would likely burst by tomorrow, making their job that much more hellish. He nodded to Diambu, standing quietly with his big RPK hanging in front of him by its sling. He had both hands clasped, resting atop the machinegun.

"Just another long day, my friend." The bulky Nigerian man spat into the dirt at his feet and muttered something under his breath. Without knowing the language, Bas still understood the sentiment. It was the same one he had, that the daily grind sucked the life out of you. He made a short patrol around the block, more to kill boredom than anything else. His long, sunbaked fingers drummed incessantly against the receiver of his rifle, tapping out the drumbeat of an old Metallica song. Bas found himself wishing his mp3 player hadn't gone tits up last week. He returned to his original post and waited, watching the swamplands for more movement.

The hours passed, dragging slowly. Bas found himself half wishing that the boys in black would pop back up out of the bushes, waving their stupid flag and firing like amateurs. He was more than a little disappointed when it didn't happen. The sun was beginning to dip into the western horizon, and with it the wind began to die. Diambu, being the shift supervisor, told his men when to leave. He asked for a volunteer to help him light the body pile. Having nothing better to do, Bas raised his hand. His supervisor nodded and then dismissed the others. The pair of men lugged the fuel cans out to the body pile. Bas spat, trying to get the taste in the air out of his mouth. He set the cans down and pulled his shemagh up over his nose. He opened the first can and hoisted it up; dousing the stack of corpses with a healthy dose of gasoline while Diambu did the same on the opposite side.

Bas emptied the second can and took a step back. He opened his magazine pouches, each carrying three of the large mags for his rifle. In the right-hand pouch, he found what he was looking for. He swapped the magazine for the one that had been resting in his rifle, pulling back on the charging handle to eject the chambered round which he pressed back into the old magazine. The newly readied bullet had the distinct orange tip of a tracer. They burned good and bright, allowing one to follow their path in the dark. They were also handy for lighting piles of insurgents who had been sent off to Allah. He took the safety off and shouldered his Galil.

Now standing next to Bas, Diambu spat on the jumble of corpses and muttered something in his native tongue. Something undoubtedly foul. Rademaker did the same, spitting on the forehead of the nearest Haram fighter. He was fairly certain it had been the idiot waving a flag just before the RPG had been fired. "Lap naai," he swore. His finger squeezed the trigger. The Israeli rifle barked as it too spat on the bodies. The tracer slammed into the corpses, igniting the fumes wafting off of them and setting the whole pile alight. Bas was immediately washed in the heat of the pyre as it sent a plume of smoke soaring into the quickly darkening sky. Diambu patted him on the shoulder and turned to leave.

The night erupted around them as rifles chattered across the plain. There was a deafening roar. Bas knew that sound well enough. Two rocket-propelled grenades blew the body pile apart, knocking the Afrikaner into the dirt. The world was twisting insanely around him as Bas fought his way up to one knee. Flashes of light blossomed before his eyes, obscuring the very real muzzle flashes of his opponents. He stumbled away from the fire, lurching toward the nearest house where he could put something between himself and the latest batch of fighters. He pressed his back to the wall and readied his rifle. The starbursts still filled his vision, a symptom that shaking his head did nothing to clear. His left ear felt wet. Bas touched the spot, his fingers coming away sticky. "Fok," he cursed.

The tall Afrikaner pulled a plastic case from a pocket, popped it open, and stuck one earplug in, protecting the injured ear from further harm. It stung, and there was probably dirt trapped in his ear. The spots began to fade, becoming less brilliant and less frequent. Bas shouldered his Galil and stepped away from the corner. Figures were beginning to appear through the thin light of the flames, tossed across a wide area following the RPG bombardment. He centered his sights on the first one to appear and jerked the trigger. The shot clipped the insurgent's shoulder, knocking him off balance. He careened into a burning corpse and tumbled over it. Bas' second shot kept him there. Several more appeared, firing their AKs blindly into the city. He lined up the sights and squeezed. A dark spurt of blood fountained out of one man's chest. He dropped his rifle and stumbled backward, collapsing into the sand and jerking spasmodically.

A long burst of automatic fire peppered the wall to his right and Bas ducked behind the wall again. Seeing clearly, he spotted Diambu. The bulky Nigerian's body was slumped against a wall, his chest glistening wetly in the dim firelight. He seethed, feeling his pulse thud like a drum in his good ear. Footsteps shuffling through the sand announced the arrival of Bas' third adversary. He pulled his rifle sling up over his head and grabbed the weapon in a tight two-handed grip, moving his firing hand to the top of the butt stock. The footsteps were right on top of him. Bas Rademaker stepped around the corner with murder in his eyes, swinging the rifle's butt in an arc that collided with the terrorist's skull. Momentum kept him moving forward, smashing into the Afrikaner and sending them both sliding into the dust. Bas felt his rifle ripped from his hands at the same time the insurgent's AK jabbed him painfully in the groin. The two men tumbled before coming to a rest, separated by six feet or so.

The Afrikaner was up first, showering sand as he jumped onto the Boko Haram soldier still face down on the ground. He seized the fighter by his shoulders. He pulled the insurgent's head off the ground, a skull swathed in black so as to make him faceless. Bas slammed him back into the dirt, a hollow thump sounding below him as he repeated the motion. He dropped the limp body and searched for his rifle. At the edge of the grasslands, a hyena barked. Bas found his Galil, half buried in dirt close to the wall. He scrambled toward it, trying to rise and being thwarted by his damaged eardrum. The hyena laughed again, much closer.

Bas paused for a moment, listening for the creature again. It was unusual for hyenas to approach an active conflict, especially alone. They were scavengers. They generally showed up long after the carnage to pick bones and run off with severed limbs. Several other members of the mercenary force had arrived to clean up the remaining Boko Haram fighters. Their rifles fired sporadically, eliminating insurgents wherever they cropped up. Bas grabbed his Galil in one hand. Motion at the edge of his vision flickered before he was slammed to the ground by something striking his back. Rolling onto his back, Bas saw one last Haram fighter standing over him. The black clad man held a machete in his hands. He lifted the blade high overhead. Rademaker ground his teeth and waited for the strike.

A blur of motion crossed his vision, taking the insurgent with it down the alleyway. A surprised yelp was cut off, turning into a gurgling shriek. The man went quiet. Bas sat up, feeling the ballistic plate in the back of his vest shift. The two pieces of the broken ceramic composite ground against each other with each movement. The hyena barked again, right next to him from the sound of it. Bas almost jumped out of his skin. The mangy creature was not in fact standing near him. He pulled the knife out of his boot, a British commando knife with a double-edged blade. He edged toward the mouth of the alley. He ran one hand through his blonde hair, slicking it back with sweat. Bas' foot snagged. Peering down in the darkness he could barely make out the black swathed figure of his opponent. He grabbed one shoulder roughly and turned the man over.

Stringy red ruin met Bas as the corpse rolled onto its back. The face was stripped clean, the ribs pulled apart and organs missing. His nose filled with the reek of it, forcing Bas to double over and disgorge his stomach contents. The vomit splashed into the open body cavity, immediately causing a second purge as the stench intensified. Darkness surged out of the alley, a physical force that blasted Bas backwards onto his ass. There was a splash of warmth against his face before the Afrikaner could sit himself up. His tailbone ached in protest, but Bas pulled himself to his feet and searched around him. Nothing. He wiped his face, taking care to keep the mess out of his eyes. His hand came away warm and sticky. Glistening fluid slicked his palm, with darker ribbons of blood swirled throughout. Bas felt his gorge rising again and quickly wiped his hand across his pant leg. The liquid smeared, leaving a slimy trail down his thigh. It reminded him of snot, or some other mucus type fluid. He gagged and tried to put it out of his mind. He turned his head left and right, surveying the aftermath of the attack.

The street was empty, quiet except for the crackling of flames as they spread from the bodies to dry grass and woven baskets. An alarm sounded, calling the fire department to action. Bas Rademaker did his part, stamping out little blazes with his boots, drowning the larger ones with sand.

Finally, two and a half hours later, the last of the fires had been snuffed. Bas found himself staring at the burnt wreckage of their corpse pile, limbs and torsos alike scattered across the area. There was also a decent amount of what he could only describe as smeared gore. He spat in the dirt, trying to rid his tongue of the foul taste from earlier. His eyes trailed over the carnage before coming to rest on a body slumped up against a wall. Bas ran to where his friend lay dead. He checked for a pulse and breathing, but he could find nothing. Diambu was gone. The tall man straightened his friend and superior out, crossing his arms in a dignified pose and closing his eyes. He laughed to himself. It was so cliché, so well worn an image that he'd never considered how it would feel to actually perform the actions. It felt numb, mostly. He wasn't sure if that was because of the adrenaline slowly melting away, but he didn't really feel like examining the feeling further.

Bas found a sheet nearby and pulled it down, draping it over his confidant's corpse and tucking its edges underneath him. He fetched the man's machinegun and set it atop the body. He turned around to look at the chaos surrounding him. Checking his watch, Bas promptly decided it was time to leave. He wasn't being paid for this. He wasn't even on the clock. His volunteering for the task had brought nothing but trouble. It was time for a drink, a shower, and a good long stretch of bedtime. Rademaker snatched his rifle out of the dirt and stalked off toward his flat. He stopped and peered through the dark, out into the tall grasses of the marsh. A pair of yellow eyes flickered in the darkness. They bobbed in the light of the fires as the hyena cackled again. Bas spat and turned away, making for his shower and refrigerator full of hard Russian beer.

Bas sat in a chair, his short-cropped hair still dripping from the shower. His right hand was filled with a large brown bottle, its red label covered in Cyrillic lettering. He listened to the radio spit static and snippets of music. Bas chewed the inside of his lip and stared at the dusty Israeli rifle leaning against the wall. He grimaced. At least he didn't have another shift tonight. He couldn't fathom going to work with anyone other than Diambu running the shift. The gargantuan bastard had always smiled, no matter the monotony, and rested his hands on that RPK of his. Bas took another swig of the stout Russian ale and cursed under his breath. He stood and adjusted the towel around his waist. It was a good idea to prepare himself for tomorrow night's shift.

He opened the top drawer of his dresser. Pushing aside his myriad socks and moisture wicking underwear, he grabbed the big pistol hidden there and checked it over. The safety was on and a round was in the chamber. The pistol was all steel, not one of the newer polymer designs. Not that he disliked the new pistols; he just appreciated the heft of a steel pistol. He dropped the magazine and inspected it. The holes in the side showed that it was filled to capacity with the nasty .45 caliber hollow points he preferred for fighting in closer quarters. He brought the pistol back to his bed, sliding it under the pillow. Bas clipped the magazine pouches onto his vest. The rear plate made a grinding sound.

"Fok," Bas swore under his breath. He pulled apart the Velcro fastening at the back of his vest and fished out the plate. It came out in two pieces. A pair of roughly matching jagged edges had split the plate from corner to corner. Bas dropped the halves and they smacked loudly on the floor. His downstairs neighbor rapped loudly under his feet with a broom or something similar. It could've been her cane. Slicking his hair back, Bas walked to his closet and reached up above to the high shelf. He grabbed his spare plate, the only one he had at the moment, and returned to place it in his vest. Finishing up, he stifled a yawn and looked at his bed. He would definitely need sleep before tonight's shift. Bas Rademaker climbed into bed still naked and closed his eyes.

Bas' dreams were troubling. He was back in the alley, knife in hand. His ears hurt as he was blasted with a peal of mad cackling from somewhere in the shadows ahead of him. He shuddered. A shape lumbered out of the darkness. Stepping into the firelight, he saw the faceless visage of the last Boko Haram fighter as it stumbled out into the street. The chest cavity gaped open, carved out and displaying the ribs and spine across his back. The hyena, wherever it was, yipped and barked. Bas dropped his knife as a burning yellow pair of eyes flickered in the blackness above and behind the shambling corpse. It swiped the insurgent out of the way and crouched, its blunt, gore-stained muzzle jutting into the firelight.

Bas jerked awake, lying in his bed, drenched in frigid sweat. He smelled the creature's putrid breath. He sat upright, fearfully glancing around the room. Empty except for himself. He smelled it again, the pungent odor of decaying meat. It took Bas a moment to realize that it was his neighbor's cooking he smelled. He sniffed. The old hag was fond of fermented dishes. It had helped him get the apartment pretty cheaply, though in the three months since he wasn't entirely certain it had been worth it. The sun outside was drooping toward the western horizon. Bas dressed himself in a fresh set of clothing and pulled on his gear. Lastly, he grabbed the Sig Sauer out from under his pillow and tucked it into its holster. He exited his flat, descended the stairs, and strode across the street to the nearest restaurant. The aroma of this food was far more pleasant than his neighbor's. He ordered a plate and sat at an empty table.

Bas ate slowly, as much savoring the food as trying to put off his shift for just a while longer. He finished the last of the goat meat and wiped his face. Paying his bill, the tall Afrikaner left the café and meandered toward his post. A pillar of smoke announced that the day shift had gathered the bodies and set them alight again. Good, Bas thought. Maybe this time they could be left to burn without any further disturbances. Surely, the mercenary team had to have made a sizable dent in Haram's local forces. Bas Rademaker nodded to the man he was replacing, a short man of Asian descent. He nodded back and left, walking in the opposite direction of Bas' rental. He slung his M4 type rifle around his back and pulled his hat lower on his head as he went.

Bas took up his position, checking his Galil over and remarking on the shiny new areas where the coating had been gouged by the rocks and tumbling resulting from last night's fighting. He watched the sky, seeing considerably more clouds overhead than he could recall having ever seen here before. His shift partner showed up soon after, another dark black man like Diambu. Though he wasn't nearly as tall.

"I'm Bas," the Afrikaner said, extending a hand. His partner smiled widely, his bright white teeth a brilliant contrast to his smooth, almost coal colored skin. He shook Bas' hand briskly.

"Raphael," he replied. "It's nice to meet you. It's sad about Diambu, though." His eyes darkened, an expression that Bas was positive he also wore. He looked the shorter man up and down, assessing his posture as well as his equipment. Raphael carried one of the modern variants of the AK, polymer furniture replacing the traditional wood. Sitting in a holster across his chest was a pistol, H&K by the look of it. He stood straight and tall, his bearing that of a professional. Complimenting the rest of his weapons, a short-handled tomahawk hung from his belt. He nodded westward. "Almost time for the shit to hit the fan again."

Bas watched the orange circle dip below the horizon, leaving behind a smear of reds and purples across the clouds in the growing twilight. He laughed mirthlessly. "Let's hope not. I've had enough excitement for the past couple of nights." They both nodded and watched the marshlands. It was the only place where one could be concealed from sight near the city of Bol. Bas tensed the muscles of his back, feeling soreness there from his encounter the night before. He stretched his neck back and forth, trying to loosen the knots. As the last traces of light washed away from the night sky, a Hyena once again barked in the shadows far away. Bas shuddered.

Across the narrow street, Raphael did the same. "It's not natural, you know."

"Hmm?" Bas turned caught off guard by the unexpected statement from his new partner.

"That hyena, wandering the marshes all alone." The dark-skinned man gestured vaguely toward the shores of Lake Chad. "It's not a natural thing. Hyenas are pack animals. They scavenge in groups, carrying away carcasses together to eat later, things like that. This one doesn't have a pack. Frankly," Raphael's shoulders rose and fell as though he were suppressing a shudder, "it gives me the creeps."

Bas chuckled and asked, "Why is that?"

"Some story my mother used to tell my brother and me." He smiled faintly, looking off into the marshlands." One of those old 'be good or else' type stories, you know? Anyway, she told about this creature. The *bultungin*. Maybe it had once been a man, maybe not. But it was usually a hyena. It wandered the night, barking and cackling, searching for carcasses to eat. Most of the time, it was a hyena like any other, but it could transform into a terrible beast. The thing was huge, a horrific mix of both man and hyena. It would stalk villages for fresh prey, taking children who were out after dark, that sort of thing." He gave Bas a conspiratorial look.

"Anyway," he continued, "that story always scared the shit out of me as a child. I got older and never really thought about it. Then one night I was out with my friends, just wandering the streets, making a nuisance of ourselves. You know, kid stuff. Then I heard it. That damned cackling laughter. I waited to hear more of them join in, but there was just the one. It barked and yipped and made all sorts of noise. I freaked out and went home right away. I never left the house after dark until I'd finished growing up and moved away. I don't know," Raphael said, "being back around the lake just brings it all right back to the forefront for me." He shivered again.

Bas nodded. In the darkness, the hyena barked again. Its call sounded as though it were mocking the man for his story. The hair on the back of his neck prickled, causing Bas to try to smooth it with a hand. He wouldn't say it, but he was feeling more than a little wigged out by Raphael's story, especially considering the dream he'd had today. He was beginning to think that the blazing Chadian sun wouldn't be such a problem for him. He could get switched to day shift pretty easily. The chill crept down Bas' arms and chest. He shook his head. Was he really considering taking the day shift just because of a dream and an old wives' tale?

Of course not.

There were also the things he'd seen. Surely something monstrous had torn apart the insurgent who had almost killed him. Nothing else could have emptied that body of its organs so quickly. Dread washed over Bas as he recalled his dream. Could that thing have been what had bowled him over in the alley? And if so, why? Why would it run away from him instead of mauling him? If it was anything like the beast in his dreams, it could've easily overtaken him and killed him. Bas shook his head. It was ridiculous, even considering such an idea. There was no hyena monster stalking the area and murdering people. Doing his best to fight back the dread he felt, the Afrikaner focused instead on the empty swath of desert between Bol and the thick growths of greenery bordering the shore of Lake Chad. He stuck his finger gently into his left ear. It ached. He'd have to go to the clinic after work tonight and see if there was anything they could do. Or at least a few large aspirin they could give him.

Lightning flickered in the clouds overhead, answered shortly by a low rumble. Bas grimaced. He hadn't been expecting rain, nor had he been told to expect it. He looked over to his partner.

"Is this what you meant by the shit hitting the fan?"

Raphael laughed. "This is definitely not what I was thinking."

Bas felt the first drop hit his face, spattering against his upper lip. The night had just gotten more interesting. A brilliant bolt of white struck near the lake, carving a purple and green swath through his vision. He blinked his eyes rapidly. This would be fun. A second bolt struck in town and Bas watched the lights die.

"Kak," Bas spat. Across the way, Raphael chuckled.

"You've got that right, friend."

The Afrikaner was surprised. His native tongue, the Dutch-derived Afrikaans, wasn't terribly common outside of South Africa. He looked at his partner.

"I spent a few years in Johannesburg as a child," Raphael replied. "In the typical way of children, I learned all the vulgar words first." He smiled.

Bas smirked. "Good to know." The thunder rumbled louder, the rain picking up to a steady pour. It was warm enough to keep from being too chilly, but the cool water remained uncomfortable as it slowly soaked into his vest and clothing. He shook water off of his rifle, trying to keep it from getting too wet and slippery.

Nearby, the hyena barked. Bas twitched, not expecting the beast to still be around with the storm going. Raphael cursed under his breath. "Scary stupid shit!" He yelled into the darkness.

Bas laughed. It helped to take the edge off. The thing was really beginning to grate on his nerves. Another lightning flash threw the area into stark contrast for a split second, leaving Bas blinking his eyes. The impression stuck in his vision mirrored the landscape beyond the city's limits. It was the same stretch of ground he'd been staring at for weeks. In the violet and neon green images burned into his vision, though, there was something else out there. He blinked his eyes rapidly, causing the colors to flicker before his face.

Whatever was out there looked tall and thin. It could've been a stand of reeds or something similar, but it was too far away from the marsh. And it looked like an animal. The sky was split by another bolt. The thing was gone. Bas rubbed his eyes. Christ, this job was getting to him. The roar of the thunder, directly over his head, died away. There was a second rumble, this one much quieter. Much closer. Hot, humid air blew down his neck. It smelled of rotten meat. Bas froze, his every instinct screaming to him that if he moved he would die. Raphael made a strangled sound. Unlike Bas, the Nigerian moved quickly. He flicked the safety lever down on his rifle as he brought it to his shoulder. A single shot burst from the muzzle with a flash of flame, smacking wetly into whatever was behind Bas.

Air whipped at his back as Bas saw Raphael vanish in a blur of movement. There was a strangled cry followed by viscous tearing and snapping. Bas shook himself free of his fear induced stupor and thumbed the safety lever on his rifle. He turned on the flashlight mounted on its hand guard and rushed toward the black alley. The searing white beam cut through the shadows as he approached. Bas heard the rumbling again. A pair of bright green orbs hovered in the darkness ahead, just beyond the circle of his tactical light. His blood turned to ice. The eyes, for that was what they had to be, towered over him by at least half a meter. Bas hoisted the muzzle of his Galil.

The light swept up, taking in the shredded corpse of Raphael, his tattered face still bearing the silent scream of his death. The flesh was ripped wide open, exposing portions of the skull in a gruesome display of savagery. The ribcage was rent open and ropy innards were spilling out onto the sand. Bas fought down the urge to retch and swung the light up toward the burning green eyes. The circle of illumination poured over a set of long, clawed appendages. They sat knuckles down in the sand as though they belonged to a gorilla, though they were bone thin and covered in rough patches of light fur. The hind legs were the same. The light crept higher, exposing a distended belly topped with wide, bony and hunched shoulders. A slobbering mouth dipped into the illuminated circle, dripping crimson gore onto the dust below it. The snout was short and broad. The eyes came into view, large and hateful. They burned into Bas like a pair of branding irons. The face was round, spotted fur covered the entire surface except for the darker hair of the snout. The ears were rounded, perked forward to catch the slightest change in Bas' stance. The large nose sniffed loudly at the air and the creature's chest rumbled deeply. It pulled a severed arm out of its maw, a very humanlike gesture. The beast barked, a demonic cackle that hurt Bas' head with its earsplitting volume.

The Afrikaner mercenary clenched his jaw, his knees going shaky, and squeezed the trigger of his Galil. The rifle jumped against his shoulder, the brilliant muzzle flash dazzling him as his finger contracted again. Bas fired two more shots, crimson holes blossoming in the monster's chest and gut, before its claw flashed out and knocked the rifle away. Bas recoiled, clutching his left arm close to his body. Warm, sticky fluid coated his hand. White-hot pain drowned his senses. He was dully aware of being struck again, slamming against the wall and crumpling into the dirt. His vision began to clear.

Bas wished it hadn't. The monster's head darted down. There was a gruesome crunch and Bas' whole leg burst into scarlet waves of agony. It was eating him. For a panicked moment, the tall man couldn't sort his thoughts. He gagged as a fresh surge of pain gripped him. His eyes blurred with stinging tears and Bas muttered a silent plea for it to end. He twisted, trying desperately to free himself of the beast. Something solid jabbed his right hip. He froze.

There was a sickening pop and Bas felt himself fall free of the monster's grasp. He rocked onto his other side and drew his Sig from its holster with trembling hands. He disengaged the safety and gripped the pistol hard. The sights lined up over the thing's snout and he squeezed. Training was forgotten as Bas hammered the beast with round after round. Blood spattered against him with every shot, crusting his face and hands in grime and gore. Eight shots rang out; Bas continued to pull the trigger. It took him a moment to realize the pistol was empty. He cursed himself and removed the empty magazine. Bas fumbled a fresh one from his vest and slid it into place. He shoved it home and racked the slide, feeding the first round into the chamber. This magazine he emptied as well.

The monster didn't move. It slumped over him as hot, black blood pumped onto the sand from a dozen or more holes. Bas swooned, his vision darkening around the edges as though he were looking up from the bottom of a well. He shivered. Christ, when had it gotten so cold? The heavy, laborious breathing of the beast rattled to a halt. Bas spat at it weakly, managing only to wet his chin with the frothy saliva. He laid his head back. Perhaps, he thought, it was time for a nap. Bas Rademaker closed his eyes.

***

His blue eyes opened slowly. Bas rubbed one hand through his short blond hair and looked up. The night was dark, humid with an approaching storm. He sat up in his chair. Gazing out over the roof, he stared toward the marshlands that bordered Lake Chad. A hyena cackled in the reeds. Bas tensed, the muscles in his neck and shoulders coiling almost until they hurt. Several others joined in with the first, a chorus of mad laughter that drifted over the plain and echoed off the walls. Bas exhaled and rested his hand atop his weapon. Leaned up against the parapet, Diambu's battered RPK sat with a full box of ammunition clipped to its underside. The belt ran from the mouth of the box up into the machinegun's feed. The pale Afrikaner sat down again and looked down at his leg. A prosthetic limb extended from just below his knee, terminating in a booted metal foot. The stump ached with the extra moisture, the electrical charge that was saturating the atmosphere around him.

Bas lifted a cigarette to his mouth, joining it with the lighter clutched in his right hand. A set of jagged scars twisted over his left arm, terminating at his hand. He flicked the flint on the lighter and set the cigarette tip to glowing. He shut the lid of the lighter, extinguishing it, and took a long drag on his smoke. He flexed the fingers of his left hand. He watched as the little finger curled obediently. The other three hardly budged. They hurt too, throbbing with every beat of his heart as the clouds drew closer. They weren't much good for manual tasks anymore, but at least he could hold a cigarette between them. Bas listened to the thunder as it answered the flickers of lightning over the lake. The hyenas scattered, fleeing the rumbling storm as it crawled toward the outskirts of Bol. A last hyena barked, a shrill titter that turned his veins arctic instantly.

His coworkers had told Bas that when they found him next to poor Raphael's remains, a hyena had died on top of him, riddled with bullet holes. He questioned them further, but the thing had apparently been just a plain old hyena. Bas dismissed them, not daring to speak the words that he'd been thinking. They would have thought he was crazy. He had taken to the night shift again after he'd recovered, the cool night air being easier on him and his injuries than the scorching sun. He had felt safe, knowing the beast was gone. Almost a year had passed since the attack. Work had been slow, but Bas didn't mind. He'd had enough of insurgents and explosions, midnight raids in the name of their god. A few troublemakers here and there still attacked the town, but nothing like the Boko Haram fighters.

Bas listened intently. The storm rumbled, menacing as it blew toward town. He felt the first few raindrops hit his face. The hyena cackled again, much louder, much closer. Bas lifted the RPK and settled its strap over his shoulder. He pulled the charging handle and released it, hearing the bolt slam home. The pale blond mercenary stepped up onto the parapet. He fought down the chill that raced along his spine. A long, thin shape darted across the plain. Bas shouldered the big machinegun, turning off the safety.

"Fok jou, lap naai," he breathed. His finger touched the trigger, dragging it smoothly to the rear. Something crunched on the roof behind him. Bas froze. The stench of rotten meat wafted over him. He inhaled, lowering the RPK to his hip. He planted his prosthetic foot and twisted, swinging the machinegun around to bear on his closest foe. White light bloomed in his face, the strike blinding him as a long, clawed arm knocked him from the roof. Bas felt the air rush past him. He landed on the street with a crunch.

On the rooftop, the bultungin barked, its hideous laughter drowning out the thunder.

Isobel Blackthorn's
Shopping List

Creamy berry flavoured yogurt - size large. I like to eat it straight from the tub. Comforting, no fuss way of eating breakfast or lunch. For when the creative flow won't let me leave my desk.

Garlic - fresh and juicy and tons of it. Who cares about bad breath.! I take no chances...!!!

Dark chocolate - for when I'm feeling unnerved by what has just flowed from my pen.

Smoked salmon - as much as I can afford. Tasmanian is best.

Steak - to pan fry rare with loads of cracked pepper, French mustard and heaps of garlic. I like to lick the plate.

Paper napkins for steak juice dribbles on my chin

Capers - for a sharp and unusual tingle on the palate. Not consumed with chocolate.

Brussels sprouts - by the truck load. They are my candy.

Red wine - for mellow evenings and rude health.

Ignominy

Isobel Blackthorn

I knew visiting the Lang Cove remand centre would be something I'd have to endure, but after that first visit I never wanted to go back there again. The place was grimy from floor to ceiling and the ungrateful swine wouldn't even look me in the eye. Some brother he's turned out to be. Had guilt written all over him. Reckons he's found a top-notch lawyer who specialises in his sort of cases. So who will pay for that, I wonder? I knew he'd done it. I knew because I was the one down on my hands and knees mopping up the mess. I'd never suffered ignominy quite like it, not in all my living days. The recollection put me in the worst of moods. I better not get called as a witness if he thinks for one moment I'll lie on his behalf. Commit the crime, do the time, that's what I decided as I regarded his knavish face.

I've always cleaned up after him. Right from when we were kids. Started with the time he vomited up our mother's pea and ham soup, all down him it went and all over the coffee table, oozing rivulets onto the deep pile of the carpet. I'll never forget mopping up that sickly mess. The putrid green of it, the dots of red meat, the slime that lodged in the corrugations of the old grey dishrag I used. The acrid smell that I couldn't seem to get off my hands. And Kevin just sat there, the goon, coated in his muck, a picture of innocence. It was down to me to change his clothes. Wash him down. Make him brush his teeth.

He was four at the time but I knew he'd done it on purpose. I would have been ten by then and I'd been assigned the household chores while our mother went to work or slept. She had a job at Kitties in the city and worked four nights a week. I had no idea what a men's club was and she never said. Off she'd go all dolled up with her high heels stuffed in her handbag, and she'd come back the next morning looking haggard and take herself to bed. Took me another year or two to cotton on to her craft.

All I knew back then was we had to tiptoe through the long days of childhood, for to wake our mother was to invite the wrath of Thor.

Those were the years after our father walked out with our mother's sister, Aunty Flo. Last we heard of the happy couple was an airmail letter sent from New Zealand announcing the birth of their twins. It might have been addressed to 'the discarded,' because that is how it felt when our mother read the words aloud. She tore the letter into four and threw it in the bin. It was left to me to explain to Kevin that his daddy was never coming back. That he'd been replaced, not by one baby, by two. Kevin was never the same after that.

The remand centre visit had consumed the best part of my day. Back at the train station, I tugged on my gloves and inched a step closer to the platform edge to let a woman with a pram pass behind. I had to resist an urge to thrust my gloved hands in my pockets. I felt sure all eyes were concentrated on the black ink stains on each of my fingertips, although my gloves were hardly see-through. Finger printed! I blamed Kevin for that too. I'd thought to wash off the ink in the station's lavatory but I didn't get further than the entrance smell.

I cast a sly eye at the others on the platform. All the women appeared scruffy I succumbed to a moment of disdain. I'm a sensible dresser. There's an outfit for every occasion. I suppose our mother taught me that. I thought when I'd left for the visit that a tweed skirt suit and knitted cardigan would be appropriate attire. That the officers would take one look at me and decide I was a good sort. They didn't. They treated me much the same as they did everyone else. With disdain. I was photographed and body scanned as well. I had to leave all my belongings in a locker. I was only allowed to take in loose change for the vending machine so that dear younger brother of mine could buy himself a snack. By the time I was seated facing the shrivelled excuse of a human I felt like going to the vending machine myself and buying a can of Coke to shake and spray all over him pretending it was acid. I sat there in front of him picturing his face melting away, the sizzling, the puckering, the brilliant red of his flesh paring open to the bone. It was probably what kept me there for the duration of the visit.

The morning was made so very much worse by the appearance, at the entrance desk, of the mother of Kevin's cellmate, the hoity-toity Mrs. Tompinkson, who had to ruin my regalia by dressing up in silk. Silk! Her makeup was lavish too. I never wear make up. I prefer to remain plain Jayne, my features, once described as delicate, allowed to be what they are now I've passed my prime. Even though when I look in the mirror sometimes all I see reflected back at me is the face of a battle-axe. Which seems awfully unfair. Why does life spoil the good and the true? Curse us with worry lines, a furrow to the brow, a downward curve at the mouth?

I was feeling sorry for myself by then. The train was a minute late and a cold wind, thick with diesel exhaust, rushed down the platform. The man beside me took a step forward. Bowler hats are back in fashion, it seems. My view of the railway tracks was obscured by them in its entirety.

The train pulled up not long after and the doors whooshed open. Once inside the carriage, I hesitated. Should I stand or sit. The man seated by the door had shunted over but he hadn't left a good deal of room and it would mean my thighs would be pressed up against his and I wasn't having that. So much for Weight Watchers. Last month I thought I'd lose a few pounds but it felt like starvation so I gave up.

The seated man didn't look all that savoury, but if I stayed standing there was every chance I'd lose my balance. As the train pulled away, the carriage swayed and I instinctively reached out to hold onto the handrail, before pulling back my gloved hand hovering near a smear of something brown.

I held a plastic strap instead, adopting a sideways stance, feet well apart, and raised myself up to my full height. I should have left the umbrella at home. It proved an additional appendage I could have done without. Could have done without that hard cover omnibus of *The Mysteries of Udolpho* in my handbag too. It belonged to our mother, gifted her by one of her regulars at Kitties. I was ten pages in and thought as I left the house that morning I might as well take it with me. Gripping the plastic strap, I could feel the weight of the tome pulling down my other shoulder and I felt distinctly lop-sided

The train lumbered on, pulling into station after station, the crowd thickening then thinning again as the bowler hats got off. The last housing estates at the fringes of the city gave way to open country. Shadows lengthened in passing fields, fingers of dark crawling over blankets of green. The sky was thick and heavy, bearing down. A vacant seat presented itself opposite the man seated by the door. I took it, placing my umbrella sideways across my lap. The man's gaze wandered about above my head. I was disconcerted by it. Self-conscious and awkward, I opened the clasp of my handbag and felt about inside for want of an occupation. I thought of extracting the book but decided the sheer size of the thing would attract attention. Besides, I'd be unable to turn the pages without removing my gloves.

I could only imagine what the others would have thought of me if I had. The bowler hats would have boxed me up a thief or a shoplifter, for they are the sorts of crimes befitting an old lady in tweed. I hardly looked like I dealt drugs. I couldn't be a rapist, could I? So what did that leave? Murderer? No one would think that of me. I'm not the type.

The man was distracted by his phone, which emitted several bars of Wagner's Parsifal before he had a chance to answer it. At first he didn't speak, the other party apparently having much to say, but when he did I was struck by the timbre. He had an odd way of laughing at whatever was being said, and I speculated that he might work in a grubby office off a narrow laneway, somewhere forgotten, seedy, grim.

He was a tubby, lank-haired sort of man of about forty, and there was a greasy shine to his face. He was scruffily dressed in an open neck checked shirt beneath brown corduroy, attire that seemed to me somewhat dated. Perhaps corduroy was back in fashion, although his outfit had the shabby appearance of the clothing bin. There was a large stain on one knee of his trousers. An old stain, ingrained, the sort that had never been treated to a proper wash.

My assessments fed a growing revulsion. I had it in mind to change to another seat but I didn't want to draw those guileful eyes to myself. I wished I had Antonio with me. Antonio would have given me someone to talk to, or he would have stood in front of me and blocked my view of the stranger and I wouldn't have recourse to yield to my misgivings.

Damn Antonio. Try as you might, you can't undo time and bring back the past.

Things started to go horribly wrong from there. They always seem to when I think of Antonio, my first, and my last love.

We met one night when mother got wasted at Kitties and it was down to me to go pick her up, quite literally, off the pavement outside. I was twenty by then so she must have been forty and a little too old for the trade. Antonio was security. A man as wide as he was tall, all kind eyed and honey smiles and as he helped mother stagger to her feet his hand brushed mine. In the time it took to get her into the back seat of the car, we'd arranged to meet for lunch the next day.

I'll never forgive what she did.

Through the windows the evening turned to black. The screech and hiss of the brakes, the grinding of metal on metal, the clatter and sway of the carriage as the train pulled into the next station, it all pressed upon me as though magnified by the strains of the day. A stretch of fence outside the carriage window was smeared with fresh graffiti. Garish splashes of color. None of it made any sense. I wanted to close my eyes to the chaos of it, but I kept staring, kept my gaze slanted away from the man opposite, watching him in my side vision.

As the train pulled away he pocketed his phone, and his gaze returned to the spot above my head. I was forced to stare down at the floor. The carriage emptied save for a young lad at the other end, leaning against the door. There we were, the three of us, on a metropolitan train reaching into the countryside to deposit the outlier commuters. Rows of vacant seats, the shiny cream and blue of the paint on walls and poles, the Perspex screens, it was meant to be all so clinical, like a hospital ward. That's how I wanted it to be, but my eyes picked over every bit of muck, and there was such a lot of it. Needed a scrubbing brush and bucket of ammonia right through the whole interior, top to bottom.

Outside, a few lights flashed by out of the darkness. There was only one more stop before the end of the line. I eyed my two companions hoping both stayed put when I stood up.

Neither moved as the train slowed.

I grabbed the straps of my handbag, propped my umbrella under one arm, and sat up, ready. The noise as the train came to a standstill was cacophonous to my ears. When at last there was no movement I made for the door and hit the exit button. It was then I noticed the tubby man in corduroy rise to his feet.

One wide step off the train and I made my way along the platform.

Sensing him behind me, with all of his grease and his filth, I quickened my pace. I was being stupid, I knew, for there was only one exit. We all had to leave the station by the same gate. Him and me, I mean. Just him and me.

Once through, I headed down the narrow, poorly lit lane to Main Street. He did the same. There was another route he might have taken, to the car park on the left. Perhaps he didn't have a car. Or he'd parked it in the street. Yes, that's surely what he'd done. Still, I resisted an urge to break into a run.

When I reached Main Street I turned left.

So did he.

I crossed the road.

He wasn't far behind me.

My heart began to thrum in my chest. I told myself not to be irrational. To keep an even pace. The street was lit well by lamplights and shop fronts. I cast a quick eye up ahead but there was no one else around.

I wanted to stop and turn. Pause by a shop window, fiddle with my handbag, let him pass. I wouldn't let myself.

I heard a car in the distance, heading our way. I kept walking, willing the car to stop, park, another human to get out and occupy the street. But the car went on its way, disinterested.

I had to make a turn up ahead. This would be the test. If he carried on walking I could relax.

My feet felt like dead weights. Like a child, I started avoiding the cracks in the pavement. It occurred to me I could simply turn around and head back up Main Street. Hope the public telephone was working again.

The kerb arced and petered out a little way into the lane. I could hear his footsteps, firm, dull, steady. Ten paces on and those footsteps were still there, right behind me.

The lane was short and linked to my own. Another thirty paces and I'd be on the home straight, not a hundred feet from my front door. I would be heading left. Mine was the only dwelling that way so he had to be turning turn right at the end. He had to be turning right at the end because I didn't know him and I never have visitors.

The trouble was, he didn't.

When I reached the little lane that led to my farmhouse beyond the outer reaches of the village and made my veer to the left, he was still right behind me. My breath caught in my throat. I succumbed to a rippling panic in my belly. I felt heavy and weak all at once. I gripped my handbag in one hand and my umbrella in the other, my weaponry. I prepared to turn.

The last street light illumed a circle of ground. Fat clots of red earth were heaped in long lines down the length of field, leaving deep furrows, splayed open to reveal the tender soil beneath. With sudden resolve I swung round, umbrella raised, handbag to the ready to swipe him, the hardback, omnibus *The Mysteries of Udolpho* sure to bowl him over.

The man put his hands up to his face and cowered.

I hesitated; let my hands fall to my sides. I couldn't hit him. There was nothing to defend.

'Why are you following me?' The words left my lips like a growl. Suddenly, I had the upper hand.

He explained, in short, incomplete sentences that he'd been directed to a house down the lane. He'd been told the woman there would help him find his missing sister. He meant me. Whoever it was had sent the man to me.

To my house.

No one ever sends anyone to my house.

'You are Miss Celina Parkmore?'

'That I am,' I said. But I'm not *the* Miss Celina Parkmore. She lives in the village at the end of the line. A private detective who I understand from local gossip had pinched my name out of an old telephone directory when she set up her business about ten years back. The cheek of it!

When I'd first been told about this pseudo Miss Parkmore I half expected mistaken phone calls, even a visitor, but no one phoned and no one came. As the years passed I forgot she even existed. The relief I felt standing there before that tubby man in corduroy was so exhilarating I almost laughed.

I put on one of my inviting smiles and suggested he accompany me for some refreshments. I had to force myself to set aside his lack of hygiene as I spoke, which is something I am proud of, for it took quite some effort. He thanked me and we walked side by side after that, along by the furrowed field, all the way to my garden gate. Removing my gloves, I extracted my keys. He stepped to one side as I opened the front door. My equanimity was fully restored as I crossed the threshold. Ensconced in my parlour, the man introduced himself as Terry. He proffered his hand. Conscious of my stained fingertips, I took it, not enjoying the hot sweaty overly soft flesh on my own. But I'm not a rude woman. I didn't pull away, deciding I would wait until I was out of sight before cleaning my palm. I think it was his handshake and my overwhelming need to erase it from my skin that caused me to offer him the soup.

Homemade, of course. He only paused for a second before nodding obsequiously.

Antonio's favourite.

It's rather good in fact, made from my own leeks. I've always grown a good stout leek. I don't skimp either; use the whole plant, the green and the white. Sometimes I take the trouble to dice the leeks finely. Other times I cook the soup for a goodly while. I have been known to mash the soup into a thick pulp.

But I was in a hurry that morning to catch the train to Lang Cove remand centre to see Kevin. Thinking of Kevin dampened the atmosphere. Scrubbing my hands in the kitchen sink I had an urge for a gin and lime. My mother's ruin it was, and she kept the gin in the freezer in the summer. In the winter she left it tucked away on the top shelf of the pantry, which was where I kept it too, in exactly her spot, right in the centre next to the biscuit tin.

As I brought the soup to a boil, I downed a tumbler, enjoying the tart heat in my throat. Sip after sip, stir upon stir, ladle to the ready.

When I handed him a bowl and spoon on a tray, Terry told me the soup was his favourite. His eyes lit up and he looked like a little boy, and I saw Kevin in his seat, Kevin as a naughty little boy of four.

Terry hunkered over his soup. I stared down over his shoulder realising I'd forgotten the bread. Can't have soup without bread. I invited him to go right ahead and make a start while I cut him a thick slice of white.

His face went all boyish again. I don't think he was a much-loved child. It felt good, all of a sudden, to be making up for his lack of mother love in a single act of kindness on that cold and lonely night. Walking back to the kitchen I confess to noticing a warm glow in my belly that wasn't caused by the gin. But it made me think of gin so I poured myself another before I cut the bread. After all, I'd earned it. I'd been through a lot that day, what with the visit to the remand centre, the train and then that horrid walk home.

It was then I thought the bread was a bit stale so I popped it in the toaster. What with all the clatter and moving about I couldn't hear a thing beyond the kitchen walls. I couldn't hear Terry in the parlour. I pictured him sipping his soup from his spoon as I sipped my gin, taking my time as the old toaster took an age.

By the time I'd buttered his toast and made my way through to the parlour, Terry was keeled over, rasping. The soup was half-finished, sitting on a tray with the spoon submerged. On the carpet at his feet was more soup, soup that had made its way inside his belly and out again, a congealed mess of grey.

I kept hold of the toast and watched. He kept grabbing at his mouth and gagging. The noise was wretched. I'd have slapped him on the back but I had my hands full. Besides, I didn't want to get closer. The smell in the room was rank. I backed away, reluctant to get involved, recalling that day some months before when I was forced to clear up the bloody mess that Kevin had left in the same spot. I knew there and then I wasn't going to clear up after another man.

Terry was making a terrible racket. I closed the door on the parlour to block out the noise and went back to the kitchen. I was peckish after the gin so I ate his toast, dunking the ends in the saucepan of soup, still hot on the stove. Gripping the toast between my ink-stained fingertips, I looked into that soup and I heard my mother's voice warning me of the perils of badly chopped, undercooked leeks. Too stringy, she'd said. Get caught in the throat. You could choke to death, she'd said to me one cold winter's day, knife in hand, hacking at the long smooth stems of the leeks.

Since when was I ever going to take note of her words, not after she snaffled my Antonio. Ran off with him to Ibiza, and me and Kevin never saw either of them again. Although, standing in the kitchen eating Terry's toast, I had to admit she was right. Leeks do need a lot of chopping and cooking. But I could hardly be blamed for being in a rush to make the soup that morning, could I? I had a train to catch.

No, I'm not to blame. The harsh truth of that dreadful day is simple. Whoever sent tubby Terry to Miss Celina Parkmore should have issued the correct directions.

Alex Laybourne's
Shopping List

Food for the kids (I've got 5)

Snacks for the kids
Drinks for the kids,
Whatever the kids sneak into the trolly when I am not
looking,
Bin Bags
Milk
Eggs,
A deep freeze pizza for dinner
A guilty conscience knowing I'm trying to be healthy, but there
is no money left for me to eat right.

Mi Casa Ciguapa

Alex Laybourne

The trees parted as the forest gave way to a small clearing, which gave the couple a breath-taking view of the valley beneath them. The lake was close to a perfect circle in its shape, and the water was an impossible shade of blue. It seemed to glow in the late afternoon sun. Dotted around the lake, which was not overly large, were four small villages - one on each point of the compass.

Jennifer and Jacob Chambers were high up in the mountains, higher than they had planned to climb, but the trail they half found was too enticing to be refused. Still, they could see delicate tendrils of grey smoke snaking into the air, which told them that the towns below while small, were certainly populated.

"It's all so beautiful," Jennifer remarked, leaning against her husband. She linked her arm through his and rested her head on his muscular upper arm.

"It's amazing. We couldn't have picked a better place." Jacob answered.

High-School sweethearts, they had been married three days before, and had flown out to the Dominican

Republic the day after, landing in Santiago, before taking a charted bus into the mountains. The company offered a unique package in so far as they arranged supplies and transport; the events of the holiday, however, were left entirely up to them. There were six couples on the trip, and while each had bonded well, they went their own separate ways once they were dropped off.

Both Jacob and Jennifer were avid hikers, and neither enjoyed lazing around by a pool all day, so the trip made for a perfect honeymoon. They had planned to hike by day, camp and make love by night. They had a set number of peaks they wanted to try and hike during the ten day trip, but that had changed the moment they gathered their things from the bus.

The last couple ready, Jennifer and Jacob found themselves with all the time in the world to choose a route that suited them. It was Jacob who had found the trail. It started as a small path, which branched from the main trail they were following and disappeared into the trees. The path was lined by orange coloured flowers; a vibrancy of colour unlike anything that either of them had seen before. The size of Jacob's hand, the flowers gave a sweetly perfumed aroma that lingered on the senses. A melodic birdsong cut through the trees and danced around them.

They had decided to follow the path until it ended. There was nothing on the map that indicated a trail in the area, but after four hours they had yet to turn back or see any sign of the trail ending.

"I think this would be the ideal place for us to set up shop for the night." Jacob suggested as the same birdsong came through again. "The sun is starting to set, and quite frankly, I don't think I can keep my hands off you for much longer." Jacob dropped his pack, scooped his wife into his arms and kissed her.

Their tent was quickly assembled, and as the sun dipped behind the mountains opposite them, they sat arm in arm, lost in a perfect place. The small gas stove heated up a tin of soup, which they shared, and followed up with a fresh mango.

"It still feels strange," Jennifer began.

"What, being married?" Jacob cut in,

"Well, yes, that too, but I meant the weather. It's February, the sun is almost set and it is still around eighty degrees." She answered, turning to face the man she loved. "I could stay here forever." She smiled and kissed him. They collapsed into the tent, entwined with one another, and made love in a foreign land while the same birdsong that had guided them all day continued to play. It grew louder and louder as the source of the tune drew closer to their tent.

The following morning, as the sun crested the horizon, Jennifer woke with a start. It was not as the result of a nightmare, but rather a form of precognition. Something roused her from sleep; what it was, Jennifer did not know. Moving quietly, so as not to disturb Jacob - Jennifer checked her phone. She was surprised to see that it was already seven-thirty. Climbing out of the tent, Jennifer stretched and felt her eyes immediately drawn to the footprints on the dusty ground. They started at the door to their tent, moving away from it, towards the woods. *Jacob must have needed to pee* she thought with a childish chuckle. Starting the gas cooker once again, she poured some water into the pot and began to boil it for coffee. Supplies were left at the bus drop off site every two days, so there was no need to be shy with the caffeine.

Forty-five minutes later, Jacob emerged, stretched and immediately grabbed the steaming cup of black gold being offered to him.

"Good morning," Jennifer kissed him, and turned back to the view of the lake, villages and mountains beyond.

They stood in silence, both watching the world beneath them. Neither spoke, for there was no need. While Jennifer made breakfast, Jacob studied the maps that they had been given.

"There has to be something marking this trail, it's too large not to have been discovered before." He spoke as his meal was delivered to him in a military style mess tin.

"Yeah, it surprises me, but hey, it can be our little secret." Jennifer giggled as she moved the coffee cup and food out of the way, to straddle her husband.

"True, but, I just want to make sure we don't lose it." Jacob said between kisses.

"What do you mean?" Jennifer asked, her passion withdrawing as curiosity arrived.

"Well, I just mean, we need to go back for supplies tomorrow, but I would love to come back this way and see what else is up here. Wouldn't you?" Jacob tilted his head and looked at this wife. "Can't you feel it? There is something about this place...." Their embrace had ended.

"Well, I guess we could spend another day or so, but I would like to do the honeymoon trail, too." Jennifer insisted.

"It's a deal."

The temperature increased by the minute. They ate slowly, quietly. Occasionally their eyes would meet in a smile. A sudden noise from the trees behind caught their attention. Jacob spun around, excited by the prospect of seeing local wildlife. As an amateur photographer, Jacob always had a fascination with wild animals; they were great subjects to work with. He was therefore surprised and shocked at what had caused the disturbance. A figure standing on two legs, with skin was so tanned it appeared golden. It had long black hair that hung loosely over its shoulders. The figure – a woman – was naked. She smiled at Jacob. Their eye contact was fleeting, and in the fraction of a second between Jacob turning his head, and Jennifer following suit, the figure was gone; vanishing into the shadows, like a ghost.

"Did you see that?" Jacob asked. His stomach fluttered. He felt light headed, even a little queasy, as the birdsong once again filtered through the trees.

"See what?" Jennifer asked, answering the question without realizing.

"There was… somebody standing there… a woman. I saw her." Jacob stumbled over his words. He shook his head, and the wave of giddiness passed.

"Where?" Jennifer asked as a shiver ran down her spine.

Jacob rose to his feet and walked towards the trees. "Here, she was standing right here… she was… naked… I think. She was beautiful." He added under his breath and out of his new wife's earshot.

"Jacob, Jacob listen to me, there was somebody by our tent last night." Jennifer blurted the news.

Jacob spun around, his mind a whirl. The birdsong fogged his mind. Something wanted to pull him back towards the trees. He knew she was still there, he could feel her watching him. "What do you mean? Where? How do you know?"

"Well, there were footprints by the tent this morning when I woke up." Jennifer looked around the camp. While Jacob was sure he could feel the woman watching him still, Jennifer could feel multiple eyes, staring at her from every available inch of coverage.

"Footprints, leading up to our tent," Jacob repeated what he had heard, for the melodious tune drowned out some of the words.

"Well… actually no, they were leading away from the tent. I just thought you had gone for a pee or something in the night. Did you?" Jennifer asked, looking at her husband with fear etched onto her face.

"Um… yes, yes I did. I went for a pee in the trees." Jacob lied. He tried to tell himself that he did so for his wife, to save her feeling anything hurtful, but he knew that too was a fabrication. He had no understanding of why he lied. All he knew was that he had to keep Jennifer calm, otherwise they would never move further along the trail.

"Then who was that?" Jennifer asked, her nerves not settled.

"I don't know. One of the locals, maybe." The answer came to him as he remembered the view of the lake and the four villages that surrounded it. "She was probably one of the villagers. We both said it; this route isn't on the map. They probably aren't used to seeing people up here. That's all." Jacob embraced his wife and kissed the top of her head.

"You think so?" Jennifer asked, still unable to shake the feeling that she was being watched.

"I'm sure of it. Now, why don't we pack up our things and get moving. There is still so much to see." Jacob had a way with words, and it was their honeymoon after all. What he said made sense, and so Jennifer made no real argument. Besides, putting distance between themselves and the village would mean they shouldn't stumble across anybody else.

Jacob packed away the tent and gathered their supplies. Just as he was fastening the straps of their packs, he heard it again, the song. Only it came from down the trail, back the way they had come. His head snapped up, hopeful of a second glimpse at the woman, but there was nothing. Only the trees and the path they had followed.

"Hey listen, Jen," Jacob began, grabbing the pack and turning as he spoke. "If you want, we can go back the way we came, hit the main trail and see where that leads us." He smiled and fastened the pack over his shoulders.

"Only if you're sure," Jennifer tried to hide her relief.

"Come on, let's get going, it should be a quicker trip back down." Jacob hoped he didn't sound too eager to be off. He felt relieved when Jennifer appeared just as happy to hit the trails.

They disappeared down the trail, and only Jacob cast a glance back over his shoulder, and there, in the centre of the clearing he saw something, dancing in the rays of the rising sun. Its form was too subtle for a casual glance to truly perceive, but Jacob was certain that there was something there. It's form flirting with his eyes, teasing him.

The trail was thicker than they remembered in places, and on particularly steep incline from the day before became a steep descent, which slowed them down for over an hour. The temperature continued to rise, and sweat soon glistened on their foreheads.

The morning passed uneventfully, their conversation ranged from the house they were looking to buy, through to the impending job cut announcement at Jennifer's firm. Her job was safe, but plenty of others were on edge. Having lived together in one form or another since the end of high school, the traditional honeymoon trepidations were of no consequence to them.

"I don't remember there being a fork in the road," Jennifer spoke as they came to a halt before a split in the trail. The moment they put the campsite behind them, her nerves had begun to calm. Now, deep on the trail, heading back towards the mapped areas, the sweet birdsong their only additional companion, and with the sweet aroma of the flowers once again the fragrance of choice she felt decidedly foolish. They probably gave the woman the fright of her life. Even if she hadn't seen her, Jessica could imagine the look on her face at finding strangers camping in her backyard.

"We wouldn't have noticed it; we were walking the other way." Jacob studied the path with deep intent. "It must have been this one." Jacob pointed to the left hand fork.

"How can you tell?"

"Footprints, see?" Jacob pointed a little further down the trail. How about: There were fresh sets of impressions, the direction of which clearly pointed towards the clearing. "The other path is clean, so it had to be this one." Jacob reasoned. Jennifer had no better logical conclusion, and so they made their choice. It did not take long for them to realize that they had made the wrong choice. The path they took descended on a gradient much steeper than their trail of the previous day.

The path snaked through the trees, and in places was little more than a route conjured by their own eyes.

"Where are we going?" Jennifer asked as they stopped for a drink.

"I don't know." Jacob finished folding the map and placed it back in his pocket. "I can't find any of this on the map. However, the lake we saw last night is, and there is a small river that runs through the mountains. We should be right on top of it. There are a few trails that cross it." He looked at Jennifer, whose face showed a look of concern.

"So we are lost?" She offered, knowing how hard it was for Jacob so say the words.

"We're not lost, we are just off-piste." Jacob smiled. Both had a keen sense for adventure, and so smiled at the excuse, and got back to their feet.

The trees around them changed and so did the ground underfoot. The earth became darker and softer, the aroma of the earth; dense and peaty replaced that of the flowers. Moss covered the trunks of most trees and the leaves took on a dark green colour, which at times seemed almost black. The air became damp, and the humidity increased until their clothes were soaked, and their muscles ached. It was only when they finally came to the end of their descent that they realized what had happened.

The trail had brought them down to the same level as the lake and villages. In doing so they had passed through a low-lying layer of mist, which hovered above their heads; a false sky which obscured the rest of the mountains from view.

"Great, well, at least we found the river." Jennifer grunted, taking an unsuccessful swipe at a fly, buzzing around her face.

"Jen, we found more than that. Take a look at this place." Jacob whispered. The intonation of his voice expressed the sheer wonderment of what he was seeing.

Jennifer turned around and looked at their surroundings. The soil and hills had given way to a stone floor. They had entered a valley of some sort; with the thick mist layer it was impossible to see what truly stood above them. Ahead of them, the river flowed. The water a little wild from the low-grade rapids. Wild flowers bloomed along its banks, and a kaleidoscope of butterflies fluttered from flower to flower, oblivious to the attentions being garnered upon them.

"Wow, this place is…"

"Beautiful," Jacob answered, grabbing his camera; he did not want to waste another second.

Jennifer could not disagree with him. The valley was cool, peaceful and without any doubt the most beautiful sight she had seen. She didn't even bother to ask if Jacob wanted to push on any further. It was clear that they were done for the day. It wasn't ideal, as their supplies were running low, but as long as they got an early start in the morning they would be able to reach the meeting place before dark; maybe even catch up with one of the other couples they had met; a gay couple from New Zealand, who had been travelling the world for a year. Having survived a cancer scare a few years before, remission had prompted them to stop waiting and start living.

Jennifer stopped daydreaming and turned back to Jacob, but he was gone, his attention at least. He was lost to his artistic world. Jennifer was used to it.

Setting up their camp was easier than she had expected, and with Jacob still taken by the sights, and wandering ever further away, Jennifer decided that she would check out the river, maybe even take a wade to ease her tired feet.

Jennifer walked along the stony bank, watching the floor, listening to the relaxing flow of the river; the gentle clash of water and stone. The rapids were by no means wild, and the water was not deep enough for a boat, not anymore, yet Jennifer walked until the water calmed. Looking back, she couldn't see their camp, the valley floor had, unbeknownst to her, crested a rise in the earth and taken her over the other side.

Kicking her shoes off, Jennifer dipped her toes in the water. It was freezing. So much more than she had expected. It gave her pause, but eventually she waded through the water until she stood knee-deep. The arctic water soothed her aching feet in its fiery-ice-embrace. She groaned in pleasure. The water was crystal clear, and Jennifer could see her toes wiggling beneath the surface. She also saw a few fish swimming with the tide. They were tiny, not more than an inch or two in length, and looked oddly like worms, their bodies propelled not by fins but rather by the writing bodies. They were jet black and paid no mind to the feet that had appeared in their path. Jennifer stood still, amazed by how smooth the stones were beneath the surface. She walked through the water, feeling the will of the river tug at her ankles. It was strong given the shallow depth.

Jennifer looked down at her feet, watching for more fish, or any other sort of wildlife. What she saw made her pause and crouch down. Reaching into the water, Jennifer picked up what she thought was a large stone, which protruded from the riverbed. She had almost stubbed her foot on the piece. Jennifer pulled her hand from the water and jumped back to her full height the instant she realized what it was that she held. What Jennifer had first thought to be a rock was in fact a bone; a human bone.

The tug of the tide changed, however, and without warning Jennifer was pulled from her feet and fell beneath the surface. An invisible force pressed against her, keeping her head buried in the water. The rocks, which had been so smooth, felt rough against her skin as she was dragged along the riverbed. The clear water became a swirling pink broth as the water became wild once more.

Jennifer struggled as hard as she could against the current and managed to break the surface long enough to choke down a lung full of air. In the second she was above the water, she became aware of her captors. They were laughing and singing all around her. As her brain fed off the oxygen she so desperately gasped for, she was conscious of a certain familiarity in the sounds being made around her. Before she could understand what it was, she was pulled down under the surface and whisked away. Faster and faster the current pulled and Jennifer was powerless to resist. Her lungs burned and her vision began to dim. She opened her mouth to breathe and water surged into her body. Choking, gasping, every spasm of her throat pulled more water into her lungs.

Jennifer fought until her arms and legs became heavy, and only when they no longer obeyed the commands her brain gave did she think about Jacob. His image flashed inside her mind, and her thundering heart slowed, and she was hauled from the water. Her body was heavy, and her legs were numb. Jennifer could not feel the ground beneath her feet. Slowly, she opened her eyes and came face to face with her killer. The woman was holding Jennifer suspended by her wrist. She was naked, her long black hair stuck to her body, clinging to the gentle swell of her breasts. Her grip was like iron and she stared into Jennifer's face. Her eyes were black and cold. She blinked, and licked her lips before speaking. Her mouth opened to reveal row after row and jagged teeth, which spiralled into the back of her mouth and down her throat. For a while no sound came, and then slowly, like an echo in reverse, the birdsong filtered into Jennifer's ears. It grew louder and louder, echoing in Jennifer's head. The melodic tune increased to a deafening pitch, so loud that Jennifer could not hear her own screams above the noise until… her eardrums burst. Blood showered from her ear canal and suddenly, the song was gone; in its place were words.

"You should never have come here. You are not welcome." The voice threatened, all traces of melody and beauty were gone from it.

"Then… let us go… we will go…" Jennifer wheezed, her lungs were still half filled with water. Looking down, Jennifer coughed as she saw that she was being dangled over the edge of a waterfall.

"Silly child, it is too late for that. You entered our land, brought us an offering. We will never reject a new offering. Our loins are starved. It has been too long since children graced these woods." The voice continued, although Jennifer saw, with her ever failing eyesight that her mouth did not actually move; it was frozen into the same toothy smile.

"Jacob…" Jennifer stuttered.

"Such a fine specimen of a man, his offering will be welcomingly received by my sisters and I. You however, are a distraction. We feel the love he has for you. You must die." The creature growled, and a thin black tongue flicked out and ran over the front row of teeth.

"Why? Why are you doing this?" Jennifer's body had turned cold; her breathing rate had slowed not because she was calm, but because her heart no longer had the strength to beat.

"Because he must feel something, something other than love," the woman hissed.

"Why? Just let me go, let me go now, nobody has to know." Jennifer screamed, using her last ounce of stress.

"My sisters will know, I would know. Your death is required. Only the giver of love can be the one to break its retched hold." Four more women appeared in the blurred peripherals of Jennifer's vision. Each one a carbon copy of the first.

"Who are you?" Jennifer fought to expel each required syllable.

"We are your end, we are his future, we are scorn. Driven to the mountains by people like you, jealous because of the desires our beauty arouses in men. He wants us now, our song will guide him home, and we will welcome him to our beds." With that, the woman released her grip and Jennifer fell, connecting with the rushing water half way down the waterfall's face. The force of the water increased Jennifer's descent, and its thunderous roar drowned out her cries. She was still conscious as she crashed into the water, narrowly missing the rocks. The tide collected her body and set it on its final course, while in the deeper waters of the small round lake it fed into, it lay in wait. The Goldrug was always hungry, and while the Ciguapa had their own use for human flesh, the Goldrug could think of no tastier morsel. Its relationship with the sisters was unconventional, but being the last of its kind, survival had forced it to seek an ally. Knowing that humans tended to enter the mountain in pairs, but with only the male half being of any use to The Sisters of Ciguapa, they had been more than happy to send the females to him.

Jennifer's body somehow survived the fall, and while only the most basic of human functions remained active by the time she flowed into the lake, there was more than enough consciousness to understand what was to be her fate, when the giant creature broke the water, its jaws, which was almost as wide as the lake itself, closed around her. The body, surging up from the deep thrust itself into the air and gave a triumphant and satisfied cry before crashing back down to its slumber, to lay in wait for the next offering.

***

Jacob was lost in the beauty of the valley. He did not notice that he had wandered so far until he paused to stretch his back, which had turned stiff from the constant crouching. Turning, he saw that Jennifer had erected their tents, and as the birdsong once more echoed around the valley, he lowered his camera and with an overpowering lust headed back towards the tent, and his bride.

Before Jacob arrived at the tent, he knew that something was amiss. The ground was disturbed; wet footprints had danced over the rocky ground, making it look as though someone had drawn the foxtrot for him to practice. The feet moved away from the tent, heading straight towards the river. A shiver ran through Jacob when he realized that the song, which had so enticed his senses all day, now came from within his tent.

"Jennifer?" He called out; a sense of unfathomable dread caressed his spine and made him shiver. "Is that you?" Jacob called out, following the footsteps, his heart racing harder with each step he shadowed. Whoever it was, they had not been alone, and there were clearly different sized footprints. The first ones had started outside the tent. Jacob paused, as he remembered what Jennifer had said about the footprints outside their tent when they had woken that morning… in the clearing.

Without hesitation, Jacob opened the tent, throwing the entrance flap wide. A blinding light filled the tent, and the overpowering scent of the flowers that had lined their trail the day before filled his nose. He was drunk on their aroma within seconds and high from it not long after. They all lay waiting for him on the floor of the tent. Five identical women, each naked, their long black hair fanned out on the floor beneath them, a blanket for their love.

"Who…" Jacob began, but the five women opened their mouths and the birdsong erupted at full volume. His head swooned and as he fell towards them, their arms and legs reached for him.

Their limbs pulled and tugged at him, genitalia erupted all over their bodies, as every point of contact became a penetrative point. Their bodies quivered and they cried out in unison as even the most fleeting contact with the male sent their minds into rapture. Arousal made their bodies sleek, and oiled with their passion.

Jacob lost himself in the heady aroma of their embrace. Their hands held him down; nails raked his flesh drawing blood along the length of his spine. Jacob gasped in surprise and his mouth was filled with a succulent breast, which suckled him into oblivion. A strange salty taste filled his mouth, and Jacob drunk it down the same gusto that one of the lovers used on his cock. Her mouth was taking him all and still he thrust. Listening to her gag with each forceful movement fed his passion, and caused him to pull harder on the teat that nursed him. His head grew heavy from salty nourishment he was given. His limbs grew weak, and at the moment he realized what a mistake he had made, Jacob understood that it was too late. The mood in the tent changed, he was no longer the one making love to them, he was a toy, a plaything for the tribe, and they meant to have their way with him.

The world melted away as they took turns to straddle him; writhing their naked bodies against his. Skin on skin, it felt as if a power surged through them, jumping from them to him and back again. Each contact they made was an experienced in arousal. Jacob cried out as the waves of ecstasy rolled over him, again and again, he felt no need to slow or stop. The passion consumed him, their scent; their cries of passion incensed him. It drove him over the edge of his own sanity and tumbling down a ravine into a distant twisted world, where pleasure was all that mattered. Reaching out in a moment of clarity Jacob grabbed the woman closest to him, his hand closing around her throat as his hand entered her. His fist disappeared and the cries of the woman ran through valley.

The tent spun. Colours and images flashed before Jacob's eyes. As he ravaged the women, one after another, he felt the pain of his activities begin to eat through the membrane of his arousal. The coppery smell of blood mixed with his sexual gratification, now flowed from the gasping holes that covered their bodies. He looked around and the women reached out to him. Their golden skin called to him like a moth to the flame. Everything about them was alluring. The merest sight of their virginal flesh. The rise and swell of their breasts, or the sweet nectar that flowed from their loins, ranging from being smooth and hairless to densely populated thick brush. Globs of his excitement clung to the hairiest cunt as if she were saving it for something.

"Stop," Jacob gasped, as a rare moment of clarity burst into the forefront of his consciousness. His body ached, and the tent reeked of sweat, the heady aroma of love and a strange repugnant odour - the smell of stagnant water. Looking around he saw the walls of the tent; they glistened, and dripped a viscous slime, peppered with the pink of diluted blood. He looked at the women, his grip on reality once again starting to slip, as their sirens song began to end. The beautiful golden skinned nymphs he had been lured by were no more. The veils of their disguise had fallen. Their bodies were bloated and soft, the skin purple and covered with pulsing veins. Their heads were bald and their mouths a lipless, tooth filled maw, ringed with blood… his blood. Jacobs's flesh was covered with circular wounds from his lovers' less than tender kisses.

His pleas were wasted however, for now that the veil had come down, there was no need for pretense. The women rose, their moans and cries of passion, which had rung so sweetly in Jacob's ears, now turned into a skin-tightening wail that made his whole body tense. He tried to leave but his legs would no long move. The wetness beneath him – their secretions - contained a powerful paralytic. Too late did he understand; the carnal cravings were merely the trap designed to lead the lusty to their doom.

Jacob was held down by strong arms, an unnecessary measure given the paralysis, but contact with the group was required. He was facedown, still naked. The floor was coated with a thick layer of slime, the stench of rotten fish made him gag. Their cold limbs teased his flesh, drawing blood for the fun of seeing it flow. The pain was nothing to the blistering eruption inside his skull and around his previously un-penetrated anus. There was no warning, the build-up; simply a dry insertion that ripped Jacob's shit-pipe open. His eyes water and his ass bled as the hermaphroditic creatures took their turn to pleasure him. As each creature took position and entered him, Jacob felt his cock harden, and despite the pain, he experienced the fiercest orgasms of his life while they ravaged his broken sphincter. Everything he had emptied into them was now returned, having been marinated in their bellies, the act was complete, and Jacob could feel the result already fluttering in the pit of his stomach.

That was when he saw it, just as the curtain came down once more and their loving began anew; their feet, they were…

Backwards, their ankles had been rotated half a turn, and so their every step created a reverse pathway to follow. *It was all a trap, a lure.* Jacob realized as he came too. They had left the tent, and the wet footsteps of his captors slapped noisily on the rocky valley floor. They were walking along the river. They were walking; he was being carried, slung over the shoulder of one woman. They had no need for their veils now. Their seed had been sowed, their loins quieted for another trimester. Jacob could feel the result of their union; his body swam with the echo of their song.

His head ached, a dull and heavy thump. Slowly, Jacob opened his eyes. He was held erect, chains around his ankles and chest; his arms were pinned to his sides. His feet made no contact with the floor. It was dark, and damp. As his eyes adjusted to the dim light, Jacob began to take note of his surroundings. He was in a cave, the source of the river, which seemed to emerge from within the rocks by his feet. A cramp raged in Jacob's stomach but he was unable to move given his restraints, and so he growled against the muscle knotting pain. Jacob squeezed his eyes closed and clamped his jaw shut until the agony passed. It left him spent. Looking around he understood that he was not alone. There were others tied to the walls, although it soon became clear that none of them were alive. They hung too still, too quiet. Every movement Jacob made caused him to groan in pain, and the chains to clang against the walls of the cave. Yet his cellmates were silent.

Another wave of cramp hit Jacob and he was unable to contain his cries as frustration and fear mixed with searing agony.

"Save your strength," a slimy voice croaked from the darkness.

"Who said that?" Jacob wheezed, his eyes scouring the cave for a sign of the voice's owner.

"That is not important. It is you who is important. You are strong, they will thrive in you. The others were weak; their body's flimsy and soft." The voice answered. Jacob was sure he could see something in the centre of the cave. He strained to listen, as the sound of feet slapping in the shallow water tickled his auditory senses.

"They will what…" Jacob asked as his stomach cramped once more. Only this time, the pain did not recede. It grew stronger and stronger, and felt as though his insides were about to burst. Unable to control himself Jacob lost control of his bodily functions.

Flinching, having misinterpreted Jacob's expulsion, the creature emerged from the dark. The woman was taller than the others – much taller – her body was stick thin, and her skin held a translucent appearance that allowed Jacob to see her organs pulsing away beneath the surface. Her hair was thin and wispy, her breasts sagging and flat. Her backwards-facing feet were long and the nails curled into long yellow talons. Waddling forward she emerged further and further into the dim light.

"Am I still beautiful? Would you still desire this?" She asked, the birdsong parting in Jacob's mind to form the words.

"Who are you?" Jacob said again as he gazed upon the woman, the wonder in his voice answer enough.

"I am Mother. " It stated in a matter of fact tone. "I am here to witness the arrival." Its entire body pulsed, gill like splits ran all the way down its flank; it was not used to breathing out of the water.

"The arrival of what?" Jacob asked as a new level of pain registered in his brain. His skin stretched and tore apart. It started in his genitals, his scrotum split along the seam, spilling the contents onto the wet floor of the cave. Jacob's screams were drowned out by the hailing cry of Mother as she stood to bear witness to the birth of another generation.

"Of the children," Mother answered.

Jacob felt his skin tear up the length of his body, a jagged edge being carved into his flesh. Blood spewed from his mouth like vomit as his cried were choked to gargles by the heavy clumps of placental tissue. During his evisceration Jacob felt the lives inside him growing, not in his belly, but within his body as a whole. The children he was to bear swam through his blood; they stretched the veins and arteries of his circulatory system until they burst. At which time they rode the crimson tide either to their elected birthing passage.

With the fading moments of his life, Jacob watched as waves of wriggling, snake like fish spill from his gaping bowel. They squirmed in the blood pools and with tiny mouths began to gorge themselves on his raw offal. The sound of the bird song, which had rung out and echoed around the cave through it all, was replaced by the wailing cry of a thousand hungry babes screaming for further sustenance. Jacob felt the chains begin to loosen; the slack caused the tear in his flesh to extend. Only when the split extended through this throat and onto this skull did Jacob's screams finally fall silent. The flesh cleaved his mouth and tongue in two, his jaw dislocated and in a semi-coagulated wave the placenta which had nourished his children pre-birth were vomited out into the world, pulling with them the spliced tongue and lips. The children had grown exponentially in size thanks to the eviscerating rain that fell. They jumped into the air. The largest chunks claimed by the strongest babes were swallowed whole. Jacob felt, but could not air his agony as the split completed its march up his body, cresting the top of his skull before racing down his spine, opening his back to the world, airing his vertebrae before coming to rest at the same place that started it all; his butchered anal cavity. The final wave of bodily expulsions ushered forth a faecal tide that washed the children into the deeper water and saw them carried out and into the river.

Death, which had so far eluded Jacob for so long, finally moved in. As his vision extended and his eyes flopped to either side of his body, along with the hollowed out skin flaps that had once been his face - he caught sight of the sisters. They stood in the mouth of the cave and watched their young emerge, a smile carved into the bloated watery faces.

The two halves of what used to be Jacob Chambers fell to the floor, where they would remain until the tide rose, washing him out into the great-lake where, deep beneath the surface, the Goldrug lay in wait. Its hunger ever growing…

THE END

Jason Nugent's
Shopping List

Cat litter
Hard dog food
Coke Zero
Paper Towels
Bleach (2 gallons)
Bread
Apples – Golden Delicious or Gala
Brown Sugar
Tongue, whole
Creamed corn
Saw blade – for hacksaw?
Green beans
Anti-bacterial bathroom cleaner
Pigs feet
Disposable gloves
Salted butter
Chocolate cake mix
Contractor trash bags
BBQ rub (the good kind, not the generic)
Carrots
2 Onions
Lysol
Candles (3 red, 3 black)
Eggs

Tiny Piece of Soul

Jason J. Nugent

Thin gelatinous tendrils escaped Steven's eye from the space between his eyeball and his lower eye-lid, awakening him.

This wasn't the first time.

Burning pain seared his face. He learned long ago how best to handle the agony of its release. The first time terrified him, but now it was an annoyance.

He gritted his teeth, clutched the sheets of his bed, and let it work its way out. Eventually when it did, his eye would throb for an hour or so with blurry vision, and then all returned to normal.

The small creature with six tentacles and elongated body squirmed from his eye, leaving a trail of slime down his face towards his pillow. The mucus blazed bright green and burned like boiling lead on his skin. The creature itself was a milky-translucent color, red blood flowing in veins and arteries underneath its skin.

Still, Steven remained calm. They never attacked him, only forced their way from what felt like his sinus cavities to crawl out of his eye and down his face. The pain would subside, as always, and he'd be free to clean up. Water on his irritated skin stung at first but in time it too went away.

Like the creatures.

He didn't know where they went. It didn't seem possible they'd live long or get far. Six squishy legs couldn't go that far and he never noticed them drop into the drains or the toilet. All he knew was that they left.

When the thing scurried off his bed and landed with a splat on the wooden floor, he listened for the accompanying squish-squish-squish sound as it raced towards some unknown destination. His blurred vision always left him at a disadvantage for tracking the things.

Steven's boyfriend couldn't handle it. The night the first creature emerged, Steven screamed as it forced its way out of his eye. Roberto shot straight up in bed from the frightful sound.

"Steven, are you alright?" he said. He turned on the lamp next to the bed and faced Steven only to let out a blood-curdling scream at the sight of his partner's face disfigured by a jellyfish looking creature with legs wiggling its way out of his eye. Roberto jumped out of bed, threw on some clothes, and ran out of the apartment.

"Where are you going? What's happening?" Steven called out. He clutched the thing on his face and pulled but the immense pain in his eye made him stop. He let go and soon it was free, dropping to the floor.

After that night, he called Roberto and left message after message but he never returned his calls. Text messages went unanswered.

Yet the creatures continued.

Every other night, a new creature forced its way out of Steven's eye. To him, it felt like confusion escaped in the form of these translucent little monsters. The pain of revealing his sexuality to his parents, of enduring the ridicule of his brother, the shame he felt for thinking he was an abomination; all of it left bit by bit as the tiny creatures emerged and pulled themselves out of him in sweet moments of release.

He'd been with Roberto for over a year. They were finally starting to grow close, even talking of marriage, when the creatures began their exodus.

As each monster left his eye, Steven felt one step closer to accepting himself, accepting his true identity. Not the façade his parents forced him into as a child. Not the false boyfriend to Maria he'd pretended to be. Each creature wiped away the guilt, wiped away the pain he'd endured by hiding who he was.

As wonderful as it was to feel freedom with the exiting monsters, the loss of Roberto hurt worse. He had to end the creatures if he'd have any chance with Roberto again. Or to accept himself.

****

He spent days pondering his predicament. He had no idea what caused them, where they came from, or what their purpose was. Did his feelings, his pain create these things? Were they products of his body, telling him he was all right, that he was normal?

The only thing he could do was destroy the source of their escape.

Would Roberto care if he lost an eye? Would it stop the creatures? He wasn't sure, but he had no alternative. Every day without Roberto was a day closer to becoming what his family wanted.

One night, Steven drank half a bottle of vodka just to have the courage to perform the surgery.

He'd acquired a scalpel from a doctor friend "to lance a boil" he said, and held it steady as he sat in front of the mirror. He looked himself in his bright green eyes and almost dropped the scalpel, afraid to continue. Then he thought of Roberto, and his loss, and chugged more courage. The creatures had to stop.

With his eye wide open, he slowly brought the blade closer. He didn't look directly at it, but watched himself in the mirror as if watching a television show. There was a detachment from himself as he slid the tip of the blade in between his eyeball and lower eyelid, the hiding place of the creatures.

He felt pressure from the scalpel, took another swig of vodka, and pushed it further inside.

A sharp pain made him recoil as the blade sliced around his eye. He severed thin sinewy material holding his eye in the socket, blinding it. He paused, unsure if the alcohol or the scalpel had altered his sight. Blood ran down his cheek like tears. Fitting. He'd cried so many times after Roberto left. These were the final tears. Soon they'd be together again.

Steven followed the contour of his eye, slicing at the connections holding it in place. He'd take a pull of vodka when his resolve waivered, then continue carving out his now useless eye. Throbbing pain radiated from his eye, but it had to be better than a lifetime of those…things escaping his eye, even if they were some sort of personal release. He could accept himself without them. He had to.

With the final cut, Steven wedged the scalpel behind his eye and pulled until a sickening pop indicated the eye was free, like he'd soon be. The eye fell into his hand, round and bloody. In the mirror, a one eyed man stared back at him. The empty socket filled with blood, but no creature. Steven placed the eye on the sink, chugged the rest of the vodka, and sometime soon after, passed out.

Several days later he regained the courage to look in

the mirror again. When he did, a horrific image greeted him.

"What have I done?" he said, tracing the outline of the empty orbital bone where his once green eye rested.

He'd managed to find his loose eye and store it in a glass jar he placed next to his bed, a constant reminder of whom he was and where he'd come from. Never again would he feel bad for who he was, instead claiming acceptance of himself.

A day went by, and no creature. Another day, still nothing. By the time a week passed and the creatures failed to burst forth from his empty eye socket, Steven's mood turned upbeat.

"I've won! I stopped you. I don't need you to free me. I did it myself. I know who I am. Nothing you do changes that," he said. Smiling, he thought of Roberto. It was time to mend their relationship. "Tomorrow," he said, "I'll make it right with him."

When he laid his head on his soft pillow, he'd felt a nervous energy rush through him as he anticipated once again meeting Roberto, sleep eluding him for several hours.

Steven woke in the middle of the night to a familiar sensation. Out of his good eye, a soft, gelatinous tentacle wormed free. The burning pain of anger and shame and relief returned. He shot up in bed.

"No more, it's over! I can't do this anymore!" he screamed as the creature pulled itself free, slid down his face, and scurried away.

Erin Lee's
Shopping List

78

Mason jars
Food coloring
Rabbit's feet
Nail polish – black and gold
Vinegar
Bleach for the floor
Vodka
Ice
Carrots

Rabbitt's Feet

Erin Lee

Jack

Hoodoo legend will tell you that it's not just the left hind foot of a rabbit that's lucky. The foot's gotta come from a rabbit shot or otherwise captured in a cemetery. It's true. I'm a lot of things, but not a liar. You can look it up on Wikipedia if you don't believe me, if you have that kind of time. There are other superstitions too. Some say that you have to do it in a full moon, or a new moon. Others say it matters whether or not the rabbit is alive. They say it has to be on the 13th or a rainy day. At least a Friday.

Not me. I don't believe any of that. You see, I've been doing this a long time. I've studied all the ways. I've got my own ideas about what makes a rabbit's foot lucky. But we'll get to that soon. We have all kinds of time. It takes at least five minutes for them to really bleed out. Except that last one, she was a fighter. Just my type. Or not. I change my mind on that from year to year.

Today, I've got a screamer. That won't last long. She'll shut up when she accepts her fate. It's what they all do. Yammer, yammer, yammer. Beg, plead, beg. Then, when they see it in my eyes, they surrender. I tell them they should feel lucky. They get to live on, forever, with their pretty little feet.

"Not every broad gets to be one of Rabbitt's lucky ladies; forever treasured and kept on display. You weren't gonna be anything anyway," I say.

"I said, shut up!" I scream, hating them for making me this way.

***

Daddysgirl1985

I admit it. I like it rough. A simple fetish isn't about to scare me. I've been that way since I was sixteen and my high school boyfriend spanked me on his parent's waterbed between English and Chemistry. What I would give to go back to those days; his warm hands, eager eyes. Two kids, a dozen rubbers, good porn, a flogger and a pack of Lucky Strikes. Everything flashes in front of me. I don't have a lot of time, so I'll get to the point. I've never been afraid of my sexuality. I figure, use it while you can. Use it good.

"I'll do anything you want. I swear! I'll be good."

I probably should have known better. My friends warned me. My father too. But why listen to a man who only showed up when I turned eighteen and it was too late for Mom to go after him for child support? Not much of a daddy there. More like sperm donor. I wonder if things would have been different, had he been around. Who could really blame me for answering the advertisement? Not like "Daddy" was going to pay tuition. I mean, what girl in her right mind turns down a free mani-pedi from a harmless old guy? I guess I'm just unlucky. "Sugar Daddy, please apply" and "Seeking Arrangement." Only, there was no sugar to this daddy.

"Please, Mister. Please!"

Me: I take what I can get. You see, I've been doing this a long time. I've met hundreds of guys. Fuck you, "Daddy." You too, Mom, with your parade of men. It'll be different for me, I told myself. And it has been. I've always taken precautions. Googled them, told friends where I'd be, met in public places, used safe words, even made them take pictures of their licenses. But Mr. "Jack Rabbitt" – how did I ever believe that was really his name? — said he was a widow. I didn't see any harm in meeting him at the cemetery. He told me he wanted to show me his wife's grave; said it was their anniversary. I felt bad for him. I mean, the guy was ancient. Like fifty.

"It doesn't have to be this way! Please, Mister!"

Truthfully, I would have been less naive had I gotten into a van marked "free candy" with windows covered in trash bags. I don't know what I was thinking. Getting sloppy, I guess. Tuition bills are due soon and I haven't had a decent haircut in months. I should have just taken the semester off. It's not like I'm learning anything I can't learn in the streets. I can see the van now, covered in blood red footprints. "Hey, follow me." *Idiot.*

***

Jack

I started collecting in 1993. I've gone through all the colors of the rainbow, and back, twice. I'm back to indigo - the perfect combination of azul, purple and fuchsia. I need to get back to the craft store for more Rit Dye. Ain't nothing like a rainbow to make a man feel— finally—lucky. Too bad I can't take the feet out with me, to the store. At least I can't lose them, all lined up on my shelf. They say losing um is bad luck. Not for me. Not no more. Jack Rabbitt is not a loser. Fuck you, "Dad." What do you think of me now, Old Man? You watchin this shit?

How do rabbits compare to women? Well, don't get me started. My late wife, Sophie—whore that she was—is the perfect example of this. For one, they breed. You try getting excited about a namesake and having it come out three shades of pigment too dark to ever be called your own without snickers from the guys at the station. Fuck that.

"Shut up, I'm trying to think! Ain't got no time to listen to this crap." I think of the guys at the firm, who make fun of me and ask me the last time I got laid. If only they could see me now. Jack Rabbitt. That's with two t's. The name fits me.

Rabbits, like women, are tricksters. Ain't nothing like a pretty woman to ruin a man's dreams, take his land, and leave him nothing but memories. A man, a smart one anyway, has got to make memories of his own. So every year, on the anniversary of the day the broad finally left me, I go hunting. Tonight was no different. Pretty little thing. Pretty little feet.

"Oh, does that hurt? Oh, I'm so sorry. Where's your daddy now, kinky-money grubbing little thing? Karma's a bitch, ain't she?"

***

Daddysgirl1985

The mani-pedi wasn't even that great. Mr. Rabbitt had made a special request - which he call and pick out the polish ahead of time. I don't like purple, no matter how fancy of a word you want to use for it. I should have argued, or just never shown up for the appointment. I'm more of a French manicure type of girl. But I wasn't about to put up a fight. Indigo was his wife's favorite color, the color of the dresses at their wedding, he said. Like I said, I felt sorry for the guy.

"You gotta let me go. Please, Mister! I won't tell anyone, I swear! Please? I'll do anything you want. Just like I said I would. Please!"

It doesn't matter what color, I suppose. Now, everything's red. Like that old boyfriend's sheets, the first time he took me home. I remember how he bawled them up and shrugged; told me not to worry about it. Promised he'd wash them himself so his mother and sister wouldn't see. Asked to go again. "Just one more time." That one time became three, and back again.

Men, and boys, are all the same when you think about it. They only want one thing. It's what I've counted on. It's how I've paid my way through community college looking good and eating free. I haven't paid for a meal in over a year. My eyelashes and dirty talk bought me anything I needed. Now, I wish I'd done things differently; seeing as there will be no more. I'm beginning to drift, and feel no pain. Red swirls at my feet. I wonder if he'll clean it up; hide it from authorities.

***

Jack

Stupid bitch. All she had to do was listen to me. I might have let her go. I actually kinda liked her. Called herself "Daddysgirl1985." I've done that before—set um free—when I ran out of dye. But not this time, she's too much of a fighter. Argued all the way home. I told her I just wanted to be able to see them in the light – the fancy toes I paid for. "No, not tonight," as if she had a choice. And then, she gave up the fight. I'm not sure I liked her as much then. It doesn't matter.

"Shut up!"

Chained to a wall in my basement. Like the others before. Squirming and trying to reason with me.

"Sorry, bitch, but your tits aren't that great and I'm not in in for those. Breeder."

What is it with women who think that a quick tongue and willingness to swallow will get them somewhere further? If I wanted that, I could pick it up for twenty roses and a whole lot less risk and hassle. Dye ain't cheap. Neither is gasoline.

"Stop the screaming, whore. You should be thanking me. I thought you said you liked little games? A girl like you is fun to play with – your words!"

Stupid me. I'm out of fuchsia too. Getting sloppy. I guess it happens to the best of us, with time. I watch her, motionless, except her chest, still moving up and down. Heaving, if she had more fight. More like conceding. Pathetic. It won't be long now. I can see her surrendering. I feel myself grow hard. I adjust. I don't want to admit to myself that there's something kinky about that moment when fate surrenders and destiny falls to its knees. I refuse to call this a fetish. I touch myself anyway. A man has needs. Go ahead. Judge me. I dare you.

"There, now, that's better. Silence."

***

Daddysgirl1985

Silly, silly me. I should have told Kate—my roommate—where I was going. They'll never find me or the dozens he's said have come before. I need this to go fast. He's staring at me. Sick, sick man. I tell myself not to fight it. There's no point in arguing. I know this by the jars—tiny painted toes, missing the big one so there's four—and colors that surround them. I wonder what he does with them, the big ones. It doesn't matter.

I'm glad I left my butterfly toe ring at home. He doesn't deserve it.

At least I can't feel it anymore. My eyes are closed, head is back, and I'm ready to move on. I don't want to see what becomes of the rest of me. If he could do that to my foot – my feet? I can't leave. I want to take all that's left of me and scream. I want to ask him why and make him, too, bleed. I close my eyes and imagine using my fingernails to carve his eyes out. I open them, telling myself I don't want to be like him. He seems pleased. I hate him. I stop squirming. I forget to breathe. Panic eats me, the same way I imaging him sucking on those feet.

He sits there in a chair, sipping coffee, chewing nicotine. I want to spit. On him. At him. I want to hop up on my right foot and hit his growing bulge. He sits there, getting off to my silent prayer for it to be over. I lay there, on a cold floor, chained to a wall, wondering if it ever will be. Reminding myself that I did this to myself. I've always been good at owning my own shit and admitting when I was wrong. I should have trusted my gut when he asked me to come home with him "just to show off those pretty little feet." I thought there might be something in it for me. I mean, nothing wrong with a few roses. I told myself, he just wanted company. I would have given him more than that. Chains don't scare me.

***

Jack

Getting um here isn't as easy as you might think. There are ways you have to do it, so you don't get caught. Two decades and no one has a clue. They just go missing. Pretty little girls with perfect tidy lives, never to be seen again; unlucky little things. I'm not a gambling man, as funny as that may seem. I don't take chances. And, well, I have luck on my side. Times twenty-two, now twenty-three. I only keep the left ones. The right ones? I eat. Like rabbit meat. I tell them I'm going to do it too. Most of them believe me. I think they can see it in my eyes. I like that. I like the respect.

"That's a good girl. I'm so pleased."

She chokes on saliva. I chuckle, remembering how that whore spit in my face and told me I'd make a horrible father anyway. I'm tempted to cover her mouth with my hand, just to watch her eyes bulge. But that would take the fun out of it; watching the struggle. I look at my watch. Two more minutes. If I'm lucky, three. I already miss her screams. Her black eyes, wide, and staring at me as I fondled her feet. A good pair of ankle restraints and there ain't nothing to it. Who has time for rope? Please. Not me. Not anymore.

I close my eyes and stroke it off; thinking about the last time that whore fucked me. She rode me into another planet. I had no idea it wasn't my seed. Took her three minutes. Maybe less. No woman could ever get me off like that. Not without pantyhose and feet. Jackrabbit style, she took me. Lucky me. Shoulda made her bleed.

"Stupid slut."

Plenty of time for bleeding now. They leak, those feet. It just comes pouring out like a fine wine and, oh, so tasty. I can't wait to drink her sweet nectar. I'll save it, like I have the blood from the others, for special occasions. If you freeze it right, you can keep it longer. Never more than a month. I just don't have the willpower. Never did. I admit it, in some ways, I am weak.

Minutes are counting down. Three. Two. Her breaths become so shallow I want to kiss her. I'm tempted to breathe the life back into her, just enough, so she stays with me longer. But that wouldn't be very gentlemanly.

Harder, faster, as her breaths become softer, further in between…

"That'a girl. Easy now…"

***

Daddysgirl1985

Dying isn't as hard as you might think. Looking back, I can't say I have a lot left to live for anyway. Cranked out mom and a half-brother twice as bad. The high school guy traded me in years ago for a girl who had a better ass. Funny, he used to say she was ugly when I was feeling insecure. But all men—and boys—are the same. Like rabbits, hoping from one bed to another, breaking hearts. They don't care about the bruises they leave on us, the stains on their sheets, or anything more than getting lucky.

He chokes his cock like he's on the clock. If I could, I'd yawn. I don't have time for this. There are places to see and things to do. He didn't give me time or room for goodbyes. I'm not sure who will even care, when I die. So it's okay. I wonder what it will be like, in heaven or in hell; wherever I'm headed. I refuse to live with regrets. I'm not that kind of girl.

I write my obituary in my head, tuning him out. I wonder what they will think of me, when I'm dead. I'll be the girl who fell for the guy with the lines on the Internet. They'll call me dumb and naïve. Some may even say I asked for it. Ha. If they could only see me now. I'd do anything to do things different. Regret comes in every color of the rainbow. "Nothing in life is free," my mother's warning screams at me.

He's a monster with a black soul. Yes, I want to forgive him. I'm weak and there's something in his eyes that makes me think he can't be all bad. I wonder who he could have been, had he made other choices. I wonder who didn't love him and turned him cold. I wonder if he's ever known love at all.

I exhale one final time, feeling myself lift fully from the floor. No man has ever lifted me higher, not without suspension rods and the threat of a crop. I look down at him, lonely old man, and smile. Color blinds my eyes. It comes in every color: red, orange, yellow, green, blue, purple, indigo. Indigo. Indigo.

Free.

***

One Year Later, Jack

Sometimes, I wonder if I'll ever be free. No matter how many pretty little feet I collect. No matter how soft they are, what color they are, and how lucky they might be, no matter what the legend is. And so, I buy more jars – hoping to increase my odds and somehow even the score. And again, tonight, on my anniversary, I'll go hunting. But this time, things may be a little different. I've done quite a bit of thinking since the last girl. And for now, while this day drags on, thinking is all I have time for.

"Did you file the Leary affidavit?"

Okay. Maybe not. Who can think with this guy around? Roderick has never had social cues. It's lost on him that I'm busy in thought. For my meager $19 an hour wage, I'm supposed to jump right up. I'm supposed to say, "yes, Master." *Fuck that. I'm the one in charge!*

"Yes. I did that last week." *Prick.*

"Any word on a court date?"

"Nothing yet. You'll be the first to know."

"Thanks, Jack."

"Yep."

"So I have this list. The partners and I put it together. We need it done by the end of next week."

I don't bother to look up from my computer screen. I know what the list will look like. It will be at least three pages long. It will include things I'm considered not qualified to do. Of course, I'll do it anyway, and better than any of them would. I'll do it for twenty percent of the price they will bill for it. I'll do it with a smile, while they buy flowers for their mistresses and wives.

"Thanks, dude," Roderick says, almost like we're friends. I wonder, sometimes, if it's guilt or just his inability to tell from my body language that I'd rather share office space with Hitler.

"Yep."

Out of the corner of my eye I can see him check his wristwatch. My computer reads 4:17 p.m. and he's already making his exit. *Wow. A whole six-hour day. He's making a record. Better than the other guys, I guess.*

"Well, it's about that time. Can you lock up?"

I nod. "Always do."

"Great. Thanks, bud. Don't work too hard."

Always do.

The moment he's gone, I push the list he left on my desk into a drawer. I'll deal with it another time. It's not like they'll be checking. Right now, I ain't got time for that. I close out of the firm's database and pull the hours for Gold's Gym, just to be sure. Women who take care of their bodies also take care of their feet. See? I'm smart. And, usually, I plan ahead. But not the first time. The first time was before I knew about luck and pretty little feet…

The first one was the landlady. The old bag lived upstairs. Before you go judging me for knocking off a Q-tip, hear me out. This woman wasn't your ordinary brownie-baking grandma. To me, that wouldn't really matter. All my things are objects. I've never met a person that I thought of as anything more than that - a thing. Well, except Sophie, but you know how that turned out for me if you've been paying attention. If not? That's fine. I don't expect you to. I ain't stupid.

Anyway, the old broad was always making problems for me. Wasn't bad enough my old lady was screwing the neighbor, and the neighbor's son. Naw, the old bag had to report on it too. She was always telling us to keep the noise down, Sophie's screaming and hollering and my music. Once, she even called the cops on us for playing a little Zeppelin. I mean, really. Who does that?

Things with Sophie were about to boil over. The ink on our divorce papers was dry only eight months and the cheating bitch was still sleeping on my couch. I'd had enough with coming home to new "friends" in the apartment, stacks of dishes, and a pot pipe on the kitchen counter. I was tired of handing my paycheck over to Sophie, who'd quit her job a year before because it was "too much" to be standing on her feet all day cutting hair. She said I didn't understand because I had a "pussy's" job.

That's how it was with Sophie. If you weren't working all day in the dirt or somehow using your hands, you weren't really working. She missed the memo somewhere that being Tweed's punching bag was job enough for ten people. She had no clue what kind of patience and man it took to put up with their condescending stares. And, for what? So she could get her nails done for the cable guy? Screw that. I showed her I could use my hands. I used those hands to knock off the old bag upstairs – the one who said Sophie could stay as long as she wanted because, technically, she was on the lease. The same broad that told me my rent was late and it'd mean a $50 fee.

I didn't keep left foot and I'm glad. I knew nothing about canning back then and she wouldn't be the kind of thing any collector could be proud of anyway. That's the great thing about the old ones; you can just leave them in their chair. Somebody finds them. The walk in, they clean um up, they have a wake and a funeral, they charge a million bucks. They say she was a lovely lady who lived a lovely life and was mother of, friend of, sister of, daughter of. It's just what they do. Just things.

But Sophie? She knew. Somehow, she knew. She was gone two days later. Ran off with the neighbor. Just like I always knew she would. Took the kid too. From what I hear, she's been through three more. She bounces, one sucker, one thing, to the next, making them pay for her till they catch on. Then, it's on to something better with a thicker wallet. Sophie and I were a lot alike in that way, I guess. Anyway, back to the old broad. Somehow, it doesn't feel like it was even me – it was so long ago. It's almost like watching a movie. Still, I think of her, every year on my anniversary - right before hunting…

***

"I just don't understand why you and Sophie can't keep it down, dear. My hearing is horrible and I can still hear everything."

"Look, I'm hardly ever even home. If I could control that woman, don't you think she'd already be out of here? It's not like I signed up for this and you're the one making me keep her here."

Nora shook her head, "No, dear. That's not me. Besides, she has that baby."

"But it is! You said her name was on the lease. That kind of locks me in, even with the kid. I can't kick her out. I've already tried."

"Why can't one of her boyfriend's help her? They are here all day anyway. And what kind of man let's his wife run around town like that anyway?"

Jack swallowed the things he wanted to say, sucking in short breaths of Momma-knows-best, and biting his lower lip. He spoke with purpose, when he finally did: "Don't. You. Think. I. Would. Do. Something. About. Her. Boyfriends. If. I. Could?"

"Kids. I just don't understand how young people do things these days. If they aren't shacking up, it's this. Don't you know a real man wouldn't stand for this? Didn't your father teach you?"

That was it. It was all he needed. Sophie's face came flashing before his eyes: Her snide glare, the way she laughed at him when he questioned her son's paternity, how she claimed she didn't know how to iron.

Jack walked closer to her, the old woman who'd been nagging them since before they'd even signed the lease. The woman who'd interrupted their love making a million times and told Sophie to stop her screaming. The same woman who informed him, at least once a week, that she was screaming again during game shows and making it impossible to watch the first round of the evening news.

Nora kept talking as he stood over her, both hands in fists but moving toward her neck. She talked about how she was thinking of raising the rent and asked him why he smelt that way. She talked and talked until he couldn't stand it any longer.

Jack reached for a throw pillow on the back of her couch, only a few feet from the old bag in her rocking chair. She smiled, assuming he was going to use it to help prop her up – like the nurse who came in a few times a week to check in on her. Instead, he grabbed her by the back of the head and shoved that pillow into her mouth. He held her there, through her screams and flailing arms.

He held her there while she prayed and said goodbye to her son and the women in the Red Hat Society. He pushed the pillow further into her mouth, wishing she would hurry up and die. That last thing he wanted to deal with was Sophie and more talking, more questions.

Finally, her hands went limp, resting on armrests she'd used to balance her coffee and the remote control. When he was sure she was gone, he turned the television down, put the pillow back and closed her mouth. He left her, sitting in that chair of hers: Death by natural cause. *It's what the newspaper said. But for Jack, it was his first introduction to karma. And, man, was it addictive.*

***

Daddysgirl1985

I've been dead a year now. Or, maybe, it's that I've been free. Either way, I've had a lot of time to think about things. I've gone over nearly every memory. Sometimes, it doesn't even feel like me. It's like watching a movie. Or, more like being part of a dream. Other times, it's a nightmare, seeing where I went wrong and what I might have done different. Mostly, I just laugh at the irony. I was killed by a man fixated on karma and getting lucky. I spent so many years trying to look good and take care of myself, putting vanity ahead of pride, that it was my feet and a stupid manicure that finally brought me to my demise. It's just ridiculous.

But, that's the way life can be—especially when you trust a man with the last name Rabbitt, with two t's.

Currently, he's sitting in his cubicle counting the hours. He plans to hit up the local gym to celebrate an anniversary with a wife who was never really his. I would know. I've met her. She's had a lot of time to think too and has even more regret. She was victim number two. And hers was the first foot he kept. …I digress. This is supposed to be about me, not him: The man who stole my life from me.

At first, I thought it was purely sexual. A freak with a foot fetish—I wasn't in the position to judge kinks with a few of my own—who thought it was cute I had Daddy issues. Now, I know, it was about the power. And power, well, let's face it; has a way of turning people on. So in that way, I can't say I blame him. I mean, I get it. I really do. I'm the girl who was desperately seeking Daddy. Or, I was, anyway, until I became nothing more than an unlucky foot dyed indigo in Rabbitt's nasty Mason jar collection. But before that? Oh, there was something nice about playing baby girl in a man's arms… I haven't forgotten. I could never forget. If I'd only stuck with my first Daddy. I close my eyes and remember.

***

I stretch across Daddy's full-sized bed, looking up at burgundy walls; wondering what's taking him so long. It's been hours, it seems, since he left. I know this isn't true, but even a few minutes without Daddy seems like a lifetime. Daddy feels the same way about me, I can tell. He misses me and gets grumpy the minute I leave his side. But he doesn't whine about it, not like I do. I try to be good, but it's hard. With him only a room away, a pacifier in one hand, and curled up in his blankets, it's easier. I'm twenty-four years old and something about a pacifier still calms me. I know, strange.

Red, any shade of it, has never been a color of mine. I think of it as harsh, mean, or even violent. Red reminds me of blood. It scares me. Red's the kind of color in a horror movie where you can only watch with one eye peeking out from the covers. Daddy's sheets, like his walls, are red. I prefer purple and colors like indigo. Still, lately, this color is growing on me and I find myself drawn to it. I throw fabric red rose petals into the air, now sucking on a green apple lollipop, waiting for Daddy to finish cooking a roast two rooms away. It feels like he will never come back and I'm tempted to reach into my bag to pull out some glitter. Glitter bombs are the best. They remind Daddy of me when I'm gone. I can't let Daddy forget me; but he promises he never could.

Daddy is the best cook. It doesn't matter if I eat ten pops before dinner. I'll eat anything he makes me, including the broccoli. I like it when Daddy brings me milk in my purple Sippy cup with dinner. I'm not so good at finishing my milk. His red and grape Kool-aides are better. I don't mind red Kool-aide. It makes my lips look pretty. The prettier, the better. Cause Daddy's kisses are the best. And red lips are good for pouting.

"Are you ready, Lil One?" I laugh, but not out loud. Just the concept of other people hearing two grown adults talk and act this way still seems comical to me. I feel lucky that Daddy understands and sees nothing strange about this at all.

I can't hold the lollipop in my mouth. Just the sound of his voice makes me want to jump up, hug, bounce on the bed, and hug him. I want to beg him to play with my princess parts and smother me with kisses. But we've already played—once—today and it's already 8 p.m. Daddy doesn't like pushing off dinner.

"Yes, Daddy!"

"Come, sit at the table, before it gets too cold."

I put my lollipop and pacifier on the nightstand table Daddy moved there just for me. I spring up to join him at the table. I can hardly stand it, watching him cut my meat. Daddy has huge hands: the strong hands of a carpenter. I imagine them palming my butt cheeks and wish I could get in trouble, just so he'd spank me. I'm tempted to skip the broccoli.

"Daddy, you don't have to cut my meat. Your dinner will get cold."

"I have to take care of you, Baby Girl."

"Yes Daddy." I melt. I think he sees.

There's a way certain men move that I've never been able to avoid noticing. How they move their hands tells me a lot about them. The way Daddy cuts the pork roast—precise, confident, sure motions—tells me he knows what he's doing. I know he's good at his job. He spends his days building things. Daddy is a perfectionist. But watching him, with that knife, cutting that meat, reminds me of the way he uses his teeth on me. Daddy knows how to move; and not just his hands.

He's watching me. I pretend not to notice. He cuts every piece of meat, but one, and tells me to tell him when I'm ready for him to cut that too. He reminds me to eat my vegetables.

"Daddy! I'm a good girl! I always eat my vegetables."

Dinner melts on my tongue and I beat him—like always—to a clean plate. When I'm not with him, I eat slowly. With Daddy, I eat quickly, wishing we could do pet play so I could lick my plate clean. He's that good of a cook. He laughs, telling me his special seasonings are not much more than salt and pepper. The trick, he says, is drying herbs out and crushing them, or something like that. I can't really focus. I can't pay attention. All I can think about is the knife in Daddy's hand and what it would be like if he put it to my throat: *Yes, please.*

Daddy never plays right away after dinner. He says he needs time for his food to settle. But, like with everything, we've found compromise. Just because Daddy doesn't want to play, doesn't mean he won't play with me. I crawl back into his rosy sheets, sucking my lollipop and asking him to snuggle me. I stare at him with my big, black eyes: the ones that get me anything I want from Daddy. He grins, again, watching me.

"Daddy, this lollipop is good."

"Well, you were a good girl and ate all your dinner."

"I'm always a good girl."

"Yes, Little One, you are."

"I love this lollipop forever. I want to buy a hundred of them."

"It's kind of small. Not like the one we had before," he says, referring to the Toys R Us pop.

I shrug, slurping at it. Then, I take it from my mouth, push it toward him, and offer him a lick. "But it tastes awesome. Here. …Try!"

He takes it from my hand but doesn't lick it. Instead, he looks at it, then at me. I squint, trying to read his eyes in the dim light, wondering what he has in store for me. He says nothing. He pushes me, gently, back on the bed. Propped on Daddy's big red pillows, I forget to breathe. I watch him, as he lifts the hem of my black mini skirt, exposing my thighs. I squirm, but with the wall behind the pillows, there's nowhere to go. I reach down and pull up my thigh high stockings – pink with ruffles to match the too-small-but-so-cute tee shirt I'm wearing. He takes my wrist into his hand like it's nothing, placing it behind my back. I know better than to fight and leave it there, wishing I'd had time to adjust the other stocking. He presses into me.

Finally, with his stubble scratching my neck, he speaks into my ear. "Little Girl, you weren't good this week. Tell Daddy why he should reward you?"

I'm dizzy. I can't breathe. I have no idea what he's talking about. Sure, I threw glitter all over his floor, even hid confetti in his work stuff. Yeah, it was me that threw a fit that he wasn't paying enough attention to me, threatened to show the boys my private parts. But that was a good week, for me, really.

"I don't know," are the only words that come out. He smells like oranges, garlic, and this organic body wash he pays too much for. "I'm sorry."

"What should Daddy do with you?" His hand is on my right thigh, pushing it against the bed, so my legs are spread. I'm not wearing panties. Daddy has a rule: No panties in my bed. I try to follow the rules. Most of the time.

"I don't know." I want to scream. I want to yell at him exactly what he should do. I feel myself wanting to be big. I feel the words "fuck me, hard!" and "doggie, please!" and "fuck being little! I want to be your whore, you fucking pussy!" coming to my lips. And, as if he can sense it, he reaches across me for my princess pacifier. He puts it in my mouth and I suck at it, grateful for the reminder, wondering where the lollipop went.

I don't wonder long.

Daddy gives me a hard look: "Don't move. Stay still."

A moan escapes me, through the pacifier. The room begins to spin and I can feel myself beginning to float away.

First, he uses his fingers. One. Two. Three. Four. Next time, I'll ask him to count them out. *Keep your mouth shut. You aren't in charge. Trust Daddy. He knows what he's doing. Daddy is in charge.*

His hands, frankly, all of him, are bigger than I've ever had before. I'm still not used to how he fills me. I can't imagine ever settling for anything less again. I only want my Daddy. He moves his fingers inside me like an artist; reaching places I haven't been able to find myself. Every worry, problem, ounce of pain disappears. I want more. And more. And more.

I arch my back and tell myself it's not time. I have to wait for Daddy's permission. I want to give in to him, and I know he wants it too. Daddy's not like other dominants. Daddy loves when I cum. But I don't want it too soon – that one thing I can control. I want to savor every second of him, all of him, inside me. This annoys him. I don't care. I am a brat. He is stubborn. This is our dance and we do it well.

"Cum for Daddy," he says. "Come on, Baby Girl, give it to Daddy."

I shake my head, sucking at the pacifier, moaning. "Nooooo."

He plunges four fingers into me, faster, harder. And then: "Pop!"

I gasp.

I strain to sit up. I look down. Between my thighs, past Daddy's hands and my princess parts, is the thin white stick—the very end—of my Cherry lollipop. He smiles at me, pushing me back down.

I can't breathe. I'm dizzy. All of me is about to leave this room, but can't. I don't want to miss a moment of Daddy's attention. It's too good, too sweet, like the sticky flavoring covering the insides of my thighs as Daddy works me. He fucks me hard, stirring my insides with the lollipop and then taking it fully out, stopping right at my hole, twisting and another "pop!"

I can't help it. I cum. Over and over. I cum again and again, spitting out the pacifier, begging Daddy for more. He isn't listening. He sucks at me. He holds my clit between his teeth, flicking it with his tongue and eating the cherry off me, all while fucking me. The round candy is hard and warm and Daddy has no intentions of stopping. I let waves of cum ride over me, ready to surrender.

"How many licks does it take to get to the bottom of a tootsie pop, Little One?" he asks, looking up at me with a grin, and going right back to work. He takes turns with the pop, his hands, and his tongue. He doesn't care that his face and hair are covered in red proof of our love. And suddenly, he pulls out of me. He hands me the pop.

"Here. Suck on this. And don't move." He leaves the room.

Again, I'm grateful for the plug in my mouth – this time born of the candy store. I want to beg him to stay, not leave. I'm tempted to call him a fag and ask him if his dick is so limp he can only fuck with props. I keep my mouth shut, knowing that will only wind up with me not being able to sit right for a week. Still, I'm tempted. I suck on the lollipop, eating up my own juices and looking down at the mess he's left between my legs. I close my thighs and they stick together. I giggle, wondering how his face must feel.

He's been gone forever. I decide there's no harm in finishing what he started. I lower the pop to my princess parts and 'pop' it in myself. No matter how hard and fast I try, I can't do it like Daddy did. It's never the same without him. I manage to cum, turning my head into his pillow so he doesn't hear, before he returns to the room. By the time he returns, I'm happily sucking the pop, smiling at him.

Daddy's smiling bigger. He holds two popsicles, still wrapped in white packaging. Through them, I can barely make out the flavors: Orange and grape.

"Pick one."

I pick orange. I like to keep him guessing. Daddy's known purple is my favorite color since before he knew my name.

"I pick both." Daddy says, removing wrappers from each Popsicle and moving toward the bed.

I try to cover myself. My skirt isn't close to long enough. I take the lollipop out of my mouth to protest. He raises his eyebrows. I put it back in my mouth, lay back, and close my eyes.

Coldness invades me. It bites at my insides and Popsicle juice immediately starts running into my ass. It doesn't stop Daddy, who starts fast and hard, like he left off, with the lollipops. This time, his mouth is almost hot on my clit as I fight the urge to push him and the freezing treat out of my private parts.

"Daddy! It's freezing!"

He laughs. "Yes. It's melting, Little One."

I want to beg him to stop. But then, I don't want him to stop. He takes my cunt into his mouth and slurps at it. It reminds me of a hot summer day. He laps at me like he hasn't had anything to drink in months, like he's starving. The coldness begins to fade, replaced by numbness, except where his mouth is. Where his mouth is the fire. I want to cum. But I don't.

He takes the half-melted orange out of me, replacing it with the grape. Again, coldness invades me - deep. It feels like it will go on forever. I beg him to eat me. I need his warm mouth on me, to make it easier. But he resists. Instead, he fucks me with the Popsicle until it's only a stick – which he hands me. I can't feel anything, pain or pleasure. Only need. For Daddy.

Daddy gives me the rest of the orange Popsicle. He instructs me to finish it while he finishes me. He scolds me, for being so sticky. Calls me a dirty girl. But I know he's pleased. And its only seconds before I can feel again – this time, him, inside of me. *Daddy's Girl. Forever. Pass the lollipop, please.*

***

Jack

Hoodoo legend will also tell you that it's not just rabbits feet acquired in the right conditions or on special occasions that bring luck. Look it up if you don't believe me, but hoodoo will also tell you that the right conditions also bring protection and spiritual connection. I do believe in that. You see, I've been doing this a long time. I've studied all the ways. I've got my own ideas about what makes the conditions right. And, how we stay connected. That last one? Daddy's girl? I bet she still thinks of me, as I do her. But we'll get to that later, when I visit her foot. We have all kinds of time. I told you before, it takes at least five minutes for them to really bleed out. This one might even be quicker. Not my type like last time. More interested in free weights than making a man feel like a man. But that's okay. There's always next year. I've got the red dye ready. Karma's a bitch. Oh, look! She's begging with her eyes. Time to unzip my fly… *I'm a lucky guy. Forget about the feet. The rest of you is* **mine**.

"Not every broad gets to be one of Rabbitt's lucky ladies; forever treasured and kept on display. You weren't gonna be anything anyway," I say.

"I said, shut up!" I scream, hating her—a grown assed woman—for crying for Daddy. I mean, for Christ's sake. People have issues with foot fetishes? *Freak.*

End

John Barackman's
Shopping List

- One-eighth inch thick copper sheet. 24" x 36"
- Sample package five watt resistors, various ohm values
- 3 watt tri-color LEDs, star heat sink, 200 count.
- oxy-acetylene gas tanks
- Portable electric air compressor - 2 HP, 4.6 gallon, 5.3 CFM
- Two tickets, Makers Faire, Santa Clara, CA
- John Deere R1025 tractor with tiller attachment
- Tickets, Steve Hackett, City Winery, Nashville
- Black Box Cabernet Sauvignon
- Set plastic wine glasses

The Vulture

John Barackman

Jason got word of his layoff package just as the last firecrackers of July exploded their paper shrapnel guts onto the black asphalt behind his condo. Dave, his manager at Robotix, Inc. had called Jason to inform him of the bad news but also to offer to relocate him should Jason accept. Dave waited patiently for Jason's response.

"But Dave", he replied after hearing the details of the offer, "It's all the way across the country in Tennessee for God's sake!"

"The office is closing Jason; you are always free to take the severance package of course...." said Dave.

"OK, so if I accept, I am promoted to manufacturing head and I get a six month sabbatical to move and get my shit together before starting the new job?" Jason asked.

"Yep, that is about the size of it. Pretty sweet offer I would say. Someone high up the chain really likes you." Dave replied.

So he, Jason Jackson (In his head Jason hears his best friend Bob's boisterous exclamation: "Never trust a guy with two first names!" accompanied by a hard slap to his back) accepted the offer. The small San Francisco regional office of Robotix, Inc. would be no more.

Jason, the lead Systems Engineer, would soon be moving to the Headquarters and primary manufacturing facility of said Robotix, Inc. located in the small rural town of Springdale, just a smidgen less than an hour south of Nashville, Tennessee. Why locate in such a small town? He had asked his superiors when the opportunity had presented itself.

"Because land is cheap. Labor is cheap. And local authorities leave you the hell alone" came the reply.

Rural Tennessee. Cow and fucking corn whiskey Tennessee, thought Jason.

As he hung up on Dave, 'DJ,' as Jason referred to his music loving, and oh so sarcastic internal voice, whooped in Southern twang: *Yea Ha! Go Git'em Cowboy! Grab Your Banjo – we're gonna have a Hoedown!* Damn and double damn.

##

Eight weeks later, after selling his condo, he was on the road. Thank God the San Francisco Bay Area housing market was hot and Jason got a great offer only two weeks after putting his place up for sale. But all of that work! After all the packing, cleaning, staging, arranging for the shipping and storage of his furnishings, the endless trips to The Salvation Army and to the dump, camping out at the local coffee shop as endless parades of prospective buyers inspected his home, he was exhausted.

As Jason drove from San Francisco, over the Sierra Nevada and Rocky Mountain ranges to Denver,

Colorado via Highway 50, then East to Kansas City, Missouri on Highway 70, South to Fort Smith, Arkansas by way of Highway 49, then East again to Nashville, Tennessee, fast approaching on Highway 40, he had felt better. Good even. *The United States is fucking BIG,* he thought, but fortunately this gave him much needed time to clear his head. Nice that Robotix, Inc. was paying all his relocation costs and six months of time off. At least there was that.

Two hours later, Jason was on a narrow two-lane country highway nearing downtown Springdale. Curves, steep drop-offs on both sides, and plenty of 18-Wheelers going far too fast, made the going precarious. Jason gripped the steering wheel tight, sweating in concentration as he muttered curses at the truckers who seemed to not care that they were nearly blowing his small sub-compact, stuffed to the gills, as it was, with what little of his possessions he could bring along. He slowed as he neared the four-way stop at the edge of downtown Springdale. *Just a scrape in the road is all it is,* Jason commented to himself as he looked at the rather limited length and breadth of the town center. His inner DJ suddenly cued: 'The long and Winding Road,' sung by Paul McCartney, just as he came to a full stop. *I always hated that song AND the fuckin' asshole that sung it!* thought Jason sourly, now in a very bad mood.

Jason, waiting his turn to cross the four-way stop, looked to his right. He was looking at a corn field (there were miles and miles of corn fields), the stalks cut recently into short stumps by a harvester. But what Jason focused on were the vultures. Dozens of them circling in the air very near to his car, another dozen on the ground, feeding on an obviously very dead cow. Ugly birds, Jason thought, and even uglier dead cow. The cow, in full rigor mortis, was on its side, hooves stiffly out facing Jason, head flat on the ground, it's tongue, long and purple, stuck out its mouth. Jason imagined black cartoon X's on the cow's eyes. The vultures had ripped open the cow's abdomen and were eagerly feasting on its guts. Jason noticed one vulture perched on the ground at the back end of the cow. The vulture was looking right at Jason. As soon as Jason's eyes caught those of the vulture (at least that is the impression that Jason had – *but how could that be? It's was just a stupid bird!* he thought), the vulture dove its head neck deep into the anus of the cow, rutted about, pulled its head back out into the air, its head covered in gore, in its mouth a piece of long sinewy intestine, and ate, gobbling the intestine thread with exaggerated thrusts of its head. Resisting the gorge that rose in his throat, Jason hurried across the intersection. *Jesus,* he thought with disgust, *I was considering stopping for lunch but I think I will put a hold on that.* The Extended Stay which was to be his 'home away from home,' at least until he could buy one of his own, was beckoning just past the town center. It was a welcoming site.

##

Four weeks passed and Jason still resided at the Extended Stay. Despite hours and hours of house hunting with his Real Estate Agent, Mark the 'Make It Happen Man,' Jason remained house-less. The two offers he had made thus far, although both made above asking price, were beat out by all cash offers.

The 'Make It Happen Man' had said rather colorfully: "Well I reckon the market in the Nashville area is hotter 'n a painted hoochie coochie on a wild Saturday night."

A sellers market in Po-Funk'in-Dunk Tennessee. Well who could have predicted that? Jason thought crestfallen.

His inner DJ: *Shucks as they might say round these parts.*

Thanks for that idiotic tidbit! replied Jason to himself, growing more frustrated by the minute waiting, as he was, in his room for his agent to call with more leads.

Jason decided to head to the Piggly Wiggly grocery store just across the street from his room to grab a six pack of Yuengling beer, his new favorite.

Chug-a-lug, chug-a-lug. Make you want to holler hi-de-ho, went his DJ.

Jason was at the checkout, beer tucked safely under his arm, cash in hand for the barely out of her teens cashier to grab. *No beauty queen,* thought Jason as he did a quick and discrete once over of the cashier, *but cute enough.* Jesus he was horny. And lonely.

"You have yourself a nice day, Darling. Y'all come back now and see us again!" the cashier said cheerfully to him.

As Jason headed for the exit, he noticed the man standing at the public bulletin board. The man was at the extreme end of skinny and lanky, a stooped posture, scraggly gray thinning hair, and a long hooked beak of a nose. The man's clothes were too small for his frame and threadbare. He wore, what Jason thought, was a far too feminine, almost girlish jacket, fur lining the lower edge. The man suddenly leaned forward to read a posted notice in a comically exaggerated way. The image of the vulture plunging its head into the cow's asshole immediately leaped to Jason's mind. 'Vulture-Man' coined Jason. Without pause, 'Vulture-Man' turned and looked square at Jason, cackled a laugh, and said in a thin reedy voice:

"You will be interested in this house Mr. Jackson" long dirty forefinger jabbing at the notice. "Just on the market today. But be quick!" he was now pointing that dirty forefinger at Jason, "It won't be available for long! There are other men just like you who would want this." The man then quickly turned and, limping on a game leg, walked out the store, never looking back.

What the fuck was that? How the hell did he know my name? thought Jason. Despite the weirdness, Jason was far too desperate *not* to look. He read, then yanked down the notice. Stuffing it into his pocket, Jason first walked into the grocery parking lot (*Vulture-Man has vanished. Flew away I suppose,* thought Jason) then across the street to his room. As soon as he was in and his door safely closed, he called Mark the 'Make It Happen Man'.

After picking Jason up from the Extended Stay, Mark said: "I don't know how I missed that house in my screens. I mean there it was big as life when I typed in the address you gave me. Weird. And perfect for your needs too! Nice big colonial, lots of privacy, completely remodeled, and exactly in your price range!"

As they approached the house down a long, tree lined lane, Jason said: "Wait. This road is the driveway?"

Mark: "Yep, fifty feet wide and one-thousand feet long. Like I said, very private."

Jason became excited when he saw the house as they approached, "It's beautiful! Look at that wrap-around porch!"

Jason imagined sipping mint juleps while quietly rocking in a wood rocker chair.

Why not? *If ya can't beat 'em, join 'em!* said DJ.

One quick look at the wood and stone interior, at the expansive lawn out back, and, to top-it-all-off, behind the lawn was a wooded acre with stream running through it to boot. *Jesus H Christ on a Stick*, Jason thought, *I've never owned a forest before!*

Jason said firmly, "I don't need to look any further Mark, let's put in an offer ASAP." Walking back to the car, Jason noticed the house on the adjacent property, another big colonial, nice, but a tad bit run down. "Needs some paint...." Jason nodes to Mark. Mark glances over to the house next door and replies:

"Now that is what I call a true 'Fixer upper.' It's an eyesore, I know, but don't worry, in this market, someone is bound to buy it, raze it, and build something big, new, and beautiful. Make this, and all the other properties around here go up value too!" said Mark.

Jason, in confusion, thought: *Raze it? It doesn't look that bad to me....*

On the drive out, on the side of the long driveway to the left, at the tree line, Jason saw the woman. She was stunningly beautiful. Model beautiful. Thirty-six, twenty-four, thirty-six brick shithouse beautiful. Just standing and looking at him. Smiling. "Wow, I hope all the neighbors are that gorgeous. And that friendly!" exclaimed Jason.

"What woman?" asked a puzzled Mark as his head swiveled about to find her. When Jason looked back to point the woman out she was gone.

##

After sending the seller's agent the offer back at Mark's office, Mark said to Jason: "The seller's agent wants you to be aware of some things about the house."

"Oh?" Jason questioned.

"Well nothing that big but a bit on the uncomfortable side if you know what I mean. It may be why there are not any other offers come through yet... but... well the owners, a married couple, vanished not too long ago. FBI investigated but they are not sure what happened, and the case is still open. Leading theory is that they borrowed some money from a loan shark; the husband liked to gamble, probably couldn't pay the Sharky off, and decided to skedaddle. Ownership of the property was deeded back after the default to a holding company that held the loan papers."

After a moment, Mark continued: "Also, there are multiple complaints filed with the local Sheriff about a next door neighbor yelling crazy shit and shooting his gun off in the middle of the night. He's nuttier than a squirrel turd from what I hear. So far as I know, based on what the other neighbors about the place are sayin', no one's been hurt by this nut bag so nothing to worry yourself about."

Jason thought on this a moment but with his strong desire to get the hell out of the Extended Stay, his instant love for that amazing house, not to mention his lust for his soon to be hot ass neighbor, Jason told Mark to go ahead and make the offer anyway. 'Make it Happen Mark!' Not three hours after the offer was in, the offer was accepted. Mark was astounded.

"In all my days I never...." he pronounced. "No counter offer, no contingencies, no waiting for other offers to post. And in this market! Blessed is Sweet Baby Jesus!" he continued. After staring at the email from the seller's Agent a moment longer and making click-click sounds with his tongue he added: "Well you're gosh darn lucky partn'r, I will tell ya that! Congrats! The property is yours!"

DJ immediately played Pharrell Williams:
Because I'm happy.
Clap along if you feel like a room without a roof.
Because I'm happy.
Clap along if you feel like happiness is the truth!
And for once in a long while Jason was.

##

Returning to the Piggly Wiggly for a second round of Yuengling beer before heading back to the Extended Stay, Jason was energized at his good fortune. *Let the Celebration Begin!* DJ crowed in his best Ringling Brothers Master of Ceremony voice. *You Betcha Ass!* replied Jason to himself as he grabbed the six-pack off the store shelf and headed quickly to the checkout counter.

"Y'all having a private party? Sounds like fun!" the mildly cute but obviously sweet tempered cashier said in a chipper twang. It was accompanied by a wink.

"Yes. Just some much needed stress release after a very hard couple of months." Jason replied to her but thinks: *If only she was 10 years older I'd be all over that!*

Heading for the exit he again passed the public bulletin board. He noticed the missing persons postings lining the top edge. There were more than two dozen. Jason was quick to note something odd about the black and white milk-carton pictures staring back at him from each of the postings. Usually the missing are children – smiling pretty young girls, the photos copied from their sophomore high school photos. These, all of them, were of middle-aged men. "Missing: Daniel Liefmore, Age 42, last seen walking home from the Saddle Up Bar and Grill, downtown Springdale." Jason read from one. And so on. *Sure a lot of middle age men go missing in Springdale,* Jason reflected with a stab of dread. Jason was turning 40 in two months. *I see a bad moon a-rising. I see trouble on the way...* popped into Jason's mind. John Fogerty was always a favorite of DJ.

##

It took a further three weeks at the Extended Stay for Jason to complete all needed closing documents, secure the home loan, and arrange for his possessions to be transferred from storage to the new property. Jason met the locksmith at the new home whom promptly changed the locks, handing Jason the keys when completed, and, at last, Jason was in his new house. Great Jesus Jumping Jehoshaphat was he glad to be finally relaxing in his new digs! *Pizza delivered hot and fresh. Check. Six pack Yuengling chilling in the refrigerator. Check. Rocker on the back patio. Check.*

"And my ass in the rocker. Check!" said Jason aloud.

##

Jason, in the rocker, scanned the tree line at the back of his property. Sycamore, Bur Oak, Black Walnut, Osage Orange, some upwards of sixty feet tall grew thickly. Wild Grape, Virginia Creeper, Passion Flower, and Poison Ivy wound around the tree trunks veining up to the top story filled his woods with a think green mass. A wall of trees and vines. In a distance, probably an adjacent farm 'over yonder,' Jason heard the sounds of cows mooing and bawling. *Perhaps the farmer is removing the calves from their mothers for slaughter?* He questioned to himself.

As he listened to the cows bawl, his eyes wandered to the treetops. Then his eyes moved above the tops. It was then that he saw the kettle of vultures circling above the tree line. Jason saw that perhaps 50 vultures were gliding gracefully, silently; some is small tight circles, others in wide sweeps above the tree line. *Is there a dead cow in my woods?* thought Jason. A particularly large vulture - "Must be a fucking pterodactyl!" Jason said out loud to no one in particular, was making lazy swoops just above all the rest. Just then one vulture broke from the kettle, sailed toward Jason, and landed on his lawn not fifteen feet from where he sat. The vulture stared at Jason a moment, hissed at him, then lifted off to fly in the direction of the front of the house. *What the fuck?* thought Jason. Just then his front doorbell rang.

Jason reached the front door and spied the man on the threshold through the stained glass inserts. *Vulture Man! What in the Name of Hell-Fire?* thought Jason to himself. Jason opened the door with a snap. "Yes?" he said to the man in not a particularly neighborly way. Jason felt a bit flummoxed by this strange man being on his doorstep.

"Hello there, neighbor," said 'Vulture Man'. "I have a little welcoming gift for you" as 'Vulture Man' shoved a Tupperware container toward Jason. "It's intestine stew. Made it fresh myself." Jason grimaced but grabbed the Tupperware from him with unease.

This is going straight down the disposal, thought Jason.

"I'm the 'Crazy Neighbor' that I'm sure everyone has warned you about! We met briefly at Piggly Wiggly if you may recall...." came his thin little reedy voice followed by the cackle laugh. "My name is Roudrich Gerlach and I'm not all that crazy really; the neighbors only talk like that because of the way I look. And... everyone shoots guns in their backyard around here anyway. What's the big deal?" His eyes momentarily look downward in what Jason assumed was embarrassment. Looking back to Jason he continued: "But I'm just here to make your acquaintance, official like, is all" Roudrich finished.

As Roudrich said the "- make your acquaintance -" he did a weird forward thrust with his hands that reminded Jason of a praying mantis, accompanied by a little head nod, his Adam's apple bobbing fast up and down. Jason was so thoroughly creeped out by this weird little man that he wanted him off his porch and pronto. Jason began:

"Uh, well nice to meet you, uh, Roudrich, but I'm kinda busy and...."

Roudrich broke Jason off mid-sentence countering:

"I'm also here to introduce you to someone special. She told me to officiate the introduction and she is someone you don't ignore! Have you meet your next door neighbor yet?" he said loudly. In a low giggly whisper Roudrich added: "She is a real looker! I've had a go at her a time or two myself." Roudrich then lifted his right arm up from his side and with hand flat like the wave of an aristocrat to the masses, pointed across the yard. Jason's eyes followed and he saw the woman, the knockout, the brick shithouse gorgeous beauty queen standing just outside the front door of the house next door. She was waving.

"Y'all come over and see me sometime y'hear!" she yelled across to Jason.

Damn, thinks Jason, *how could I be so lucky?* As he waved back.

Sometimes when you win you lose, piped in DJ.

Shut the fuck up! Jason thought sharply back at DJ as Jason continued to wave. And smile. Big, stupid grin smile. There was some residual unease in the pit of his stomach, however. Jason could not quite place his finger on why.

##

Jason was back in the rocker, beer in hand. It was the cool of evening. Jason tumbling the events of the day around in his head when he heard a screen door open and close just to his left. He looked across to the back of the house next door and sees the woman. She was on her back patio wearing a long sheer lacy robe. It was see-through and she had nothing on but a G-string underneath. She looked up at Jason, and pulled the robe apart. Jason's eyes drifted downward. Her exposed breasts were big and beautiful. She beckoned him with her right hand forefinger to come to her. He did. As he walked across the lawn from his house to hers, Jason felt as if he were floating on air, gliding toward her. He thinks: *So this is what it is like to be under the spell of a woman.* DJ played 'Witchy Woman' by the Eagles as he walked. As he drew close, he noticed she was wearing a necklace. Hanging from the necklace, just above the midpoint of her breast, was an amulet. Had Jason known ancient Egyptology he would have recognized the amulet as that of the deity Nephthys, deliverer of the dead to her son Osiris, God and protector of the underworld. As she led him into the interior of the house he couldn't help but notice how dark, dank, and dusty the interior was; it smelled strongly of rot and mildew. *How weird that a woman would keep her place in such poor shape,* he thought, but quickly turned his thoughts back to the beautiful form that was now heading into the bedroom. He followed and soon was lost to the perfume of her glorious body.

"Valda" was the name she whispered in his ear.

##

A couple of hours later, as he walked back to his house alone, Jason noticed just how exhausted he was. He thought: *Am I coming down with something?* Instead of feeling a rush of energy from the amazing sex he just had, he felt drained. The thought: *A vampire just drained some of my blood,* popped into mind. Jason laughed at his own crazy idea. *It has been a long day and I just need to sleep*, he thought. Jason headed straight to his bedroom, pulled off his clothes, dove into bed, and immediately fell fast asleep.

Several hours later, in the deep of night, Jason woke suddenly with a snort and a start.

"What? What? Huh?" He said in a sleepy haze. He wiped the sleep from his eyes, looked to his right to the clock on the nightstand: "Shit. Three AM!" he exclaimed then looked to his left. There, next to the bed was the apparition of a woman. She looked to be in her forties in age. She was floating in the air, her legs slowly fading from view into nothingness from her knees down. Whiffs of smoke floated around behind her upper body and head. Her hair was a wild, tangled mass. To Jason she looked like the image of a woman on a black-and-white TV screen, strangely two-dimensional, all in shades of gray. She was looking with eyes wide open into round orbs that were intensely staring down at him. Jason rubbed his eyes thinking he was still dreaming. But when he looked again she was still there. Where her mouth should have been was instead a round jagged hole. The flesh surrounding the hole where her mouth would have been appeared to puff in and out as if she were silently screaming something to him. Jason looked at her eyes again. He thought, *she is desperately trying to tell me something!* Then, suddenly, she simply faded away. The puffs of smoke went "Poof!" and she was gone.

##

Afterward, rattled by the appearance of the ghost, Jason could not sleep. Despite his physical exhaustion, he got dressed and went to the back porch to let the cool night air comfort him. *Did I really just see a ghost?* he thought to himself. But without some better explanation of what he had just witnessed, he had to conclude he had. He was sitting in his rocker looking into the dark of his back yard and mulling this over when he saw the fireflies - thousands of them flashing their chemiluminescent abdomens, on and off, on and off, as they flew in random loops above the grass.

"Beautiful" he said to the night air, temporarily forgetting about the ghost. Temporary was the key word because as his eyes began to adjust to the dark he saw the 'Ghost Woman' floating at the back of his yard just at the tree line. She glowed a soft whitish chemiluminescent light matching that of the light of the fireflies. When he looked upon her she suddenly drifted backward into the trees, her glow looking like a candle lantern as if carried by an unseen person walking deeper into the woods. The fireflies, in unison, followed her. Their lights, it appeared to Jason, merged into pumpkin sized balls of phosphorescence dancing about the woods as if the fireflies were attending a ballroom dance.

Jason, wondering if he was still asleep in his bed, all of this a very vivid nightmare, got up from the rocker and walked to the trees, following the parade of dancing ghost lights. When he reached the trees, Jason walked a dozen steps inward. The dancing lights, reminding Jason of glowing jellyfish, were circling in lazy arcs above and about the Ghost Woman. She was floating just above a slight indent in the earth, the shape and size reminding Jason of the sunken-in look of an old moldering grave. She was emphatically pointing down at the indent as she stared with those orb eyes at Jason. He was about to step in for a closer look when a loud voice boomed behind him:

"Hey what's up man? You out for a bit of night air like me? Can't sleep?"

Jason jumped. Turning around he saw it was Roudrich. Jason, being badly startled by the sudden outburst yelled at Roudrich:

"What the FUCK guy? You trying to scare me to death? What are you doing on my property anyway? This is private property GET OFF!"

"I'm sorry," said Roudrich, but Roudrich's eyes were mischievous Jason saw, "I didn't mean nothing. Just taking a walk is all. I'll leave you be then. Sorry to disturb your privacy...." With that Roudrich turned quickly and headed off into the woods.

Homeward Jason assumed. *Thank God. Jesus that guy gives me the creep-ass heebie-jeebies*, thought Jason. Jason then returned his gaze to where the Ghost Woman had been. She was gone along with the dancing jellyfish. Lights out and nobody home.

The next day Jason was so disturbed by all that had happened he decided he needed something to protect himself with. *After all, I am alone out in the boondocks of America,* thought Jason.

In space no one can hear you scream, quoted DJ.

Jason drove into town to the local Guns-R-Us Emporium. *We have thousands of weapons to choose from!* The bold words of the sign reflected as he drove into the parking lot. *Why should he not?* opined Jason, *everyone in Tennessee has at least three guns and a shit-load of bullets to match.*

Soon Jason walked out with a brand new Beretta PICO 380 pistol and two boxes of shells. A 'purse gun' Jason chuckled to himself.

Now you just need the matching purse! quipped DJ.

Jason had never felt the need to own a weapon before, but as he headed home, he felt an unexpectedly comforting emotion with the weapon next to him on the car seat. When he arrived he quickly popped into his house, carrying the gun and .380 rounds with him, into his bedroom, loaded six shells into the weapon, and tucked it under his pillow. The rest of the rounds went into the nightstand drawer. As he walked back out to his car to fetch the six-pack of Yuengling Beer (he had also made a quick stop to Piggly Wiggly) he spied Valda watching him cross his driveway. She waved him over. *God help me but there was just something wickedly fun about that woman,* he thought, *also something very disquieting* he added to himself.

Who Cares! Time for a booty call! shouted DJ in joy as Jason sauntered over to where Valda stood.

Jason and Valda headed into her house together.

Several hours later, at dusk, Jason was walking back to his home. *I feel so fucking tired!* he thought. In fact he felt like getting down on all fours and crawling back to his house. How was it that a few hours of sex (and great sex at that) could leave him so drained? Was he sick? Did the mosquitoes in this area carry malaria? While he had suffered multiple mosquito bites while camped out at his back porch he doubted there was any malaria. He was in fact so weak that he stumbled and fell, hitting his head on the steps as he attempted to climb his back patio stairs. "Dammit to Fucking Hell!" he yelled in pain and anger. It was all he had to make it back to his bed. He was fast asleep in minutes.

Jason dropped into the first stages of sleep over the next several hours, into deep sleep for a period before entering REM sleep. He dreamed. It was a nightmare. In his nightmare Jason heard a noise in the hallway. "Clack, Clack, Clack," went the sound. Jason recognized it as the sound of birds talons clacking on tile as the bird hopped forward. A big bird. A very big bird. "Clack, Clack, Clack!" The sound grew loader as the bird hopped down the hall approaching his bedroom. He was suddenly floating above and looking down at his bed. In his dream Jason found himself to be a ghost. He was black and white. A two-dimensional image that floated above the floor. He was looking down at the two people sleeping in the bed. The missing husband and wife. Jason knew this. Jason also sensed how much in danger this couple was, but he, being a ghost, was powerless to help them. "Clack, Clack, Clack!" echoed in the hall. The head of a giant vulture rounded the corner of the hall and peered into the bedroom. The vulture, six feet tall, entered the bedroom and approached the bed. "Clack, Clack, Clack!" In his nightmare Jason knew it to be a 'She.' Around her neck lay the Nephthys amulet.

##

The couple continued to sleep. Jason tried to warn them but he had no mouth, just an empty hole, where no sound would emit. The vulture's eyes began to glow red. From the middle of the chests of the husband and wife a smoke appeared. It swirled and eddied its way up and into the eyes of the giant vulture. Jason knew that the smoke was their souls and if he did nothing the souls of these two people would be vacuumed out of their bodies and consumed by her. Jason was trying to scream but nothing would come out. His eyes bulged out into round orbs in his head from the effort to scream. The man and woman were shriveling up as the vulture sucked them dry. *Scream Dammit Scream!* Nothing. The man and woman clung to life as their souls continued to be sucked from them. A second vulture, this one smaller, a 'He' thought Jason, came into the bedroom. "Clack, Clack, Clack." The smaller vulture had gripped in its left wing a large knife. With the knife, he cut first the woman's heart out, then the man's. A white whiff of puffy smoke rose from each of their chest wounds. The smaller vulture placing the hearts, still beating, onto his outstretched wings, presented the hearts to the larger Vulture. She ate the hearts with great thrusts of her head, gulping them down whole. Then suddenly, Jason found himself floating behind and following the smaller vulture as the vulture dragged the couple away to the woods to bury them in shallow graves. As the last few shovels of dirt were thrown on the man, nearly covered in dirt but for the face, Jason saw that the face was his own. At this, Jason woke from the dream screaming. His bed sheets soaked in sweat.

##

It was still dark as the thunderstorm began. Jason was standing in his bedroom. The flashes of lightning briefly illuminating his face in the mirror on the wall facing him. He saw his face, extremely weak with fatigue, but with determination; he knew what he needed to do. He quickly dressed, grabbed the gun from under his pillow, stuffed it under his belt, his cellphone placed into his left pocket, walked to his garage, grabbed a shovel, and headed out to the woods. He looked across at Valda's house just as another lightning flash light up the yard. He saw the house, in that brief flash, as it truly was: a wreck. The house had fallen in on itself on one side, it was moldered and in ruin. Plywood covered the windows. The door broken in and battered. Teenagers had graffitied the exterior: 'Burn This Shit Down!' in red spray paint along the back wall. As the light of the lightning strike faded, Jason once again saw the house as he first saw it: a large colonial mansion in need of some paint. Jason turned, resolute once more, and trudged to the tree line.

##

He entered the forest and made his way to the depression that he had seen the Ghost woman point to. He got to the spot then leaned his shovel against a tree behind him momentarily to wipe the wet of the rain from his face. A flash of lightning illuminated the area. Jason could see more depressions just like this one scattered in the woods. Just as the last of the light from the lightning flash faded, he saw something twinkle near the top of the depression he stood at. He recognized it as the Nephthys amulet, startling him. Just as he leaned in to get a closer look Jason felt the sharp burst of pain at the back of his head. A ring like a bell burst out into his head as he lost consciousness.

Jason found himself floating in a deep dark abyss as if under water. He could see the surface. Jason, his physical self, was now laying in the depression next to the water's surface. He could see standing, behind his physical self, Roudrich, pulling the shovel up from the back of his head of his physical self and discarding it to the side. Jason was sinking into the abyss. In the distance, Jason saw lights heading toward him, like the light of a swarm of fireflies. As the swarm approached he saw floating in the middle of the swarm the Ghost Woman. She looked like a normal woman this time however, a rather pretty woman. Jason realized she was, in fact, the wife in the missing couple. She swam to him and pointed up to the water's surface.

"Swim up" she mouthed to him without sound. He began to swim upwards.

As Jason neared the surface again he heard voices. Roudrich and Valda were talking as they stood over his limp body.

"I think he is still alive. Although I don't know how. You nearly sucked him dry," said Roudrich.

"You were the one who almost killed him with that shovel you groveling idiot!" Roudrich lowered his eyes in supplication at the scorn in her words. She continued: "Thankfully he *is* still alive. I am hungry. Get your knife and bring him to the house!"

"Yes Mistress!" he said as he hurried to bid her wishes. Valda then left to return to her house.

DJ played the Rolling Stones 'Sympathy for The Devil' as she walked away.

After she was gone, Jason fought with every ounce of energy he had remaining to regain consciousness. He knew he had only moments before Roudrich's return. The water's surface, so close yet so far, seemed forever to reach. Just as Jason broke through the surface and regained consciousness, however, he realized Roudrich was indeed back. Roudrich was busy tying a rope around Jason's ankles. A moment before Roudrich was able to cinch the rope tight, Jason pulled the pistol from his waistband, aimed at Roudrich's head and fired. 'The Vulture' fell to the ground; gore painting the ground red and white. This time dead was dead. Jason kicked the rope off his feet, pulled the cellphone from his left pocket and dialed 911. He collapsed back to the ground and groaned.

##

A week later the police were nearing the end of their investigation. The yellow 'Police Line Do Not Cross' tape, still up across the entire front of the forest, would likely be up for several weeks as the police continued to dig for additional evidence. The head of the crime task force, Captain Williams, was walking toward Jason as he watched from his porch. As Captain Williams reached him he said "Looks like we found sixteen bodies in all. Almost all are men, probably going to be a lot more before we are through. We think these are the men missing from around the Springdale area," the Captain said, adding: "We found the missing couple who previously owned this property too."

Jason just said "Oh Wow. That is truly terrible." and left it at that so that the Captain could continue:

"It appeared from the condition of the two bodies that the man had had his body cavity cut open and the woman was shot in the mouth close range."

"Ung...." Jason was all he could manage to say, as he was now feeling sick to his stomach.

"Some of the graves are very old however but...." the Captain continued, ".... all lines of evidence point to the killer being Roudrich so they can't be as old as some of the guys in the investigating crew think. You did us a favor Son by killing that sick bastard."

"What about the Valda woman? Do you know where she may have gone?" Jason said as he glanced across at the ruin of the colonial next door. Jason did not mention that he had been hallucinating the house in a significantly newer shape then it appeared to everyone present now. Jason also knew some of the graves would prove to be much older than the Captain was willing to believe. But he kept his thoughts to himself. He didn't want them to think he was a lunatic like the late Roudrich.

"We found no reports, no believable reports that is, other than yours, of a woman living at the old Stewart mansion." said Captain Williams, "You said you did not feel well the last several weeks – are you sure you didn't just imagine a woman living next door?"

"Perhaps Captain, perhaps." Jason lied.

"Well funny thing, the way you described her looks and behavior and all...." he said as he looked back at the tree line, "My Grandmamma told me scary bed time stories when I was a lad about just such a beautiful woman that lived at the Stewart mansion in the early 1800's when it was still a grand mansion. After her husband died, he was a Stewart too I believe, she went crazy, luring lonely men in to the mansion only to kill them then eat them.

Made some kind of pact with the Devil, Grandmamma said, and the Devil turned her into an 'Empusa,' a female demon that haunts nightmares. The neighbors finally had enough and rounded up a' hangin' party. But when they got to her place to finish her off she had vanished. Never to be seen again. Other than some local crazies filing reports about seeing her ghost walking these here woods...." After a moment pause, the Captain continued, "The house was left to rot where it stood. My Grandmamma told me only buzzards would roost in the ruins after that." Returning his gaze to Jason he continued:

"My Grandmamma believed she was a living She-Devil who still haunted these woods. She warned me never to play around these parts." He paused, then added: "But that is just superstitious nonsense Mr. Jackson." he said firmly, looking squarely at Jason.

Jason replied simply, "I'm sure you are right Captain."

Both of their gazes turned to the rotten remains of the Stewart mansion. They were silent as they reflected on these events. Jason had his suspicions that Captain

Williams secretly did not believed these things to be "…. just superstitious non-sense" however.

##

That evening, when all the police had cleared the property and gone home, near sun set, Jason was convinced he needed to do one more thing. Closure. He got up from the porch and headed for his garage. In the garage he grabbed the five gallons of gasoline he used for his lawn mower and his box of extra long barbecue matches. As he marched to the Stewart mansion. DJ playing the Talking Heads song 'Burning Down the House,' he saw a committee of vulture, at least fifty, had landed on the lawn between him and the mansion. They were all looking at him silently. Valda stepped out onto the back porch from the interior of the ruins.

"Jason!" she called "You don't need to do this… you can join me! I will please you as I have…. As much as you could ever want! No more loneliness. I will be yours!"

Jason kept marching toward her house. As he crossed the property line from his property to hers, the vultures began to peck and bite at his legs. Some flew up to scratch at his face with their talons. Valda, knowing now that Jason was not going to stop screeched:

"I will kill YOU! I will claw your eyes out! I will eat your intestine for breakfast!"

But he continued on. As he reached the corner of the mansion, he began to pour gas on the wood ruin. The vultures frantically clawed at his back, Jason batting them away as much as possible without stopping. He walked from one side of the mansion to the other pouring gas as he went. He then pulled a match out, struck it on a rock, and threw the match onto the gas soaked wood. It caught immediately.

"Jason No! Jason No! What Have You Done!"? Valda screeched.

As the flames grew and spread, she started to hiss at him, and as she hissed, her form began to change. She was shrinking, growing gray and old, the skin of her face wrinkling into, first, an old lady, then a hag. She continued to transform. Her arms shrunk and became wings. Her body bent forward and her neck elongated. Her mouth and nose elongated to a beak. Her legs became thin twigs and her feet turned into talons. She was transformed to a giant vulture. As the flames of the mansion became a conflagration, she screeched once more and lifted off in flight. The other vultures lifting off into flight to join her. Together with her at the head, the kettle of vultures turned east and flew, inline, into the darkening of the growing night. Then they were gone.

##

Six months had passed. Jason was, yet again, on his back patio, a can of Yuengling in hand. He was this time joined by his girlfriend Marcia, the cashier at Piggly Wiggly, a little young for him he admitted to himself, but he liked her and she seemed to like him. She was, despite her looks, twenty-eight years old. A nice glass of chilled chardonnay rested in her hand. Sorry Yuengling. Ben Harper & The Innocent Criminals were playing on Spotify. DJ was silent for once. Jason was happy. His job at Robotix was doing well. Someone had purchased the property next door and a brand new house was rising up, where not too long ago, the ashes of Stewart mansion lay moldering. He was beginning to get into the country life. Marcia even talked him into some line dancing at the local Wild Horse and Bull Riding Bar.

Shit Howdy! said DJ.

The End.

Serena Daniels'
Shopping List

Brownies
Corn
Chicken
Cookies
Rice
Pizza
Cupcakes
Ice Cream
Hamburger
Cream of Chicken soup
Cream of Broccoli and Cheese soup
Tuna
Tortellini
Cinnamon Buns
Chocolate Bars
Soda

Blood Feast

Serena Daniels

"Is everything ready for tonight Maude?"

Dr. Maude Anderson turned to the sound's origin and her colleague Dr. Nick White strode up beside her.

"Everything is in place," she replied as she turned back to the setting that was behind the viewing window that was set up between the test room and the observation room. In just a few hours, they will find out if years of research will pan out or dash the hopes that had built up over the course of attempting to find a solution to the countries' current problem.

"Fantastic! Years of research and countless hours of sleeplessness will be rewarded for our hard work!" His eyes glazed over in excitement as he too turned to the set up.

'Or everything will have been all for nothing,' she thought wryly; all too aware that it would be too easy for this final experiment to fail and years of effort to go down the drain.

"You believe this is going to fail, don't you? Don't deny it, the look on your face says all;" he said, facing her now, his features stone.

"It just seems like something that you can only think of in science fiction and even then with only a small margin of working like now;" she said firmly knowing that this was true.

"It's the best that we could think of, we've been over this before; we have no other options!" His voice boomed at the final part and she barely suppressed a flinch; she should be used to his angry mood regarding any talk of failure by this point and he has yelled louder at others who had actually went so far as to protest the nature of this project.

"I'm fully aware of that fact Dr. White;" she shot back coldly. "I only wish that we had a Plan B for if this goes south!"

"Well, we don't! This is our one and only shot to prevent society from complete collapsing!" The stress was evident in his voice and the tension was palpable; they were glaring at each other, a standoff regarding one of the biggest decisions that would affect the future of their entire country.

"I'll go check on them, see if they will be ready;" she said frigidly and made it clear that she wasn't backing down, just checking for last minute flaws. She reluctantly turned her back to him before she made her way to the elevator; once inside she had to swipe her identity card before she was able to press the button that would take her to the basement.

The sight that greeted her when she emerged calmed her a little bit; the other scientists were calmly working on their notes as they examined their assigned tanks. They all looked up as she walked in, it was so quiet that her footsteps were clearly heard and they waited for her to speak.

"I have received our next orders," she began and they became even more attentive; "they want them tested tonight!" She waited for any objections, anything to calm her nerves; but her face was close to falling when she noticed the people in the room glance at each other and wondered what could be going wrong to warrant such a reaction.

"So the rumors are true then Dr. Anderson? They really want to see if we have been successful?" Dr. Casey Peck was the first to step from the crowd; her voice was quiet and almost fearful.

"Unfortunately yes," Maude saw no reason to keep her feelings hidden; this would be the final moment working together regardless of how it all ended. "Is there a problem Dr. Peck?"

"Everything," she was still quiet; "especially the morality of it all.... and the what ifs."

"I assume that you all feel the exact same way?" Maude's tone was gentle now and all the others in the room turn away in confirmation. "It's unfortunate, but the higher ups feel differently and what are we but the lowly drones who must obey; on a more serious note, how are they really?"

"As good as they can be," Dr. Peck said and motioned for Maude to look at the tanks for herself. Maude took up the silent invitation and walked past each tank, of which there were twelve in total. When she reached the last one she touched one gently and allowed her expression to become more emotional.

"You are the key," she whispered; "you will be either our savior or you could very well be our destroyer." Her hand slid down from the tube to her side and she heaved a sigh before she steeled herself and walked back to the elevator and faced everyone.

"Please have everything ready by sundown in a few hours;" she announced as the doors opened and after pressing the button for the top floor left one final message: "and pray for the best, even if it turns out for the worst."

The top floor was reserved for the scientist's sleeping quarters, which is where she was headed because she had a feeling that she was going to need the energy to deal with the unveiling that was going to happen in such a short amount of time.

Her sleep was still restless; despite the pills that she had popped and kept on hand for times like these. She had a very bad feeling about tonight.

#

Her alarm ringing was both a relief and a dread.

'This is it, years and years of research, experimenting and general brain wracking have led up to this moment; with the potential to blow up in the faces of everyone in existence,' she sighed as she got up and checked herself in the mirror to make sure that she was presentable before she left her room.

She felt nothing but trepidation as she rode the elevator down to the observation floor and it didn't alleviate when she heard voices on the other side of the doors because she was well aware just who the voices belonged to: army soldiers and government stooges. Both were here for the demonstration but for different reasons; the former were there to restore order if necessary and the latter were there to see if their pet project would save humanity.

Everything about her was stone as she gave the expected replies to all the "isn't this exciting" and "this will be our savior for sure"; she saw Dr. White's expression out of the corner of her eye.

'I'm not going to screw your pooch Nick, you're going to do it yourself since everyone knows that this

was all your idea and if this fails....' and so she kept on pretending that everything was okay despite the truth being that many things could go wrong. When she had a break, she discreetly looked at her watch and saw that it was time and she looked to her colleague and he nodded in acknowledgement before he took out his phone and called the basement dwellers to inform them to drain the tanks.

"Ladies and gentlemen," Dr. White announced as soon as he got off the phone; "I am pleased to announce that it's time for the demonstration that all our years of hard work and determination have led up to. I am very proud that you have placed your trust, that the very population have placed their trust in us to get through this extremely difficult time."

'That's putting it lightly,' was Maude's only answer.

"But I am confident that I have found the solution to all of our problems! Just over a decade ago was when our country began to panic as our population soared and the result was the surge in the homeless population; however a more pressing problem was the lack of food to feed all of our people. As the top scientists in our fields, the government placed me and my esteemed colleagues in charge of finding a solution for this food shortage while helping to lower the population."

"I am happy that I have undertaken this journey and I'm sure that my colleagues will agree,"

'Or not.'

".... so without further ado, may I present: Project Blood Feast!" When he finished the lights in the observation room shut on to illuminate a single long table that was big enough for twelve people; the settings only consisted of spoons and bowls that were filled with a dark red liquid.

"What's that in the bowls?" someone asked.

"That's non-coagulated cow's blood," Nick was still taking the lead and Maude was more than happy to let him. "That's how the project got its name; among other reasons."

"What exactly does this project entail?" a government worker asked.

"Well to be honest it was difficult to come up with an idea with regards to food shortage," Nick confessed; "as there aren't enough of any of the food groups for everyone to subsist on, we wondered how exactly we could change that. Being named the head of this project placed a burden on me, if we are being truthful, and I felt that I had to work the hardest to come up with the solution and bring it to life."

'Nice bending the truth there, Nick.'

"It actually came to me while I was sleeping...."

'Actually it was from watching a Dracula movie.'

".... I realized that what was needed was to wring a new food source from an already existing one - but how? The answer was surprisingly simple: blood but a new problem emerged; how can we sustain on blood, as it is indigestible by us? Perhaps I should demonstrate just what we've done before I continue with my explanation."

He walked to the intercom and clicked it on; "bring them in but don't seat them just yet."

"Yes sir," came the anonymous male voice before it clicked off and the door to the audience's right side facing inside of the room opened. A male scientist came in first but he was followed by the first of the wheeled gurneys that had small figures strapped down and the audience couldn't help but gasp and Maude grimaced.

They were children, all twelve of them and if it weren't for the restraints one would think that they were sleeping peacefully; however, they were just barely identifiable as small humans. Their skin was very pale, with tints of gray; their hair was wet from being in the tank but an oily sheen could also be noticed. They were clearly emaciated, their fingers were boney and their hospital gowns hung loosely on their frames.

"Are those children?"

"They are," Nick said proudly; "genetically engineered to fit the parameters of this project. We have picked apart and put back together their DNA in order for them to be able to subsist on nothing but blood."

"Where did you get the materials to create them?"

"From the egg and sperm banks; it took many, many tries for us to perfect their new sequence. But I am sure that we have been successful as there are no damages or holes in their DNA."

"Isn't this immoral?"

"If they were human than yes it would; however I prefer to see them as more sub-human as their DNA has changed too much to be considered human anymore."

'And there's the justification!'

"They are sleeping because it helps their growth and they are currently at the perfect age to test them out; which is why you are here today, to witness this glorious new age for science and humankind!"

The crowd began murmuring, some unsure, others were excited; what they all had in common was that they were raring to go and see if the time (and the huge amount of money) was worth the results. Dr. White, being the smug bastard that he was, waited until the reactions were reaching fever pitch before he clicked on the intercom again.

"It's time, you know what to do!"

"Yes doctor!" The com clicked off and the doctors in the room began taking little bottles full of adrenaline out of their coat pockets and prepped the syringes before they injected the patients to awaken them. Twelve sets of eyes opened slowly before they blinked from the intrusion of the harsh lighting; the doctors removed the straps as the children began to experiment with movement.

The doctors helped the shaky test subjects off the gurneys as they took their first steps toward the table; their noses sniffed the air, as if scenting something strange.

"I didn't expect them to have a heightened sense of smell;" Maude heard her colleague whisper incredulously and that caused a shiver to creep up her spine. She was not a geneticist, she was recruited for her expertise in general human anatomy; she was supposed to attempt to predict how things might change from the children's new DNA. Now she was a bit more perturbed as she hadn't thought of this; she also noticed something else that she hadn't predicted.

"Dr. White," she managed to croak out before he turned to her; "I think they may have some sort of blindness."

"What do you mean?" he hissed too low for anyone to hear.

"Look at the way they move their heads," she whispered as she pointed to what she had noticed.

The children looked confused, they kept looking at the light and turned their gazes away after a second; but made no indication that they could see the scientists, the bowls or even the table, they were just unfocused and the doctors on the floor were just noticing this as well and shot each other concerned looks.

The young ones steps were now a bit steadier and they were sniffing the air with more confidence; their non-seeing gazes now changed from sniffing in the direction of the bowls to their handlers and back and forth as if testing something.

This made Maude's stomach drop, she had imagined so many scenarios in which something went horribly wrong; but if the thoughts that were currently running through her head were coming into fruition, then it will be her worst nightmare come to life. The worst part is that no one else seemed to have noticed and now she was torn between running for her life before things went to hell and staying while praying that she was wrong.

The scientists were setting them at the table now and stood back waiting; the children simply stared at the bowls in front of them despite not being able to see them. The continued to sniff experimentally at the blood soup and one of them (best guess was a girl) even stuck her tongue out and touched it gently before dragging it back in to taste it.

She gagged and spat angrily before she hissed, the others reacted and began to mimic her noises; the way they swiveled their heads towards each other made it appear as if they were communicating with each other. After a minute the noises didn't stop, but became quieter and they were almost chirping; the complete and sudden stop in sound was more deafening than the chatter itself.

That was when all hell broke loose.

They turned their sightless gazes onto their handlers before they leapt at them, toppling their chairs over in the process. To the horror of the observers, the children dove straight into their prey's throat and they could plainly see the blood that sprayed copiously from the severed jugular. The sounds of the flesh, muscle and bone being ripped apart from what could only be sharp teeth were clearly heard despite the distance between the rooms.

The scientists' screams were also heard; they were loud and their bodies thrashed about maniacally until the last of their blood had been drained out and they became motionless. The area on and around the table was painted crimson; not much of their original colors were left and it was indistinguishable from the meal that the scientists were attempting to feed the little creatures.

The two bloods must have mixed together as once their first feeding frenzy had finished, they turned their attention back to the bowls and sniffed them carefully and drank a little but the taste of human blood could not override the foulness of a bovines' as they became furious and threw their bowls around or banged them furiously on the table. Either way, pieces of porcelain littered themselves around in the giant puddle of blood.

No one moved or breathed loudly; everyone was simply too scared at what they had just witnessed.

'I knew it you son of a bitch! I fucking knew it!' Maude swore, as she was frozen in place, too shocked to be able to move; too scared at what happen next. Of course, Dr. White took charge; he turned to everyone present.

"Everyone, we have a procedure for an emergency like this!" He turned on the intercom; "bring in the hush up squad!" The doors inside burst open and a large squad of uniformed gunmen ran in.

"Fire!" The leader shouted and everyone immediately obeyed; rapid gunfire reverberated throughout the area and the spread was so wide that every single child was hit directly. Maude could not help but close her eyes, not willing to look at the carnage or its aftermath; no matter how much she had protested against this, these were still children after all. Her eyes were still unopened even after the noise had died down and there was a deathly silence.

"What the hell?" Someone shouted and she instinctively opened her eyes to see the incredible sight of the creatures still moving. They let out loud, angry roars before they leapt at their attackers; who began firing again in a panicked state until that dreaded clicking of empty magazines became rampant. The mutated children showed no hesitation in moving in for the kill and took out the squad in no time at all.

For the second set of time nobody moved, mainly because they were too shocked but they were also even more scared than before. Even the people from the military could do nothing as they had not brought their weapons in with them and they did not want to end up adding the already painted room.

Everyone breathed harshly in unison when the creatures suddenly whipped their gazes in their direction and began to slowly make their way towards them; some stalked upright while others crawled slowly, their noses did not stop sniffing the whole time.

'How could they smell us through this glass? Are their brains and noses that advanced?' Maude wondered as they crept closer until their noses pressed up against the glass. Without warning, they all began to bang loudly against the glass and everyone in the observation room jumped a couple feet in the air and Maude could swear that she smelt urine from at least one person that was near her.

"Don't panic," Dr. White said calmly; "this glass is bulletproof-" he was cut off by the sound of the glass cracking loudly. Over a dozen different spider webs were forming from the fists of the little vampires and they were connecting in a foreboding manner until small chips began to fall onto the floor and everyone began to back away; Maude was the most squeamish and was attempting to make her way to the exit before anyone else.

It was only a few seconds later that the explosion of glass happened, showering the extremely unlucky few that were the closest with the army of small projectiles; the force also knocking them back along with a few others. The ones who were cut were screaming in pain from the stinging and a couple of them were clawing at their eyes in an attempt to remove the embedded shards.

Maude had not wasted any time in getting the door open, just as the vicious ones hadn't when the attacked the observers closest to them; she knew that she should have started running immediately, but she couldn't help but glance back first as did the others. She could now see clearly just what kind of damage they were capable of; she saw the more of the details of the rips taken from the flesh as they hungrily devoured the screaming meals as if they hadn't just had a banquet.

Unable to take in the sight any longer was when she finally came back to her senses and the kick in of her survival instincts; she just ran out and blindly so, not really taking in what directions she was headed. She could barely hear the others who were going in the same directions as her and who went other ways, but they were distant to her brain, a buzz that she pushed away in her attempt to focus on her own survival.

She also had ignore the sounds of the creations escaping and devouring whoever they were able to get their hands on; she has heard more screaming this night than in her life and that included movies. After more time of blind running and unable to hear any companions nor the screeches of the abominable children did she stop to regain her bearings and think of a plan.

'I don't think I can run anymore and they've proved that they are too fast; there's no way I can outrun them, I have to think of a place to hide! But where, their sense of smell is quite powerful and they're probably tracking me right now if they're not too busy with everyone else! Think, what could possibly hide me or block their sense of smell? Hell if I know! But I have to do something! Hang on, they are quite emaciated with very little flesh,

how can I use that to my advantage? Wait a second, the cafeteria freezer! What have I got to lose?'

Her only apparent option firmly planted in her mind, she tried to take stock of where she had ended up in her haste to flee the disaster zone; but her mind was blank and began looking on the walls for one of the maps that were scattered around the facility. She eventually found one that was by the nearest elevator and just kept herself from groaning in case their hearing was as good as their sense of smell.

'I'm literally on the opposite side of the cafeteria and one floor below!' she thought ruefully; *'I can't take the stairs, that will take way too long, but I'll be a sitting duck in the elevator! I have to make a decision and fast!'* Her decision was made as soon as she heard that horrible screech from somewhere down behind where she had come from; she couldn't tell how far away it was but she wasn't about to sit and wait to be chowed down, elevator it is!

She quickly pressed the up button and waited with uneasy anticipation as she heard it move, the doors opened quite fast and she wasn't sure if that was a good or bad thing. She saw one of the mutated girls leap from behind the corner into her hallway just feet from her so she dashed inside, hit the button for the floor above her and hammered the close button. As soon as the doors slammed shut, she heard the sound of the body hitting it; leaving the physical evidence of a huge imprint that bent inwards towards her.

'Damn that was close! They're going to get in sooner or later; they broke through bulletproof glass so this will not be hard for them! Come on damn it!' She swore at the elevator car that suddenly felt very claustrophobic; her heart was racing, her pulse was pounding and she was sweating enough to fill a swimming pool. Without warning (save for another

angry screech) the moving box shuddered harshly causing her to collapse to the floor before halting; to make things much better, the lights also went out.

'Fuck!' She started breathing more heavily as her eyes darted around looking for a way out. She could tell that she was stuck between the floors and that there was no chance of getting the heavy doors open so that left her only option as the ceiling. There was an emergency hatch built into the top of all elevator cars and the wall barriers on the inside were perfect enough for her to stand on while she opened it.

'Here goes nothing!' She stood up on the barriers as she pressed her hand against the hatch; it was heavy so she gathered up what adrenaline-fueled strength she had and shoved the hatch with a mighty heave and it flipped open with a loud bang. She lifted herself out and took stock of her situation.

While she was indeed stuck between floors she didn't have far to go to reach the top but that would require climbing via one of the cables and rope climbing was something that she had failed at in gym class; however she had no other options left if she wanted to live through this. Yet a part of her hesitated, did she want to spend the rest of her life running like this? Why not just let her life line end here, she had no family and likely had no friends considering how long she had been cut off from the outside world to do this project.

It was her survival instincts that decided for her when the car suddenly jerked, almost causing her to fall, and she heard that now all too familiar screech. Without anymore hesitation, she jumped as high as she could and grabbed onto the cable and shimmied up until she was level with the door she was looking for but was not relieved to see that the doors were open enough for her to get through; because there was a dead body jammed between them.

'They had to have separated in order to hunt all of us, they have a pack mentality and yet they don't if they behave that way; unless they plan ahead.... this would indicate that they are more intelligent than they made themselves out to be.' Maude shook her head to clear these thoughts, this was most certainly not the time to be in scientist mode; this was life or death and she couldn't afford any kind of dawdling.

She took a deep breath and tried to drown out the noise below her (no matter how fierce it sounded) and swung as hard as she could towards the door. With a heavy object below it she didn't get it very far even after a few tries; realizing that any progress would be futile, she swung as close as she was able to before jumping.

In a panic, she realized that she had little to grab on to; with little choice she grabbed onto the dead man's head and hoisted herself so that she could grab one of the open doors. With a bit more effort she climbed onto the body with one side of her body turned inside and made her way onto the floor breathing a sigh of relief and nonchalantly wiping her bloody hand on her lab coat knowing that it didn't matter whether she did it or not. Plus, she was fast getting used to the gore fest that had become her night.

She quickly turned to the posted map beside the elevator, desperately searching for the fastest route possible to the cafeteria/kitchen. Once she memorized it, she ran full speed (or as much as she was able to) to her destination; she had just turned her first corner when she heard that horrible sound come from behind her, almost echoing off of the sparse walls and empty halls.

She had reached the closed doors that led to her possible sanctuary when a couple of them popped into the corner of her eye; luckily the doors weren't locked and she pulled one open with ease before she slipped inside. But her luck did fail when she tripped over a steel leg from a chair that hadn't been pushed in properly and couldn't stop herself from falling hard to the ground.

The blood drinkers had fully entered now, all twelve of them and raced towards her. She managed to push herself up and propel forward to her chosen hiding place; dodging all the appliances that littered the large kitchen into what she hoped would save her: the freezer. She prayed for the first time since she was a kid, that their skin and bones wouldn't be able to handle the cold and that they would eventually leave her alone.

This particular freezer certainly lived up to its name, the cold penetrated her bones as soon as she was inside; despite knowing that it was futile, she shut the heavy door behind her nonetheless and waited. Only a second or two ticked by before the sound of them hitting the door was clearly heard and the dent appeared.

This door held up better than the elevator's as they took a couple more tries and it was still firmly shut. For some reason, one had the idea to stick some of their bony fingers under the door and immediately howled from the cold; it sounded like it was in extreme pain. However, something peculiar did happen next: it began sobbing pitifully.

"Mama!" a female voice cried tearfully; her voice was harsh from being unused for so long. Maude was so startled that she stumbled and slid on the floor and tumbled down for the second time, just barely grabbing onto a shelf to regain her balance.

'They can speak?!'

She was more creeped out by the fact that she called her that; did that mean that they wouldn't hurt her? Or was it just a clever ploy to get her to come out?

'I can't stay in this freezer forever and I'm already starting to get extremely cold; I don't think I have much choice other than to come out.' Taking a deep breath,

she opened the door to the sight of the injured mutant curled up in a fetal position. Instinctively, she touched her head and was barely aware of how all other ones had arrived and were crowded in a circle around them.

The female looked up at Maude and reached up to her before she gently buried herself in the human's neck and bit down; but not savagely like with their previous prey, it was almost loving. Before everything went black, Maude felt that something inside her was changing and she embraced it.

#

Her stomach was rumbling when she woke up, but the food around smelt sickening. Her vision wasn't the same, she could see her babies but they were more like heat signatures then actual individuals. They came up to her and rubbed her lovingly; she didn't resist.

"Okay my children; let's go show the world what we are made of."

David Clark's
Shopping List

5 gallon pail
Trowel
25 pound bag of cement
Shovel
Garden Hoe
Spool of bailing wire

JACK

David Clark

JACK is a simple man. He owns a modest farm with pigs, cows, and chickens. On his property sits a simple single bedroom farmhouse with an attached garage. It is not large by any stretch of the imagination, but it is adequate for his needs. There is an old traditional looking red barn with vertical planking lining the outside. It has large double doors in the center of the front, with an opening to the second floor directly above doors. To the left of the barn is a simple workshop with a variety of wood and metal working tools that he uses to keep his farming equipment running. There is a worn path in the grass that connects the house to barn and from the barn to the workshop. The path continues on from the workshop a few feet and then branches off in two directions. One way leads out toward a large lake. The other way leads up a hill toward the only drinkable water source on the property that he uses to provide the livestock water. The well has a stacked stone wall extending about 4 feet above ground. There is a wooden 4x4 post on either side of it. The posts cradle a pipe with a rope tightly wrapped around it. One end of the rope is attached to a bucket. There is a hand crank extending from one side of the pipe that when turned causes the bucket to raise and lower.

JACK has the same routine every day. Up at 5 am, eating a quick breakfast and then he and his beloved head up that hill to fetch a pail of water. They walk back down the hill and down the path into the barn to feed and water the livestock. The trip down with the water is treacherous and they have both fallen down it several times spilling the water, only having to go back up again and start all over. Milking the cows and collecting the eggs takes up most of his morning. By noon he is done changing out the hay in the barn and then it is time to feed and water the livestock again. He uses the afternoons for equipment maintenance or the occasional slaughter of a pig that has matured enough to provide a food source.

JACK goes through this routine day after day without change. He believes he could take care of this farm with his eyes closed. One afternoon he was in the workshop cleaning the carburetor of his trusty tractor when he heard giggling coming down the hill. He stood there for a minute listening. Peering out of the window he sees his beloved coming down the hill, but she is looking back at the top and giggling the whole way. He starts for the door and then wakes up the next morning in bed. He gets up and starts his daily routine of breakfast, up the hill to fetch a pail of water, and then to tend to the livestock. He finishes changing out the hay and then feeds and waters the animals again. The afternoon, there is no maintenance to perform. It is not a free afternoon either. He has a very special job to take care of.

JACK grabbed his keys and headed into the garage to take a trip to the store. Out the backdoor he went and into his trusty truck. It's not the most glamorous vehicle in the world. It has its dents, a good amount of dirt and dust with hints of rust peeking through. The remaining few spots of green paint are sun bleached and showing every bit of the 23 years of hard wear it has been through. The driver door opens with an old familiar sound, not a squeak but more of a scraping of metal on metal with no lubrication between the two pieces. As he climbs in, the leaf springs in his suspension squeak as they move to accommodate his weight in the cab. The door closes with the same scrape and a slam followed by the sounds of a few components inside the door still shaking. He pulls out his key and puts in the ignition and performs the one consistent act in his life for the last 23 years, he turns it and hears the engine roar to life after just a few seconds of delay. There is no spitting or sputtering, it purrs like a high performance machine. He loves his truck and takes care of the engine himself. It is his work truck, and without it he would be lost.

JACK pulled out of his garage and down the dirt driveway to the road that runs in front of his property. Taking a right toward town he drives for about 20 minutes until he reaches the small quaint town he lives near. There is a gas station, a diner that closes at 9 each night, a movie theatre, a few clothing stores, a grocery store, and the target of this trip and most of his trips to town, the hardware store. Pulling in and parking in front of the store he turns off his trusty truck, exits, and walks inside. Moving with purpose, he walks down the aisles in the store gathering the items on his list. He grabs a 25-pound bag of cement, a shovel, and a large 5-gallon pail. He purchases the items and exits the store. Loads each item into the bed of his trusty truck as he begins his trip home. He has a task to take care.

JACK turns into his dirt driveway, but does not pull into the garage. Instead he follows a worn path off to the left around the house back towards his barn. He stops just in front of the barn door and shuts off his truck. He exits the truck and pulls open one of the 2 heavy wooden barn doors. The barn is illuminated by the sunlight penetrating the cracks between the wood slats skinning the outside walls. He walks midway into the barn and retrieves and oil lantern from a peg sticking out of a vertical support. He has kept the barn original, no electricity or plumbing. Producing a lighter from his pocket he lights the wick. He's adjusting the wheel on the side back and forth until just the right amount of light is illuminating the general area.

JACK retrieves the items he purchased earlier from the bed of his truck and takes them to the back right corner of the barn. The barn is still, no sound beyond the restless movement of a pig or two coming in and out a livestock door he put in the back left side wall a few years back. The rest of the animals are outside in their pens for the day. He puts down the newly purchased supplies and explores the rest of the barn for the other tools he will need today. Behind him he hears a new rustling, but it doesn't hold his attention, his mind is focused on his task. After a few minutes of looking and gathering, he returns with what he needs to the back right corner. He lays out the tools side by side next to his workbench. Lined up in a row are his pruning shears, metal shears, spool of bailing wire, trowel, and garden hoe. He takes a deep breath and reviews in his mind what needs to be done to ensure he has everything that he will need. Hearing the rustling again, only louder, he rolls up the sleeves of his shirt and mutters to himself, "Let's begin".

JACK picks up his pruning shears and scissors them open. Studying her shirt, he develops his plan. He carefully inserts one blade under her shirt through the V-neck being careful not to cut the skin and slowly closes the handles making the first cut. The sound of the blades is overpowered by the sounds of a muffled scream and the sudden jerk of the workbench. He opens them again, sliding them down further this time preparing to make another 12 inch cut. Closing the handle, he cuts through the last bit of her shirt. Again another scream and more jerking of the bench. Each disturbance of the workbench is more and more violent. His mind is focused and he doesn't notice the movement, nor does he hear the continual sound of someone screaming as loud as she can through rags shoved in her mouth.

JACK moves now to the sleeves of the shirt; he cuts through the arm openings toward the cut down the center of her shirt. The cuts form the shape of a Y allowing him to remove the shirt completely without having to move her arms or head. Opening the shirt up he plans his next point of attack. He cuts each bra strap off her shoulders and then attempts to cut down the center of the frilly undergarment. Being careful to not nick her flawless lily-white skin. His attempt to cut through is foiled by the underwire that provides her support. She was graced by God with nice D-cup sized breasts that he enjoyed many times, but now they sit there heaving up and down in the way of his goal. He looks at the assortment of tools gathered beside him and grabs the metal shears. They were not gathered for this reason, but they will work. With one quick cut the bra is now in 2 halves. He grabs one cup with one hand and the other cup with his other hand and opens it up as if he were opening a book. This book usually was a happy ending, but today the ending would not be a happy one.

JACK moves to her lower body and examines her pants. Deciding it would be easier to unbutton the waistband and unzip them as far as they would go than trying to cut through all that doubled up denim in the waist. He completes this operation and then looks at the legs. Starting at her left ankle he begins cutting up with the intention of meeting the opening created by the zipper. The first cut is difficult because the cuff area is also doubled up. Cutting through the cuff with the pruning shears he keeps moving up the legs. The denim is causing the cut to stray off of a straight line and he is growing frustrated. What goes unnoticed is it is the constant jerking of her legs and not the denim causing his cutting to be uneven. Using one arm and all his body weight he steadies the leg he is working on and continues cutting. Now cutting above the knee across her thigh the pants are tight against the skin. He is going very slowly to avoid scratching her skin. Finally reaching the crotch area, he struggles with cutting through the seams. After several minutes and attempts he has worn the fabric down into submission and the cotton fabrics making up the denim frays open. He moves to her right ankle, positions himself to use his body weight to steady the leg and begins cutting in the same manner as the left leg. After a few minutes, both pants legs are cut from bottom to crotch. The denim lays open on the workbench.

JACK is down to one garment left to remove. The most delicate garment of all, her white cotton hip hugger panties. He stands there admiring her beauty for a moment and then back to his task. Using a method similar to what he used to remove her shirt, he scissors open the pruning shears and slides one blade under her waistband and goes halfway down toward her crotch. Before making the cut he steadies himself, his target is moving up and down rapidly with each muffled breath with an occasional long outward or inward movement with a muffled scream. He presses the blades together and makes the cut. Moving to the left leg he inserts one blade of the shears in through the leg until the blade reaches the center cut and makes a cut. He repeats the same steps on her right leg. Opening up the fabric she is now laying there on the workbench completely naked in all her beauty. He pulls out a handkerchief from his pocket and wipes the sweat from his forehead.

JACK walks back up to her head, opens the sheers and pokes the edge into the skin of her neck just above the collarbone. As the blade pierces her skin, a skinny river of blood starts to flow from the point and down the side of her neck. The blood does not bother or distract him, nor does the screaming and violent shaking of her body. Working the blade side to side to create a bigger opening, he finally can get about a half inch of the blade underneath her skin and begins to cut. Cutting a half-inch at a time over her collarbone toward the top of her breasts. A silence falls over the barn. No animal is making a sound, the blades of the shears are so covered in blood they make no sound when they close onto each other, and the shaking and muffled screams have come to an end. Blood is now running down her entire upper torso in what seems to be gallons every minute. It falls off the workbench like a powerful waterfall, but the hay covering the barn's dirt floor easily soaks it up. At the top of her breasts he stops cutting and moves to her right side where he can get an angle to cut across to the left and up. He continues this cutting through the top layer of skin and some muscle until he is about 2 inches' shy of her shoulder. He moves around to the left side and performs the same cut toward her right shoulder. Back at her head and continues the cut across her breastbone down the center of her 2 beautiful breasts. He feels the blade scraping against her breastplate. Working now in the softer tissue of the abdominal cavity he is very careful to not damage any of the internal organs. The cuts continue a half-inch at a time until he reaches her navel.

JACK moves to the lower torso, opens the pruning shears, and inserts the top of a blade into her open cunt. Her whole body jumps. He begins cutting in quarter to half in cuts up through her clit and across her pelvic bone, pausing a few times to wipe the blades against the edge of the workbench to clean the cutting surfaces. The amount of blood, bits of skin, and hair are interfering with the cutting of the blades. A half an inch at a time, moist cut after moist cut, he finally stops about 4 inches below her waist. The normal smell of the barn is now replaced with the overwhelming and unmistakable iron-metallic scent. It is one he is not only familiar with, but also comfortable with. He has spent many an hour slaughtering a summer pig in that very barn. This really seems no different.

JACK cleans the blades again on the edge of the workbench and then readies himself for another cut. Using the point of the blade he opens another point to start a cut, this time on her left ankle. Blood no longer rushes from each new opening. The volume in her body has been reduced to only what gravity restricts from rushing out of exposed or opened veins. He starts cutting again working up her shin a small cut at a time, scraping the bone several times. Once at the knee he curves the cut inside around the kneecap being careful to not cut any muscle or tendons holding the joint together. He continues up her thigh, which is a little easier to cut than her shin due to the higher fat content. Once he reaches her hip he begins to curve the cut toward the center of her pelvic area and eventually intersects the cut that connects her cunt and waist. Backing away, and cleaning the blade, he moves to her right foot and repeats the same procedure with the precision of a surgeon.

JACK puts down the pruning shears, now coated in a layer of half congealed blood and skin fragments.

Starting with her upper torso, he grabs the intersection point of the vertical cut and the cuts coming in from her shoulders and pulls the skin back to expose the anatomical wonder that is the human body. He stretches the skin to gain better access, working, pulling and even tearing at times to open it up for better access. As he releases the skin much of it flaps back into shape like a spring-loaded door. This was not something he had prepared for. He walks off to survey the barn for the correct tool. Looking at various instruments and cabinets, he finds a baby food jar converted into storage years ago that now contains exactly what he needs. While walking back over to his work area he unscrews the top and pours out a handful of finishing nails into his left hand. Back at the workbench he puts all but 1 of the nails down. He reaches down and pulls a flap of skin back and with just his own strength he pushes the nail through the skin and down into the wooden top of the workbench. The wood was more receptive than he expected thanks to the blood it has been soaking in for the last several hours.

JACK finishes pinning all the skin back and she is just lying there like a bizarre old-school anatomy exhibit. He reaches down and grabs the next tool. Choking up on the handle a little, he raises the hoe and then plunges it into the chest cavity turning it back and forth creating a hole in the soft tissue. He repeats this over and over, with each strike producing a splash of various fluids and tissue with a sound that can only be described as the repeated bludgeoning of a watermelon with a sledgehammer. He pauses to wipe the sweat from his brow with a handkerchief, unaware that each swipe of the cloth smears blood and other biological matter across his face. The hoe makes another plunge deep into the cavity below her ribs but still hits bone, this must be her spine. The movement with the hoe changes from a violent thrusting to a pulling and dragging as what is left of the almost liquefied liver, stomach, and stringy intestines are pulled out and allowed to slop onto the workbench and then the floor.

JACK moves his focus to the legs, pulling the skin back from the cut toward the workbench, pinning it down with a finishing nail every few inches. She is petite, not a lot of fat content. He wonders to himself what is he going to do here. Looking down at his tools and back at his work, he does not have a solution. He walks through the barn looking for another solution. As he passes the door he sees his workshop just across the yard. Making the journey to his workshop he retrieves what he needs. He walks back pulling the end of an extension cord the whole way until he once again stands at his workbench in the back right corner of the barn. Plugging in the tool he gets back to work.

JACK plunges the router bit into the left shinbone just above the ankle and slowly works his way up her leg making a channel in the front of the bone. Fragments of bone, tissue, blood, and muscle fly out in all angles. The heat of the router bit spinning against the bone causes a searing of the bone and tissue creating a smell that overpowers the existing smell of blood that was absorbed into every surface of the barn. At the knee he pulls the router up and repositions at the thigh. There is more tissue here and he pushes harder as he turns the power on again. The sound of the bit is muffled by the soft tissue it is cutting through. He feels the difference in cutting through the thigh as compared to the shin and realizes he is not cutting into bone yet. He completes a complete pass up the thigh stopping at the hip. Soft tissue and muscle is sprayed out at a radius of at least 20 feet from the workbench. He repositions where he started and makes another attempt at the thigh pushing harder in the channel he created, striking bone this time.

JACK backs up and admires his work. He has one leg to go. What he is having to do to prepare her legs is taking longer than he expected, but he is almost done. Not worrying to clean off the router bit before starting again, the router is plunged into the shinbone of the right leg cutting a smoking groove up to the knee. His least favorite is next, the thigh, but this is the only one left. Starting the first pass just above the knee he is paying more time and attention to perfection than he did in his previous attempt. Ripping through muscle and tendons he finishes his path. Moving back to just above the knee he leans over and uses his weight to make sure the bit cuts into the bone on this pass.

JACK sets the router down next to the other tools and grabs the pail he purchased earlier. Walking out of the barn and up a hill using a very warn footpath he fetches a half pail of water from the well. He returns back into the barn and sets the pail down next to his tools. He turns his attention to the bag of cement. Reviewing the instructions before pulling at the flap on one of the corners to open just a few inches of the top edge. This opening forms a perfect spout for pouring. Not just dumping the entire contents pouring, but a controlled and measured pour. Using that spout he pours about a quarter of the powder from the bag into the pail of water. Thinking to himself, this is not the best way to mix cement, but I can mix it like a grout and it should work. Grabbing the shovel, he thrusts it down into the pail and begins to mix the contents. Stirring and sloshing the contents to ensure everything is mixed together to form the consistency of peanut butter. As it begins to thicken he begins to strain to move the shovel and now has to use both hands. He imagines he looks a little like an old fashioned milk maid using a butter churn, moving the shovel with two hands up and down and left and right. After several minutes he stops and lets go of the shovel to test the consistency. It stands up straight for a few seconds before starting to fall to one side. It is perfect.

JACK uses the shovel to deliver a dollop of mixed cement into the exposed abdominal cavity. Using the blade of the shovel to lightly pat it down flat while spreading it out to ensure it is filling all the crevices. There are a few voids left so he retrieves a little more from the pail and fills them in. Giving the area a final smoothing he puts down the shovel and picks up his trowel. Using the edge of the trowel he gathers some cement and then delivers it into the channel he carved in the right leg. Repeating this step, like a mason building a wall, until the channels in both legs are not only full, but also are neatly smoothed over to provide a nice, rounded contour.

JACK switched the trowel to his left hand and used his right hand to grab a glob from the pail and smears in her pelvis area sealing up her cunt for the last time. Using one more handful, he finishes filling any remaining voids and opens he sees. Switching the trowel back to his right hand, he takes his time going area by area smoothing the surface to nice flat, almost slightly rounded, but even surface like a true craftsman.

JACK puts down the trowel and wipes of his hands on his work overalls. The cement creates moist gray smears mixing with some of the semi-drying blood splatter from earlier. Over time those stains will blend in with all the existing ones, adding character to the garment he has owned for years. With his partially clean hands he picks up the bailing wire spool and positions himself alongside her upper body. He removes each of the finishing nails used to anchor the skin to the bench, releasing the skin to return to its normal position. Some of her skin does move back to its original position, but most of it just stays where it lay. Using his left hand, he pinches the skin together at the top edge of the cut at the base of her neck and uses the sharp edge of the bailing wire to push through both sides of the skin. It took more effort than he thought to pierce the skin. He pulls the end of the wire through and back around to the original side and moves down a few inches and pushes through both sides of the skin slowing stitching up the holes and being careful to not tear the skin. The cement is still very wet and moves around as he stretches the skin over it. A few areas require him to adjust the contents of her body to ensure the skin on each side of the cut touch. Each adjustment caused an oozing of water, cement, and blood to bubble up over the already closed areas leaving streaks of red and gray running down each side of her. Reaching the end of the vertical incision the bailing wire is cut with the metal snips. Moving to the cut that goes from the right shoulder and sews it up until reaching the intersection with the vertical incision. Finishing the same on the left, he decides to take a break for a couple of minutes to let the cement setup better in the legs before starting work down there.

JACK heads outside the barn only to return just over 20 minutes later with a freshly washed face and hands and now pushing a cart. The cart is a deep-binned cart with a large wheel on each side and a set of legs in the form of curved metal looping down from the axle then curving back and then down to the ground to form back legs. The metal loops back up to support a wooden handle that extends off the back of the cart. He parks the cart beside the workbench and then goes back to work. The break worked out just great, the cement firmed up enough to be workable. He grabs his bailing wire and sews up the cuts in both legs from bottom to top, cutting the wire with his metal snips once he reaches the top of each leg. While sewing up the pelvic incision he didn't stop when he reached the lower part of the cut he made and sewed the exposed lips of her heavily used pussy. These lips will never spread again.

JACK put down the bailing wire and grabs both legs together. Carefully sliding her body at an angle toward the edge of the workbench. He repositions the cart in position to catch her if he gives her one more tug. Using both hands he tugs the legs and she slides off into the cart with a loud echoing metallic bang. Wheeling the cart out of the barn door and then to the left down a footpath they have worn for years to fetch water. With great effort he pushes the cart up the hill being care to not lose his footing and come tumbling down. Once he reaches the top of the hill he pushes the cart to the well. Once at the well he reaches down and cradles her body in his arms for the last time lifting her up to the edge of the well. This takes more effort than he was expecting, but she has gained a little weight. He sits her up on the well's stonewall and watches the red and grey liquid streaming down the wall.

JACK gives her one final shove and listens for several seconds before he hears the distance splash of her body hitting the water below. He sits there for a few minutes looking at the water, looking at the sky, and looking at the path down the hill. Struggling to understand how everything came to this point, resigned himself to just accepting it was done and time to move on. She had it coming. This was their hill. It was special. She was stupid and she knew better. Jill knew not to go up their hill with the wrong Jack and ride his beanstalk and fondle his magic beans. She knew better. She said it was because he was always clumsy and falling down, but whatever. It was done. Time to move on. Maybe I should have dinner sometime with Mary and her Lambs, or Little Bo Peep and her Sheep.

Donna Maria McCarthy's Shopping List

A Raven
A Donald Trump wig
Theresa May's psychiatrist
Elixir of life
Gothic Mansion in Transylvania
Bats if the Belfry is on offer
The Queen's business acumen
This is not a political protest it's just that
Donald's hair gets him noticed
Theresa's psychiatrist must be a miracle worker
And the Queen is the wealthiest landlord I know
Lifetime supply of acceptance
Insurance policy for continuing to laugh at myself
Men In Black memory eraser so as you forget the political

protest
Ruby slippers as will save on flights home
And lastly, Supper with Alfred Hitchcock

Follow Me.... Follow You

Donna Maria McCarthy

'What was that?' The old woman, whose sandwiches had kept the party of tourists satiated, jumped as the coach veered and swerved, only just managing to avoid on-comers.

'Keep your seats, Please!' Vernon, the middle-aged tour guide, puffed out his chest, though ashen.

The loud crack against the side of the coach had terrified everyone as they pulled into High Gate Cemetery.

Vernon once again took the stage. 'Nothing more than I have come to expect!' he said, raising an eyebrow along with a whoop from the crowd. They had been in his palm the whole journey... tales of Vampirism and sinister goings on that were never explained so well as they were by Vernon - Vampire Hunter, Destroyer... Nemesis.

'I have a nose for it!' he exclaimed wildly, waving his arms about. He was a true evangelist...

'And they for you, it would seem,' came a voice from a shadowy figure that had lurked at the back; never speaking, not even to refuse a damp sandwich from Edith - instead holding his hand up in disgust.

'Tell me,' he spoke again, 'there are laws, are there not - protecting laws?'

'You mean,' Edith eyed him warily, 'that you believe Vampires are regulated by Brussels?' Her banal comment made him chuckle, 'If only from the Ediths and Vernons of this world.'

'Come along!' Vernon hustled and bustled. 'If we are to catch one of the beasts, we must move fast and together. Crucifix?'

'Check,' replied his followers.

'Holy Water?'

'Check.' All quite proudly showed him their armoury.

'Steak?' A rancid lump of meat was hurled from the back by the unenthusiastic stranger. He gurgled with laughter as he stood up, towering over all before crouching as quickly he made his way through them, casting shadows on strained faces that couldn't take their eyes off of him.

He pushed Vernon violently aside and leapt from the coach.

'Well!' Vernon said as the others rushed to his aid, 'how rude!'

'A disbeliever, Vernon?' Edith wiped his face with her snotty tissue. Vernon pushed it aside with repulsion. 'Yes, Edith - *and a fool*!' he shouted after the figure with trembling lips as it disappeared into the cemetery.

'Come, come.' Vernon was braver than his limited mind would ever let him know. 'Let us descend upon the creatures; the hour is late.'

'And just about right,' Edith said, excitedly.

Once again the old woman, who insisted on stealing all the punch lines, irritated Vernon. He thought he wouldn't mind all that much if she was taken, then shuddered at his own lack of conscience.

The group huddled together, whispering fearful words and holding onto each other's jackets.

Vernon opened the gates, the bewitching moonlight lighting their way. He suggested ditching the torches, his grievance being that as a group they were not wholly embracing the experience, and that he had gone to considerable effort.

'It is very cold, is it not Vernon?' Edith came up beside him, shaking visibly. 'Has been so long since I've felt warm, I am sure I cannot feel *anything*.'

'Yes, Edith, but still –' He threw up his arms in desperation, '– you were very aware of the particulars of this experience – of the times, of the season. I must say that I find it a little embarrassing that a woman of your considerable years … well…'

'Oh for sure they are considerable, Vernon,' Edith was enjoying the attention, even if it be from a *numbskull* such as he.

'Yes,' Vernon continued, irritated by the woman's constant interjection. 'That is all then, Edith.' He pushed her from him and stalked away from the group.

Confidence was not something Vernon lacked, at least not here amongst creatures he had never seen – nor in moments of introspection, really believed in. Still, those thoughts were shrugged off, put down to the lack of hard evidence and the endemic ignorance of the populous.

Looking back at his party, Vernon thought they appeared diminished. 'Edith!' he cried, suddenly fearful – not of Vampires, but of his reputation and license, both acquired through much brown nosing and studious research into who to apply to.

Terrified that she had fallen, frozen to death, or worse, suffered a heart attack, Vernon rushed back towards his group… there were *many* missing!

'I thought I told you people!' Vernon looked crazed, almost to his knees as they sheepishly encircled him as they stared at the ground. 'Stick together – is that *so* difficult?'

The group muttered their responses, which served only to aggravate him more.

'Edith and the others?' He growled. 'We must find them, mustn't we? You bunch of idiotic misfits!' But before Vernon could continue, a shrill cry stopped his heart. He crouched to the floor in terror and began to pray, 'Heavenly Father, protect me.' He tried to continue his prayer but stopped short, noticing Edith's Sketcher shoes and inflated ankles on the ground by his hand – along with her purple-gummed false teeth.

Angry, Vernon knocked the falsies away from him, sending them skittering across the cold, hard cemetery dirt. 'Edith! You stupid, stupid old woman!' he shouted as he stood up. He raised a hand to hit her, hit *it*…

Towering over him, snarling through bared teeth, Edith screamed as her body convulsed, shaking in unspeakable ecstasy as she tore at his flesh. As if in unearthly encouragement, the others of the group shrieked and reveled in the carnage. Eyes rolled back, Edith tore Vernon's heart from his chest and held it before him as he clung to his last few seconds of life, in which his eyes and mind still knew absolute terror.

'Tut, tut, Vernon,' the shadowy figure kicked at Vernon's spilled, sprawling guts with his boot, stretching out the sinew and grinding it into the ground. 'Vindicated at last, but with none but we Vampires to see; it is as pitiable a discovery as you are.'

They then delivered Vernon unto the nothing. 'An utter bore,' the shadowy figure clicked his teeth and saluted a decidedly dead Vernon, 'you might still be alive had your shadow been more worthy, had it cast more than silly shapes beneath our beautiful moon.'

End

Megan E. Morales's
Shopping List

Salt N' Vinegar Chips
Salt and Caramel Peanuts
Dole Jello.
Oreos.
Tomatoes.
Cilantro.
Tortillas.
Knee High Socks.
Snapple.
Pot Pie.
Snickers.

Danvers

Megan E. Morales

Chapter One.

It was 1973, and the start of a great revolution of Hair Bands and getting high. But, while people were rocking out to their favorite rock stars and getting high on ever stronger pot, along with anything else that provided a buzz, the government was cooking up something way bigger in the background.

You see, they had found out a way to once and for all vanquish leprosy, but didn't actually want to get rid of it, not in the slightest. The powers that be figured the disease would be an efficient way to get rid of their enemies - the Japanese, the Soviets, or anyone else who should come their way.

And yet, someone else had different ideas.

The person's face was hidden by a mask, yet no one paid him much heed as he passed through security, using the pass codes he knew well from working in the building. He grabbed the precious vial that was contained within a rather small suitcase, and ran out of the building before the alarms had the chance to set off, their whirling red lights and claxon horns shattering the afternoon.

Oh, this person had big plans indeed. He would destroy New York from the inside out, and the good folk of the city would never know what had hit them!

With ease, the man hopped the large fence as the police guards with the German Shepherds espied at a him, and he flipped them off in mock salute.

He got into the Jeep that awaited him, and raced out of the government owned parking lot, and on his way to freedom. He now had the serum he'd so coveted, but who to choose as his first victim?

The man in the mask looked around as he drove, his fingers thrumming with impatience against the black leather wheel, and sighed loudly as no one suitable attracted his attention.

And then, just as he was about to give up, someone did catch his eye.

She was walking all by herself and audibly snapping gum in her mouth, her long, dark brown hair swaying as she rubbed her arms to warm herself against the chilly weather, despite the long, white coat she wore.

The man pulled over after a moment's contemplation of the woman, grabbing his bat before clambering out of his car Casually, he strolled over to her, the bat hidden behind his back, and he inhaled deeply when he smelled warm vanilla and cinnamon sticks.

He almost felt bad about this.

Almost.

The woman heard him walking behind her. She turned around, tiny wisps of fine hair flying about her face, her eyes, large, grey with flicks of green, stared up at the man.

And before she had time to scream, he'd brought the bat down.

Chapter Two.

Eloise Warren couldn't quite remember what had happened as she awoke to find herself on the hard, cold cement ground by a garbage can. Some of her hair was stuck to the ground with congealing blood, and she realized she must've been laying there for quite a long time.

She groaned.

Every little part of her was sore, and Eloise wondered if perhaps she'd fainted. She held her face in her hand as she sat up, and desperately tried to think back. And then, after a moment or two, it all started to come back to her, in small but painful pieces. Someone had knocked her out by hitting her across the head with a baseball bat. But why just leave her here, with her purse intact, cell phone in her pocket and absolutely no indication of sexual shenanigans?

Weird.

Eloise didn't remember the man's face at all, and she knew she couldn't go to the police if she couldn't even remember that vital piece of information. And so, with that, she grasped the trashcan with shaking fingers and hauled herself up.

She began to walk, slowly at first, until she was confident in her balance, and pointed herself in the general direction of home, she damn well needed a coffee to soothe her nerves.

But, as Eloise began her walk home, she noticed that there was no one else on the street.

On any other day, Eloise wouldn't really have noticed, as she tended to keep her head low - this was a popular street and people were rude and pushy. But this total and absolute absence of people struck her as odd. A chill, creeping sensation crawled up along her spine, and Eloise began to run.

It felt as if someone – *something* – was watching her, and she didn't like it. Not one bit. And as she ran, Eloise scratched at her arm, shoving up her sleeve to glance at the angry red skin patches that crawled up her arm like they were threatening her.

She gagged at the sight of her blemished skin, an icy rush of terror flooding her senses.

Instinct told her that that this had something to do with the man who had hit her with the bat – she should've ran when she had the chance… but her mother had always told her that she was a slow runner, and that would never change.

The wind whistled in her ears as Eloise continued to run in what felt like slow motion, and she felt like her legs were starting to go numb. She persisted, though and when she eventually stopped and sagged against herself to cry, a pinprick feeling started to take over her.

Eloise lay there against the ground, her brown hair spread around her head like a dirty halo, sighing as she tried to force her legs to relax.

After a few moments of silence, she heard a loud *BOOM.*

Eloise propped herself up to her elbows, her eyes widening when she saw President Nixon up above her on the holographic television. He shuffled some papers around on the grand Presidential desk that so many other presidents had used before him, before finally speaking.

"As many as you may now know, there has been an outbreak of leprosy; an infectious disease that causes skin and nerve damage. Please stay where you are, and someone will come and find you. Effective immediately,

New York City will be cut off from the rest of the United States - until further notice." The screen went black.

"Oh god," Eloise wept to herself. She stroked her throbbing arms that burned to the touch, and just knew in her gut whatever was causing that was surely killing her.

Eloise began to look around for someone – *anyone* – but had to close her eyes when all she could see were limp corpses whenever she looked.

Were those bite marks?

Some of the dead bodies had their throats torn out, others had intestines were hanging out like glistening pink snakes – and poor Eloise struggled to hold in her breakfast from earlier that morning as she tried her very best to figure out how long she'd been unconscious; it must've been quite some time for all of this death to have happened in the city she knew so well.

After what seemed to be an eternity, Eloise heard the sound of someone whispering. Clambering to her unsteady feet, she hid behind a tree, peeking around its rough trunk at two men she stood not too far away, just around the corner. She strained to make out what they were saying, catching only something about them needing to find more food or else they'd go hungry.

Eloise had a tough decision to make she knew she would either have to appeal to the strangers' human nature – something she very much doubted they possessed, given the nonchalant way they appeared to be tearing people to pieces or kill them so she search for some help.

She sighed.

Then, once the two men were firmly turned away from her –she had no desire to see their eyes as they died – Eloise plucked the knife she always carried in her purse and slit their throats.

It was all too easy.

The two men fell to the ground clutching their throats, gurgling with their own blood, anger burning in their eyes, as if furious at being were bested by some slip of a girl. Eloise snorted her derision at the pair and stared down at the monsters that had themselves killed so many people.

She wiped her bloodied blade against the verdant leaves of a nearby bush, and studied the smeared blood them with morbid curiosity.

Without warning, the sickly-sweet smell of lavender and honey wafted to spray about her in thick, sickly fumes. Eloise wanted to cover her face, but her limbs just felt so heavy; and in no time at all, the mist covered her entire body.

Eloise dropped to her knees, then slumped to the cold concrete and fell into a deep, uncomfortable sleep, that cloying scent following her into her slumber.

Eventually, men in masks came upon Eloise as she slept.

"We'll help you, I promise," said the man who carried her away. He placed her gently in the back seat of his Government issued minivan, his mask never once leaving his face, remaining there with her as his partner drove them away from the hellish, death-strewn streets.

Eloise awoke to find herself on a pure white cot with fluffy pillows beneath her head. She stretched out her legs, but was unable to move her arms as they were cuffed to the bars. Eloise figured that she couldn't really blame her rescuers for that one – since people out there were eating other people – she wouldn't want to take the chance either.

A pitcher of water sat next to her bed. It contained with precisely six ice cubes that circled lazily inside of it, as if someone had just set it down. Eloise eyed it with a gnawing thirst, before yawning loudly. She caught a whiff of her own sour breath and realized that she hadn't brushed her teeth in quite a long time.

"You're awake!" a nurse chirped merrily as she walked into the room, her long, brunette ponytail bouncing behind her.

Eloise disliked the woman already.

"Why am I here?" Eloise demanded to know. She let out an over dramatic sigh when the nurse didn't answer her, but instead paused briefly to thumb at a button that perched on her hip. She smiled at Eloise, flashing a painfully regimented set of teeth that were clearly bleached.

A doctor dressed all in white strode into the room, grinning at Eloise like some proud father – just who the hell did this man think he was?

"You are a very odd case, Miss Warren – you haven't eaten and yet you've killed two people in cold blood… most odd indeed." He sat himself down next to her on the small, wheeled stool, hitching up his heels to roll closer to the bed.

"It was killed or be killed," Eloise told him, not caring to meet the doctor's questioning eyes. She didn't bother to ask *how* he knew that she killed two people - she figured it would have been made rather obvious by the fact that the two mens' throats had been sliced open by the knife she still had about her person when the lavender smell got to her.

"That's very true," the doctor replied. He snapped his fingers at the nurse, who obediently returned with a syringe full of white liquid. Eloise cringed – she hated needles.

"What I'm about to give you – is nothing more than antibiotics. You haven't transitioned yet, so this will ensure that you don't." He told Eloise as he pressed the needle all the way into the dark blue of her vein. He depressed the plunger and the white liquid disappeared into Eloise's arm.

"What do you mean *transition*? Are people turning into zombies out there?" her voice was barely a whisper.

"I'm afraid so – at least, in a way." The doctor told her. "You see, the man who injected you was a lunatic who had aspirations of kick starting a zombie apocalypse; he wanted people to believe that they were becoming zombies without actually doing so. Sci-fi nerds, eh?" He sighed an exasperated sigh, shrugging as he wrapped bright blue bandage around Eloise's arm.

"Although, once an infected person gets a taste of human flesh, something inherently primal happens and they just can't stop. We can't stop the disease's progress at that point – heaven knows we've tried." Another heavy sigh. "I guess we're lucky that President Nixon put the wall around New York."

"Jesus," Eloise gasped..

"Can't help you there, Miss!" the doctor said, with a sincere smile. He tipped her a wink with a sly look on his face before dismounting his stool and walking briskly from the room.

Eloise watched the doctor go, saw him and checking something off of his list before walking into another room along the hallway with a smile on his face.

Eloise let her head fall back onto the soft sanctuary of the pillows.

Wow.

Chapter Three.

Eloise was released later that week as what few symptoms she had disappeared just as the good doctor had promised. Everyone at the clinic sighed in relief and began to look at her like her recovery was a sign from God or some such; an accolade that Eloise wasn't sure was deserved.

She was asked if she wanted to stay or leave, and she decided to stay to help the others that the paramedics brought in almost daily. Outside of the hospital, everyone was still trying to eat everyone else, and aside from the obvious dangers out there, Eloise knew that she could do so much more here; her life in the world beyond was pretty much over.

Much to Eloise's distaste, she saw them experimenting on the infected, those too far gone with the disease to be saved – their only redemption the hope of their virus riddled bodies helping others. Of course, she didn't say anything, she simply bit her tongue and turned a blind eye, because what else could she possibly do? They had saved her life, after all

Eloise also saw strange food coming in and out of the cafeteria, it looked to her like some kind of pies, oddly enough they were never offered to her; and she had a gnawing, sickly feeling that she knew the reason why – their contents were less than savory and they were reserved for those who couldn't be helped, but who still needed to eat so they didn't die the slow, undignified death of starvation.

Some bright spark had the idea of using old crop dusting airplanes to spray New York, a last ditch attempt to halt the spread of the insidious virus and save what remained of the populace. Eloise couldn't help but wonder when she heard the news, that is was remarkable that no one had thought to do it sooner, and even allowed herself the thought that perhaps Nixon had actually encouraged the endemic to continue as some sick science experiment – the man clearly couldn't be trusted.

And then it was time to wait.

Wait to see if the people outside we cured, if the sickness had been stopped, if New York would ever be the same again.

THE END

The Truth Artist's Shopping List

MATTRESS

STOOL

COOKING POT

BOWL

SPONGE

DETERGENT

KNIFE

The Basement

The Truth Artist

A Young Man lies on a mattress in a small room. A woolen sheet covers his quivering body. A small lamp illuminates the concrete walls. In the corner of the room a Demon sits upright on a stool. The eyes of the Demon are black and stare blankly into space.

YOUNG MAN
"Aeurgh... Aeurgh..."

The Demon gets up, approaches the Young Man...

DEMON
"Hey... Hey..."

The Young Man suddenly wakes up...

YOUNG MAN
"What? Where am I?"

DEMON
"You were having a bad dream"

YOUNG MAN
"I'm tired... I need to sleep"

DEMON
"It's early. I'll prepare you a warm shower and some
breakfast"

Kitchen. A table, some chairs, the Demon stirs a hot pot.

Bathroom. The Young Man takes a hot shower. Steam fills
the area.

DEMON
" I prepared you some oat meal. Take your time and enjoy. I
will go fix your bed with some clean sheets."

The Young Man sits at the table.
The Young Man lies on his mattress. The Demon pulls the
stool closer to the Young Man holding a book in its hand.

DEMON
"Long time ago, lived a young boy and his grandma.
Grandma took very good care of the boy. She cleaned up
after him, fed him fresh food, and sang the boy to sleep..."

The Young Man is fast asleep. The Demon sits in the corner
of the room staring blankly into space...

Kitchen. The Young Man eats his oatmeal. The Demon comes in...

DEMON
"Tomorrow you will have to make your bed and clean the bathroom. I will leave a sponge and some detergent under the sink. Make sure it is sparkling clean."

DUM! DUM! DUM! DUM! DUM!!

The Young Man jumps out of bed. The Demon is no where to be seen...

DUM! DUM! DUM! DUM! DUM!!

YOUNG MAN
"Yes? What is going on?!"

No one answers. The Young Man gets up and opens the door. The Demon stands there staring at him.

YOUNG MAN
"You scared me"

DEMON
"Get to work"
The Young Man scrubs the bathroom clean, makes his bed, and goes to the kitchen. The bowl sits on the table. The Demon stands upright staring into space.

YOUNG MAN
"The bowl is only half full?"

The Demon does not answer and continues to stare into space.

The Young Man is fast asleep. His body quivers and is covered in sweat.

YOUNG MAN
"...AHHHHHHHHHHH!!!!"

The Young Man jumps out of bed. No one is there.

The Young Man takes a hot shower, gets dressed, goes into the kitchen. The hot pot is filled with oatmeal. The bowl sits empty on the table.

The Young Man is fast asleep. His body quivers and it is covered in sweat. The Demon sits on a stool in the corner of the room.

YOUNG MAN
"Aeurgh... Aeurgh..."

The Demon gets up, approaches the Young Man...

DEMON
"Hey... Hey..."

The Young Man suddenly wakes up...

YOUNG MAN
"What? Where am I?"

DEMON
"You were having a bad dream"

YOUNG MAN
"I'm tired... I need to sleep"

DEMON
"It's early. I'll prepare you a warm shower and some
breakfast"

Kitchen. The Demon stirs a hot pot.

Bathroom. The Young Man takes a hot shower. Steam fills
the area.

DEMON
" I prepared you some oat meal. Take your time and enjoy. I
will go fix your bed with some clean sheets."

The Young Man sits at the table.

The Young Man lies on his mattress. The Demon pulls the
stool closer to the Young Man holding a book in its hand.

DEMON
"Long time ago, lived a young boy and his grandma.
Grandma took very good care of the boy. She cleaned up
after him, fed him fresh food, and sang the boy to sleep... One
day his grandma disappeared and the boy was left all alone.
He cried and cried but no one came..."

DUM! DUM! DUM! DUM! DUM!!

The Young Man jumps out of bed. The Demon is no where to
be seen...

DUM! DUM! DUM! DUM! DUM!!

YOUNG MAN
"What is going on?!"

The door creaks open. The Young Man gets up and opens the
door. The Demon is not there.

The Young Man takes a hot shower, gets dressed, goes into the kitchen. The pot is empty.
The Young Man sits on the mattress. He is weeping...
YOUNG MAN
"I'm hungry... I can't sleep..."

A book sits on the stool. The Young Man gets up and picks up the book. He opens it and goes through all the pages. Nothing is written.

DUM! DUM! DUM! DUM! DUM!!

The Young Man jumps out of bed. The Demon is no where to be seen...

DUM! DUM! DUM! DUM! DUM!!

YOUNG MAN
"I am tired! Leave me alone!!"

The door creaks open. The Young Man gets up and opens the door. The Demon is not there. There is a note on the floor. The Young Man picks up the note and reads it...

NOTE
"Clean the bathroom and make your bed"

The Young Man scrubs the bathroom clean and makes his bed. He goes into the kitchen. The pot is filled with oatmeal.

The Young Man is fast asleep. The Demon sits on a stool in the corner of the room.

YOUNG MAN
"Aeurgh... Aeurgh..."

The Demon gets up, approaches the Young Man...

DEMON
"Hey... Hey..."
The Young Man suddenly wakes up...

YOUNG MAN
"What? You are here. I thought you had gone and left me all
alone..."

DEMON
"Don't worry I will never leave you completely alone"

YOUNG MAN
"Is it time to get up? Do I have to clean the bathroom?"

DEMON
"The bathroom is clean and I prepared you some oatmeal"

The Young Man takes a hot shower, gets dressed, goes into
the kitchen. A box sits on the table...

YOUNG MAN
"What is that?"

DEMON
"I brought you a present"

YOUNG MAN
"Really? Can I open it?"

DEMON
"Sure. Open it"

The Young Man opens the box. A small cage sits inside the
box. The Young Man pulls it out... There is a mouse in the
cage.

DEMON

"I brought you a friend. Whenever you feel lonely feed it and
it will talk to you"

The Young Man is fast asleep. The cage sits on the stool. The
mouse starts to squeak louder and louder. The Young Man
gets up and feeds the mouse from a small container of food.

MOUSE
"Thank you! That was very tasty"

YOUNG MAN
"You are welcome"

MOUSE
"Would you like me to sing you a song?"

YOUNG MAN
"Sure"

MOUSE
"One night I was lying on my bed... One night I was reading
a book... The book was about a little boy who lived with his
grandma... Lalalala... His grandma was sweet and took care
of the little boy... One morning I woke up... One morning I
took a hot shower... Lalalala..."

The Young Man takes a hot shower, gets dressed, goes into
the kitchen. The pot is empty.

The Young Man sits on the mattress. He is weeping...

The Mouse begins to squeak louder and louder... The Young
Man gets up and feeds it.

MOUSE
"That was very tasty. Why were you crying?"

YOUNG MAN
"I'm hungry and I can't sleep"

MOUSE
"Eat some of my food"

YOUNG MAN
"But then you won't have any"

MOUSE
"That's alright"

The Young Man eats from the small container then goes to sleep.

DUM! DUM! DUM! DUM! DUM!!

The Young Man jumps out of bed. The Mouse is no where to be seen...

DUM! DUM! DUM! DUM! DUM!!

YOUNG MAN
"What is going on?!"

The door creaks open. The Young Man gets up and opens the door. No one is there.

The Young Man takes a hot shower, gets dressed, goes into the kitchen. The bowl sits on the table and is completely full. The Young Man finishes the bowl and goes to the pot to get some more. As he fills the bowl he notices something bulging through the oatmeal. He scoops out the dead mouse and runs to the corner of the kitchen...

YOUNG MAN
"BEURGH!! AARGH!!!"

The Young Man vomits out the oatmeal.

The Young Man is fast asleep. His body quivers and it is covered in sweat. The Demon sits on the stool in the corner of the room.

YOUNG MAN
"Aeurgh... Aeurgh..."

The Demon gets up, approaches the Young Man...

DEMON
"Hey... Hey..."

The Young Man suddenly wakes up...

YOUNG MAN
"What? You killed the mouse and put it in my food!!"

DEMON
"What are you talking about?"

YOUNG MAN
"You know damn well what I am talking about!!"

DEMON
"You had a bad dream. Let me prepare you a hot shower"

YOUNG MAN
"I don't want to take a shower! I want the mouse back and I want some clean food!!"

DEMON
"You better watch your tone young man"

The Demon exits the room and locks the door...

YOUNG MAN
"Hey?!"

The Young Man attempts to open the door...

YOUNG MAN
"Open the door!! Open the damn door!!!"

The Young man sits on the mattress and weeps...

YOUNG MAN
"Why is this happening? What did I do wrong?"

Something rolls up to the Young Man's feet. He picks it up. It's the Mouse's food container.

YOUNG MAN
"I didn't mean to eat its food! I was starving and the mouse offered it to me!!"

DUM! DUM! DUM! DUM! DUM!!

The Young Man jumps out of bed.

DUM! DUM! DUM! DUM! DUM!!

The door creaks open. The Young Man gets up and opens the door. No one is there.

The Young Man goes into the kitchen. The pot is full. The Young Man dumps it in the bin.

DUM! DUM! DUM! DUM! DUM!!

The Young Man jumps out of bed.

DUM! DUM! DUM! DUM! DUM!!

YOUNG MAN

"What the fuck do you want?!! Im tired!! I'm hungry!! And I want to fucking murder you!!!"

The door creaks open. The Young Man rushes into the kitchen. The pot is empty.

DUM! DUM! DUM! DUM! DUM!!

The Young Man jumps out of bed.

DUM! DUM! DUM! DUM! DUM!!

YOUNG MAN
"Come in here you coward!! I'm gonna fucking chop you up and eat you motherfucker!!!"

The door is suddenly locked. The Young Man rushes to the door and bangs the shit out of it.

BANG!! BANG!! BANG!! BANG!! BANG!!!
YOUNG MAN
"I'm gonna kill you!! You hear me motherfucker!!!"

The Young man sits on the mattress and weeps... He picks up the book and pretends to read...

YOUNG MAN
"Long time ago... Was a little boy and his grandma... His grandma was mean and ugly... She fed the boy rotten meat and read him horror stories to put him to sleep... He had bad dreams and his stomach hurt so much... One day the little boy stole a knife from the kitchen and murdered his fucking grandma!!"

The Young Man is fast asleep. His body quivers and it is covered in sweat.

YOUNG MAN
"Aeurgh... Aeurgh... AHHHHHHHHH!!!!!"

The Young Man suddenly wakes up. The door creaks open. The Young Man gets up, opens the door, no one is there. A knife sits on the floor. The Young Man picks it up and goes into the kitchen. The pot is empty...

YOUNG MAN
"I'm hungry motherfucker!! What am I going to do with a knife? Kill myself?!"

DUM! DUM! DUM! DUM! DUM!!

The Young Man wakes up.

YOUNG MAN
"Stop banging on the fucking door!! I'm fucking tired!!"

The door creaks open. The Young Man gets up, opens the door. A note sits on the floor...

NOTE
"Clean the bathroom and make your bed"

The Young Man scrubs the bathroom clean and makes his bed. He goes into the kitchen. The hot pot is filled with oatmeal.

YOUNG MAN
"Finally! Some fucking food and I don't give a fuck if your fucking eyeballs are in this I am eating!!!"

The Young Man eats out the pot. Live cockroaches are mixed in the oatmeal...

YOUNG MAN

"BEURGH!! AARGH!!!"

The Young Man vomits everything out. Picks up the knife he had left on the table and rushes into the room. No one. Rushes into the bathroom. No one...

YOUNG MAN
"Where the fuck are you?! You coward piece of shit!!!"

The Young Man sits on the mattress. His face is pale. A cockroach crawls out from underneath the door...

SPLAAAT!!

The Young Man squashes the creature with the book. It is stuck on the book. The Young Man opens the book and pretends to read...

YOUNG MAN
" Long ago was a little boy and his grandma... The boy loved his grandma so very much... She was damn fucking ugly and fed the boy swarms of cockroaches."

DUM! DUM! DUM! DUM! DUM!!

The Young Man wakes up.

YOUNG MAN
"My friend! Good morning!! I can't wait to see you!!"

The door creaks open. The Young Man gets up and opens the door. A note sits on the floor...

NOTE
"Clean the bathroom and make your bed"

YOUNG MAN
"You are damn sure I will!"

The Young Man scrubs the bathroom clean, makes his bed, goes into the kitchen. The pot is filled with cockroaches.

YOUNG MAN
"Finally some fucking food! I love you man!!"

The Young Man empties the pot into the bin. Takes a hot shower. Goes to sleep.

DUM! DUM! DUM! DUM! DUM!!

The Young Man wakes up.

The door creaks open. The Young Man gets up and opens the door. A note sits on the floor...

NOTE
"Clean the bathroom and make your bed"

The Young Man scrubs the bathroom clean, makes his bed, goes into the kitchen. The pot is filled with cockroaches.

YOUNG MAN
"BEURGH!!"

The Young Man vomits.

YOUNG MAN
"Listen! If you can hear me I'm sorry! I'm sorry I ate the mouse's food! I'm sorry I got mad and said terrible things! I'm sorry..."

The Young Man collapses to the ground and passes out.

The Young Man suddenly wakes up. Blood trickles down his forehead onto the kitchen floor. Cockroaches all over the place.

YOUNG MAN
"No... No... No... I'm tired man... What do you want from
me? I want to sleep... I want to eat..."

The Young Man gets up and drags himself to the room.

DUM! DUM! DUM! DUM! DUM!!

The Young Man wakes up.

The door creaks open. The Young Man gets up and opens the
door. A note sits on the floor...

NOTE
"Clean the bathroom and make your bed"

The Young Man scrubs the bathroom clean, makes his bed,
goes into the kitchen. The pot is empty and no cockroaches
can be seen.

DUM! DUM! DUM! DUM! DUM!!

The Young Man wakes up.

The door creaks open. The Young Man gets up and opens the
door. A note sits on the floor...

NOTE
"Clean the bathroom and make your bed"

The Young Man scrubs the bathroom clean, makes his bed,
goes into the kitchen. The pot is empty.

The Young Man sits on the mattress. His face is very pale.
His eyes stare blankly into space.

DUM! DUM! DUM! DUM! DUM!!

The Young Man wakes up.

The door creaks open. The Young Man gets up and opens the door. A note sits on the floor...

NOTE
"Clean the bathroom and make your bed"

The Young Man scrubs the bathroom clean, makes his bed, goes into the kitchen. The pot is still empty.

The Young Man sits on the mattress. He picks up the book and turns it around. The dead cockroach is still there. He grabs it and puts in his mouth...

YOUNG MAN
"BEURGH!!"

The Young Man is asleep. His body quivers.

YOUNG MAN
"Aeurgh... Aeurgh..."

The Young Man suddenly wakes up. The door creaks open. The Young Man gets up, opens the door, no one is there. The knife sits on the floor. The Young Man picks it up and goes into the kitchen. The pot is empty.

YOUNG MAN
"I can't do it. I don't want to do it. Please..."

The Young Man is asleep. His body quivers.

YOUNG MAN
"Aeurgh... Aeurgh..."

The Young Man suddenly wakes up. The door creaks open. The Young Man gets up, opens the door, no one is there. The knife sits on the floor. The Young Man walks past it and goes into the kitchen. The pot is empty...

YOUNG MAN
"I'm dying already. What's the point?"

DUM! DUM! DUM! DUM! DUM!!

The Young Man wakes up.

The door creaks open. The Young Man gets up and opens the door. A note sits on the floor...

NOTE
"Clean the bathroom and make your bed"

The Young Man scrubs the bathroom clean, makes his bed, goes into the kitchen. The pot is still empty.

The Young Man sits on the mattress. He picks up the book and pretends to read...

YOUNG MAN
"Long time ago, lived a young boy and his grandma.
Grandma took very good care of the boy. She cleaned up
after him, fed him fresh food, and sang the boy to sleep..."

The Young Man suddenly weeps...

YOUNG MAN
"Grandma where are you? I need you grandma..."

DUM! DUM! DUM! DUM! DUM!!

The Young Man wakes up.

The door creaks open. The Young Man gets up and opens the door. A note sits on the floor...

NOTE
"Clean the bathroom and make your bed"

The Young Man goes into the kitchen. The pot is no longer there.

DUM! DUM! DUM! DUM! DUM!!

The Young Man wakes up.

The door creaks open. The Young Man turns over and continues to sleep.

DUM! DUM! DUM! DUM! DUM!!

The Young Man lies motionless. Suddenly the Demon appears from behind the door...

DEMON
"Hey.... Hey...."

The Young Man turns over...

DEMON
"It's early. I'll prepare you a warm shower and some breakfast"

The Young Man does not answer.

DEMON
"The bathroom is clean and I will make your bed"

The Young Man continues to remain silent.
DEMON
"You don't look at all interested"

YOUNG MAN

"I am dying and I am tired of all this"

DEMON
"Don't be dramatic. Come on get up let's get you cleaned up"

The Young Man turns his back on the Demon.

BANG!!!

The door violently slams shut.

The Young Man falls asleep. A Voice suddenly beckons the Young Man...

VOICE
"Hey... Hey..."

The Young Man continues to sleep.

VOICE
"One night I was lying on my bed... One night I was reading a book.... The book was about a little boy who lived with his grandma.... Lalalala... His grandma was sweet and took care of the little boy.... One morning I woke up... One morning I took a hot shower.... Lalalala..."

The Young Man opens his eyes and turns over. The cage sits on the stool....

MOUSE
"How are you my sweet friend?"

YOUNG MAN
"...I thought you were dead?"

MOUSE
"What are you talking about? Can't you see I am still here?"

YOUNG MAN

"I must be dreaming"
The Young Man turns over and continues to sleep. After some time the Young Man wakes up. The cage is no longer there. He gets up, opens the door, goes into the bathroom and takes a hot shower. He looks into the mirror. His eyes are black. He gets dressed and goes into the kitchen. The pot is empty. He opens the kitchen closet and pulls out a bag of oats, fills the pot with water from the tap and pours some oats inside.

The Young Man returns to the bedroom...

YOUNG MAN
"Hey.... Hey...."

The Demon lies on the mattress. His body is quivering and covered in sweat.

DEMON
"What? Where am I?"

YOUNG MAN
"You were having a bad dream"

DEMON
"I'm tired.... I need to sleep"

YOUNG MAN
"It's early. I'm preparing you some breakfast"

The Demon gets up and follows the Young Man into the kitchen.

YOUNG MAN
"Have a seat"

The Demon sits at the table. The Young Man fills the bowl.

DEMON

"That tastes really good"

YOUNG MAN
"You're welcome"

Josh Darling's
Shopping List

Bullets
Bleach
Windex
Condoms
Bottled Water
Frappuccino
Rubbing Alcohol
Gauze Pads
Matches
Hot Sauce

Kill the Architect

Josh Darling

He knew he looked delicious and they wanted to devour him. Standing off against them in the cool autumn air, he'd become the High Plains Drifter in the center of the empty New England mountain town. In the movies, the gunslinger fought *mano-a-mano*. In real life, there were no rules and he was facing off against a dozen or so ruthless killers. He didn't break eye contact with the alpha. A glance away and the pack would charge. A growl rumbled from the German Shepard's crinkling snout. It was signaling the pack to get ready. His fingers twitched, warming up for the grab.

His hand bounced down. From its holster on his left leg, he pulled a modified neon orange pump action water gun. With a hard squeeze, he fired on the alpha mutt. The red fluid soaked the dog's face, recoiling, it squealed.

Seeing weakness in their leader the pack ran. The alpha dog left behind, sniveling on the ground. The crying animal rubbed its paws over its snout.

Dent slid the water gun into its leather holster. On the opposite side, he kept a holstered revolver. His homemade dog repellent doubled as a condiment. He reserved eating it for when he needed to show people it was safe.

Walking down Pearl St. the Windsor Hotel caught his eye. Six stories of ivy-covered brick and paint peeling off weathered wood. The building was an old woman with good bone structure; anyone with an eye could see she was once beautiful. In her prime, she was a reminder of the robber barons. The Rockefellers and P.J. Morgans of the world had the fortune of going extinct a hundred years before the rest of humanity.

The State University, a town over, drew enough visitors to support a four-star hotel. He figured the place must have filled around this time with the parents of out of town students. In the winter, skiing would pull in the tourists. He'd lectured at the university once; their labs had some nice gear. He hoped it was still there.

Dusty art deco crown molding framed the concierge's desk. At the end of the room, a tarnished brass banister ascended along a staircase. His parents took him to places like this when he was a kid. Tonight he would find a room by a fire exit and not worry about the wind chill. In the morning, he'd go to the roof and see if he could find the University.

In the air was an aroma from a long time ago. He filled his lungs to capacity. Memories surfaced of good times in high school and college before he became "serious." Knees bent, he stepped toe-heel-toe-heel following the odor.

Reaching the restaurant attached to the hotel, he stopped. There were three of them and he listened to their conversation as a matter of safety.

A man's voice, "Sky, we've been here three days and haven't found anything, not even a fresh turd."

"Maybe he's using the bathrooms," a woman said.

"Maybe he's not real."

A second male voice, "Sky and Harmony, you need to check your negativity. We'll give it another day or two then head back to Peace Land."

They'd chosen a table in the middle of the room. The circular seating allowed them to check the others' back. Their assault rifles leaning against the rim of the table waited for action as they passed a joint. The three were early twenty-something white kids with dreadlocks piled on top of their heads. Dent tried not to smile at the idea of hippy kids with assault rifles.

The woman with translucent white skin passed a burnt down joint to the man next to her. Seeing the young woman, Dent felt the tension in his back release. The men weren't violent towards her. He'd seen too much of that. One loud footstep and they looked at him.

Dent put his hands up, "I come in peace."

They gave him a look of prey frightened by a predator.

He smiled, "Name's Dent. I'm just passing through. I mean no harm. I smelled the dope, heard you guys talking, and thought I'd say hi."

The young man facing him with a light brown beard started, "I'm Jeff. That's Sky and Harmony."

Jeff paused. Sky and Harmony gave syncopated greetings, raising their hands in limp waves. Jeff cleared his throat, "We're from Peace Land."

"Never heard of it, where's it located?"

Harmony handed Jeff the burnt down joint. Jeff pinched it while speaking, "We'll wait till we get to know you a bit better before discussing that." He sucked the cherry of the micro-roach down to his thumb and forefinger.

"Mind if I join you? It's been days since I've talked to anyone."

"If you're looking for extra food, we don't have any," Harmony's tone perplexed Dent. The comment was rude but his tone calm. Dent took off his backpack. With the load off, he dug his knuckles into his lower back, heard it crack. His body creaked and cracked, they'd know all about this in 20 - 30 years. Provided they live that long.

Dent pulled out a chair. Sitting he smiled, "You kids come to town to party?"

"We're not kids, man," more calm from Harmony.

He didn't mean to be rude but he couldn't stop glancing over at the woman. She was lean and muscular, healthy looking and attractive. Most of the people he came across doubled as apparitions of starvation. This group looked healthy. Her moon-shaped face reminded him of a silent movie starlet whose name didn't come to mind. Her lazy eyelids half-covered green eyes that said "Go."

She caught him looking, "We're on a mission. We're looking for someone special--"

"Sky, no," Jeff lifted his hand, the gesture, a soft cue to stop. Jeff coughed, "The place we are from has tremendous agriculture resources and armaments. We've been able to protect ourselves from raiders and others since the plague."

"I might be able to help you."

"You like farming?" Sky asked.

"She said you are looking for someone. I've come across some people in the area. I'd be careful though. The other day I came across a guy strung up in a tree and carved, like by cannibals."

Harmony chortled, "We don't have to worry about cannibals."

"With firepower like that you don't worry about anything. Those M16? So who's this guy? I might be able to find him for you."

"In Peace Land, we've heard of a man who knows how to make things, things from before the collapse. He built an electrical generator in Sharon. In Torrington, he taught the people to weld and then they built a large-scale water distillery. Next to it, they built an alcohol still—"

"Tell him about the dam," Sky said. Her eyebrows lowered, her lips pursed together.

Dent wondered if more women collected in Peace Land who'd survived the brutality following the plague.

"North of the Massachusetts Connecticut border, he built a hydroelectric dam. People started having electricity again." Jeff said.

Reading people was a survival skill new to Dent. He improved with each interaction. Jeff's eyebrows made a triangular peak. The look was questioning, no, despair?

Dent smiled, "So you're looking to find that guy? I might know where you can find him."

Jeff grabbed his rifle, winged it over Sky's head, and pointed the barrel at Dent's face. "Take us to him."

"Easy, what will you give me in return?"

"I'll let you live, Sky," Jeff said.

She leaned into Dent. Gravity pulled down the front of her shirt exposing the top of her bra. He could smell her. Not perfume but her. The smell reminded him of dead lovers from years past. With a hand on his knee, she supported herself, reaching for his revolver.

His gun in her hand, she leaned back. Upright, she opened the gun's cylinder, spun it, closed it, and put it on the table.

"No bullets," she said.

Dent focused on Jeff, not the M16, "Lower that, so we can talk. I'll gladly take you to him, but if you kill me, it'll be impossible. You're looking for The Architect?"

Jeff didn't move the weapon, "We need him dead."

"Dead? He's on a personal mission to help people."

"After the plague, the world got a second chance. Now that asshole is going around, building wind turbines, making electricity—"

"Bro, he taught people how to make penicillin from moldy bread. How long do you think it will be before we have big pharma again?" Harmony said.

Dent swallowed, "You're afraid things will go back to the way they were?"

"We won't let it happen. Peace Land's army has destroyed every town with working lights. Now we need to find this asshole before he kills again."

"Kills?"

"All those towns, all those people, none of them had to die. We destroyed them because of him," Sky's eyes looked ready for rain.

***

Heading down Main St. Dent inventoried stores' display windows. The buildings were all similar. Shops on the ground level with three or four stories of apartments stacked on top. He didn't know where he was heading. He'd told them it would take three days to get there. Seventy-two hours bought excess time to come up with an escape plan. Wayne's Pharmacy & Sundries might be where they'd find a clue to the location of The Architect's lair.

"There," Dent nodded at it.

"I thought you said he was three days off," Jeff said.

"He is, but his lair is booby trapped. Give him the right smoke signal and he'll come to us."

"We got matches."

"Yeah, but can you make colored smoke using sugar, baking powder, potassium nitrate, and crayons?" Dent pushed on the locked glass front doors, "Shoot it out."

"I'm not wasting bullets," Jeff smashed the glass with the butt of his rifle shattering the glass. Jeff reached into the door feeling to unlock it.

Dent grabbed his squirt gun. Harmony and Sky didn't see the stream of hot pepper sauce coming. Hearing his companions cursing on the ground, Jeff turned; darkness and pain followed the eye full of hot and delicious pepper spray.

Jeff clutched his face, "Motherfucker!"

Dent bolted through the broken glass.

Inside, he sprinted under the "Family Planning" sign. He yanked the closest box of condoms off the rack. Panicking, he searched the store's ceiling. Then he found it, the "Cleaning Supplies" aisle. This was his first time spraying people with dog repellent, and he worried about how much time he had.

He ran to the "Cleaning Supplies" aisle. Grabbing a bottle of Windex, he headed to the other end of the aisle. He slid feet first stopping at the Clorox bottles.

Ripping open the box of condoms, he unrolled a lubricated Jimmy hat. It jiggled in his trembling hands. Unscrewing the Windex bottle, he poured half of it into the condom. The rubber bulged taking in the huge load.

Pinching it closed, he pulled a jug of Clorox off the shelf. With the cap off the bottle, he broke the safety seal with his finger. He put the opening of the condom to the mouth of the bleach bottle and inverted it.

He heard moans and grunts. One of them was on his feet. Glass crushed under boot as someone entered the store.

"You better run motherfucker," Jeff said.

"How can you even see? This shit hurts, wait for him to come out, you're not in touch with your chi," Harmony said from outside.

Jeff was closing in like he knew where to find him.

Dent tied off the soft bulbous weapon. His head was up, but he was not on his feet.

It was too late to run.

Jeff cornered the aisle turning to check his six. As Jeff's red eyes aimed the gun at Dent, the balloon flew at him.

The skin-toned latex blob lumbered through the air. Snagging on the muzzle break at the end of the barrel, it elongated. Stretching way beyond its load limit, the condom burst. The fluid surged for its target splattering on Jeff's face.

Dropping the assault rifle, Jeff yelped. The burning pain anew, worse than the hot sauce. His face reddened. An instant reaction to the hydrochloric acid created by mixing the bleach and Windex.

"Enjoy dying fuck," Dent ran for the back of the store.

A byproduct of the mixture Dent created was chlorine gas. The poor man's nerve gas would kill Jeff in minutes, way before the acid. Dent didn't want to stick around while it filled the room. It would kill him as quickly as it would kill Jeff.

Kicking out the backdoor, he was in an alleyway. He hoped that Sky and Harmony would try saving Jeff and asphyxiate with him. The fire escapes hanging above the dumpsters lead to the apartments above the stores. Frightened, he scrambled for the rusted iron ladder behind the drugstore. Two years ago, he'd never be able to make this jump, back when his morning routine was coffee and doughnuts. Now it was nothing but net. Slam-dunking the bottom rung, he rode it down, imagining a glass backboard shattering. Shit, he'd become a jock in his old age.

He ran up the fire escape's stairs breathing through his nose. The chill in the air made the sweat on his forehead numb from cold. Climbing the last rung to the roof got him out of sight. They wouldn't be able to make it through the drugstore. By the time they made it to the alley, he'd be gone.

On the roof, he gasped. It hit him. Winded, he got down. Resting his back against the ledge, he panted. Catching his breath, a gunshot got his attention. He darted across the roof and positioned himself by the street side ledge.

Sky and Harmony walked away from Wayne's Pharmacy & Sundries. He figured they put Jeff out of his misery. Lifting their canteens above their heads, they poured water into their eyes. Pain reduced, they headed a block down, split up at the intersection.

Returning to the fire escape, he collapsed back in the same spot against the ledge. It would be easy to defend and anyone climbing up would make a lot of noise. Opening his backpack, he took inventory: 30-feet of rope, his knife, two liters of water, waterproof matches, a mag-bar, a flask of whiskey, a first aid kit, a bandana, flashlight, and lots of military MREs –Meals Ready to Eat. The people of Springfield were grateful for the hydroelectric damn he'd helped them build. He'd have to double back and see if they were okay.

Or maybe not.

Sipping water, he felt his body cool.

They didn't know where he was, but they still had him trapped.

***

The building's shadows were tilting across the street when Sky returned to town. In front of the drugstore, she spun, shouting, "I know you're here I can sense your negative energy."

Ignoring her, he cut open MRE bag "Menu No. 17 Beef Teriyaki."

He ate his meal away from the ledge. When done he chased it with water.

Hearing Sky and Harmony talking, Dent moved closer to the front ledge to listen in.

Sky was on the hood of a car in the lotus position. Harmony stood, facing her. Their words decayed into echoed mumbles before reaching him. Dent missed interacting with people. Despite they're wanting to kill him, part of him wished to be in on the conversation. His loneliness was killer.

They stopped talking. Their heads pointed down the street. A black haired teenaged girl wearing a camouflage jacket held a rifle over her head.

"I'm friendly," She shouted.

The girl reminded him of his students back when he'd taught high school chemistry to pay the bills while working on his doctorate. For better or worse, he'd never do that again.

When she got close enough, she rested the rifle's strap over her shoulder. Sky and Harmony greeted her with conversation. The three of them took turns pointing in distant directions.

Dent figured, when the girl pointed, she was explaining where she came from and where she was going. When Harmony pointed, he was giving directions. Sky pointed to something distant behind the girl. As the girl turned to look, Sky pulled a knife. Embracing the girl from behind, Sky's hand came from the side and pushed the blade into the girl's tummy. Sky covered the girl's mouth, reducing the sound of her screams. Sky let go of the girl's body. Sky yanked the gun away from her.

Rolling on the ground, the girl clutched her stomach with both hands. Sky ignored her suffering noises and said something to Harmony. Harmony removed his backpack and pulled a coil of rope off the back. When he offered up the rope to Sky, she turned and pointed at a lamppost.

Harmony tossed the rope over the arm of the lamppost. One end he tied into a loop. Using this, he bound the girl's kicking feet. A black-red stain expanded on the front of her blue jeans. The stain ran from the bottom of her shirt to the inside of her legs.

Harmony and Sky worked together pulling the rope. Dragged across the pavement, the girl scratched at the impenetrable asphalt. With each tug, the girl's baseline crying spiked into screams. Nearing the lamppost, her body angled up. With another tug, she was off the ground, and her head swung into the trunk of a gray Volvo. A few more pulls and the girl wiggled in the air. Tying off the rope, Harmony grunted.

Sky stepped on the front fender of the Volvo and climbed over the car. Unzipping her jacket, Sky left it on the roof of the car. From her belt, she pulled her knife. She slid the blade into the fabric of the girl's pant leg and sliced down. At the waist, Sky undid the girl's belt then finished the cut. The girl's hands concealed the wound that flowed a red river down her chest.

Sky cut open other pant leg and hopped off the car. Standing behind the screaming teenager, she sliced open the back of the girl's jacket and shirt. Sky pulled the ripped fabric from the girl's body leaving on her bra and panties.

Upside down, the girl twisted, and jerked, like a fish fighting to live out of water. From the hole in her guts, blood striped over her neck into her black hair.

Dent froze. His mind blank, unable to process what was happening.

Sky put her hands on the girl's hips, stopping her from twisting. Sky pressed her knife to the girl's neck, with a jerk, she slashed open the girl's neck. She duplicated the cut on the other side of the girl's neck.

Sky stepped back, avoiding the puddle collecting under the girl. As the girl bucked, fighting the inevitable, Sky and Harmony chitchatted. They took turns gesturing at the horizon. Harmony kept shaking his head. Dent assumed they were guessing where to find him.

With the sun low and throwing warm tones in the clouds and sky, the girl stopped moving. With her blood leaking out at the same pace, Harmony took off down the street.

Sky pushed the tip of her knife into the flesh between the girl's belly button and the waistband of her underwear. Sky stopped her incision at the girl's ribcage. She sheathed her knife and turned away from the girl. Using her foot, she pushed the girl's shirt and coat, positioning them inches from the puddle by the car.

Putting her hands in the cut, Sky pulled out the girl's intestines and dumped them on top of the rags. Sky's hands went inside the shell of the girl. Her hands pulled out what looked like a liver, stomach, and other organs. Sky plied the guts on the girl's sliced open clothing.

Dent put his head in hands. He couldn't allow himself to throw up. He needed the calories from the MRE. If he vomited, they might hear him gagging. He needed to watch them. He needed to keep an eye on them. He needed to hold everything in.

Harmony returned with pine boards. He dropped the wood over a manhole. Sky began working her knife over the girl with the skill of practiced butcher. Cutting off her remaining clothes, Sky pulled at the skin, using the point of the blade to separate it from the muscle.

As Sky processed the girl, Harmony worked on his knees building a fire. With the girl's muscles exposed from knees to shoulder, Sky tossed the skin onto the pile with the rest of the undesirable parts. She tied the clothes around the guts in a bindle. With everything wrapped up, she carried off the unwanted parts. Harmony's waist high flame spilled shaking light into the canyon of empty buildings.

She took her time walking off to dump the bag of guts. It reminded Dent of the first time he'd killed a deer a few years back. Exhausted after his meal, he fell asleep with the carcass of the animal strung up. In the morning, he awoke to the happy eating grunts of a bear enjoying his deer. As he gathered his things, the bear would pause to shoot him a look that said, "Yeah, what are you going to do about it?" Then the bear would return to its meal.

When Sky came back, she and Harmony carved muscle off the hanging body. They roasted the meat on the ends of sticks.

Laid out on the roof, Dent listened to Harmony and Sky chat. He didn't want to watch them anymore. He didn't want to hear them either.

Above, the Milky Way revealed itself, forcing feelings of insignificance. Hiding behind his eyelids, he avoided the poetry of the universe.

He needed the cover of darkness.

***

After food and another joint, Sky took first watch. Harmony pulled a yoga mat and pillow from his backpack and laid down. Dent put on his backpack. He did his best to get his old bones down the fire escape, make no noise, and do it with his backpack on. He couldn't risk having to run and not be able to double back for it.

With the street lamps, houses, stores, and apartments' lights out, darkness became tangible. And in the pitch of extreme shadows, Dent felt safe. He took short steps, feeling with his feet. This prevented him knocking over anything he couldn't see. The last thing he needed to do was kick over a trashcan sounding off his location.

He propped the open the pharmacy's back door with a milk crate. If the door shut, he'd be in total darkness. He considered using his flashlight, but it was too risky. He sucked in a deep breath. The nerve gas should be dissipated, should be....

In the black of the storeroom, the pressure in his nose and mouth built and he couldn't hold the air inside him. He took another deep breath. The air smelled of death, not chemical. Within the tones of black, he found the door to the front of the store.

Red and orange light on the ceiling contrasted the shadows cutting a rhythm on the walls and floor. The light emanated from the fire Sky sat next to. Her assault rifle rested across her lap, her elbow on her knee, her hand supporting her jaw.

Inside his arsenal, he inhaled again. Everything he needed to defend himself was right here.

Only if this were a hardware store, he thought. Hardware stores had what he needed to make serious explosives. Tonight he needed to be fast, stable, and simple. Searching, he felt his irises stretch. He needed rubbing alcohol.

Something crawled on his face and he swung his hand in the air to get it off him. The uncoordinated movement knocked merchandise to the floor. He froze, waiting for Sky's reaction. She continued watching the flames. Another one crawled over his face. Dent twitched and it was gone. Flies were working on Jeff's body. It wasn't late enough in autumn for the cold to keep them at bay. Now, they wanted a piece of Dent too.

The M-16 next to Jeff caught Dent's attention. He wasn't good with guns. The last time he'd shot an assault rifle, his shoulder hurt for a week. He didn't want to spray and pray and miss. He needed to take them down and be sure they weren't around to hang him from a lamppost. A gun battle in the middle of the street might attract their friends and he'd be fucked. Dent put the back of his hand to his nose and inhaled.

His recipe was simple. With rubbing alcohol from the first aide aisle found, he needed a container. In the shut off freezer, he grabbed two bottles of expired Starbucks Frappuccino.

Mission accomplished.

***

Returning to the roof, he grunted lifting off his backpack. Relieved with it on the ground, he started on his project. He took rope from his backpack. Doing his best to tie a lasso what he came up with didn't look right. It did work as a slipknot, and that's what mattered.

Propping himself against the roof's bulkhead, he unscrewed a Frappuccino bottle. It popped as pressure released from the fermenting beverage. He didn't think anything of it. Sky spoke, her voice consonant and alert. She'd heard the noise, Harmony replied with mumbles. Dent gave it a moment, waiting to find out if the sound gave him away.

When they quieted down, Dent listened to his footsteps crossing to the far corner of the building. He poured the fermented fluid on the roof. Not knowing how long he might be stuck up here, he wanted distance from the smell of beer-coffee-barf. He would have poured it over the side of the building. But with Sky on the alert, he worried she'd hear it splatter on the pavement.

He opened the second bottle with a slow twist. It hissed instead of popping. He added the foul liquid to the puddle at his feet.

With both bottles placed level on the roof, he filled them with rubbing alcohol. Being eye level with the fluid was an old habit. Another old habit was searching for measuring lines that weren't there. With both bottles almost full, he stuffed the openings with gauze pads from his first aid kit. The pads drank up the alcohol. Touching a finger to them, they felt cold. He rubbed his hands together to be sure the alcohol had evaporated off them. He wondered if it would be better to wait for daylight or start now.

"No time like the present," He pushed himself to his feet with a grunt. Realizing he'd spoke to himself aloud, he listened. They didn't start talking again.

Harmony lay next to the fire. Sky, rifle in lap, used a bucket as a makeshift seat. She gazed into the flames. The fire illuminated the inverted carved up body above a pool of black blood. Harmony would be his first target.

Dent lit a match and cupped his hand around the gauze pad wick. Igniting, it burned with a blue flame.

Memories of all the times he'd sucked in gym class came flooding back to him. All the times he was picked last for teams. All the times kids told him, "You throw like a girl." He shook his head, *why didn't I take more bottles?*

With a gentle underhand toss, the glass bottle traveled downward. Falling through the air the flame went out above Harmony. Landing next to his sleeping head, the bottle shattered.

Harmony sprang up, "What the shit?"

He started wiping the fluid off his face and jacket. He grabbed one of his dreadlocks and sniffed it, "Fucking booze." Putting his fingers to his nose, he inhaled. Making a face, he jerked his head back.

Sky aimed her gun into the darkness searching for a target.

Dent lit the second Molotov Frappuccino. With a

bang, he felt the air compress by his cheek –*that was a bullet whizzing by*. Dent chucked this cocktail with the same graceful underhand throw as the first.

The flame flared up as the incendiary device left him. The bottle was a few feet away from Harmony's head when the fast air current extinguished the blue fire on the wick.

"Fuck," Dent said.

Flash. Bang. Another bullet zipped by his head.

Watching his failure crash between Harmony's feet, Dent didn't move, figuring himself dead anyway.

The liquid between Harmony's legs pooled. The alcohol crawled to the fire behind him. Igniting, the fire swam upstream for Harmony. Before he could react, the fire jumped onto his pants cuff.

Harmony yelped, "Shit!" swatting at the flames on his leg. This touched off the rubbing alcohol on his hand. He flapped his arm, attempting to wave out the flames creeping along his jacket sleeve. The burn distracted him from the flames climbing his pants leg.

The fire burst to life around Harmony's head radiating light and heat like a beacon. He screamed as his jacket and shirt lit up. His hands beat against his head. He pulled his jacket off and slapped himself with the flaming article of clothing. His confused attempt to beat out the flames worked against him. The motion stoked his flaming hair and clothes. Sky split her attention. With her gun pointed at the ledge, she'd glance over at Harmony, then back to her line of fire.

Dent wanted to call out, "Stop, drop, and roll." What they teach kids in elementary school if you catch on fire, but fought the impulse. After a school year of arguing with a parent about the creation of the world, he decided to let the ignorant have their cake and eat it too. Though, Harmony's cake was getting burned.

After beating himself and spreading the flames

didn't work, he fell to the ground and rolled.

It didn't take that long for Harmony to put himself out. Smoking tattered rags clung to his burned body. He screamed, "I can't fucking see."

Sky stood over Harmony. Dent couldn't make out her words over the distance, but her tone was calming. Harmony moaned.

When Sky finished talking, Harmony shouted, "You mean my whole face! Kill him! Fucking kill him! Find him and shove that gun up his ass!"

Sky turned, faced the building, and lifted her gun. Dent ran from the ledge. Tar and splinters flew into the air as high caliber bullets pierced the roof. She strafed the top floor of the building. No amount of wood or plaster was going to stop .45 mm rounds. Some of the bullets went through windows, some penetrated bricks and cement, but they all made it through.

Dent cried out, "Fuck! You hit me!"

He'd been shot before and didn't feel it right away. His ears rang from the gunfire. He felt himself up checking for bullet holes. Finding none, he shouted, "You got me. It hurts so bad. Before I die, I want to tell you, I'm the one you're looking for. I'm the one they call The Architect. Hell, Dent is a nickname too. Please."

Dent grabbed his lasso and tossed it on top of the bulkhead. With a hop, he grabbed the bulkhead's roof and pulled himself on top of it.

Harmony made noises, a mix of hums and whimpers and crying.

"I'm in a whole hell of a lot of pain here so I'll be square with you. I booby-trapped the fire escape. You're going to have to come up through the stairwell in the building. Please don't eat me," Saying the last part felt weird, like something from a children's book.

With a bang and muzzle flash, Sky shot out the lock

for the stairwell leading to the apartment's front doors and the roof. The old New England building had to be built in the 1920s – 30s and the wooden steps reported her distance. Ascending, her footfalls increased in volume as she neared.

Lasso in hand, he thought about asking her, "How do you spell gullible?"

Her footsteps clunked at the top of the stairwell. Dent tuned out Harmony's wailing. With Sky under him, it created an artificial silence.

A cold jolt of fear twisted in his guts. She wasn't moving. There was the sound of metal sliding along metal and a click --she was reloading. There would be no chance of her running out of ammo.

A rifle shot startled him and his whole body flinched. Catching himself, Dent bit his lip. He didn't know if the wood beneath his feet creaked and she didn't know where he was.

With the lock shot out, she kicked the door open. Dent leaned forward. The gun's muzzle protruded from the doorway. She didn't charge out as expected. She took her time, sweeping the gun, searching for her shot. All clear, she dashed a few steps out the door and backed up slamming her back against the bulkhead. She moved like a soldier. Spinning around the corner, she checked her six, the same way Jeff did.

Dent dropped the lasso around her neck. With a jerk, he hoisted her into the air. Her hands went to the rope around her neck. Dent felt her legs scissoring and the weight of her in his back muscles. The rope burned his fingers. Keeping her suspended took a fast toll on his old bones. Freed she'd have that gun on him, ventilating him in seconds, and in minutes she'd be making a pate out of his liver.

He jumped down behind her. Pulling the rope over his shoulder, he ignored the pain in his knees from landing. Sky's body slammed into him. Bending forward he lifted her off her feet and onto his back. She didn't weight more than one-twenty and was easy to lift. He pulled tighter. Sky kicked at the air.

Her gun bounced off his ribs, it dangled attached by the strap over her shoulder. Panicking she clutched at the rope around her neck and didn't reach for her gun. Breathing in, her lungs pleaded for more. She made an awful noise, as air dragged down her constricted windpipe.

The kicking stopped as she convulsed. It felt awful, when her struggling ended, he rolled her off his back onto the roof. Dent loosened the rope from her neck. With one hand, he held her up. She was light and tying her upper torso was easy. Dent wrapped the rope around her arms and laid her down. Getting her wrists together, he bound her hands. If she was alive, he didn't want any surprises.

He put his ear to her chest. The sound of Harmony wailing in the street returned to the foreground of noise and he couldn't hear anything. With his hand, he covered his exposed ear.

Her heart made a weak thump. It had been so long since he last touched a woman. He kept his head to her warm flesh. Her heart made a succession of weak thumps, it was revving up. She'd awaken in minutes.

Dent got on his knees and patted her down. He pulled the knife from her belt and a lighter from her pocket. He didn't want to chance her burning through the ropes. He stood, taking her gun to the other side of the bulkhead, closing the door to the roof on the way.

From the street below Harmony's suffering noises persisted.

With a foot on the ledge, Dent debated shooting Harmony out of mercy, if he could make the shot.

Wheezing, Sky came to. After a few minutes, her

breathing became regular. It didn't stay regular for long. Coughing and huffing jumbled with her sobs. He got down on his haunches. The rope marks on her neck showed in the moonlight. He hoped she wouldn't be angry with him when she saw them.

"You okay?" he asked.

"I failed everyone, all the people I love, you're going to kill us all," She said.

"I haven't taught anyone how to build a nuclear bomb and I don't eat people. Do you even realize how many people thought it was safe seeing you? A woman not being held down by a dozen guys. How many people have you killed?"

"You need to help Harmony," Sky's lips turned downward, her face a classic tragedy mask. Her trickling tears glared in the moonlight.

Instead of responding right away, he said nothing. He wanted her to wait, "No, no I don't."

"He's in pain."

"You were trying to kill me. The girl aside, how many have you butchered along the way? Do you have any idea how hard it is restoring electricity, lights, medicine? You know helping people? Some of which were my friends. There are so few people left in the world and you're busy killing? Where the fuck is your moral compass?"

"But the world is perfect now. We don't have an evil oligarchy ruling over us."

"Didn't anyone tell you when you were a kid, knowledge is freedom? The only bill I had was property taxes. I had solar panels on my house and I distilled my own water. I wasn't a survival nut, just a cheap chemistry researcher. Everything else is ridiculous nonsense. No one ruled over me and I don't want to rule anyone or hurt anyone. Hell, I've been setting people up so they can build hospitals and even have pre-natal care.

I've asked nothing for that beyond the supplies to make it to the next community to help them."

Sky snorted, swallowed back her sobs, and halted her crying. With her bound hands, she pushed off the tears on her face, "Are you going to kill me?"

"I hope I don't have to."

"Are you going to," she kicked herself for starting to ask the question. After murder, there was the other evil that men do.

"No Sky. You're a bit young for my taste, no pun intended."

"So, then what?"

"I can't risk you going back to your people. I don't know what I'm going to do, but right now, I'm going to rest."

He gagged her with a bandana. He carried it with him in case he needed a tourniquet. Leaving her by the fire escaped, he rested by the building's front ledge. He got a light sleep. Harmony's groaning kept him from getting real rest. At sun up, he removed Sky's gag, waking her.

"You hungry?" he asked.

She nodded.

"You eat stuff other than people?"

She nodded again, "Please help Harmony. The noise he's making is terrible. You got to do something."

He walked to the ledge. Below, the pack of dogs he'd met yesterday had their alpha reestablished. They advanced in ranks behind their commander toward the man on the pavement.

He said it for her to hear, "I'm going to let nature take its course."

<End>

Jovan Jones's
Shopping List

Fifth of Jack Daniels, Newport 100's, Bleach, deck of playing cards, pretzels, Miller High Life, *Charlotte Observer*

The Night Crawler

Jovan Jones

Hungry squeals and sharp pains throughout his body rousted Delano from his slumber. Through the fog of his cold breath he saw his longtime friend, Betty lying next to him on the hard, wet, concrete floor. Her eyes were wide and frightful, like she had been surprised and then immediately put into a cryogenic state. Her skin was ashen and filthy from exposure to the sewer's innards. Delano's soiled body shivered in the dark corridor.

"Betty," Delano whispered. "Are you alright?"

He waited anxiously for her response. Betty's mouth moved. Relief overcame fret, as he first thought she was dead, but she readied herself to speak. *Everything will be alright. We're getting out of here alive,* he thought. Her head tumbled toward him on a rubbery neck. She stared blankly. Her usual vibrant brown eyes had darkened into black voids.

"Betty?"

Her lip curled, and her mouth fell open. A gnarled

black and red stump that resembled a chewed piece of steak lay in the spot where her tongue once was. Delano attempted to push up on his haunches, but a heavy foot stomped down on his neck. Disgusting, malodorous goo dripped onto his face. His stalker stood over him with the intent to satisfy the hunger that ached inside his treacherous belly. Delano readied himself for the inevitable. *Please forgive my trespasses.*

***

Thick tobacco smoke filled the air. Balls clicked as they crashed into each other and rolled on the green felt tables. A jazz quartet serenaded the room through the old fashioned cantaloupe colored jukebox in the corner. Near empty beer bottles housing only backwash and cigarette butts littered the tables. Betty, a curly brunette in her late forties swept the room, while clearing the tables of trash. The crow's-feet amidst her mahogany eyes, wrinkles in her brow, and swollen knuckles on her calloused hands with tobacco stained finger tips tell a tale of her survival through rough times. Westside Billiards was a rest haven for her, whereas for others it was a trap.

"Corner pocket," said a weathered faced man with an unlit stogy between his smoke and coffee stained chompers. His opponent anxiously chalked his cue stick. There'd been a hundred dollar wager on the game. Delano Fucciata also known as, The Prowler owned the toughened mug concentrating on the cue and eight ball. He picked up the moniker in the late seventies, while hustling pool in Los Angeles. He'd gone from pool hall to pool hall within a twenty-four hour period unburdening some of the iciest sharks for over sixty grand.

A fellow hustler recognized him in a billiards joint

in Hollywood, and pulled him to the side. He said, "Man, I just saw you in Inglewood, and now here." His gaudy pinky ring shone in the fluorescent light. A grimy grin crossed his face like a gator's fishing in the bayou. He declared, "Don't worry. I won't expose your cards. I respect your hustle, but you won't get a game out of me. You're like one of those nocturnal predators in the jungle eating all of the unsuspecting prey. You're a wily prowler."

The cue stick glided smoothly between Delano's fingers. He took the shot. There was a lot of green to the corner. The cue ball cracked the eight. With a forceful thud it fell into the corner pocket, but the backspin on the cue caused it to roll backward into a pocket.

"Looks like a scratch, old man," crooned the once anxious, but now cocky young man waiting for Delano to shoot. "Pay up." He curled his fingers back and forth. Delano slapped a C-Note in his palm.

He donned false disappointment and anger, and then challenged the victor to another game.

"This time double up—two hundred," Delano said.

"Make it three, old-timer," the sucker responded.

Delano frowned, but smiled inwardly. He asked, "What's your name, son?"

"Tucker."

Delano smirked.

"What?"

"Nothing." *Just the fact your name rhymes with sucker,* he mused.

Delano racked the balls. Tucker unnecessarily chalked his cue stick and stooped into shooting position. Betty waltzed by and gave Delano a knowing smile. He ignored her as he watched Tucker break. The balls scattered across the table. "Stripes," Tucker claimed, while going to work. He made three balls in a row, but missed the fourteen trying to kiss it into the side pocket.

Delano wiped the table clean of solids, and ran the eight down into the corner. Tucker paid up, and played again for three hundred dollars. Delano knocked the eight in off the break. He asked the young fellow if he wanted to go again. "Double or nothing," he said. Delano knocked the eight ball in again off the break. Tucker reluctantly handed over the money, and turned down an offer to play again. Delano shook his hand and headed for the kitchen.

"Hey, Will. How's it going?" Delano asked the dishwasher as he gave the man's shoulder a friendly squeeze.

"I'm good," Will said. He stopped rinsing the beer mugs in their rack and added, "I saw that ass whooping you put on young blood. It felt good to see you in action again, like the good old days."

"We're still here, Will. We're still here." Delano smiled and sauntered to his office in the back. Will and Delano had been running together since the eighties.

He took a seat behind a modest wooden desk. An old yellowing computer monitor and keyboard sat on top. He pulled his chair close, and placed his fingers on the keyboard. Before he started his work he turned to a picture of an olive skinned, wavy haired woman with a nice sized mole under her eye. She was stout with big cola colored eyes and full lips; his wife, Vivian now resting in peace. The only woman to possess his heart still possessed it from the grave.

"I love you, baby," he said. A doleful smile creased his cheeks. He kissed his fingers and touched her picture. *Amore mio.*

Delano worked on a proposal to host a local billiards tournament hosted by radio station WRFX 99.7; a classic rock station out of Charlotte, North Carolina. In his younger days he'd taken part in tournaments like that, and as a proprietor he'd hosted a few. He quickly realized unless the venue was held at an exclusive hotel and casino in Vegas or Atlantic City the pot was light and not worth his time. The money was in clubs like his; hidden in plain view, after hours with pros that rather stay inconspicuous. Betty appeared in the doorway.

"You want some coffee, Daddy?" she asked in her southern drawl.

"Yes, Love thank you," he said. Betty traipsed to the kitchen.

Let me go, please! No, please!

Shut up, bitch!

"Just like you like it. Two creams, two sugars." Betty sauntered in with his steaming cup of Joe.

"You hear that?" he asked.

"What?"

"Sounded like a woman in trouble."

"What?"

"Get Will. Quick!" Delano barked.

Betty hurried into the kitchen and yelled for Will to come into the office. When he stepped in he saw Delano stuffing a pistol into the back of his pants. Delano motioned for Will to follow him out the back door that led into the alley.

"What are you doing with that?" Will inquired with an inflection of angst.

"Just in case old friend you never know." Delano looked back at Betty as she started walking behind Will. "Stop right there. Keep an eye on the joint for me."

"Well . . . wait a sec," Will protested. "What's going on?"

Delano disregarded the question and entered the ally. Tucker stood adjacent to an attractive blonde with big cerulean eyes. He had a dangerous looking scour on his face.

"What's going on Tucker?" Delano asked. The young man's anger was evident from the deep creases in his face. Will sidestepped Delano to protect his friend from any potential harm, and to protect Tucker from possibly being killed.

"This isn't any of your business," Tucker replied, and spit on the ground.

Delano put his palms out in front of him in a surrendering gesture. He said to the pretty, but clearly terrified young woman, "Go inside. I'll call you a cab."

Tucker glared at his girlfriend. "You better not move."

Delano stepped closer to Tucker. Will was behind Tucker in arms reach. The guy was drunk and unstable. Delano peered into Tucker's glassy eyes. He said, "Look kid, come back tomorrow. I'll set up a table for you, and some pals if you want. You can hustle all night if it suits you."

To everyone's surprise Tucker's head dropped, and he rubbed his temples. It appeared the hot air had been let out of the balloon. He looked at his girlfriend and scowled, then turned toward Delano. "I apologize for disturbing your place of business. It's just that it has been a *long* day. I thought it was turning around when I won that money from you tonight, but then I found out that I was deceived by you too." He slurred his words.

"Me too?" Delano looked at him strangely.

"Yeah, that pretty little . . . thing that you're protecting over there is my fiancée." He paused to stop himself from vomiting. "She enjoys evening walks in the park, champagne and bubble baths, and sleeping with my best friend." His neck crooked as his head dove into his chest.

"Will, call the kid a cab huh? I'll walk her to her car," Delano said.

"He drove," the girlfriend said pointing to Tucker.

"I'll call you a cab." Delano shook his head and escorted her back inside. Will slapped Tucker on his back and walked with him down the alley.

***

It was four in the morning when Delano officially closed his place. The ordeal in the alley drained him. The hours of operation had no effect. He rarely got up before noon, besides the world was more peaceful in the dark morning hours. He pulled down his Murphy bed and collapsed onto it. Delano clicked on the tube and set it to an old black and white film featuring theatrical gangsters in slick suits, fedoras, and exaggerated street thug accents.

Delano's eyelids grew heavy. A cigarette burned between his fingers. He smashed the half smoked square into a glass ashtray, and turned the T.V. off. The sun would be up soon. It was a little after five and the occasional vehicle would splash by. While his day came to an end it was beginning for others. His worries and the tension from the day had been jettisoned. The sandman pulled the drapes on his eyelids just as the main character in the movie pulled a switchblade from his coat pocket.

Get away from me!

The distressful shouts from a woman jolted Delano out of sleep. He turned to the clock: 5:35. *I've done my Good Samaritan thing already today. You're on your own.*

He fell asleep. 5:37: Loud raps on the door woke him. Palpitations beat in his chest like a drummer boy reading the troops for battle. Delano swung his legs out of bed, slipped some shorts on, and grabbed the shotgun from the closet. This time the visitor at the door pounded it. The thudding from the door vibrated the window in the kitchen.

"Who is it?" he asked. "Got nothing for you here."

"Please, let me in," a woman's distressed voice pled through his door. She knocked with woodpecker-like rapidity.

Delano moved slowly to the door. He raised his eyes hesitantly to the peep hole. The knocking ceased. He could hear her breathing through the door.

"Please . . . let me in," she begged in a nervous whisper.

He aligned his eye with the peephole. She had her back turned toward the door. He only saw her curly red hair. For a moment she stood motionless, and then she turned with frantic eyes. She got ready to scream, but someone slammed her into the door; knocking it into Delano's face. He jumped backward, fumbled with the gun, cocked it, and took aim at the door. The sound of splinting wood induced hard, fear driven palpitations. Through the bottom of the door blood stained the matted champagne colored carpet. The crimson substance spread as if the floor itself had sustained a wound. He crept cautiously to the peep hole. Images were distorted from the blood splashed on the glass. Beastly grunts resonated on the other side of the door.

He swung open the door, ready to fire on whatever rabid animal was out there. Nothing. The stairs in the hallway creaked. Delano leapt over the puddle of blood to the top of the stairs. There was a woman being dragged by her feet to the bottom. Her arms were limp over her head. They plopped down from the steps like dead branches falling to the ground. She appeared to be staring directly into his face, but life was absent in those eyes. The scene reminded him of a large fish being drug off the deck of a boat.

"Hey!" he cried; giving chase in his underwear and shotgun.

Delano hurried downstairs and stepped into a puddle of what appeared to be saliva. It smelled rank and diseased. The front door to the building hung open. The jamb had been broken and the door hung on a single hinge like a condemned man hanging from the noose. He peered down the street, but didn't see a soul. The sound of heavy metal clanging, like a container of some sort, snatched his attention. He surveyed the area. Except for an old rusted car parked on the street inhabited by the usual homeless man bundled in it the street was empty.

***

Delano remained on edge from the previous night's events. Pinpricks of angst shimmied through his nerves like maggots crawling through rotten meat eating away at his sanity. The usual peace he found in the pitter pat of the rain only stirred an association with the monstrosity he'd encountered the night before. Every noise bombarded him with the possibility of his violent demise. What was it? Why was it stalking the streets now, or had it always been present? Worst of all: When was it coming for him?

"You want anything before I get out of here?" Betty asked; breaking his troubling reverie.

"Fix me a Reuben if it isn't too much trouble."

Betty nodded and headed to the kitchen.

Delano fumbled with his pack of cigarettes. He found it difficult to remove one from the pack, because his hands shook from bad nerves. Once he got it together he lit it, inhaled deeply, and then released a burst of anxiety through a cloud of smoke. He leaned forward at his desk with his elbows placed on top rubbing his brow. Delano attempted to block out the parasitic nightmare engulfing his thoughts.

"Here you go," Betty said with his sandwich in hand. "What's going on, sugah?"

He contemplated feigning ease, but the stress gnawed at his psyche like termites in a dilapidated hovel.

"Sit down." He pointed to the chair on the other side of the desk. "I think someone . . . something is stalking me."

Betty hesitated to respond. She recognized terror in his face. Something troubled him. She felt the fear coming from him, like a draft of cold air from a poorly insulated space.

Delano sat back, extinguished his cigarette, and immediately lit another.

"You're really bothered by this, aren't you?"

He nodded.

"I can tell. You haven't offered a lady a cigarette."

Delano asked her to excuse his manners, slid the pack over to her, and lit her cigarette once she put it to her lips.

She asked, "Do you know who it is?"

Delano hesitated. Betty noticed a slight tremor in his usually steady pool shark hands. To comfort him she put her hands atop his. He exhaled and explained, "The other night while I was in bed a woman came banging at my door."

"You didn't have any more blue pills?" Betty teased.

Delano smiled, but didn't respond to her good natured ribbing.

"Did you know her?"

"No."

"What did she want?"

"She was trying to get away." He shoved away from the desk and sat upright. "I should have let her in."

"Was she in trouble?"

"She was."

"Delano, tell me what's going on," she urged

"The woman was murdered in my building. I know,

because when I eventually opened the door she was being dragged off the stairs," he said. He shook his head and continued, "If you could have seen the look on her soulless face. It was terrible."

Betty started to interject, but he cut her off with a raised index finger.

"Naturally, I called the police, and they took my statement, but I'm afraid they won't find the killer."

"Did you see the killer, Delano?" Betty asked; her fingers toiling in her hair.

"I didn't see the murderer that night. I saw him, or I should say *it* the next night."

"You've got to contact the police. What did he look like?"

"Like I said, I saw *it* the other night."

Confusion colored Betty's wrinkled brow. She tilted her head slightly to the right, and gave Delano a questioning look.

"I know this may seem crazy, but please listen to me. I'm not crazy. I took the train home the other night. The rain quit for a while, and I was glad to get some air. I strolled down my block. I felt someone's presence. I didn't hear or see anything peculiar, but you know that feeling you get when trouble is near?"

"Certainly," Betty agreed.

"It was eerily quiet. The hairs on the back of my neck stood up. The sounds of my own footsteps rattled me. I stopped walking and looked around. I thought I saw a shadow trailing me, and then suddenly disappear behind a building. I looked around. Once I gathered my wits I turned.

"'Get inside quick! The beast is amongst us!' The homeless man that lives in an old jalopy outside my building stood so close to me, that if I'd stuck out my tongue I would have tasted his eyebrow." Delano shivered violently for a second, as a chill ran through him. He continued, "The guy has been sleeping in that car for months. He's never bothered anyone that I know of. He's never bothered me; however that night I actually *saw* him for the first time. His cataract eyes were crazed. Madness bellowed from his throat."

Betty watched as he recounted his story. Delano was in the moment—on the block, being confronted by the creepy vagrant. His skin was riddled with goose bumps, and his usual Mediterranean hue exhibited a ghostly pale. Delano took a breath and placed his palms on the desk, as if to stabilize the shivers now noticeably running through him. He commenced his story.

"I gave myself some space and moved back an arm's length from the man. The malodorous stench of garbage and liquor punched at my nostrils from the rotten toothed cavern that was his mouth. He said, 'Once it gets your scent its appetite grows for you.' I asked him, 'What are you talking about?' He told me about a creature that lives in the sewer. He called it, 'The Night Crawler'.

"I asked him if he'd seen what happened to the woman from the other night. Had he witnessed the killing? 'Not the killing, no,' he said. 'I saw it drag her into the sewer. That's where he feeds. He shares his spoils with the rats, and in return they follow his command.' 'How do you know?' I asked. He just looked at me and then flashed a decaying grin. I left, leaving him as he persisted into a lunatic's guffaw.

"That same night I couldn't sleep. The rain vexed me. Usually I'm comforted by the sound of rain, but that night it sounded like a hundred maniacs tapping at my window, beckoning to enter so they could tear me apart."

Betty gasped. Delano had drawn her into his story. Her imagination had her looking for something within the shadows of the corners of the room. What? She didn't know, but she was about to find out. Delano settled into his chair and aligned his body with hers. His face transmogrified into a painful mix of terror and disgust.

"I thought perhaps I'd made too much of the matter. Surely the homeless man was putting me on. He knew the woman was murdered in my building and concocted this monster tale to jerk with me. That's what I thought, but I'll be damned if it didn't." Delano slammed his palms on the desk, and shut his eyes. He said, "I'm sorry, I just . . ."

"Go on, Delano it's alright. Tell me what happened."

"I saw it."

"What did you see?"

"*It*, goddamn it. It!" Delano turned his pack of cigarettes upside down and snatched one as it slid from the pack. He lit it, took a toke, and continued. "I'm sitting in my room and notice fog on my window. I didn't think anything of it at first, but then it was expanding and receding, expanding and receding. You know, like when you look inside of a display window close up.

"Irradiating white eyes stared at me through the window. They were so bright I didn't realize they were eyes until I brought my face closer to the window, and saw them enclosed in crusted burgundy orbs. Its pupils were iridescent. I desperately wanted to jump back; to scream, but I couldn't move. It had me trapped in its gaze. I supposed I was paralyzed by its splendid gruesomeness. The creature wiped away the water from the rain with its large hand. Its hand was like a man's, but the finger tips were open, and it didn't have fingernails. Its hand moved along the window like a snake. It took those hollow finger tips and placed them on the window. They were like suction cups. A tongue slid from each fingertip; licking the glass.

"It wanted to taste me. It wanted to devour me. I know, because when I looked in its face it was drooling like a mad dog. Lightning flashed. I caught a good look at the Night Crawler, as the homeless man calls him. At first glance the creature looked human, but as it shifted and stretched it was evident that this was no man. The electric blue light from the lightning and the dim yellow street lamp revealed its deep red color, almost brown, kind of like a cock roach. Strange white hairs flecked its glossy crimson skin. They moved like sea anemones attached to a coral reef. Two large slits in its torso had several short arms of bone with no flesh and sharp points extending from them.

"I heard scratching in the walls. Tapping noises came from the roof, but it was more than the rain. The Night Crawler drooled more heavily now. A fork shaped black tongue with ochre colored taste buds the size of dimes extended from its mouth. They were moving; crawling along his thick tongue like flesh eating beetles dining on a carcass, and then the squeals came."

"Squeals?"

"Yes, the squeals were coming from the rats. I'd never seen so many rats in my life at one time. They gushed from the manhole in the street like water from a geyser. They fell from the roof and passed by the window. It was literally raining rats."

"You didn't call the police?" Betty asked.

"Call the police?" Delano looked at her incredulously. "And tell them what? I got some kind of man eating monster outside of my bedroom window. Come now. I think the guy's hungry."

"This is too . . ."

". . . Much. I don't blame you for not believing me. I didn't want to say anything, but hey. Who the hell else could I tell?" Delano shrugged. "This was a bad idea. I'm sorry that I exposed you to this nightmare."

"No, please finish telling me what happened," Betty implored him.

Delano inhaled deeply, and relaxed the tension from his shoulders.

"Go on, Delano I'm listening."

"I actually did pick up the phone to call the police. If anything they would have brought animal control, or something for the rats, but the phone was dead. I'm positive the rats chewed the wire, and of course you know I don't believe in cell phones."

"I bet you wished you had one that night."

"Damn right, but listen. The creature backed away and turned. Its vertebrae were exposed and it was covered with some type of white goo. It dropped down into the manhole and the rats followed. They were spilling in like someone had pulled the plug and they were going down the drain. They didn't . . . didn't."

Betty started to speak. Delano stopped her with a raised hand.

"They didn't go back empty fanged. They toted human remains; flesh, bone, innards. They even had feet with the sneakers still on them for Christ sake."

Delano conveyed the happenings of that evening, and Betty listened as fear crept in, and disgust crawled under her skin like searching vile fingers. He explained how the homeless man came knocking on his door that night, and he'd reluctantly let him in. The man told him that the Night Crawler had an appetite for him now. It had a whiff of his fear and with every day that passes by it grows hungrier for Delano.

Delano asked the man why he hadn't been eaten by the creature. He said that he was grabbed one night by one of his awful hands, but when the fingers licked him the Night Crawler growled and tossed him in the street. The man reasoned that the years of filthy living and internal sickness probably saved his life.

"Well, I'm no spring chicken, and not in the best of shape. Why me?" Delano had asked.

"Haven't you ever had an aged steak? The flavor is delicious." The homeless man displayed that hideous grin again.

***

Delano sat in an easy chair peering through the window of Betty's apartment. She figured it a bad idea for him to be alone after the strange story he'd laid out for her. It was almost time to open Westside Billiards. Betty hummed along with the classic rock song playing on the radio and caught a glimpse of him staring blankly out the window.

"I can run the joint tonight. You stay here and relax. You need a night off," she said.

For the first time in several minutes he moved. He responded, "No, I'm fine." He presented a false smile of reassurance. "I need to get out."

She shrugged, and finished putting her mascara on. A heavy knock at the door jarred Delano from his seat. Betty went to answer it.

"No, wait!" Delano cried.

"Delano, it's fine." Betty answered.

Will stood at the door in his golf hat and worn blue jeans. "You ready to go?" he asked Betty, and then turned his attention to Delano. "My man, what are you doing here?"

"We're just hanging out," Betty answered for him.

"Are you riding with us?" Will asked.

Delano nodded and grabbed his coat.

The night was unseasonably warm and the moon had a luminary effervescence. The street was ghost town-bare. Water drained into the sewer sonorously. Delano thought about the Night Crawler washing down the woman from the other night's flesh with that filthy street water. It probably waited down there salivating over the thought of eating him.

They approached Will's old sedan. Delano pulled on his cigarette like a death row inmate granted one just before execution. His nerves were shot. The shadows looming in the dark corners of the street seemed to be in motion. Delano looked. Oh, he looked thoroughly for those bloodcurdling lunar-like eyes with the iridescent pupils.

The urge to run grew with every step, but where? Would he be able to outrun that *thing* he saw the other night? Maybe if he stayed away from his street he'd be safe? That was its home, nowhere else. Of course he would be safe. Why hadn't he thought of that before?

"Jesus Christ!" Will shouted and jumped on top of his car.

Betty did a rapid high step like a football player in training.

"What? What is it?" Delano frantically scanned his surroundings. A squirt of bile entered his throat.

"A rat!" Will let out a high pitched shout.

"Everybody get into the car," Delano said fighting back his own foreboding. "Stop overreacting."

Will and Betty threw themselves in the car. Delano chuckled. He needed that laugh. For the first time in a couple of days he felt easy. He slipped in the backseat and they headed to the club.

Beady red dots bounced to and fro in the moonlight. Rats. Hundreds of them trampled one another hissing and squealing. The Night Crawler stood in their midst tossing them pieces of human flesh like they were pigeons in a piazza. Its massive chest expanded, as it inhaled deeply. Saliva dripped from its rapine mouth as Delano's scent entered its nose. The tiny arms of bone protruding from its torso opened and closed like greedy hands. It removed the manhole and dropped inside. His army of rodents followed behind.

***

A popular eighties' rock tune blared from the juke box. Patrons of Westside Billiards shot pool, drank beers, and chummed the night away. Delano felt easy. He needed the normalcy of his everyday life, especially after dealing with feelings of shame he began to encompass when he confessed what he'd seen of the Night Crawler to Betty. He felt the whole time he spoke she looked at him strangely, like he was some head case in a sanatorium.

Delano smirked. *I know what I saw, and if you would have seen it* you *would've crapped in your bridges.*

Will, Betty, and Delano sat at the bar throwing back Vodka and tonics after hours. They shared a few laughs.

Betty's laughter came to an abrupt stop. Delano and Will continued to chuckle as Delano refilled their glasses with happy juice.

"Did you guys see that?" Betty said. Her bottom lip quivered.

Delano's eyes widened. He suspected what she'd seen.

"What is it, Betty?" Will asked.

"I saw . . . something outside the window toward the front."

"What did you see? Is someone out there?" Will squinted and started for the door.

"No!" Betty and Delano cried in succession.

Will laughed. "Okay, you two." He waved his index finger at them. "I'm not that gullible. I know a practical joke forming when I see one. You might as well cut the crap and try again some other time."

A loud bang came from the office door in the back. The grin Will had diminished into a stoic glare. He double timed to the kitchen and pulled a six shot revolver from under the dish sink.

"You have a gun under the sink?" Betty asked in surprise.

"How long have you known Delano?" Will raised his eyebrows.

Betty shook her head. "No, no, you're right."

Delano stared at them both.

Another bang at the door, but this time the door jamb's wood creaked under the strain. Someone or something breathed heavily on the other side, and just as suddenly as the commotion began it ended. The sounds of scratching at the windows took their attention from the door. Red-eyed rats clawed at the glass. Two rats scurried from the kitchen. Delano ran into the kitchen. Rats flooded upward through the drain. Their bodies expanded as they returned to their normal girth after crawling through the tight space.

"We have to get out of here, or these pests are going to tear our bodies apart," Delano said.

"Is it out there, Delano? Is it the Night Crawler?" Betty asked.

"Yes and its appetite for me must be insatiable. You two may have a chance. It wants me."

Will's face contorted like he'd sucked a lemon. He said, "What wants you, and what is a night crawler?"

Delano explained to his friend. Will wasn't skeptical at all, besides *something* was beating down the back door, and the grunts coming from the other side of the door didn't sound like a man's. The door knob shimmied violently. Delano grabbed his pistol from the desk drawer. He motioned for them to run for the front door. Will twisted the doorknob.

"Wait!" Delano hollered. "Let's think about this for

a minute. Maybe we should wait it out?"

"Look, man we have guns. Now I don't know about you, but I rather take my chances shooting this thing than trying to fend off a hundred rats with six bullets," Will said.

"He may be right, Delano," Betty said looking at the rats hissing and starting to surround them.

Will shoved the door open, stepped back and readied his gun. Delano took a position by his side with his pistol also in the ready. Betty stood close in between with her hand over her mouth. Will released a sigh, relaxed his arm, but kept his gun pointed out in front of him. Delano stayed ridged; his arm straight and his eyes open. They didn't see anything unusual in the dark parking lot or street.

"I'm going to take a look around the corner," Will whispered.

"Don't, Will you have a death wish? Let's get the hell out of here," Betty said.

"She's right. You two go. It wants me," Delano said.

"Shut up. We all go, now come on." Will grabbed Delano by the collar and Betty by her elbow. He pushed them toward his car. Rats scampered at their feet; some tried crawling up their legs only to be beaten back by disgusted hands.

"Oh my God, oh my God." Betty slapped at the vermin.

"Get in the car," Will bellowed.

They got in.

"Oh, shit," Delano said almost inaudibly. "We have to go *right* now."

Will went to stick his key in the ignition, but not before catching a glimpse of the Night Crawler. It was coming directly for them. Its teeth dripped with frothy slobber. Will dropped the keys on the floor, and quickly retrieved them. He fumbled with the keys before getting them into the ignition, but after a few miscues he did it. The Night Crawler leaped onto the hood of the car. The metal hood wrenched under its weight. They yelled out and were temporarily frozen in terror from the creature's appearance. Sharp shark tooth shaped bone extended from its thick muscular legs. Deep guttural rumbles, like a crocodiles escaped from its throat. It pressed its face into the windshield, cracking it and causing both Betty and Will to scream. Will pulled his gun and shot once into the windshield. Will and Betty covered their ears desperately trying to lose the ringing in them. The Night Crawler let out an angry roar and jumped down from the hood.

Will started off, but the gun blast disoriented him. He came dangerously close to hitting a telephone pole as the car momentarily skipped onto the curb.

"Let's see where the son of bitch goes," Delano said to himself with a little more moxie than he felt.

He saw the Night Crawler crawling into a drainage hole across from Westside Billiards. It dislocated its bones and flattened out until it crawled on those bony arms extending from its torso, and slid through. It left a trail of steaming yellow and red blood. Will hit it. *It can be killed! Of course it can be killed. I'm going to kill it.* Delano looked at his gun, and felt a sudden burst of courage. Will almost got into an accident at the intersection running a red light. Delano stared at the street; oblivious to the near danger, wondering what direction the Night Crawler was going.

***

Will chain smoked while he paced the living room. The three of them decided on going to his place seeing it was the furthest from the club, and Delano's apartment was certainly out of the question.

"It's been two years since I smoked; two *years* Delano. Explain this shit, brother. What the hell is that thing, and why is it after you . . . us?"

"It's like I told you at the club," Delano said.

"Sorry if I wasn't attentive, but there were legions of rats scurrying around the goddamned joint."

Delano delivered the spiel again. Betty made coffee and sandwiches. She spilled the hot liquid all over the carpet her hands shook so badly.

"We should call the police," Betty suggested.

"What will we say, Betty?" Delano's frustration mounted and it exposed itself through a cacophonous banter. "Um, yes there's a. . . I don't know what the fuck he is—ugly bastard with creepy white eyes, werewolf teeth, and oh yeah arms reaching from his belly, and tongues in his fingertips after us. Can you send a unit to pick him up?" He waved a dismissing hand in her direction. "Get the fuck out of here."

"You know what, Delano fuck you! You two jerks pacing the room like junkies on a bad high twiddling your thumbs; at least I brought a solution to the table."

"You're right, Betty I'm so. . ."

"Save it," Betty snapped before making an about face in the direction of the bathroom.

Delano lay stretched out on Will's old couch, while Will slept in his recliner. Delano felt something tickling his fingers and opened his eyes. A long rat tale slid over his fingers. He yelped, and sat up. The commotion woke Will.

"What happened?" Will asked.

Like an alligator emerging from the marsh striking out at its prey the Night Crawler seeped from the shadow in the corner of the room and snatched Will into its bosom. Its bony torso arms locked around his rib cage, holding him in place while it took a bite out of his shoulder. Blood spurted like water from a Roman pond.

Will's painful scream intertwined with the sickening sound of crushing bone.

"Shoot it!" Will cried.

Delano grabbed his gun, fired, but missed hitting the lamp behind them. The Night Crawler looked at Delano with hungry, vicious eyes as he started in on Will's neck. Will struggled in its grip, and then silence. His eyes rolled to the back of his head. Fear rendered Delano inert, as he watched his friend being eaten alive by the monster. The Night Crawler released him and chewed on the flesh of his neck, but Will didn't fall to the ground. Tremors pulsed through his body keeping him on his feet. He resembled one of those old plastic football players bouncing on the metal electronic football field.

"Will!" Delano reached for his friend, but it was too late. Death had made his rounds.

Will collapsed. His wound stopped bleeding. The skin rolled like an ocean's tide under the man's pale skin. His eyes had been sucked inside his skull, and his body shrunk. Will was being eaten from the inside out. A red worm crawled between his gold teeth from his emaciated mouth. Several others followed through the openings of Will's body. They emerged from his nose, eye sockets, and began to spill from his pants legs. Delano followed them with his eyes. They leapt onto the Night Crawler and embedded themselves into his skin; their white color returning. They'd sucked the blood from Will and transferred it to the Night Crawler.

With one swift motion the Night Crawler snatched Delano by his throat and knocked the gun out of his hand. Those queer eyes roamed Delano's body. Delano felt the tongues from the creature's hand licking his flesh. A mound of saliva spilled from between the monster's mouth. Delano shut his eyes tight. There was nothing he could do. *Tho I walk through the valley of death . . .*

An ear piercing scream resounded from behind the Night Crawler. Betty stood in the hallway with her hands over her belly, as she stumbled backward. The monster tossed Delano through the living room window and grabbed Betty. With cat-like movements it hurried her into the street, removed a manhole, and dropped in. Betty's screams tailed off until they couldn't be heard.

Delano sat upright. He was concussed, and cut badly from the glass, but the adrenaline pulsating through his body allowed him to go into the house, grab the gun and enter the manhole after the Night Crawler. There may have been a chance to save Betty. He told himself, besides the damned thing had just eaten his best friend. It should've been full. Then a horrible thought crossed his mind. *He's going to feed her to the rats.*

He opened the manhole, and latched onto the ladder. During his descent he slipped and fell awkwardly; twisting his ankle. Delano splashed around in the diseased water trying to get up. Feces smashed between his fingers as he hoisted himself to his knees. He winced with pain as he stood. The fetid odor of the sewer combined with his nerves brought hot bile up from his belly. It splashed in the dark, rank water under his feet. Once hunched over he noticed human bones scattered around him within the spherical walls of the sewer. It was dimly lit by flickering fluorescent lights half burnt out. A human skull smiled at him from afar. A grey rat spilled out of an eye and scurried down the corridor.

Help me!

"Betty!" Delano called out. "I'm coming!"

He quickly limped along the stream of bio-hazardous debris. Water dripped from the ceiling landing on him, bringing the sensation of fingertips tapping on his shoulder. The cruddy walls were laced with layers of filth. Everyday household trash lay at their base. A sharp pain ran through his gut. A few steps ahead of him lay a plump ball with sleeves and pants legs. *Oh no.* He inched closer and carefully giving himself enough time to mentally deal with what he was going to see. Tiny flesh colored hands extended from the sleeves. A fast food container covered the head. Delano slid down the dirty wall to his bottom alongside the . . .

I'm hungry momma!

"It's a doll," Delano said aloud through a madman's chuckle." It's a doll!"

His head crashed against the wall. He blacked out.

***

Delano whimpered at the sight of his friend. The bellies of the rats were full with her flesh. Their menacing, greedy beady eyes yearned for more. They wanted him, but their master had dibs. The Night Crawler stood on Delano's neck. The strange white hairs on the creature twirled about on its glossy dark red flesh. The creature's pupils bounced around its eyes like pin balls searching for the prime meat. The malodorous saliva dripped into his mouth as he let out a silent scream. It tasted like sour milk. The Night Crawler bit down on his chest ripping the flesh away with one swipe like a ferocious pit bull. The pain and sight of his exposed chest cavity almost made him pass out. The Night Crawler chewed on the meat; savoring it. The homeless man's words came back to Delano. *"Haven't you ever had an aged steak? The flavor is delicious."*

The Night Crawler bit down again, this time chomping through his rib cage to get to his heart. Complete darkness fell over Delano's eyes. He could hear slurping sounds, and greedy grunts, until there was no sound; no feeling only a world of cold blackness.

Nick Swain's
Shopping List

Soda pop and cheeseburgers
First Editions
Horror movies and Film Noir
Pointier-toed cowboy boots
Sharper straight razors
Bubblegum and shotgun shells
More and more Rock 'n Roll records
A Tommy Gun and a hundred-round drum, see
Black Harley Davidson heritage softail, chopper, with white wall tires
A place in Transylvania, with a good view; say, somewhere on a mountain top?
A date with Winona Ryder…… this turned into a Wish List……

Archie's Beachside Paradise

Nick Swain

Summer has arrived in the town of Saint Betsie, a quiet community with a population of just under 7,000 on the coast of North Carolina. On the strip, the aromatic scent of salt from the sea and suntan lotion from the flock of young girls in bikinis fills the air; seagulls peck at scattered scraps of food left behind as children fresh out of school for the next three months' glide by on roller-skates, passing the older, long-haired teenagers hanging out between the record shop and the store that sells taffy. The ocean is calm, its horizon profiled by countless outlines of fishing boats coming and going. The beaches are packed, more so than usual, even for this time of year. Hundreds upon hundreds of beach umbrellas impale the sandy shores by the water, providing shade for those of the crowd who'd come waiting for a show. See, something very strange happened in the community of Saint Betsie the night before. Something very… curious. And now its beaches were swarmed with townies, fanatics, and bible thumpers alike - every one of them watching the stage to see what might happen next.

The skater's urethane wheels roll staunchly over the ridged cracks, carrying them to the end of the walkway where pavement turns to sand. Where the island of, "Archie's Beachside Paradise" restaurant stands alone, neighboring the more mainstream businesses along the strip. Behind the tropically ornamented building, a man with dark hair pulled back in a short ponytail, sporting a single golden earring in his left ear, leans against the brick wall smoking something that looks suspiciously like a joint. A white apron strung around his neck drapes over the t-shirt and jeans he's wearing. Using a rock to prop open the door he'd just come out of, he could still hear the radio inside; Led Zeppelin's "Black Dog" leaks out from the kitchen as he carefully blows clouds of smoke in the other direction. The young man's name is, Mickey Hanson: the head chef (and today only chef) to the steadily declining business of Archie's Beachside Paradise, owned by Archie GiaVante - who Mickey thought closely resembled Al from Happy Days; short, heavy set, thinning hair, and a nose like a toucan's beak. But not at all timid, like the lovable burger joint owner from television. Archie was a rather emphatic type, and today he'd gone out to negotiate the terms of how much red snapper he was to purchase from his brother in law, Larry; who was a sap, as Archie had emphasized several times. Mickey knew that no matter how much fish Archie bought, Larry would be lucky to get even a quarter of what they'd be worth on the open market.

At least Archie's absence meant that he could step out in the sun and burn one for a little while. And Melina would be there any minute. He'd called her from Archie's office after he'd gone, and told her he had at least an hour (if Larry wasn't feeling particularly strong that day) to spare out back, before "Toucan Sam" returned. Melina, who was a waitress at Archie's herself, immediately agreed to walk down to the beach to see him, even if only for a short time. Melina: short, perfectly built, and blue eyes to go with her soft, blonde hair. She wore it just like Marilyn Monroe in that movie The Misfits. She and Mickey had grown intimately close over the last year, and he really did believe that he loved her. And more importantly, he felt that feeling was reciprocated.

As the song on the radio changed to something by Credence that Mickey didn't recognize, he did his best to remain inconspicuous to those passing on their way to the beach. Especially to all those men in suits he kept spotting. It was far too hot for someone who wasn't a cop to be wearing a dark suit, and the last thing he needed was for one of them to sneak up from behind and ask him what was in his hand.

Gee, Mickey thought. *I can't believe Archie took off, today of all days. The beaches are packed and we're the only business closed temporarily until the owner can get the very food it needs to operate.*

Mickey wanted business to pick up just as much as Archie did. He enjoyed cooking; he had for as long as he could remember. He especially enjoyed cooking seafood. There were all kinds of dishes he could create with the array of ingredients any decent kitchen had to offer. And one special ingredient he always used, more for superstitious comfort than for taste; some habits die-hard.

As Mickey did his best to keep his smoke rings in tact against the mercifully cool summer breeze, he saw her. As if in a hazy dream, she was coming to him from across the short patch of desert, on her way to kiss him. He couldn't wait. He met her halfway in the sand, embracing her in his arms, even lifting her a little as they kissed. One of several kids passing let out a catcall whistle as another began to applaud. Mickey let her down, and even in the days blinding rays he could see the blushing of her cheeks.

"Hi," she said.

"Hi yourself." Their fingers intertwined, and they held hands as they ambled towards Archie's.

"You better not let the boss man catch you smoking this back here," she warned, taking a puff from the joint Mickey had just passed her.

"It's alright. He still thinks it's some kind of French tobacco."

They both laughed; then the laugher turned into a prolonged giggle that so many people with a slight buzz have to offer.

"Can you believe all this? Look how many people are out here!" she spoke with a tone of childlike wonder. She gave her boyfriend back his joint and wrapped her arms around his torso.

"Believe what? What're all these people doing here?"

Melina let go of him and went from a state of total amazement, to total incredulity. "You mean… you haven't heard? GOD, Mickey! How could you not have heard? It's all anyone's talking about!"

"Not all of us have the day off, you know. Some of us have to work for a living."

If she noticed that he was making a joke, she didn't show it.

"I can't believe you haven't heard! What the heck were you doing last night?"

"I helped my old man move some furniture. Then I crashed."

But that was a lie.

"Haven't you listened to the radio? I can hear it."

"I just turned it on when Archie scrammed. Are you gonna tell me what's going on?"

"Well *I* didn't see anything, but I heard about it on the news. And Debbie said she heard all about it this morning, but…"

For a second, and only a second, Mickeys ability to cogitate was totally impaired; he didn't know if it was because Melina had mentioned the name Debbie, or because he just saw another group of men all dressed in the same style suits arrive on the beach and merge with the crowd.

"…Mickey. Mickey, did you hear me?"

He came to and looked back to her. "What?"

"I said, it came out of the sky…"

It came out of the sky!

"… and crashed *in* the ocean."

"What? What're you talking about?"

"Geez Mickey, I always have to repeat myself to you! I said, the woman they interviewed on the news said that she saw some sort of green light darting across the sky last night, and that whatever it was went crashing into the ocean!"

He couldn't help but titter. "You mean… like a UFO?"

"Well, she didn't say that…"

"No, of course she didn't. Hell Melina, I guess I've taken you to the Drive-in one too many times."

"Oh, shut up!" She barked at him, plucking the joint from his fingers. "I'm serious. What do you think all these people are doing out here? What about all those guys in suits down by the beach?"

Mickey's smile died. So, she had noticed them too. Or the news had and told her. Either way, *something had happened.*

"Alright, go on."

"Go on nothing, that's it," she said, inhaling the smoke in a surprisingly deep and experienced way for someone as delicate and attractive as she was. "No one's found anything, yet. Only a bunch of creeps on TV are saying anything. But I'll tell you, Mickey… some of them looked really scared." And suddenly, so did she. Mickey grabbed her by the waist and pulled her to him.

"Hey, don't worry about it, ok? I'm sure it's just some dumb prank, or a false report that got out of hand. They'll have some poor bastard's mug shot all over the news before the end of the day."

"Ok," the word was muffled against his chest, but it sounded dubious to him.

"Listen, I've gotta get the kitchen ready before Archie gets back. He's actually making make me taste test this snapper before we sell it. Can you believe that? Archie's never missed out on a chance to make a quick buck."

Melina was grinning again. "Ok," she said. "Be good, I'll be down at the beach for a little while. Debbie said she'd meet me down there."

"Oh?" Mickey asked through a waning smile.

"Yea, so maybe if you're back here later, I'll see you?"

"Yea, I'll come back out."

They kissed goodbye, then she let go and made her way towards the beach. Before she left she turned around and hollered: "Stay safe!"

Mickey nodded and forced a grin.

It wasn't until she was out of sight that he remembered the roach, and that Melina had walked off smoking it. Normally he'd laugh at that, but right now, he was feeling a little disquieted. He knew there couldn't be any truth to the insane story Melina had just told him. Or the purpose of all the people gathering at the beach. Flying saucers, green lights, men in black suits – that was the stuff of 50's sci-fi, not the mundane real life of the stranger friendly community of Saint Betsie. But still, as he took one more glance across the shores and the vast body of water that was as crowded with ships as its beaches were with bodies, he wondered.

Archie showed up about ten minutes later, toting a single plastic bag of fish. He looked ten years older than before he'd left. His hair was uncombed and standing straight up like he'd been tugging at it, and there was a layer of stubble on his face that Mickey must've missed before. He never fully buttoned his brightly colored hibiscus-patterned shirts, but now it was only held together by a single mismatched button in the middle. He dropped the bag by Mickey's feet and immediately laid in. "Alright kid, hurry up with this will ya? We need to get goin' an see if this snapper is any good before I open the doors for those eager-to-sue yuppies out there."

"I still don't understand. You've bought snapper off Larry hundreds of times, and never once asked for a taste test. You starting to doubt me, Al?" Mickey joked in his best Richie Cunningham voice. Archie knew damn well who he looked like.

"Don't break my balls, kid," Archie said in his heavy Brooklyn accent. "It ain't you. It's that sap, Larry."

"What'd he do now?"

"Nothin' I know of, but I'm suspicious. You heard anything about that crazy shit goin' on outside?"

Mickey's throat was suddenly dry but he forced the words out. "Just a little."

"Yea. Like what?"

"Just… you know… what've you heard?"

Archie took a deep breath, like he'd heard too much and didn't know where to start. He shut the door and felt himself over for a cigar. "I've heard all kinds of crazy shit," he muttered, biting off the tip of his stogie. "But what's on my mind is all the fish them fellas out there are catchin'. Sure, they look alright, but they're all bringin' in so much of 'em. It's just whacky; Larry included, guy made me such a good deal on a haul, I couldn't take it seriously. And you know Larry; he doesn't know what the fuck a good deal is. Anyway, we talked by his boat for a whole hour while I tried to figure out how he made a score like that. He said everyone's makin' scores like that today. Says the fish are just beggin' to get caught. I still didn't believe him, so finally I decided to wait until after I tried it."

Mickey couldn't believe his ears. First, Melina with UFO's and men from Area 51, and now Archie, with tales of miraculous quantities of fish appearing and practically leaping into the fishermen's nets. "You think something's wrong with them?" he asked.

"That's what I wanna' find out, kid. You gotta admit, there's something weird going on around here. And I just hope they ain't a part of it." Archie said pointing a finger at the bag of snapper. "Now let's get to it. There are a lot of hungry people outside, and every minute a few of them go and take their business somewhere else."

Mickey had a lot more he wanted to talk about, a lot more he wanted to ask. But he fought off the desire. After all, everything that was going on outside was nothing more than pure nonsense. It had to be. Just like that War of the Worlds hoax on the radio all those years ago. As soon as someone takes all this spaceman stuff too seriously and hurts themselves, or someone else, it'll all be over. Besides, he was ready to try a little of that snapper himself. Even if your passion and occupation isn't cooking, the munchies have a way of turning anyone into a gourmet chef. So, instead of prolonging the conversation about the freak show outside, Mickey smiled stupidly and said, "Ok, boss man. I'll gets right on that."

Archie gave a smirk that he camouflaged by spitting out a piece of tobacco. "Yea, yea." He said. "Now remember, kid. Make it that way you usually do. You know, put that kick in it."

Now Mickey's smile was sincere instead of mocking. "Always do."

"Good. Some fries too! And some onions."

"Yea, I know I know. The usual boss man."

"Well, then get to it. And next time you go out back close the door, ok, Pepe Le Pew? This place reeks of that skunky French shit!"

Mickey cranked up the radio, knowing Archie wouldn't care while there weren't any customers, and got to work. As Mick Jagger sang for shelter, Mickey went about with the ingredients: mustard sauce, honey, ground turmeric, ground red pepper, garlic powder, and salt. Plenty of salt. He'd even whip up another quick side dish to go with Archie's sliced deep fried potatoes. A nice sautéed spinach, seasoned with garlic, salt, and pepper would go perfectly. First came cutting off the scales, and taking out the eyes. Not exactly the most appealing part. The first peculiar thing Mickey noticed about the snapper was how dense it felt. It seemed like it weighed an extra half a pound or so. He pressed his fingers against the fish's body and squeezed here and there. It was tough, like the pigskin of a football. It was a little ominous when he'd press the fish's belly and its mouth would open a little, like it was silently speaking to him. That thought both amused and terrified him. He enjoyed a fright night horror movie plot as much as anyone else, but he'd had enough of it for one day. He had other things to worry about. *Important* things, like what Melina and Debbie might be talking about down at the beach.

Debbie Harris was Melina's long time best friend.

She was also the woman Mickey had spent the night with. Last night, and several nights before.

He meant it when he thought that he loved, Melina. He really believed it, and he was sure that she was the woman he'd marry - not today, or anytime soon, but eventually.

Yea, eventually.

But sex had a way of insidiously tempting people into the forbidden zone. Like when Debbie had made it perfectly clear in the locked bathroom during his birthday party two months ago, that she wanted him. Even if he was with, Melina. He couldn't resist. And he didn't regret it quite as much as he thought he would. She'd done a good job of being discreet so far, but how long could that last? How long *would* it? And would Melina believe it?

I'll deny, he thought. *No matter what. And she'll have to pick between one of us. Debbie, or me. Nothing to do about it right now. I just have to kick back, and relax.*

Normally, Mickey would have been able to do that. The sweet smell of garlic was surprisingly more prevalent than that of uncooked fish. And that helped. But then Mickey noticed the second strange thing about the snapper when he took the scaler to it. Its skin just seemed to peel off. One gentle, thumb eased slice across and the first layer was off in a matter of seconds. When he tried for a second slice, one of the snapper's eyes popped out. That was more startling than anything, and it took Mickey a moment to be able to laugh at himself for the way he'd jumped when it happened.

"Get it together, man." He whispered to himself, picking up the eye on the floor and shooting it into the trash ben like a basketball in a hoop. He took out the fish's other eye - to make sure history didn't repeat itself

- and got back to work with the scaler. He whistled along with the last thirty seconds of the song on the radio before it ended rather abruptly and the voice of the middle-aged deejay (who spoke like someone who spent their evenings at the "locals only" surf sections of the beaches) came on.

*"Well alright, cool dudes and cool dude's chick's, that was the Rolling Stones hit, Gimmie Shelter. And we're gonna' be playin' some more crunchy sounds for you in just a little bit. But right now, I wanna' talk about this far-out madness going on, and I **know** you all know what I'm talking about..."*

Mickey's attempt at relaxation seemed like it would only become more insurmountable as he finished up with the scales and started cleaning the meat. Willing for the commercial gibber jabber to end and the crunchy sounds to return. He wouldn't chop the fish up yet until he'd finished cleaning it, and rolled it in his constant ingredient. It was creeping him out; watching the raw fish lips continue to move when he held it tight enough.

"...We have got all kinds of wild reports coming in, man..." The deejay went on. *"... and I'll tell you, there is no sign of this thing slowing down. Alright, here's some news I just got; So, I thought all of this 'thing coming out of the sky' business was just here, on the North Carolina beaches. Who else thought that? Well dig this man... There are as many as **fifty** reports of similar sightings on the coasts of South Carolina and Virginia. That's right! People there are saying the same funky stuff we're hearing around here. Green balls of light shooting across the sky, green lights crashing into the oceans. We're even hearing reports of men in black, in each of the cities. Man, can you believe..."*

Mickey was relieved he'd finished up with the knife before deejay Gnarly said that last bit about the men in black, because he probably would've slipped and hacked off a finger. All he could do was keep on cleaning the tough, skinned snapper that he had to make hastily and delicious for Archie's absurd surprise taste test, and listen.

"... so, here's a question. If all these things from the sky landed in the water, and we know about it, how has no one found anything? I mean someone has got to be out there looking for these things, I just feel like if something was out there then someone would have found it, right? Alright, let's go ahead and take some calls, go ahead caller you're on WPPL, what do you think about all of this?"

"Yea, I'll tell ya what I know..." Now the voice on the radio was old and raspy, almost inaudibly twangy. *"...I know them fishin' spots's more crowded than a whorehouse on Friday. I also know it ain't just fishermen out there on them waters. I saw at least a dozen ships out there, filled with them doe-eyed, lab-coat wearin' scientist types. Anyway, it was pretty damn obvious to me that they was out there lookin' for somethin' in the water, and I'll tell you somethin' else you won't be hearin'! I know for a fact that them boys found somethin' out there. You go far enough out, just clear outta sight of the docks; an you'll come across a'whole gang of 'em. Couple of guard boats there got fellas with rifles. Boys won't let ya through to get a close enough look-see at what the bigger boats are doin'. But I'll tell you and all the rest of the folks listenin': my sixth sense ain't ever wrong, and if I'm right..."*

Mickey shut the radio off. He'd heard all he could stand about what was going on outside. And that's all the radio was going to talk about today. It seemed like the *only thing* people were going to talk about today. He'd have to get lost in his work in silence. But that was ok. Right now, silence was golden.

Now all that was left to do was debone the fish. Mickey always thought that was something Larry should have taken care of himself, but Archie thought he was so dumb that he'd ruin the snapper trying. But it didn't take too long, and after that he could start up the grill and make magic.

But first the special ingredient: Cinnamon.

Yes, that was all. Plain old cinnamon. Most people would be baffled to know he did that to their fish. That just wasn't an ingredient you associated with snapper. Or any other kind of fish, really. But that was the superstitious part of it. Something he'd picked up off his grandmother when he used to help her cook. She'd picked it up in the old country and kept it up in the states. She claimed that cinnamon had a magnanimous and spiritual power to cleanse different kinds of bad energy. And according to her, bad energy could come in any form; even dead meat. Mickey never understood how she could believe in such things; she was certainly smart enough to know better. But he supposed it was just the way she was raised, and he never questioned her about it. And the food was so damn good he went on with the tradition himself. And every time he used it, he would think of her.

He was starting to feel levelheaded again. Livening up now that no one was here to contaminate his mind with the conspiracy bug. It was all beginning to seem sort of funny to him. Hundreds of people sweating it out under the scorching sun, throwing their money away, and staring out at the ocean with the same kind of spectacular awe that children have while watching the lions sleep at the zoo.

Poor suckers, he thought.

All of them standing around like mindless zombies,

waiting for something completely insane that they'd eventual realize was never going to come. Followed by the inevitable feeling of embarrassment, accompanied by stupidity that would finally become the shame that would send them back where they'd come from, heads down and pockets turned out. Mickey was even starting to feel better about the situation with, Melina. So, what if she was at the beach with Debbie? She was always with Debbie when she wasn't with him. And Debbie had made it clear that she could conceal a secret, why should today be any different?

He gave an exultant little shuffle dance and whistle as he unzipped his bag of cinnamon and reached in for a handful. He bobbed his head up and down, as if the radio where still on, and sprinkled cinnamon out of his hand and onto the skinned fish on the chopping board. Brown snow powdered down into the dead snapper's eye socket and along its raw flesh.

I'm too young to be this stressed out about these kinds of things, Mickey thought. *I've got nothing to worry ab-*

It screamed. It was *still* screaming.

The eyeless corpse of the sea creature he'd been slicing and dicing let out the most unnatural scream of agony about a second after the first grain of cinnamon touched it. The kind of shrill, high-pitched shrieking of some sort of feral beast caught in a bear trap; ripping its own limbs apart in a vain attempt to free itself.

Mickey was frozen; consumed with incredulous terror that rendered him unable to grasp what he was seeing. His eyes were so wide and bulging it felt like the pressure would cause his own eyes to pop out. He felt his heart pounding implacably against his chest plate, like it was going to the rhythm of a rock 'n roll song. Mickey thought it would burst any moment.

Now the skinless pink fish was flopping around on

the chopping board. The shrill cry had become a deep, gurgling sound.

"…Sweet Jesus…"

It was coughing. The fish corpse, was coughing. It stopped flopping around and its mouth began to open. Not in the dumb, lifeless way as it had while Mickey was scaling it, but like it was being stretched by something forcing its way out. As the ridges of its mouth tore open, Mickey could see that there *was* something fighting its way out; something was tearing through the dead fish's mouth and squirming its way into the world.

A slim, slimy kind of black gunk - sludgy in its appearance, began to pass the snapper's lips and solidify. And then Mickey could see eyes… Four, darker toned, beady black spider-like eyes on top of what was starting to look like a tiny, scaled beak. It oozed farther out, and the beak slowly opened and revealed hundreds of small, jagged teeth all over the inside of its mouth. It looked like a black, scaly slug that had the mutated skull of a crow. The scream returned, but now from *its own* mouth.

Mickey had the strongest desire to shout out for someone to get their ass back there and see this… this thing. Not only so that he could be sure it was really happening, but so that he wouldn't have to be standing there alone *with it* in the kitchen. But all the courageous stamina he seemed to be able to conjure went into not pissing his pants.

The last of the things disgusting worm-like body crept out of its former host and plopped onto the stove. It wasn't done transforming. It rolled back and forth over the burners, its menacing spike-filled beak giving off sporadic screams as it did.

Then it began sprouting legs…

"Arch!" Mickey finally managed to yell. "Holy shit,

Archie!"

They were like insect legs, six of them. And as they grew from what was presumably its torso, they let out a disturbing crackling noise as they bent that made Mickey sick to his stomach.

"JESUS CHRIST, ARCHIE WHERE THE FUCK ARE YOU?"

No one was answering Mickey's desperate cries for help, and he felt like running. Running right out the door while this thing was still in the midst of its bazar, painful, and rapid alien puberty spell. But then he thought about what might happen if he left that thing in the kitchen. It could hop down and go right after him, or it could go out of the other door and towards the public. Towards Melina.

Without further contemplation, Mickey grabbed the knife by the cutting board and brought it down on the mutating creature. The thing sliced like butter and was immediately in two pieces. Both its beady pairs of eyes shot to Mickey's and sent a sinister chill through him. The beak-half looked as though it were snarling at him, and the bottom half – with only two of the boney legs left- crawled back towards the cutting board. Its mangled top was already morphing itself back to full length, growing two new legs.

Jesus, Mickey thought. *I only made two of them*!

The cinnamon; the cinnamon hurt it! The cinnamon!

Mickey reached to the floor with a cupped hand and scooped up a handful from the brown mountain of powder he'd spilled from the bag when dropping it. He threw all of it on top of the small monster on his stove and there was another horrible, blood curdling scream, this one even more shrill and echoing than the last. The creature began jerking violently in place. And then it seized up and twitched, like it was having some sort of seizure. Even in the tiny black eyes, that he could only catch in flashes now, Mickey could see all the excruciating pain and agony any living thing feels as it dies… slowly.

The smell of sour, burning flesh unlike any other filled Mickeys sinuses and made him gag. The thing on the stove had stopped moving, and it looked like a giant slug with legs that had just been melted with salt.

It was dead.

A laugh actually managed to slip past Mickey's gritting teeth. "How you like that, huh? What now you ugly little freak?"

Suddenly, Mickey heard the rattling of a dish to his right. Before he could even remember that the bottom half of that thing had squirmed away while he took care of its top half, it was on his face.

It had completed reassembling itself into what it had been before being chopped in two, and pounced from the counter to Mickey. Six, skinny legs wrapped themselves around Mickey's head, and he could feel the thing forcing its way into his mouth. He was powerless as it stretched his mouth out like it had the dead fishes, and pushed its way over his tongue. Mickey stumbled blindly around the kitchen; knocking over the trash barrel and a pile of dirty dishes stacked by the sink, tugging with all his strength at the thing straddling his face. He could feel the slim at the back of his throat now, and then there was a sharp, sudden pinch that started in his brain and worked its way down his spine.

It was in his head…

Mickey tumbled backwards into the rack of condiments and fell over with it. Now the pain in his skull was excruciating, and its body was almost all the way inside of him. His arms went limp, and suddenly he was no longer able to control them. They wilted by his sides and Mickey realized that he didn't have any control anymore; the thing inside of his head was running the show now.

Its spider-like legs unraveled themselves from Mickey's head and glided into his mouth with the rest of it. And then disappeared. Just before his sight went out, Mickey could see blood gushing from his nose, down his apron, and onto the floor. It felt like a strong hand with razor sharp talons was mercilessly clutching at his brain. And then suddenly, and only briefly, he could sense *its* thoughts. *Its* intentions. Suddenly he knew that even if he hadn't added a toxic ingredient – that turned out to be cinnamon, of all things – this thing still would have gotten inside of him. That was what *it* wanted - to be cooked and eaten. By us. By human beings. The visitors from space were very real, and they had not come in peace. They'd come to invade; and it was a sneak attack.

There was another sudden, sharp, final tightening around his brain, and then sweet release. Mickey Hanson, head chief of Archie's Beachside Paradise, lay dead in his kitchen.

Archie waddled through the kitchen doors sometime later and found Mickey manning the grill and putting the finishing touches to the greens and friend potatoes. Archie first thought, was that somehow, he looked… different. "Ay, kid."

"Hello, Archie." It responded amiably enough.

"If you were lookin' for me sorry it took so long. Larry came back and we talked business down by the beach. Fuckin' guy was determined to sell me everything he had. Walked into my office all bug eyed an shit. Kind of like you are right now. You ok, kid? You're lookin' kinda… pale."

"Yes. I'm fine, Archie. What did Larry say?"

"Well like I was sayin', he came into my office,

actin' all spaced out, and made me an offer I couldn't refuse." Archie said, pinching his fingers in the air and doing his best Marlon Brando impression.

Mickey didn't laugh. Instead he said, "That's good. I had some myself, before I made yours. It's rather delicious. I believe our customers will be quite satisfied." He finished filling the plate and handed it over to Archie.

He took it and said: "They're gonna have to be for the deal I made with that sap, Larry. An why are you talkin' like that? All, pronunciatin' an shit?"

"I'm sorry, Archie. I'll stop if you'd like."

"Did you change clothes?" Archie asked, noticing more and more how different his head chef was looking. "I coulda' swore you were wearin' a white shirt earlier."

"Yes. There was an accident. I had to change."

"In here? Ya didn't break nothin', did ya?"

"Nothing that wasn't replaceable."

"Whatever the fuck that means," Archie said grabbing a fork and heading out to his office for that taste test he'd been waiting for. Just before going out the door he stopped and turned around. "Oh, before I forget. Melina and that little number Debbie are outside askin' for ya. You wanna go out an say hi to 'em real quick?"

"Tell them, I'd like them to come in and try the snapper."

"Sure, sure. But just one each. I ain't runnin' a charity here, ya know. Oh, and kid, did ya put that special kick in it?" Archie asked, pointing the fork at his plate and grinning.

Mickey finally smiled back and said: "This has something new."

Douglas Ford's Shopping List

Tissues,

Wine,

Razors,

Clown make-up.

A big knife.

A Cure For Clowns

Douglas Ford

Barbara needed a cure, something to fix her fear of clowns.

The answer came in the unlikeliest of places, a grocery store.

In her shopping basket: tissues, wine, razors.

She almost dropped the basket when she heard the laughter, abrupt, booming, obscene. It cut through the white noise like a chainsaw. Everyone around her froze. The old woman next to her in line squeezed a loaf of bread against her chest. Cashiers stopped scanning items and looked at their feet. At a cellular level, everyone, including Barbara, shared a momentary understanding that to make eye contact with the wrong person would be dangerous. This laughter exposed everything, everyone. After that sort of laugh, someone most certainly would die, probably whoever looked first.

But they all looked eventually.

The laughter came from one of the baggers, an olive skinned man with big, floppy, asymmetrical ears and a mouth disproportionate to his face. His features suggested a mental disability, and the laughter confirmed it. He didn't have all his marbles, Barbara's ex-husband would have said. Whatever made him laugh, he kept it to himself. He abandoned his station behind the cashier and ran off toward the parking lot, the echo of his laughter still pulsing through the building.

The old woman clutching the bread winced at Barbara. "That kind of person shouldn't be out in public," she said. "He's a burden on society."

Barbara could feel her tears starting. At home, later, she would understand that they came from not just fear and sadness, but elation too. Part of her loved the laughter, and she wanted to hear it again. The other part wanted to run, and she obeyed this impulse, not bothering to put back her items.

Before she left, she took the old woman's bread off the conveyer belt and squeezed it in front of her eyes.

*

She took note of the bagger's schedule on ensuing trips. She learned his name--Joey--and yearned and ached for him to laugh again.

His laughter filled dreams already haunted by clowns.

Her ex-husband complained she never got jokes. The things he said about her tits and sagging ass, he meant them as jokes. When she woke up screaming because of a clown, he told her to get over it. Start getting his jokes, anyone's jokes. When he left the clown dummy for her to find in the corner of the bedroom, he said that was a joke, too. He left that to cure her, he said, but it seemed more like a murder attempt.

Unable to kill her, he divorced her.

She knew what he'd say about the thing she did to the old woman's bread. A person with a healthy sense of humor would never do that.

Nor would they return to the store with the intention of luring Joey home with her.

In her basket: wine, razors, make-up.

She said she needed help to her car, so Joey carried the bags. At the car, she told him how nice he was and asked if he wouldn't also like to help her at home? She could hear her ex-husband's voice: Fucking psycho. Fucking psycho bitch.

Suddenly ashamed, she almost took it back, but then Joey did something amazing.

He laughed again, just like before, his big booming laugh.

This time she felt arousal. "I'm not joking," she said. "Come home with me."

She hated how she sounded, like a temptress. Joey's eyebrows rose over crisscrossed pupils. He could decipher that sort of innuendo.

Horny psycho bitch.

He grinned and got into her car.

*

Working from old circus pictures, Barbara tried different make-up combinations, and her first attempts came out horribly wrong. Joey's olive skin stubbornly showed through the whiteness of the pancake make-up, so she applied thicker and thicker layers until she got it right--so right that it took resolve to redden the mouth. The ghastliness of his white face made her want to run and scream.

But she held strong.

Using the razors, she shaved his head, and then she created a perfect dome of white.

From there, she choreographed her life and his, like the ringmaster of a circus. With his white face and red mouth, he watched her live. She taught him to follow her from room to room. In the corner he stood while she sat at a table and wrote checks for her ex-husband's unpaid bills. He watched her while she cooked meals for two. He watched her bathe. Sometimes she looked at him and wanted to sink beneath the water and never come up. But gradually that feeling began to ease. She bought him a cone hat and painted blue diamonds around his eyes. Soon she could even sleep with him standing over her and wake up feeling refreshed and rested and not even start when she turned to see him in his polka-dotted shirt, barely able to stand from exhaustion.

It took weeks, but she finally pronounced herself cured.

One thing left to do.

In her basket: a knife.

She fashioned Joey a red rubber nose and taught him how to use the knife. Together, they drove to the house she used to share with her ex-husband, and when she found that her key still worked, she took Joey into the bedroom and showed him where he could stand without being seen. In his fist she placed the knife. He would stand quietly until the time came to use it.

Before she turned off the light and left him to meet her ex-husband, she kissed him on the cheek. Some of the make-up came off and she laughed.

He laughed too. Booming, abrupt, obscene. Just like before.

The old her might have run. Even now, she inched away from him.

But she practiced her newfound resolve and looked into his off-center eyes.

"What's so funny?" she said.

"You," he said.

So she was finally funny. They shared one final laugh together before she left him to do his work.

Craig Bullock's
Shopping List

Sandwich meat (possibly ham)
Bread - wholemeal
Chocolate spread
New spring for pincer
120 super strength refuse sacks
2 x tinned tomatoes
2 x Chicken breasts
Pack of 6 toilet rolls
Rice
Bacon
Twinkies
Tin of Tuna
Lilac wine x Red wine x - oh come on, white wine at least x
None alcoholic wine - wet rag

Children Of The Lilac Tree

Craig Bullock

"Come on buddy just one more swig. Don't be a wet rag!" Sometimes being an enchanted left arm had its limitations.

"No dude you've had enough. You really wanna turn into one of them zombies?" Arnold prized the bottle from Frank's fingers. "They walk round this town without a care in the world. As long as the bottle's full that's all that matters to them. You've had enough, anyway."

"Wow! When did you grow a pair of big cojones?" Sniggered Frank.

"I'm sorry man. It's just I don't want us ending up like the rest of them, that's all." Arnold inspected the label on the bottle 'THE OLD VINTER'S LILAC WINE - SWEET AND HEADY - MADE WITH ONLY THE FINEST GRAPES.'

"Whatever dude? We're done with this stuff." With that Arnold placed the rest of the bottle into his refuse sack.

#

Arnold had 'acquired' Frank a few years ago after stumbling upon a lucky rabbits foot, whilst performing the odious task of litter picking the streets of Stoke. Arnold kept the decrepit foot on his key-chain and after a particularly lonely day rubbed its coarse white fur and wished for a friend, someone to make him smile and pick him up when he felt low.

When Arnold woke the next day, he had Frank. Frank had acquired the use of Arnold's left arm and had a wealth of tales to tell the young boy. It appeared that Frank was once a famous musician who had toured the world with the greats, or so he claimed. Frank was confident, a show man, a ladies man and was gifted with a wealth of knowledge. Everything that Arnold wasn't. Arnold was never really sure if anyone else could hear Frank, as he didn't exactly have a solid group of friends to speak of. The occupants of Stoke never really paid him much attention. He felt like he was simply there to clean the streets and exist, with his ambiguous friend for company.

#

In front of the duo approached a thin blonde woman, maybe early thirties, ample breasts and good legs, swaying from left to right.

"Hoo-boy, she's a baby. Reminds me of our Mum," Frank excitedly blurted out.

"In what way? For reference, I'm ignoring our Mum part, cus that's just weird."

"She got a fine rack and she's drunk," blurted out Frank.

"Again weird, but yeah, she's kinda cute.... but she's one of them," sighed Arnold.

"Who cares? We've got half a bottle in that sack of yours. I bet she'd be on the hook and ready for anything."

"No man it's not my style," replied Arnold.

"You have no style, buddy! Seriously flash that wine."

"No dude I'm n—"

"Bet she'd even blow you off for a quick swig.... take it. Daddy needs some loving!" Frank insisted.

Frank stretched out towards the sack but Arnold shifted it out of reach.

"No dude."

As the blonde approached Arnold noted her eyes were glazed, her top was torn and her teeth black as charcoal. She snarled at Arnold as she passed, tossing an empty cigarette packet in the duos' direction.

"Pick it up yourself. Scraggy bitch!" Shouted Frank but the woman carried on walking, paying him no attention.

"Don't matter, dude. She's heading our way. I'll toss it back to her as we pass," Arnold replied with a sigh.

Frank grabbed the litter picker and snapped its jaws shut several times. "Come on buddy. Lets catch us some skirt."

Arnold looked at his arm in disgust and shook his head. "No, we've got a job to do and really did you not see the state she was in?"

"Oh come on. If you ignore the teeth and eye thing, she had a great silhouette. You don't need to look at the mantle whilst you're poking the fire."

"Dude your sick! Plus we don't have time."

" 'We have all.... the time.... in the world'...."

"Not now, Frank!" Arnold snapped.

"Louie was a good friend of mine back in the day. We shared many a stage. I could tell you a few stories...."

"We've gotta crack on," interrupted Arnold. Arnold adjusted his refuse sack and the two companions set out to clean the streets of Stoke.

#

The town of Stoke was once a vibrant and prosperous region. It made its fortune through the pottery industry and it's thriving steel works. In its hay day the skyline was ablaze with bottle kilns spewing wealth into its humble community. The people had plenty and those that didn't shared in the wealth of others, community sprit was everything. Neighbours were real neighbours back then and kids would play in the streets safe and happy all day long.

However since the downturn in industry people began losing their jobs. Communities became rundown, unemployment was at an all time high and people looked for other means of providing for their loved ones. Gangs began to rule the streets and violence was a means of survival. The kilns that once lite up the sky line now stood dormant as a relic to times lost. Even the kids stayed indoors, no longer able to play with the safety they once enjoyed.

That was until the vineyard rolled into the cultural quarter.

The vineyard was huge! It rolled into the quarter in the middle of the night. A horrendous deafening industrial reminder echoed throughout the town, its giant caterpillar tracks tore through the landscape and came to a halt in the once vibrant cultural quarter.

The inhabitants of Stoke woke to a gleaming monstrosity occupying their smog filled skyline. People were, at first, curious as to what the beast was. It was a giant dome, easily the size of a football pitch, which sat proud on its mammoth set of tracks. After several days of inactivity people became angry and frustrated that this "thing" had tore through their town without explanation. People became restless and plotted to storm the beast to discover what was in side. People were ready to take action! Well, that's what they were planning, until sample day arrived.

#

Arnold and Frank made their way towards the cultural quarter, picking up any waste in their way and condemning it to the refuse sack.

"Buddy we've pick the wrong time of day to clean this area," laughed Frank.

For miles the queue could be seen running from the gates of the vineyard all the way back to the neighbouring town. Miles and miles of unkempt individuals queued pushing and shoving ready for their turn on ration day. Each one had glazed eyes, torn clothing and covered in scratches where they had fought to win their spoils.

"Yeah. You're not kidding. We'll make our way up to the top and do this area later. Don't fancy crossing paths with these junkies I'm just gonna fill our sack with bottles and cast offs. We'll leave the smaller stuff until later."

"Or.... We could get in line." Frank tried his best to persuade Arnold.

"No chance. I told you were done. Plus we have nothing to trade." Arnold was almost sure he was trade free.

"You've got a whole bag of goodies in that sack of yours."

"No one would want this. It's just waste. Anyway, as discussed, we're done."

"Square! It would be a gas. Remember sample day? It was the greatest moment in Stoke's history. Free wine for everyone. Wow, to be there again. Even you joined in. The wine flowed freely and the ladies flowed too, if you know what I mean," winked Frank.

"Yeah it was pretty nice," reminisced Arnold. "But we've got a job to do, dude. So let's go."

As Arnold and frank walked through the streets they noticed those who had money and those who didn't. The whole town craved this wine. Those with money had bulging wallets and those that didn't had other objects of desire, paintings, crystal vases, painted pottery figures, anything of value. Arnold noticed that one guys seemed even willing to trade in the family dog for a bottle of lilac wine. Arnold and Frank carried on up the street when a guy who was missing one eye shouted out, "Oi! In line boy! We've been queuing all night."

"Tell him to do one, lose your cool bud," argued Frank.

"No," whispered Arnold as he lowered his head to avoid any other comments. "It's not worth it. Just keep moving."

Arnold and Frank continued their way picking up the litter the queuing people tossed it front of them.

When they neared the gates of the vineyard they heard the music. It was an old fashioned merry go round song, from Arnold's childhood that played through several speakers. The speakers were the size of a small bear and were attached to the sides of the mobile vineyard and signaled the start of the rationing.

The crowd began to get excited! Cheering and clawing to be served first. All civilized queuing went out of the window. As Arnold looked behind him he saw the line slither in a snake line motion. Fists flew and blood ran as the crowd attacked each other in anticipation, trying to make their way to the front. The giant anaconda was ready to pounce on its' prey. Each scale, violent and striking at itself to seize its spoils.

"Who's even looking after their kids?" questioned

Arnold.

"Like they care! They're only here for one thing, the wine."

"True," sighed Arnold.

On cue the music stopped and the crowd fell silent. Fists stopped flying, feet stopped kicking and the dogs even stopped barking, an eerie calm fell over the crowd. The large rusted gates that protected the tops of the steps that led to the almighty vineyard began to creek open. A Man in a stained purple suit and what looked like a crippled back emerged with his supportive cane, oh how the crowd began to cheer! The carnival music kicked back in as the man approached the top of the steps. In a frightful moment the old man tripped over his cane and fall, toppling over the first step and began his slow descent to the bottom. The music cut out and the collective gasp from the crowd could be heard for miles as bones cracked and howls of pain could be heard from the tumbling man.

"Oh my god! Is he ok?"

"Will we still get wine?" The questions could be heard throughout the worried crowd. When the body hit the bottom, all was quiet.... People waited with concern in their throats.... Concerns that they weren't going to get their next fix of the sweet lilac wine!

After a slight pause the music kicked back in and the Old Vinter jumped back to life and tossed his cane to one side. After much applause from the hungry crowd he opened the public gates and began the trade. Money for wine, antiques for wine.... Even hamsters for wine. Anything was trade-able and had value.

"Wow did I really just see that?" Laughed frank. "Swear that's from some old movie."

"Yeah it is," confirmed Arnold. "Lets come back later when this crowd's moved on. We're gonna have a lot of bottles to collect.

\#

Arnold and Frank returned later in the evening after the theatrics and the crowd had died down. Bottles littered the streets, where people were too eager to drink before returning home. Everywhere was quiet and the town seemed to be sleeping off its hangover. Hundreds of bottles were savagely raped of every drop and left discarded on the ground.

"It's gonna be a long night," sighed Arnold.

"Why don't you just quit and get a normal job?"

"Our mum got us this job, before she turned into one oh them," whispered Arnold. "I promised her I would do my best to clean the streets of Stoke. I used to pretend I was some sort of super hero with a destiny to clean up the mess. Guess you're the Robin to my Batman now? When the gangs moved in it just wasn't safe. But that's all over now and here we are. The gangs have gone, replaced by wine enticed zombies."

"You need a real life yoyo."

Arnold began collecting the bottles from round the back of the vineyard when he noticed a fire escape open.

"Buddy, let's take a peek. Actually screw the peek, let's get us some free wine."

"No dude I want nothing to do with this place. It's the poison to this town," snapped Arnold.

Just then Arnold heard laughter. A child's excited voice caught the wind and echoed in Arnold's ears. Arnold couldn't recall the last time he'd even heard a child, let alone seen one. Since Stoke had become so run down the children seemed to stay indoors. The laughter appeared to come from inside the vineyard.

"Ok maybe we'll take a quick look."

"And maybe free wine?" argued Frank.

"Really?"

The two slowly made their way inside cautious of what they'd find. The air smelt musky but the vines were all barren. The thing that caught their eye the most though, was the giant lilac tree that stood proudly in the middle of the dome. Its branches appeared to stretch way beyond that of a normal tree. Its majestic lilacs seemed to blow enticingly in the breeze.

Metal machinery was placed around the dome ready to pick the grapes that once existed and to squash the life out of those that were picked.... but all was empty. The vineyard looked sorry at best.

Arnold could hear laughter from what sounded like children. It appeared to be coming from the far side of the dome.

"Come o—"

Just then lights flashed at the exit and the sound of a reversing van set Arnold into panic. "Shit hide!" Shouted Frank. Arnold didn't move.

"Well, Sherlock. Move it," replied Frank.

"Sorry. I was waiting for you to move!"

"We're connected, goof. They're your legs."

"Oh yeah. Sorry." And with that Arnold hid between the barren vines.

The van backed up to the exit and shut down its engine. From out of nowhere appeared the old Vinter carrying what appeared to be a crate of wine. The door to the van opened and the Vinter placed the box inside. Next he walked to the rear of the truck and the door opened. One by one children stepped out. Obese and plump, all with an excited looks on their chubby little faces.

"Come on kids the most immersive social media experience awaits." The kids jumped out with glee all waiting for their prize thirsting on the Vintner's' words.

"Shit Frank, the kids. We've gotta do something. What's he up to?"

"Silence, my eager friend. Let's just watch for a minute."

The Vinter lead the children across the barren fields of the dome and towards what looked like a holding area. The transport truck flashed its lights and drove off leaving Arnold and Frank alone.

Frank and Arnold watched as the Vinter lead the children to what looked like some giant games console. Kids were everywhere each one with virtual reality headsets on laughing and giggling at whatever they were watching and taking part in. The new recruits were made room for but there was one child too many.

The Vinter yanked a small boy up from his headset. The boy looked starved and weak, but he had a smile like no other, cursed with the joy of social media but withdrawn from the lack of nutrition.

"This way, child. Time for the final laugh," the Vinter chuckled.

The thin gaunt looking boy was replaced at his station with the new rather healthy looking recruit.

The Vinter lead the boy towards the tree in the centre of the dome.

"We've gotta do something, Frank."

"Relax, dude. We're not even sure what's happening yet."

The boy was led to the tree. The Vinter whispered in his ear and with a grin, the boy stood, his back against the rippling bark of the lilac tree.

The branches appeared to vibrate and the lilac flowers began to fall to the ground. Without warning the tree viciously enveloped the child in its majestic arms. Screams of pain filled the room.

Arnold closed his eyes and begged for help, rubbing his rabbit's foot to calm his nerves.

"Two choices, buddy. Fight or flight!"

Arnold continued to close his eyes and hoped it

would all pass.

The screams suddenly halted and the ground began to shake and with that, he was gone.

"Shit!" Arnold jumped backwards.

The barren vines began to shake and pulse, giving birth to the ripest, largest grapes Frank had ever seen. To Arnold they looked odd and misshapen. The Vinter laughed by the giant lilac tree as all of the metal machines around the dome kicked into life and began their work.

The harvesters roared to life maiming the life from the vine with quick efficiency, collecting them in container machines that were taken to the crusher.

The grapes appeared to cry and scream like small children, their embryo shaped sacks pulverised into juice.

When the last grape was squashed the cries stopped whilst the metallic boom continued. The large conveyor belt expelled the wine, once the labels were attached to the bottles, and that's where the Vinter stood waiting.

#

"Jesus Christ! Perhaps I don't need this stuff after all," gasped frank.

"Oh god! What are we gonna do? He's making this stuff from children!"

"We...? You're on your own, buddy. If I was you I'd turn around, walk away and pretend this never happened."

"I can't. Come on, back me up?"

Just then Arnold looked up. The Vinter was looking their way tasting the fruits of his labour.

"Strangers in the night, exchanging glances...." sang Frank "Sorry, can't help myself."

"Perfection," he laughed in their direction as he

swilled the wine around the glass and took a sip. "And what can I help you boys with?"

"Nothing," replied Arnold. "Sorry. We should go."

"Maybe not. What exactly have you seen? Not that anyone would care, but please enlighten me."

"You're a dick!" Shouted Frank.

"Now, now that's a bit harsh considering all that I've done for this town."

"What? You can hear him?" replied Arnold looking at his left arm.

"Oh course I can. I hear all the lost souls of this town, the forgotten ones. If I was you I'd keep your pet in check!"

"Fuck you! Pet?"

"Now, now, listen to me children.... Wait. Where are my manners? Would you like a drink?"

"No chance," replied Arnold. Just then his left arm shot out.

"Sorry buddy. Old habits."

"No, we're good. Thank you," quivered Arnold's voice.

"Ha-ha! You sure? So, what's your problem?" Questioned the Vinter.

"You're poisoning this town and using innocent kids to do it. The people need you to move on."

"Really? Poison?" Questioned the Vinter. "That's interesting. As far as I was aware this town was horrible, crime, gangs, and general crap littering the town. Now you have zero crime. Zero gangs and no social imbalance. Everyone is equal."

"Everyone is drunk. The town is zombie-like. And what's the idea with the kids?" Questioned Arnold.

"Oh the kids? They are the secret ingredients. Sorry but sacrifices need to be made. The children help produce the perfect batch. Their souls make this stuff worth drinking. The thinner the child, the better the grape. If the child is starved, and wanting, they produce the sweetest wine known to man. So delightful and so heady. I'm not an evil man? I'm just trying to bring peace to this shitty country. I travel, I improve, I reduce crime and social imbalance. Don't blame me. This is what we all want, what we all need. Order and peace."

"Fuck me. Really, is that what you think? Kidnapping kids and doping a nation will clean the country. Never! You're crazy!" shouted Arnold.

"Ha-ha! I kind of feel you slightly agree with me. After all we're on the same team, you and I. Cleaning the streets together. You have your pathetic pincer and sack, I have my wine. Lets be honest even if you don't agree how are you going to stop me? You're just a lonely litter picker. What can you achieve?"

With that, Frank grabbed the nearest thing next to him.

"No one speaks about my buddy like that." He tore out the vine nearest and threw it at the Vinter. Children's screams echoed throughout the dome.

"Shit, buddy. These grapes really are the kids, tread carefully."

The vine hit the Vinter but obviously did little damage.

The Vinter laughed and walked back towards the giant lilac tree. On his way he picked every last remaining grape that his machines had missed and devoured each one. With every crunch, screams rang out, sending shivers through Arnold.

"No more!" screamed Arnold, as he followed him over towards the tree.

"Grow up!" laughed the old Vinter. "Oh yeah, they cant. They're dead!" He laughed to himself even harder. "Meet Rosie my little secret in this operation. The largest and most special Lilac tree. She helps with the secret ingredient."

"Excuse me," interrupted Frank. "Why would you name a lilac tree Rose?"

"It's Rosie!" snapped the Vinter. "She's named after my lost wife. I loved her so much but she was brutally rapped and stabbed by some gang. Police never even looked into it. Apparently too scared to interview those involved. That's when I started growing my own wine. It helped block out the pain. Blissful oblivion I think its called? Anyway that's when I decided to share my talents with the world."

"I'm sorry for your loss, but you can't carry on with this. It's wrong," argued Arnold

"What are you going to do? A half-wit and a pathetic washed up singer. You've got more chance of producing a hit comedy than stopping me."

Arnold rubbed the rabbits foot connected to his keys willing for an end.

The Vinter produced his theatrical cane and swung it at Arnold. Cracking it against the tree as he missed his target.

"I won't miss next time. Don't interfere where you're not wanted."

Arnold began backing away, his fears overtaking him.

"Come on bud. We can take him," tried Frank.

Arnold continued backing up, scared and feeling out of his depth.

"Dude. Man up. It's him or us. He's not gonna let us leave and think of the kids. You're their only hope."

Arnold paused and stuttered. "You're right! I made a promise to help clean these streets and this needs getting rid of. Follow my lead," he whispered. "What's that song you always used to sing? The one about the curtain?"

"My way?"

"Yeah. That's the one."

Just then Arnold grabbed Frank with his right hand and straightened both arms out to one side. With a shaky voice he began singing, "and now the end is near, and so I face my final curtain."

The Vinter look extremely confused at this point, as Arnold advanced, waltzing from side to side heading in the Vinter's direction.

"My friend, I'll say it clear. I'll state my case, of which I'm certain," shouted Arnold.

Now within reaching distance Frank grabbed the Vinter round the throat and, with some reluctance, Arnold began hitting him. The Vinter kicked back, breaking frank's grip and swung his cane smashing Arnold in the face. Arnold cried out in pain as he tasted the blood that ran from his cheek.

"Pathetic," laughed the Vinter, moving in for a second swipe.

Arnold ducked as the cane tore past his ear.

"Let's take him!" shouted frank.

The pair dived forward connecting with the Vintner's mid section, pinning him against the towering lilac tree. Just then the bark began to shake and shiver. Before he had time to contemplate what was happening the tree engulfed them all.

#

"Wow. That was tense," reflected Frank.

Two sets of grapes emerged on the once barren vines, one set of black grapes and one set of white. The lucky rabbits foot that Arnold once wished upon lay broken on the ground. The machines began to stir, pumping and hollering ready to get to work.

"Rather them than me." Looking at his new wooden appendage, Frank stretched out his branch and eased his leaves in picking up a bottle of THE OLD VINTNER'S

- LILAC WINE. The lilac tree grabbed the bottle from Frank's fingers.

"Come on buddy, just one more swig. Don't be a wet rag!"

"Do you never learn," smiled the tree. "Oh and it's Lilly, by the way, not Rosie."

"Ha-ha. Hi sweet cheeks. Think we're gonna get on just fine," laughed Frank.

PC3's
Shopping List

Bacon
Pork Chops
Ham shank
Spam
Bratwurst
Hot dogs (not beef!)
Pork tenderloin
Pork spareribs
Canadian-style bacon
Pepperoni
Pork summer sausage
Sliced black forest ham
Shiner Bock
Tums

Pigs

PC3

"So you're looking for a J-O-B, are ya?"

"Yes, sir," Kyle said, smiling at the farmer. He didn't look much a like a farmer to Kyle, who, growing up in the city and rarely leaving it, had imagined all farmers to be wearers of straw hats and overalls, and chewers of grass or tobacco, and speakers of such a country drawl that their words were barely discernable as English. He had imagined meeting someone straight out of a Steinbeck novel. But, standing before him, was a trim man in his late fifties, clean-shaven and wearing a pressed Cinch shirt tucked into pressed Wranglers. A brilliant green John Deere hat was perched atop his nicely cut hair and polished boots covered his feet.

"Have you ever worked on a farm, young man?"

"No, sir. I've lived most my life in Dallas and my folks weren't much on leaving the city limits. I didn't even know the difference between a bull and a steer until recently."

"I see," the farmer said, drawing out the "I" in a way that made it sound like a two-syllable word. "You must be attending the college down the way?"

"Yes, sir. Two of my classes are in the evening and the rest are Internet courses, so it shouldn't interfere with work."

"Oh, I don't mind working with college students and their schedules anyhow. Had a young lady working for me last year, as a matter of fact. She was an Ag major. Good little worker too. What's your major, young man?"

"I'm not sure yet. It's technically English at the moment, but really I don't know what I want to do."

"Well, no rush on deciding. I'm sure your parents told ya that. I may just make an Ag major outta you too."

The two of them laughed and Kyle said, "You never know, sir."

"Oh please, call me Ned. There are a lot worse things in the world than being a farmer. You look like a strong young man, Kyle. I'm sure you can handle it. The summer heat can get to you though, let me tell ya. You don't know heat until you're out there building a corral or tossing hay bales in 100-plus. Got to stay hydrated. Of course, I've got plenty of water for ya. Do ya reckon you can start tomorra?"

"Of course, sir-er-Ned," Kyle said. "Tomorrow would be fine."

"Excellent. As you no doubt read, it's fifty per day. Isn't much, but I'll feed you breakfast and lunch. Actually, my wife will and you should be thankful for that; I'm no cook. 6am. That work for ya?"

"I'll be here, yes sir."

After a quick meal of gas station tacos, Kyle went back to his campus dorm to struggle through a few algebraic equations before boring himself to death with a few pages from Beowulf. His roommate, Carlo, lay in bed, eyes closed and snoring, wearing headphones that annoyingly thumped base every few seconds. Kyle wondered how Carlo was managing to snooze with the pounding vibrations of hip-hop reverberating through his empty skull. Carlo's only sign of life other than snoring was to occasionally lift his right ass cheek (the one facing Kyle) and squeeze out a whistling fart. After more than an hour of reading Beowulf and failing to retain any of it, Kyle switched off his lamp and went to bed.

At 6am the next morning, Kyle was seated at Ned and Glenda's kitchen table, a spread of bacon, eggs (scrambled in bacon grease), jelly toast, grits, a glass of milk, a glass of orange juice, and a mug of coffee laid out before him. He thanked Glenda and commented that he would gain fifty pounds over the summer if he ate like this every morning.

"Not likely," Ned said. "You'll be starving by lunch time with all the calories you'll be burning. Farm work'll go right through that breakfast. You may gain a few pounds of muscle over the summer though."

Following breakfast, Ned walked Kyle behind the house and to one of several barns that dotted the property to explain the day's tasks. The morning sun already had the temperature north of 90. Kyle stuck a university ball cap on his head to catch the sweat that was already beading there. He breathed in, the air seeming surprisingly fresh despite the cattle and chickens and feed. The current barn they occupied was stacked with hay bales on one side and a John Deere tractor, various farm equipment, and several barrels of sweet feed took up the other side. Sunlight squeezed through the barn wood in brilliant rays, revealing the hay and dust that hung on the air like snow flurries.

Before lunch, Ned told him, the cows would need feeding, the steer that was being fattened up for the butcher needing five good scoops of feed all for himself. Eggs would need to be collected from the chicken coup and placed in the shade of the back porch. Areas of fencing between the cow pasture and the cornfield would need to be tightened up with bailing wire. "But first," Ned said, "you'll want to get the yard around the house mowed and weedeated before it hits triple digits."

Ned had been right: By lunchtime Kyle felt famished, hungry to the point of dizziness. The zero-turn lawn mower had been fun to operate and on the straightaways he could get it going fast enough to cause a pleasant breeze to roll across his sweat soaked t-shirt, making him almost forget how damn hot it was. The push mower and weedeater provided no such cooling sensation. Nor did fixing the fence; and he had managed to make his fingers pretty sore twisting bailing wire before he figured out how to use the fencing tool. Using Ned's ATV, Kyle had hauled sweet feed to the cows, the bull getting a little too close for comfort when he started tossing scoops of feed into the trough. Kyle was relieved not to be trampled into the mud on his first day on the farm. He had expected the gathering of eggs to be the easiest task of the day, but the inside of the tin chicken coup was a good 10 degrees hotter than outside and, upon gathering his first basket full of eggs, Kyle's hand had startled a chicken snake out of hiding beneath the hay. Ned was thankful that Kyle had found the snake that had been terrorizing his chickens and quickly disposed of it with a .410 shotgun.

Kyle gobbled his lunch—a turkey sandwich, an apple, potato chips, and a cream soda—like he had not eaten in days. Had Glenda offered another helping, he would have gladly gobbled it as well. But he settled for a mouth full of sunflower seeds as he set out to complete his first day's work. These tasks consisted of spraying grass killer around the house and all the barns, watering the garden and picking any watermelons that seemed ripe (you could tell by knocking on them; if they were hollow sounding, then they were ready to go), filling in driveway mud holes with gravel, and feeding the pigs.

Kyle attacked the grass around the farm structures with the chemical/water mixture that Ned provided, wondering as he did so how long it would take for the grass to die. Would he arrive the next morning to find previously sharp, green blades of grass had overnight morphed into brown, withered skeletons of their former selves? He then picked the one watermelon that seemed ripe and put it in his car after Glenda said he could keep it for himself (they already had three watermelons picked the previous week). The only holes in the driveway were those where Ned and Glenda turned their cars into their respective parking places beside the house. The holes were nothing more than slight depressions in the gravel, but come the next rain (the next rain could be a month or two away in a Texas summer) the dips in his driveway would gather water and turn into holes in earnest. And that would lead to Glenda's SUV getting mud on its tires, and she certainly wouldn't stand for that.

The pigs, Ned explained, were in a large, fenced in barn and they were to be fed a combination of leftover scraps from breakfast and lunch (which Kyle would gladly have eaten himself) and pig feed. There were five pigs, Ned had said, and two buckets of feed and a bucket of leftover scraps would hold them until the next afternoon. After completing the other afternoon tasks, Kyle filled the buckets as instructed, noting that the pig feed stunk far more than the cow feed, and loaded them onto the ATV. The pig barn was towards the back of the property and Kyle gave the ATV's gas pedal a strong push as he traveled the dirt path that led to it, allowing a comforting breeze to wash over him.

The barn was of a newer variety than the others on the farm. It wasn't made of tin and century old boards; instead it was bright, red steel with a large white door that could slide open and closed. Surrounding the barn was a beautifully crafted wooden fence that would do very little to keep any wandering pigs from escaping to the cow pasture. Kyle supposed the fence was meant more to keep cows from entering than pigs from leaving. Inside the corral, among the grassless black dirt and mud terrain, were three troughs, one with a waterspout positioned over it. No pigs were visible and Kyle guessed they were smartly in the shady seclusion of the barn.

Dismounting the ATV and wiping sweat from his brow, Kyle grabbed the two five-gallon buckets of feed. He pushed through the gate and emptied their contents into the feed troughs. Then, after turning on the water over the third trough, he grabbed the bucket of scraps and was about to begin dispersing it between the troughs when he looked up at the open door of the barn, the brightness of the outside world making it impossible for him to make out anything in the gloom beyond the barn's entrance. It could have been the entrance to a cavern that led down to the depths of the Earth for all Kyle could see. He walked towards it with easy steps, as if approaching a haunted dungeon.

Stepping in, Kyle noted that no rays of sunlight squeezed through cracks in this pristine steel barn. His eyes struggled to adjust, like walking from day into night, everything dark and grainy. His nose hairs curled at the stench of what must be pig excrement. He jiggled the bucket of scraps, hoping to insight some movement that his eyes could focus on. And there was movement. Against the back wall directly in front of Kyle, a large, pale form shifted and rose from its bed of mud and hay. Kyle blinked, trying to focus, the grittiness of his vision finally clearing.

He took a step backwards, towards the sunlight, suddenly confused and afraid. He couldn't be seeing what he was seeing. Some sort of trick of the light was to blame. Shuffling towards Kyle was what appeared to be an obese, naked man on his hands and knees. His body was smeared with mud and shit, strands of hay clinging to some of the messier spots. His rolls of sagging fat glistened in the dim light of the barn and dozens of flies circled his retched body. He breathed heavily and snorted as he moved towards Kyle, bringing attention to the most disturbing thing about the naked man: he didn't have a human nose; instead, wet and dripping long strands of snot, was a pig snout.

"Oh my God," Kyle said, backing away again.

Movement from his right came to Kyle's attention and when he looked, he saw the rest of them. Four more people, three women and another man, were crawling naked through the filth of the barn, grunting and staring at Kyle and the bucket of scraps. They too all had pig snouts in place of noses. The large woman in the lead looked wide-eyed at the bucket in Kyle's hand and snorted loudly, clear phlegm dripping from her mouth and hog snout. The man in the rear, who looked like he had recently bathed in mud and feces, suddenly mounted the middle-aged pig-nosed woman in front of him, his engorged penis thrusting into her unannounced. They grunted in unison.

Kyle turned to run and slipped in a patch of mud, sprawling flat on the soil, the bucket falling from his grasp and spilling its contents. With that the pig people were squealing and shambling towards him with greater haste. The pig-nosed man that had mounted the woman had either finished his spontaneous sexual adventure in a stroke or two or had abruptly become more attracted to the sight of food than the woman's wide rear. Kyle was up in an instant, sliding out of the barn's mud and into the hard-packed black dirt underneath the summer sun. Sprinting through the gate, leaving the water running into the trough, Kyle jumped into the ATV's seat, glancing up briefly to see the pig people slurping the dropped food scraps out of the mud. The head of the obese man that Kyle had first seen was dunked deep inside the bucket and disgusting sounds of greedy eating echoed from within.

The pedal was to the floor of the ATV, moving it at a speed that would normally make Kyle a bit nervous. As he pulled close to the driveway, pressing hard on the break and nearly skidding into his own car, he saw Ned walking towards him from the back porch, a concerned look on his face.

"What's going on?" Ned said in a pleasant voice as Kyle jumped from the ATV and scrambled towards his car. His cellphone was in the glove box and he intended to call 911. He brought keys out of his pocket, fumbling to find the correct one, as if he had never seen them before. "Kyle," Ned said, "What's the problem?"

Kyle spun around, shock and grief painted on his face, and said, "You have people out there! Naked people in that barn! And they… they're-"

"Kyle, listen to me. I should have told you about the pigs before sending you out there. I should have gone with you the first time, I suppose. But look son, they're just pigs. Nothing to worry yourself about."

"You're fuckin crazy!" Kyle yelled in disbelief and, finally finding the key he needed, opened the door of his car.

"Now listen, I won't have you using that kind of language with my wife within ear shot. But lets talk about this for a minute, Kyle."

"I'm calling the cops! Don't try and stop me!"

"Alright, alright," Ned said, holding his hands up in a *don't shoot* manner. "But that's hardly necessary. Those pigs are out there because they want to be. The gate isn't locked as you no doubt saw. Heck, they could crawl right through the fencing if they wanted to. I understand your confusion, I do. It's jarring I imagine if you aren't used to seeing those kind of pigs. But lets do this: You go on home for the evening and get some rest. Sheriff Simmons comes out here quite frequently–at least once a week in fact–and I'm sure he wouldn't mind coming out tomorrow. I'll give him a call. You come on back in the morning and we'll all have a little talk about the pigs. That work for ya?"

Kyle, shaking his head with continued disbelief, dropped into the driver's seat, fired up the engine, and slammed the door shut. A few miles down the road, he slowed his car from 90mph and pulled over to the side of the road. Leaping from the car, he transferred the lunch from his stomach to the pavement, where appreciative ants quickly converged. Back in the car, he grabbed his cell and punched in 911, then let his thumb hover over the green call button. What would he tell the dispatcher? That there were people with pig noses living out on the farm? *Are they being forcibly detained?* the dispatcher might ask. Well, no, but they're crawling around naked and dirty. *Are they naked on public property?* No. *Are they being harmed in any way?* Not that I can tell, but…. Kyle canceled the call.

That night he slept restlessly. Not because of Carlo's music or farts (they had more of a baritone ring to them on this night and a more pungent odor), but because of visions of the pig people crawling through the mud, staring at him, their tongues hanging out, dripping slobber. Kyle dreamed of being chased by the pig people through a never-ending landscape of mud and shit.

When he grew weary and collapsed in the sludge, the pigs tore the meat from his bones as easily as one could do an overcooked chicken leg and happily devoured him. He awoke before 5am, his t-shirt and shorts drenched in sweat. He contemplated calling the police again. Surely there was something illegal going on. People wouldn't choose to live that way, would they? And what of Ned saying the sheriff would be out there today? He could have been bluffing. In fact, he probably was bluffing. After lying in bed for another hour with Carlo snoring loudly, Kyle decided he would drive out to the farm. If a sheriff's vehicle was there then he would stop. If there was no law enforcement visible then he would drive on and call the police himself.

To Kyle's surprise a sheriff cruiser was parked in Ned's driveway. Leaned against the hood of the cruiser was a large man in a tan sheriff's uniform and a cowboy hat, and Ned stood across from him with arms crossed, talking. Kyle pulled slowly into the driveway, the two men halting their conversation to turn and watch his approach. He parked behind the cruiser and got out.

"Was beginning to think you wouldn't make it," Ned said, looking down at his watch, which read 6:30. Kyle said nothing as he walked towards the men. "This here, Kyle, is Sheriff Simmons."

"Andy Simmons," the sheriff said, holding out his large hand, which swallowed Kyle's in a snug shake. He had a bushy gray mustache and a serious look in his eyes. Kyle introduced himself and then the sheriff said, "Ned here tells me you left a little upset yesterday. Why don't you tell me about it."

Kyle glared at Ned and said, "At that barn in the back of the property, he's got people living there like animals. And they've got… they've been mutilated in a way to have pig noses."

Sheriff Simmons was nodding, his thumbs looped into the belt beneath his large gut, his eyes staring into Kyle's. "Well," he said, "let's go have a look. Ned, can we use your ATV to get down there so I don't dirty up my boots?"

"Certainly," Ned said, then gave Kyle a regretful smile.

The three men loaded into the ATV with Ned driving, Sheriff Simmons riding shotgun, and Kyle crammed onto the backbench that was usually used for carrying feed. Ned drove through the pasture at a leisurely pace, commenting on the weather and last night's ballgame as if having human beings corralled on his farm was no bigger deal than tracking cow shit across the back porch.

They pulled in front of the gate and the sheriff rocked back and forth a hand full of times before gaining enough momentum to propel himself into a standing position. With the heat of the day not yet set in, three of the pig people laid outside the barn in different areas around the fence. Kyle instantly recognized the fat man shifting his weight in a depressed patch of dirt that must have been his usual spot, the sagging flesh of his ass smeared with wet shit. Kyle hesitated walking closer, instead standing beside the ATV while Ned draped his arms over the wooden fence and looked upon the nude people as if he was watching a high-priced filly frolic around the corral.

Sheriff Simmons trudged to the fence breathing heavily. Rising from the ATV seat had apparently been a considerable workout. Sticking his hand into his front pocket, the sheriff hollered, "Here, piggy! Come on now, piggy!" From his pocket he produced a bag of dried fruit and nuts.

One of the pig people that had been laying outside hopped to her hands and knees and started quickly shuffling in the direction of Sheriff Simmons. She was younger than the other pig people and probably would have been relatively attractive if she weren't covered in filth and sporting a hog snout. The strands of blonde hair that weren't plastered to her back from sweat and mud and whatever else waved in the air as she did her hand-knee gallop, her breasts swinging in a circular motion beneath her.

Straining himself into a squatting position, Sheriff Simmons pulled out a handful of trail mix. The pig girl approached as he stuck his offering through her side of the fence. She ate happily from his palm, snorting and grunting and drooling, snot and saliva dripping into the sheriff's hand. "Good pig," he said. "You're a good pig, yes you are. Pretty little pig too!" When the female pig had finished off the trail mix and he had petted her, Sheriff Simmons stood up, his knees creaking, and wiped his hands on his britches. He looked at Kyle and said, "What is it you don't like about Ned's pigs?"

"What?" Kyle said, his arms outstretched. "They're people for God's sake!"

The sheriff sighed, looping his thumbs back into his belt and nodding. "Yessir," he said, "they used to be. But these here are pigs. Surely you can see that."

Kyle stood wide-eyed, his mouth agape.

"Listen," the sheriff continued, "you are correct in that they are physically human. But, son, they've chosen to be pigs. That's all. They've chosen to be pigs."

Kyle looked back at the pig people in confused horror. The middle-aged woman that had been quickly mounted and dismounted the day before had risen from her spot against the fence and was crawling to the center of the corral. She stopped, her face in twisted grimace. Veins stood out on her forehead and sweat dripped down her temple. A large, wet turd emerged from her backside and fell with a splat onto her right calf. Then she continued her slow crawl as if she didn't notice; as if it was no big deal that she had a steaming pile of shit clinging to her leg.

Kyle's hand went to his mouth and he retched. "Who in the world would want to live like this?" he said. "It's disgusting!"

"Why you intolerant son-of-a-bitch," Sheriff Simmons said.

"Andy," Ned said with a disapproving tone.

"Sorry, Ned," Sheriff Simmons said, looking at the dirt. "It's just… you know what this means to me. I figured they taught more acceptance in college these days." Then, to Kyle, "The truth is son, I used to be as intolerant as you. Probably more so. Hell, I used to talk ill of colored folks and Mexicans and all kinds that weren't like me and the people I loved. Not on the job, you understand. As a public servant, that would be unethical. Queers I thought were plum disgusting. And them fellas that want to pretend like they don't have a pecker between their legs, walking around in ladies' outfits; I used to have substantial fun at their expense.

"Son, when I was about your age, me and a group of buddies decided we would harass a queer boy that lived down the road from my folks. We toilet-papered his parents' house and threw eggs at their cars and right when I got done spray-painting 'MY SON IS A FAG' on their front door, his father opened it up. I stood their stunned, thinking he was probably about to stick a shotgun in my face or something. But he didn't. He looked at the work I had done on his door, then looked at me and said, 'I'm not ashamed of my son.'

"For a long time it angered and confused me that that was the only response I got out of the fella. He never called the police or anything and the next day he cleaned up all the work we had done like it was just some damage done by a spring storm. I didn't understand it. But I do now.

"You see, son, this little pig here, she used to be my daughter. I think Ned told you about her: she was an agriculture major over at the college before becoming a pig."

Kyle looked down at the pig-girl who was gently rubbing her head on the sheriff's pant leg. She snorted a soft oink of love.

Sheriff Simmons patted her head and then continued: "Having a child that pursues happiness, no matter its form, has a way of changing the way you think about things. Sure, I protested her desire to become a pig at first. Leslie, that was her name, knew I would. In fact, she told me that she had kept her desire a secret for months, feeling that something was wrong with her. You see, Leslie had felt like something was missing her entire life; something inside was hollow. She went through bouts of depression and never seemed to make friends. She even attempted suicide in high school–took a handful of pills and had to have her stomach pumped. It wasn't until she worked here on Ned's farm that she realized what the problem was.

"She found herself growing closer to the pigs than she had ever been to people. She longed for their way of life, free of the hassles and complexities of society. She wanted a simpler life; to be one with nature and the farm." The sheriff looked down at his daughter, the pig, tears welling in his eyes.

Kyle looked from the sheriff to the girl-pig, trying to determine if the whole situation was insane or if he really was out of line for finding the pig lifestyle disgusting and immoral. Sheriff Simmons' story was compelling and heart felt, but someone taking their desire for a simpler life to this extreme was… "The noses," Kyle said, "how do they get–"

"Surgery," Ned cut in. "A plastic surgeon in town does the work. He does it cheap too, using the flesh of folks who came in for other stuff, like gettin' rid of their rooster neck or their belly or sagging skin. He matches up the skin tone right good as you can see. I must say," he said gesturing towards the girl-pig at Sheriff Simmons' feet, "that pig has the prettiest little snout I've ever seen."

Kyle rubbed his temples, watching as the girl-pig ate another handful of treats from her father's hand. He looked across the corral at the fat man-pig who lay basking in the morning sun, covered in mud and feces, his tongue lulling out the side of his mouth. He watched the middle-aged woman-pig crawl along the dirt with shit still clinging to her leg, sniffing the ground and occasionally looking up at the sheriff's daughter with jealous hunger. The third woman-pig had emerged in the doorway of the barn and plopped herself at the threshold, watching the activity around the corral with lazy abandonment. They really were pigs, Kyle thought. In every way except appearance, they were pigs. He wondered if any of them ever spoke and started to ask Ned this, but then thought he already knew the answer. They wouldn't speak. No matter what, they wouldn't speak. If someone forgot to feed them they wouldn't yell across the pasture, demanding dinner. If a tornado danced its destruction across the farm, they wouldn't scream in terror. If they did these things, they would cease to be pigs.

"Look, Kyle," Ned said, "I understand if you find their lifestyle hard to accept; I really do. If you don't want to work on the farm, then I understand that too. Just let me know what you would like to do, cuz I'll need to find me another farm hand ASAP."

Kyle looked at the sheriff as he brushed his hand across the greasy blonde hair of his daughter, the pig, a wide smile visible beneath his bushy mustache. "No," Kyle said. "I'll stay. It will take some getting used to, but I'll stay."

"Great!" Ned exclaimed. "I accept that. Let's go eat some breakfast guys."

Kyle could hardly believe that he had decided to stay. Had he even consciously thought about the decision prior to making it? He didn't think so. *I'll stay* had just slipped out like one of Carlo's farts: unintentional and irreversible. Kyle was surprised by his own willingness to accept the pig people. He seemed to have an unconscious desire to deny their repulsiveness and set aside the breach of morality by dehumanization. He didn't want to grapple with the question of if it was *right* or not; it was easier to just accept it and move on. So, as the day drew to a close and Kyle found himself with the task of feeding the pigs once more, he looked upon them with new eyes, seeing them as interesting oddities, things of intrigue, rather than carriers of filth or people of disrepute.

As the days went by and the summer grew hotter, Kyle drew closer to the pigs. At first he had trepidation about feeding them at the close of the day, seeing their naked human bodies and their wholly inhuman-pig snouts. The obese man-pig in particular disturbed Kyle. His mannerisms, more than any of the others, were like that of a *real* animal. He was greedy when pig feed was tossed amongst them, often pushing aside the others or huddling over the scraps of food so they couldn't get to it. The obese pig, like any real pig, had no issue wallowing in its own, or anyone else's, excrement, smearing wet shit and mud on himself to keep cool in the summer heat. When Kyle questioned Ned about the obese pig, he was surprised to learn that he had once been a professor of sociology. A professor of all things, now a shit-covered pig. But as the days turned into weeks, Kyle even came to appreciate this most foul of pigs. For, when he truly thought about it, only this pig had fully embraced what it meant to become a pig. Only he could crawl along with a sounder of swine and be completely at home. The others, sure, they were pigs and displayed pig qualities, though not as fine-tuned. The obese man-pig, he was the real deal.

But it was the young female, the sheriff's daughter that really caught Kyle's attention. Being the newest to the pig lifestyle, it wasn't surprising that she showed the most obvious human characteristics. She seemed an outsider from the other pigs, keeping her distance from them even at times of feeding. She would linger beyond the trough and only get in to eat once two or three of the others had filled their bellies and collapsed in the mud to relax. She kept cleaner than the other pigs, choosing to seek out tufts of hay or dry patches of dirt to lay on, rather than mud and puddles of urine. Kyle even caught her using her hands one time when her mouth was having difficulty picking the feed off the ground, though she was quick to stop when she realized she had been seen. And it was she, the cute little female pig, that showed the most excitement when people, and Kyle in particular, came around.

One evening in early September, with a new semester of school looming on the horizon and with a good month's worth of 90-plus temps still to come, Kyle leaned across the wooden fence, watching four of the five pigs dunk their heads in the troughs and come up with mouths full of feed and table scraps; except for the obese pig's head which never seemed to rise, greedily preferring to stay dunked in the trough until every last morsel was gone. Only the young female pig did not join in on the feast. She hung back as usual, patiently waiting for her companions. She crawled along the dirt, looking at the other pigs, then looking at Kyle, almost smiling.

He was ready for her this time. "Here, pig," Kyle said. "Come on, little piggy." He dug into his pocket and brought out a handful of dried fruit. "Here, pig," he said, kneeling into a crouch, watching the pig that had once been a young woman named Leslie crawl curiously towards him. One of the other female pigs brought her head out of the trough, glaring at Kyle and his handful of fruits. Kyle was momentarily concerned that she may rush over and attempt to steal the young pig's prize, but she lowered her head back to the trough, apparently deciding it wasn't worth the effort.

"Here, little piggy," Kyle said again. She approached slowly, her head down, but her eyes up, staring at Kyle's face with a look of uncertainty. "It's ok," he said and shook the fruit in his hand. When she was within reach, Kyle reached out with his other hand and brushed the tangles of blonde hair from in front of her face; she flinched. She looked nervously from the fruit to Kyle, drool dripping from the corners of her mouth, mixing with strands of clear snot that lingered from her snout. "It's ok," he repeated and opened his hand. The pig, with one last quick glance at Kyle's face, lowered her head to his hand, her tongue and lips gently pulling pieces of fruit into her mouth. Ned was right about one thing, Kyle thought, this pig certainly had a pretty little nose.

Kyle found himself staying later after that. Once the chores around the farm were done, he would feed the pigs and stay to make sure the young female pig had gotten enough to eat. He would pet her and talk to her and feed her from his hand. He would watch with growing fascination and delight when she would scamper from the barn towards him with all the excitement of a puppy dog that found its owner.

He bent down beside her one evening in late September as she laid against a corral post, noting the look of satisfaction as their eyes met. A lazy grin was on her face. Kyle had gotten used to that soft smile; a smile that revealed her happiness without laying waste to the fact that she was still a pig. He rubbed her back, ignoring the brown smudges on her skin that could just as easily be dried shit as dirt. The pig nestled against Kyle and he plopped down cross-legged beside her. For a long while they stayed that way, Kyle scratching the small of the pig's back. Then she rose to her hands and knees, staring at him as if wanting something.

"What is it?" Kyle said. The pig looked at him, licking her full pink lips, her blues eyes wide. Kyle wiped beads of sweat from the pig's forehead. She wanted something, he could see that, and he asked again what it was. But of course she could not respond. She only inched herself closer to him and grunted quietly–cutely–through her snout. Kyle ran his hand along the length of her face and let it settle below her ear, caressing the pig's neck. Before he had even made the conscious decision to do so, he was pulling the pig towards him. Their lips met, mouths opening and tongues slithering across each other like mating slugs. The pig tasted salty and bitter and as Kyle pulled slowly away from her kiss, a bubbly string of clear snot hung between their mouths like a suspension bridge. The pig licked her lips and the snot strand fell away, clinging to Kyle's chin. They kissed again.

"I want to be a pig," Kyle said over breakfast the next morning, causing Ned and Glenda to simultaneously halt their eating.

Setting a fork full of scrambled eggs down on his plate and sighing, Ned said, "Listen Kyle, that isn't a decision someone should take lightly. I don't think you're ready to really consider–"

"Yes, I am," Kyle interrupted. "I understand completely. Ned, I watched the pigs all summer. I've grown close to them and I've come to love them and their way of life. I want to do it."

"Kyle," Ned said, folding his hands together and lowering his eyes like a high school principal about to lecture a student, "I know you've got a liking for that one pig, the one that was the sheriff's daughter. That's fine. I like that ya take care of her. I like that ya take care of all the pigs, but especially her. She's become a more spirited pig since you've been around, if you get what I mean. But becoming a pig yourself on account of y'all's connection is hasty, if not downright foolish."

"I know what you're saying, Ned. But you are wrong. I've been thinking about this for a long time. I don't want this life anymore. I want a pig's life."

The pig rose from the depression of packed mud in the corner of the barn that he shared with his companion, blinking sleep from his eyes, stretching his neck and breathing in the cool autumn air that had at long last arrived; breathing it in through the snout that was still healing; the snout no longer sore and bruised, but still itching with the mad fury of thousand mosquito bites. Rather than use his human fingers to scratch at his nose, the pig gently brushed it across the dirt and hay until the itch was somewhat relieved. The morning glow crept through the barn door and the pig could hear people not too far away. The sound of people made his stomach rumble with anticipation that they may be bringing food.

The pig urinated and watched the yellow stream follow a crack in the dirt and pool beneath the slumbering blonde pig. She wouldn't mind. He considered mounting the girl-pig and penetrating her, but the sound of another pig drew his attention. The obese male pig was grunting loudly outside the barn as if he was excited about something. The pig crawled gingerly to the barn door, his palms and knees still getting used to the constant abuse they got from the ground.

In the middle of the corral, on his hands and knees, facing the pasture, was the obese pig, his giant stomach sagging nearly to the ground and his wide rear covered in a mess of shit. He snorted forcefully, spewing a cloud of drool and snot into the air, his tubby body jiggling like a bowl of Jell-O. Beyond the fat pig and the fence, in the pasture, were several foldout tables with balloons tied to their ends. Around the tables was a gathering of twenty or more people, and more were walking from the farmhouse. The farmer, Ned, and his wife were among the people and they were talking and laughing and clearly getting ready for some kind of celebration. The obese pig continued his commotion, wanting someone to bring over some food.

The pig formerly known as Kyle watched with passive curiosity as the crowd of people gathered, the children playing tag and throwing footballs back and forth, the adults laughing and drinking. And then Ned was walking towards the corral with several other men around him, a young boy in his arms. When he reached the fence, Ned stood the boy, who was barely standing age, next to him and pulled a bag from his back pocket. Ned fished around in the bag and came out with dried fruit, which he tossed, into the corral, simultaneously hollering for the pigs.

"Which one do you like, Jasper?" Ned said, kneeling down beside the boy. "Come on, pigs! Aren't they good looking pigs, my little grandson?" The other pigs straggled from the barn as Ned put his arm around the boy, smiling. Ned placed several pieces of dried fruit in the boy's hand and the fat pig went into motion, shuffling across the ground at top speed, his roles of flesh rippling like disturbed waters. The boy stretched his arm through the fence and the fat pig all but engulfed his hand, sucking the fruits into his slobbering gullet. The boy pulled his arm back, a look of displeasure on his face, and said something that made Ned and the other men laugh. He put more fruit into the boy's hand and the fat pig came again, but this time Ned shoved him away. "Go on," he said to the fat pig, then, "Try another one, Jasper. Whichever one you like, birthday boy."

Jasper held his hand through the fence again, this time stretching towards the pig that had once been named Kyle. The pig advanced slowly and lowered his head to the boy's hand, picking the fruit from his hand with his lips. The boy smiled and ran his hand through the pig's hair with his other hand. He laughed as the pig's lips tickled his palm. He scratched at the pig's cheek, fascinated by the stubble that grew there. "Dis one," Jasper said.

"Are you sure?" Ned said. "He's a fine pig, but you haven't even looked at the rest."

"Dis one," the boy repeated.

"Ok. You made a fine choice," Ned said, and the pig smiled at the prospect of being called 'fine' and bringing joy to the boy. "Guys," Ned said, turning to the men around him, "grab that pig. The fire should be just about ready and we need to get him on the grill."

The pig backed away, his eyes wide with sudden terror. Panicked, he looked around the corral for some sort of sign that this was a joke. He was just an innocent pig. He was no harm to anyone. He couldn't be cooked! But the other pigs had ceased to show any interest in him, each of them crawling off to their respective areas of relaxation. Even the blonde pig, which he had gleefully screwed just the night before, was shambling indifferently into the shadows of the barn.

"No," the pig said under his breath as men walked through the gate towards him, one carrying a rifle. "No!" he screamed and leapt to his feet. "I'm not a pig! I'm not a pig!" The pig turned to run, but hands were on him, pulling and shoving. "I'm not a pig!" He jerked away and was grabbed again, their hands struggling to hold onto his flesh, slick with sweat. The pig swung, his fist connecting with a man's mouth, feeling the crack of a tooth and the splitting of a lip. They converged, pushing the pig towards the ground, his legs kicking out like a mule, connecting with someone's belly, sending them sprawling to the dirt. "I'm not a pig!" They forced him down, pressing his naked body and face onto the ground, his wet snout filling with dirt. "I'm not a pig. Don't eat me," he whimpered. And then, as he felt the barrel press against the back of his head and heard the click of the safety being switched off, the pig took his final breath.

"Damn, Ned," a man said with the dead pig at his feet. "He put up a hell of a fight."

"So I saw," Ned said, holding Jasper in his arms and smiling. "Almost like he forgot he was a pig. Glenda cooked him bacon every morning when he worked for me and I guess it never occurred to him why we raise pigs to begin with."

Jovan Jones's
Shopping List

Fifth Jack Daniels
Newport 100's
Comedy Club tickets
The Charlotte Observer
Fresh catch from local Seafood Market
Fresh veggies from local farmer's market
Books: History, Mystery, Crime, etc. — Adam Hochschild, Walter Mosley, Elmore Leonard

The Mysterious Mr. Pierre Toussaint

Jovan Jones

Officer Casey Hutton and his partner Henry Garcia responded to a call of a possible domestic disturbance at Fourth Street East and Avenue J. A rusted blue Buick Skylark and a new model white Toyota Avalon were parked in the driveway. The next-door neighbor called saying that she'd heard screams coming from the home, and was concerned for the women that stayed there. Officer Hutton knocked on the door, but got no response. Splatters of blood were on the shattered front room window and he could see through the open curtains that the living room was in disarray. He called for backup.

Two patrol cars pulled in front of the driveway. Hutton knocked again on the door. Nobody answered. Garcia twisted the doorknob. To the officers' surprise it turned. The police entered the home with their guns drawn. Officer Hutton led the way announcing their presence. Shattered bottles of liquor and picture frames littered the floor. A trail of blood led from the kitchen into a bathroom. The room had a coppery odor, like a jar of pennies. Smears of blood festooned the bathroom door like a macabre cover of a horror novel containing the tale of a disturbing crime. Water splashed onto the floor on the other side of the door. Hutton's boots sloshed through the blood stained carpet. He slowed his breathing. Garcia nodded to his partner. The officers readied themselves for the inevitable. Hutton eased the door open. Shriveled pale fingers dangled from the side of the bathtub. The fingernails were broken and stained with blood. Hutton stepped in.

The sight stunned him. An elderly woman had been bludgeoned, and floated in the tub filled with the blood from an expansive wound in her head. The other officers caught sight of the woman and gasped contemporaneously at the scene. Hutton turned the faucet off. Strands of the woman's stringy white hair wrapped itself around his fingers, as it had hung from the faucet. It felt like a dirty mop. He shuddered.

"I'll question the neighbor," Garcia said. "Let's hope she saw someone come or go."

Hutton nodded.

Garcia's heart raced like a thoroughbred's at the Kentucky Derby. He desperately tried to conjure the calm that naturally disappeared when he laid his eyes on the victim. The police officer wiped the fear induced sweat from his brow and stepped outside. He closed his eyes and inhaled deeply before making his way to the neighbor's house. On his way across the lawn he heard whimpers behind him. He turned but didn't see anyone. He looked down the block, into the backyard, on the roof - nobody. Garcia wiped under his eyes to make sure it wasn't him crying, and then he caught a glimpse of a piece of clothing hanging out from under the Buick in the driveway.

Garcia moved cautiously toward the car. Unconsciously he'd drawn his gun.

"Someone under there?" he called. "It's okay. It's the police."

He holstered his piece and hunkered down. As his eyes focused on the crying woman under the car he noticed her blood soaked blouse. Flecks of blood plastered her face. She shook like maracas in a Cuban jazz band. He reached out.

"Ma'am, it's alright now," he assured.
With a little extra coaxing she emerged and immediately leaped into his arms like a frightened child into her father's embrace. He rubbed her back consoling her. The other officers at the Lang Cove remand centre stood in front of the house with their heads bowed. The woman's eyes were bugged as they stared into the distance. Her teeth chattered like she'd been hit with an arctic blast.

"Is he still here? Did you get him? Oh, my God, mamma!" she cried before fainting in Garcia's arms.

***

Doris Sutton, an attractive brunette with dark Moorish eyes and a Mediterranean complexion to match sat in a comfortable chaise lounge across from Horus Condon, a burly man with a distinguished manor, full salt and pepper beard, and a deep voice about an octave above Barry White's.

"Do you know who I am, Ms. Sutton?" Condon asked.

Doris responded with a quizzical face. "I know you're a psychologist. I'm pretty sure you want to talk to me about what happened at my mother's home."

"That's precisely what I want to talk to you about."

"I woke up in the driveway under Mom's Buick covered in blood." Doris smoothed the wrinkles from her blouse. "It's amazing I got away pretty much unscathed."

"It is," Condon agreed, and then interjected, "except for that nasty scratch on the side of your neck." He pointed to a scratch leading from the lobe of her left ear to the center of her neck.

Doris lightly stroked the puffed skin. She diverted her eyes from Condon. Her torso shimmered. She raised a hand to her face and wailed into her palm.

"Her death still haunts me," she expressed through tears. She sniffled. "If I would've known he was coming I would have taken her out of there."

Condon leaned slightly forward. He had a glint in his eye that betrayed his practiced stoicism. "If you would have known who was coming?"

"Pierre, of course."

Condon handed her a box of tissue. He asked, "Who is Pierre?"

Doris appeared confused. She looked up from her snotty Kleenex. She closed her eyes, inhaled deeply, and then exhaled. She directed an angry gaze at Condon and replied, "He's the monster that killed my mother." Her mood changed from furious to morose.

Condon observed her body language droop from an intense stiffness to a slumping melancholy. He inquired, "Did your mother know Pierre?"

"No, but he knew her," she said, then waving an index finger in the air to correct herself. "He knew of her."

"It sounds to me that you knew, or know Pierre."
Doris nodded.

"Who is he, Doris?"

"He *was* my boyfriend, but . . ." Doris sat erect. She squinted and scooted to the edge of her seat. "You think

I hired him to kill my mother so I could collect the life insurance."

Condon didn't respond. To the untrained eye he appeared motionless, but he scrutinized Doris Sutton with the fervency of a fox seeking his sustenance within the dark of the hen house.

"Ms. Sutton, tell me about Pierre."

***

Doris watched her ex-boyfriend, Pierre shuffle into the courtroom in shackles wearing an orange county jail jumpsuit. Her heart plundered into a black abyss of loneliness and despair. The love she once felt for the man had transmogrified into a treacherous mixture of shame and anger. The latter stemmed from the horrendous murder committed by the man she had entrusted with her heart, yet shame resonated from the amorous emotions prickled from the sight of him.

His eyes roved subtly in her direction. He grinned. An uncontrollable reflex turned her lips upward into a happy smile. She quickly ducked her face under the covering of her palm to conceal her adoration. It occurred to her that she indeed, still loved Pierre. Doris peered blankly into the center of the courtroom, staring at the court clerk's computer and fell into a reverie of her and Pierre's initial acquaintance.

Doris sat in a café sipping her cappuccino, reading current events in the local paper. The café's bell chimed with the entrance of a customer. She ignored it and continued reading an article about a dispute between the granting of zoning permits to commercial contractors. The sound of the chair across from her scraping the linoleum floor grabbed her attention. Doris looked up to see a sharply dressed black man sitting at her table.

"Can I help you?" she asked, attempting to conceal the astonishment at his audaciousness.

"Hello," he replied, and then sipped coffee from his Styrofoam cup. "I'm Pierre Toussaint. You are?"

A sarcastic chuckle escaped her throat. "I'm not interested."

Pierre brushed imaginary lent from his virgin wool blazer sleeve. "It seems to me you are very interested." He nodded toward the newspaper.

Doris stared at him incredulously and then said, "You can have the paper when I'm done with it. I won't be long."

"I know you'll be on your way to work soon. The paper isn't of any concern to me."

"How do you know I'm going to work?" Doris asked accusingly.

"By the look of your sharkskin pants suit, and day planner I figured as much."

Doris started to speak, but Pierre beat her to the punch.

"And the bun in your hair." He pointed. "You appear ready for a productive day. I like it."

"Well, thank you but . . ."

"What is your name?"

"You're right. I do have a busy day ahead of me, so if you don't mind."

He arose from his chair and Doris caught a whiff of his cologne. There were notes of pine, musk, and bergamot. She closed her eyes. *Polo maybe?*

He said, "I didn't mean to impede on your ritual of serenity. I respect that you have to prepare your mind for the day ahead. I am sometimes brash, but I had no intention on being so. I enjoy the company of beautiful women and hoped to embark in conversation. Forgive me. I'll leave you alone."

Pierre turned and sauntered through the door with his steaming cup. Doris observed his thigh muscles contract through his creased slacks, as he walked away with the swagger of a Black-and-White era movie star. When she tasted the frothy cinnamon of the cappuccino on her lips she realized that she had licked them, while watching Pierre's exit. As calmly as her whetted nerve endings allowed she arose from her seat and followed after him.

She flung the door open. He was halfway down the block. His gold cufflinks glimmered in the morning sun. "Doris!" she shouted down the street. He stopped and about faced with a smile glowering with pearly whites. Pierre started toward her. Doris' heart skipped a beat. It'd been a long time since a man had approached her in a gentlemanly fashion somewhere other than online, and it made her nervous.

He offered his hand. "It's a pleasure to meet you, Doris."

"Doris Sutton, my last name is Sutton."

He shot her a smooth grin.

"I apologize for the way I acted. Please, come back and we'll talk."

"I'd love to, but I'm afraid I must take my place in the rat race." He pulled a business card from his inside pocket. "Give me a call when you get an opportunity. I'll be excited to hear from you. Good-bye, Doris."

She nodded. "Have a good day," she said, waving as if she were flagging down a cab. Doris pulled her hand down and blushed after realizing her girlish enthusiasm.

***

The day at the office proved to be a trying one. Her proposal for an event to market the latest fashion trend received more nays than a logical solution to a problem in Congress. Doris kicked off her heals, and grabbed a bottle of Jack from the kitchen counter. She poured herself a neat glass and opened Charles Bukowski's

Women in hopes of easing into a lighter mood. Her attempted escape from reality ran into a roadblock when the vociferous complaints from her elderly mother resonated throughout the room.

"My blood pressure's got my head in outer space, because some ungrateful child forgot to give her mother her medicine," Doris's mother Anne said in her smoker's Southern drawl.

"I didn't want to wake you, mama," Doris said.

"That's bull. You were trying to avoid me and you know it." She pointed an accusing liver spotted finger at her daughter.

"No, I wasn't," Doris lied. "I'll get your medicine."

"And something to eat might be nice. Old people need to eat too."

"Momma, I left you with all those TV dinners."

"I can't eat that crap! The government makes those things to control your mind."

"Oh, I forgot how important you were that the government would need to control *you*."

Anne shot Doris a murderous glare. "If I wasn't so frail, I'd slap the taste out of your mouth. You're just like your no good daddy; ugly like him too," she said with venom dripping from her plaque ridden tongue.

"Okay, mamma." Doris traipsed past her mother. The elder woman's abusive words had formed into peevish complaints of her own shortcomings, Doris reasoned; however her thoughts screamed: *I wish she would shut the fuck up!*

Doris entered the bathroom to retrieve her mother's meds. She scrutinized her reflection in the medicine cabinet mirror. Throughout her life her mother called her ugly and degraded her constantly. It affected her negatively as a child of course, but by good sense and reaffirmation elsewhere she ignored Anne's insults; however on occasion the little vulnerable girl inside of her would look out from the windows of her soul and gaze upon a lie told by the demon named Mamma.

Doris ran a finger over a few of the barely visible acne scars on her cheeks and cringed. She thought her eyes looked lopsided. *My nose is huge.* Doris fingered the area between her eyes down to the tip of her nose. She averted her eyes from the mirror and looked down into the sink. She frowned at the distorted version of her in the metal faucet's reflection. She blew a breath of frustration, lifted her head and snatched the mirror open.

"I should put the old bat in a home. At least those people would get paid to be insulted," Doris mumbled aloud, as she twisted the top of the blood pressure pills.

Once mamma was fed and medicated Doris returned to the couch and her book. Before sitting she noticed a small piece of paper on the seat - Pierre's business card. She held it against her breast.

He doesn't think you're ugly. You should call him.

***

Dr. Condon sat with Assistant District Attorney Valerie Sanchez in her office. A.D.A. Sanchez stood about five foot one, maybe two, with thundercloud-grey eyes, raven hair, and a high-pitched voice that contradicted her tough demeanor. She approached every case with the ferocity of a honey badger. She tossed a manila folder containing another case on the desk and provided her full attention to the doctor.

"What's your take on Ms. Sutton?"

Condon hesitated. "Naturally after such a traumatic event one's psych will be disturbed."

"That is certain, but I suppose I'm asking more specifically; will she be fit to take the stand?"

"I would have to say no."

Sanchez leaned back in her leather chair and interlocked her fingers under her chin. She gazed into his eyes. Condon recognized darkness in those eyes, malevolence. She possessed that cold, unsympathetic glare that so many psychopaths he'd encountered through his career had. Her career enabled her to practice the control over another human being's life. It was that power that often seduced the depravity of serial killers.

"The defense will play up the whole Pierre Toussaint thing as the gentleman there to unburden his love interest of Mommy Dearest. Doris wrestles with this, "guy", but he over powers her and murders Anne Sutton with a hammer and makes sure of his handy work by drowning her in the bathtub."

Condon nodded.

"We live in a screwed up world, Mr. Condon," Sanchez expressed while waving her hands through the air. "But dealing with depravity is my business, and I intend on handling my business. Thank you for your efforts, sir. I look forward to seeing you on the day of the trial."

***

Doris sat three rows behind the prosecution's desk. Several members of the jury had their faces twisted in disgust as they peered at Pierre Toussaint sitting erect awaiting his fate next to his less than enthusiastic lawyer. Doris wrung her clammy hands. In her seat she bounced on her toes, anxious for the verdict. Something seemed odd, she thought. Perhaps it was her paranoia of the jury, and the other spectators in the courtroom as well, obtaining the knowledge that she felt sympathy for the defendant; that she loved him, even after his atrocious act.

As if reading her mind, A.D.A. Sanchez subtly leaned forward and whispered to Doris, "You're going to rot in Hell, Ms. Sutton."

Sanchez directed her questioning to Condon, who'd taken the stand.

"Did Ms. Sutton describe her relationship with the *mysterious* Mr. Pierre Toussaint?" Sanchez asked acidulously.

"Yes."

"Can you describe that relationship, Mr. Condon?"

"I believe Ms. Sutton had been under tremendous stress during the time in, which Pierre Toussaint became a way to cope with the pressures she endured."

"What pressures specifically?"

"Anne Sutton abused her both physically and psychologically. Physically as a child and adolescent, and the psychological abuse continued up until recent events."

Doris wondered where this line of questioning led. What was the purpose? Pierre was guilty without a doubt. Perhaps they wanted to simply prove motive, and she was the motive. *You have to admit that no matter how violent, the gesture was romantic. He really did love me!*

The circus of events drained Doris. The drawn out process made her tired and ready for the conclusion, so she could press on with her life. The judge ordered recess. She watched two Sheriff's officers escort Pierre back to his holding tank, while the courtroom cleared out for bathroom breaks and a bite to eat. Doris sat in her car and drifted asleep.

***

Pierre held Doris' hand in his. They strolled along the shoreline just before dusk. They'd stayed the night at a hotel just walking distance from the beach. Over a seafood dinner and white wine they conversed, flirted, and gazed into one another's eyes through the flicker of candlelight.

"Have you ever been in love, Doris?" Pierre asked.

"Remember? I told you I was married for six years."

"*Were* you in love? Because if I loved someone I couldn't simply let them walk away."

"Like the saying goes: "If you love them, let them go.""

"That's a cop out."

"How can you say that? You don't know what's happening in someone's life. What if . . .""

"I love you," Pierre said, cutting her off.

"What?" Doris put her hand over her mouth, and then spoke before Pierre could respond. "I mean, I heard you, but I don't think you mean that."

"Why?"

"For one thing you barely know me. I know I'm not your type."

"What's my type?"

"You know, sexy, confident." She averted her eyes from his.

He stood from the table and extended his hand. "Let's go. Right now," he said firmly. "I'm going to show you who I'm in love with."

He pressed his hard body behind her, his thick member pressing against her backside, as they stood in front of a full body mirror. His full lips were close to her ears. The base in his voice vibrated through her body disturbing her pleasure center. She watched him explore her body with his fingertips. He pulled her skirt down and let it drop to the floor, then her blouse, bra, panties. She started to cover her nipples, but he held her wrist.

"What do you see?" Pierre asked, as he feather-stroked her neck with his fingertips.

"I see me," she said, sensually squirming to his touch.

"I see the glorious stroke of God's artistry. The treasure of man stands before me, like a lighthouse to the weary shipwrecked drifter. You are my angel. I will protect you. I will worship every inch of your body, kneeling at the feet of your desires." He gently turned her face toward his. "Use me how you please. I am your servant. Let me into your heart." He leaned in to kiss her.

That man don't want you. He's probably married, and using you as his whore. What would a man like that want with an ugly bird like you? Get me my medicine and fix me something to eat!

***

The vile, gravel voice of her mother resonated in Doris' thoughts. Even from the grave she'd found a way to disturb her peace. She rubbed her eyes and realized she was back in the courtroom. Everything was blurry as if looking through a muddy windshield. Sanchez delivered closing statements to the jury. The grainy world began to clear. Sanchez gesticulated, and pointed an accusing finger at Doris.

Doris lifted her hands to her face to cover her yawn. The sound of metal clinking grabbed her attention. Her arms felt heavy. Handcuffs were attached to a chain, attached to a harness that led to shackles around her ankles. Pierre's lawyer sat next to her twirling a pen between his fingers.

"What's going on?" she asked frantically.

"It's alright," the lawyer replied. "I'm more than positive the jury will rule in favor of not guilty by reasons of insanity."

His words hit Doris with the force of a NFL linebacker on an undersized wide receiver. He observed the faces of the jury. Disregard and disgust adorned a few of their faces, while curiosity and sympathy showed on the countenances of the others. The room began to spin. Her breathing labored. To cope she attempted to withdraw into her mind, like she'd done so often before.

***

Doris sat in the café she usually went to before work, sipping a cappuccino and reading the paper. The picture of a handsome black man modeling for a new line of men's clothing brought a smile to her face.

PIERRE TOUSSAINT:

FOR THE STYLISH GENTLEMAN

The walls of the café melted around her like ice cream from a warm slice of pie. With the diminishing of the café she found herself standing in the living room of her mother's home. Her mother gratingly expressed her disapproval about something Doris had no idea about - degrading her like she did ritualistically. Doris turned and went into the kitchen to grab a knife. She opened the drawer. Butcher knife, chef's knife, steak knife. *What's this?* A wood handle hammer, its chrome head shining like *an angel's.*

Momma's still fussing. Her voice is unsettling, mean, and nefarious. The hammer is calm. Its strong confidence is reassuring. *Do it!*

Doris marches into the living room, her contemptible mother hardly recognizes the rage in her daughter's eyes, and certainly ignores the Angel of Death clutched in her fist. Doris shoves the elderly woman into the window. Her head smashes into it, and a piece of broken glass slices the back of her neck. Anne's eyes bug out. She surprisingly avoids the forceful strike of the hammer by inches, as it dives and further shatters the glass of the window. Doris raises the hammer above her head.

Anne's head makes a sickening thump likened to that of a melon being smashed. Her neglected toe nails snag ever so often on the carpet, as her body is dragged to the bathroom. Anne manages to scratch her attacker's neck, as she fights for breath in the tub. The water splashes on the floor. It's cold, so cold. Doris gasps. She falls back weeping, aghast at what she's done. Sirens blare in the distance.

What kind of child murders their own mamma? I told you you wasn't no good, like your daddy.

***

The judge addressed the jury. "How does the jury find the defendant," she asked.

A stout middle-aged man stood. His pot belly drooped over his cowboy belt buckle, making it almost invisible. His shirt was stained with the day's lunch, and his hair and clothes looked as if he'd just gotten out of bed; just the type of person you want announcing how you would spend the rest of your days on Earth.

"Your honor, we the jury find the defendant not guilty by reason of insanity."

Her lawyer, who she first thought was Pierre's lawyer, shook her hand and the members of his team's as if a huge victory just took place. Doris was confused. Insane? Murderer?

I'm going to be right here for you baby. Don't worry.

"Pierre?" Doris smiled. "Pierre, my darling."

David F. Gray's
Shopping List

336

2 Cans Chili Beans
2 Cans Tomato Sauce
2 Bottles Tabasco Sauce
5 Pounds Ground Beef
1 20' by 20' Plastic Drop Cloth

Wade Flick

David F. Gray

I rapped on the shaky wooden door three times. Long seconds passed while I stood there, sweating in the Florida heat. Finally, Wade Flick opened the door and frowned. He was not pleased to see me. He never is. When I contact him I'm either out of time or out of options. On this particular night I happened to be out of both.

He was expecting me, of course. I always call ahead. Common courtesy aside I owe him a lot. It's hard enough being a cop in this day and age and a good detective is always looking for an edge. Wade was my edge.

It was almost midnight when he let me in to his small Sulphur Springs home. I had not seen him for over a year, but he looked the same. Pale, dark hair, over six feet tall and lean to the point of emaciation, he peered down at me with milky brown eyes. I did not know his exact age, but a reasonable guess put him in his mid forties.

"How's the job?" he asked, waving me over to an overstuffed leather couch.

"Same," I replied as I sat down, grateful for the coolness of the air conditioning. "No sleep, no cooperation, and no appreciation." Wade folded himself into his recliner, grabbed his remote off the nearby coffee table and muted the television. On his seventy-inch screen, Jimmy Cagney continued to dance to the tune of Grand Old Flag in silence. Wade loved the classics.

"You're here about the disappearances.... the three women," he said. I wasn't surprised. The case had made national headlines.

"All in their mid-thirties, all professional and all making good money. That's the only thing they have in common," I said. "The doctor is Hispanic, the hedge fund manager is Asian and the lawyer is Caucasian. They have no connections to each other. None of them have any family to speak of and there's no ransom demand."

"You've solved worse," Wade said pointedly.

"Given time, I can probably nail this one, especially with all the resources the Feds are pouring into the case."

"But you don't think there's time." I shook my head.

"I *know* there isn't. I think that they might still be alive, but not for long." I looked at him square in the eye. "Will you help?" Wade's nod was one part compassion and two parts resignation.

"Yeah," he said, holding out his right hand. "You know the drill." I took his hand and closed my eyes.

Once I had referred to Wade as a psychic. That had earned me a harsh glare and a stern warning not to call him that again.... ever. I still don't understand what he does, but I know that it's real. Like I said, he's my edge.

He tried to explain it to me once. Somehow he can see the connections we make with other people, past, present or future. He could track my bloodline back to Adam, if he had a mind to, or track it through countless futures to the end of the world. Even the most ephemeral connection, living or dead, could be traced.

There was a good chance that, sometime in the future, I would come into contact with at least one of the three missing women; even if it meant finding their bodies lying in some back alley. If he could find that connection, then he could tag them and through them, their kidnappers. That might lead him to a location, and with a little luck we could change their fates.

I've used Wade on three other cases, and it was his lead that broke each case. He never accepts payment or credit. He only has two conditions. One, I only come to him when there are no other options and two, I never tell anyone else. He demands absolute secrecy. If I blab our deal is off.

If he was poking around in my mind, I couldn't feel it. I gripped his hand for several minutes, kept my mouth shut and let him work. Two identical cases, one in Atlanta and one in Cincinnati, had ended with six dead, all women. I didn't know why the kidnapper had surfaced in Tampa, or even if it was the same person, but I had not been lying when I told Wade that time was running out. The last disappearance had occurred a week ago. In both the Atlanta and Cincinnati cases, all three women had been found dead ten days after the last one disappeared.

Time dragged on until at last Wade released my hand. When I opened my eyes and saw him staring back at me, I had to suppress a shudder. His emotions were running wild across his face, and the predominant emotion was terror. That scared me. In all the time I've known him, I've never seen Wade afraid.

"When this is over," he said in a low voice, "Don't come looking for me. I won't be around."

"But…"

"I mean it, Daniel. This is the last time I help you. I'm leaving town, probably tonight. Don't look for me. *Ever*. Understood?" I started to object, but that look in his eyes stopped me.

"All right," I said. Wade held my gaze for a moment, and then stood. "We have to go now," he said, heading toward the front door. I didn't argue.

We got into my car and took off. Tampa isn't a small city and it's spread out over a fairly large area. There had not been any witnesses to the kidnappings, and all of the friends and co-workers were clean, so we had not been able to narrow our search to any particular area. Wade told me to head toward the dog track, which was on the other side of Sulphur Springs, about five miles from his house. He settled back into the seat and closed his eyes.

In the 1920's, Sulphur Springs had been an upper class neighborhood, but time had taken its toll. The older houses were falling apart and the newer ones were small, barely adequate single-family homes or cheaply made duplexes. Narrow streets, abandoned buildings, and roaming gangs made the area dangerous, especially at night.

It took less than five minutes to get to the dog track. The season had just ended and the hulking grandstand was dark and empty. I stopped when I got to the intersection of Waters and Kennedy, a four-lane street that ran past the track, and waited. I didn't have to wait long.

"Over there," said Wade, pointing. I followed his finger over to the old Sulphur Springs pool club.

"You sure?" He nodded. The pool club sat directly across from the dog track. In its heyday it had been a popular retreat, but it had been abandoned for decades. Local legend had it that the sulfur-laden waters contained magical healing properties. A large two story gazebo stood over the now capped spring. The upper floor had been host to numerous parties and other social functions. The lower level enclosed the spring.

Now the pool was filled with dark green rainwater, and the gazebo's white paint was faded and peeling. A sturdy chain link fence surrounded the pool, but the rest of the area lay open. A few scattered amber streetlights accented the glow of the full moon, providing adequate illumination. I eased my car onto Kennedy and turned towards the gazebo. Wade's hand shot out and grabbed me by the shoulder.

"Stop here," he demanded.

"But…"

"I said *stop!"* I hit the brakes and pulled over to the curb. Wade was out of the car in an instant and I scrambled after him. His long stride forced me to jog to keep up. When we entered the empty parking lot that fronted the pool club Wade pulled up. He stood there, staring at the gazebo. It shimmered softly with reflected moonlight, a good fifty yards away. After a few moments Wade pointed at the glowing structure.

"The girls are in there," he whispered, turning to face me. "Give me thirty seconds, no more. Then go in and *don't stop for anything.*" His hand shot out and gripped my shoulder with surprising strength. "They're still alive, but they're not alone. Do *not* hesitate. The men holding them have killed before and they'll kill again."

"I need to call for backup," I said, but Wade shook his head.

"No time. Now get ready. Do what you have to do, Daniel." Licking my lips, I nodded. Wade released my arm and turned toward the gazebo.

"What are you going to…?"

"What I have to do, just like you," he replied, his voice shaking. "It doesn't concern you. Pray that it never does." And then he was gone. He angled off to the left, darting forward with nearly inhuman speed. Shoving my own fear into a small, dark corner of my mind, I started counting. When I reached thirty, I drew my .45 and starting running.

It took another fifteen seconds to get cross the parking lot. The bottom level of the gazebo was comprised of a series of columns and arches that held up the second floor. There were no doors, but the columns were at least five feet wide, blocking most of my view to the spring.

Halfway across the parking lot, I realized that there was a soft glow coming through the arches. *So much the better,* I thought as I reached the gazebo. The idea of going in blind did no sit well with me. I leaned against one of the columns, wasting a few precious seconds to catch my breath. Then, gripping my .45 with both hands, I stepped through the arch, and stopped dead in my tracks. I had steeled myself for just about anything.... mutilated bodies, tortured, barely alive victims.... anything. What I was not ready for was beauty.... pure, absolute, perfect beauty.

In the center of the cement floor where the spring should have been was a column of what could only be described as living light. Even now I cannot begin to describe it. I think it was maybe two feet wide, or maybe two miles, or two million miles. It penetrated the ceiling, the sky and for all I know the universe itself. I stared at the breathtaking sight before me, tears welling up in my eyes. I could sense that this.... light.... emanated from deep within the ground. It sparkled and danced within itself, glowing with every imaginable color along with an infinite number of unimaginable colors. Just to be near it made me feel whole and healed.

Fifteen years of police work had damaged me. I had seen more than one man should be allowed to see, but in just a few seconds I could feel the wounds from those years healing. I wanted to shout, to scream in ecstasy. To this day, I don't know exactly what I saw, but I know this. That indescribable column was alive, and it was aware. It sounds insane, but I felt as if I was staring at the very soul of the earth.

My hesitation nearly cost me my life.

DANIEL!

Wade's shout tore through my mind, and *only* my mind, breaking the spell cast by the light. Stunned, I tore my eyes away.

The expected obscenity presented itself.

The women were there, tied up and lying on the floor next to the light. Their clothes were ripped nearly to shreds and in the glow I could easily see that they had been brutalized. They were bleeding from a dozen shallow cuts and their faces were bruised and swollen. They were tied together, arm-to-arm and ankle-to-ankle. It looked for all the world like some kind of pagan sacrifice.

Their tormenters were there as well. Both were men, one Caucasian, one Hispanic, both middle aged, and both dressed in black. By the time I spotted them, they had already seen me. The white man, a hulking football lineman type well over six feet tall, had already drawn a long, serrated hunting knife and was coming straight at me. The Hispanic remained where he was, hovering over his victims like some kind of deranged vulture. For just an instant, I saw tiny threads of light stretching out of the women and plunging into that man's chest. The man in turn had threads reaching out of his forehead, stretching towards the light. But these threads were not made of light. They were dark. I looked at them saw corruption and death. I saw anti-light.

Wade had warned me not to hesitate, but if he had said nothing, I would still have fired. I think I would have fired even if the man had not drawn his knife. Something emanated from both of them that made me want to gag. It was a foul stench that was more.... *spiritual* is the only word I can think of.... than physical. I knew that, for the first time in my career, the first time in my *life*, I had come face to face with true evil.

My .45 bucked in my hand. I had a full clip and I divided the eight slugs evenly between the two men - four shots each, straight to the chest. The noise reverberated through the gazebo. Both men went down without a sound. I ejected the spent clip and reloaded, just in case they had friends. I took a moment to make sure that both of them were dead. Then I checked the victims.

They were alive, and conscious. I used my pocketknife to cut their bounds and got them to their feet. They struggled to stand. All three were in deep shock. I was surprised that they made it to their feet, but looking back, I think that the light may have helped.

Ordinarily, I would have used my phone to call for an ambulance, but suddenly I knew that I had to get them away from the gazebo. Their kidnappers were dead, but there was something else close by. It was a presence, and like the light, it was aware. Unlike the light, it was *not* alive. I could feel it closing in, and if the darkness that had possessed the men had been bad, this was a thousand time worse.

I led the women through the nearest arch. Outside it was dead silent, but I could feel something closing in. I got the sense that there was a desperate battle being waged in and around the gazebo. It was like walking blindfolded through the middle of a battlefield.

Somehow I got the women back to my car, and it was only then that I felt safe enough to call for backup. Two of them seemed to be coming around, but the third had lapsed into unconsciousness.

I had three patrol units on scene in under two minutes, and a pair of ambulances there in five. Ten minutes after that, my captain showed up with a forensics unit and a handful of F.B.I. agents in tow. The victims were taken away, and I spent the next few hours going over the night's events. I never mentioned Wade.

I wasn't surprised to find that the marvelous column of light was gone when I got back to the gazebo. The bodies were still there, of course. They were never identified, and because of that, the case is still open.

There was just a hint of light in the eastern sky when we wrapped things up. I would be going on administrative leave because of the shootings, but I wasn't worried. In every conceivable way they were justified. The last patrol unit pulled away and I got into my own car. I still had at least an hour of paperwork waiting for me at the station. I wanted to get it done and go home, hug my family and sleep for a month. Just as I started the car the passenger door opened and Wade slid in. I looked at him, my face asking a hundred questions. He shook his head adamantly.

"Believe me Daniel," he said, "The less you know, the better." I took a closer look at him. His face was drawn and haggard, as if he had aged ten years in a matter of hours. He held his right arm with his left, wincing in pain.

"Wade…"

"You got them out," he said. "That's the important thing. The rest…" his voice trailed off.

"That light," I whispered, and he smiled sadly at me.

"There are beautiful things in this world, Daniel; powerful, pure, beautiful things. And there are forces that want nothing more than to destroy them." He licked his lips. "You've come close to something tonight, and you don't want to come any closer." His eyes bored into mine. "Because if you do," he said, and now his voice was made of steel, "It will cost you everything.... your wife, kids, career.... *everything*." He looked back at the gazebo. "Walk away, Daniel. Please, walk away." And with that, he got out of the car.

That was over three years ago. Since then, Sulphur Springs has experienced a bit of a renaissance. The pool has been renovated and the gazebo has been remodeled and painted. I stop by every now and then and watch the kids have a blast in the summer heat.

But I don't go near the gazebo.

True to his word, Wade disappeared. The women recovered, physically at least. Mentally and emotionally, they still have a long way to go, but they're alive. The Feds took over the case, and last I heard they haven't made any headway. I got a commendation and a promotion, and I've been very careful to heed Wade's advice. I walked away from a mystery that night, and I continue to walk away. I have a good life and I intend to keep it.

Sometimes, late at night when my family is asleep, I step outside. Every so often, I fancy that I can see dark shapes hiding in the shadows, or a faint glow of perfect light hovering at the edge of my vision. I tell myself that it is a trick of the moonlight. Most of the time, I believe it. The other times…

I can't get that light out of my head. I can see it in my dreams. I can feel it in my heart. It's out there, somewhere, everywhere. Its beauty and strength constantly tug at me. I'm terrified that someday I'll answer its call, walk away from my life. I'll begin a quest that will take me out of sight and possibly even out of memory. Perhaps I'll find that light again, but maybe I'll stumble across the creatures that only live to corrupt it. If that happens…

No. I'm going to keep my life. I'm going to hang on to it with every fiber of my being. I don't know what kind of battle Wade fought that night, but it's not my fight. My battle is on the streets of Tampa, going after ordinary thieves, murderers and drug dealers.

It's not my fight.

Dear God, never let it be my fight.

#

Sergio Palumbo's Shopping List

Blood-colored Tomato Sauce
Whitish Powdered sugar
A slice of cake
Add fats and other ingredients at will…

Suicide Point

by Sergio 'ente per ente' PALUMBO
edited by Michele DUTCHER

"People's lives are in the care of the railways when
they get on a train.
The railways should remember that."
by Nina Bawden

All of the habits Patrizia did every morning since the moment she awoke at her home in downtown Lucca, were a sort of worn-out ritual of hers that would have made no sense to anyone else's attentive eyes, for sure. Nonetheless, the whole process the curly-haired, 37-year-old young woman usually followed - attracting her into the shadowy corners of her mind the same as a vampire might hear a persuasive call to a lost alley - lasted only a few minutes, but in the end it cleared her thoughts. Putting on her winter dress uniform, combing her blonde locks, preparing the bag she always had with her while on duty, these were the same actions she repeated day after day, morning after morning, before going outside and walking to the railway station.

While she crossed the ancient, medieval streets that were badly in need of repair, looking at the silent fronts of the three-story buildings along the way, she ran into only a few passers-by - given the early hour there weren't many people around, of course. Lucca wasn't born as a touristy town, even if it was 800-1000 years old. As she went past the ancient, battered city-walls and got to the tree-lined square, it was about 6:50 AM.

Patrizia knew what she had to do next, and time was going by very quickly, anyway. She briefly reminded herself of the reason why she was acting this way, why she was working down there and the goal she hoped to obtain very soon. The simple thought of her -possible- objective made her feel better. Maybe this would turn out to be a good day, an interesting day, who knew. Perhaps it would be better than the one before when nothing appreciably different had really happened, after all.

It had taken her a lot of time to be assigned to that line. After many requests, finally the railway management had accepted her application and allowed her to work on the trains going from the small town of Lucca to the beautiful medieval seaport of Pisa. Actually, that job was always going to be hers, sooner or later, as Patrizia well knew, because it was her hometown so her transfer was just a matter of time.

But, referrals from others and unspoken or unrevealed favors were the rule in the Italian national railways, so she had been given no choice but to just patiently bide her time.

Finally some of the other engineers appointed to that line had retired because of their age, and some had moved to the town where they lived, and others had been assigned elsewhere, so the exact job position she wanted was vacated, in the end. Now, the young woman simply drove the trains along that line half of the day, then returned home, within the ancient walls of Lucca at night - or early in the morning, depending upon her job schedule each day. And as soon as she was home, she happily recalled the best things she had seen or done while at work that day.

The best deeds that Patrizia tried to remember over and over again, *were the ones where she had run over people*, and the faces of the people she had *killed on tracks by using her locomotive while at work*, of course.

The **Lucca–Pisa railway** was built in 1846 and, when regular train services commenced, it was located at the beginning of an international line, *the first in the world*, actually. The line ran from the now-gone Duchy of Lucca and the town of Pisa, which was in another state at that time, before the unification of Italy had taken place. Actually, the duchy of Lucca had lost its peculiarity the following year, when all the lands of the Duchy were integrated within the Tuscan territory.

Managed by the ***Italian national transportation network*** nowadays, there were several *at-grade intersections* of the railway and some roads or paths. And those roads across the railroad were seriously dangerous and had seen many accidents over the course of the years. In order to do away with such occurrences, tunnels would later be favored, but this could turn out to be impractical in the flat countryside, just like in an area where there was insufficient space to build a roadway embankment or tunnel because of nearby buildings, for example.

Anyway, a significant amount of collisions between trains and road vehicles or pedestrians walking across the tracks had caused, so far, more than 20 deaths, as a matter of fact. Even if there had been several plans to largely eliminate many places like these on heavily used trunk main lines, all the ones along these small railroad lines still existed and remained very common along the tracks. All that seemed to be because of lack of public funding – or perhaps funds had been mismanaged elsewhere in the past. Also, the management was indifferent and didn't care too much about this situation, as it knew that the new high-speed lines were more profitable and they alone were valuable enough to have big expenditures focused on them, certainly.

It was strange to think that safety features could be greatly increased if only some **automatic warning devices** (AWDs), with flashing red lights, were placed to warn automobile drivers. Or if there had been a bell to warn pedestrians - or a few video cameras had been used to allow the human operators to be some distance from the point of intersection. But it seemed that nothing like that would likely occur in the near future... *And that was exactly what the way Patrizia liked it*, certainly.

That line was full of green shrubbery and ancient buildings with a few old manors along the way. But it wasn't just because of the scenery that the young woman had chosen that job. Along that railroad, in fact, there was a very famous point that possessed the all-time highest statistics for fatalities caused by accidents due to the train set's circulation. In particular, there was a place where most of the deaths had occurred so far. It was also known as *Suicide Point* among the train-drivers.

Patrizia desired to be the woman who abruptly put an end to another's' life. She reveled in the sight of blood seen on the victim's corpses after collisions; **she loved the act of killing itself**. If it were left up to her, the woman would have been given the opportunity to run over more and more people day by day, instead of the few she had killed so far, anyway. But she didn't want to be involved in the legal responsibilities surrounding the murders. In a way *she was a coward,* but by means of her job she had found the perfect way to continue killing people without ever being held responsible.

As a matter of fact, all the court cases about people killed along those tracks ended up with no real charges being brought against the train-drivers. This was because the evidence always blamed the peculiarity of the transit speed and the poor visual angle of the ill-reputed area. That section of track had been slated many times to undergo great improvements because of new security standards, but had never seen any new work done on the tracks because of a lack of money. Also, there was always a question about the alleged carelessness of the victim. Perhaps the dead person's true intention was to put an end to his existence for his own reasons, and this point didn't allow any charges to be brought against the train-driver's behavior in the end.

Actually, the inquiries usually stated that the accidents had occurred because the road vehicles weren't capable of stopping quickly - as required when a warning sign was present. Another reason for the accidents were pedestrians who insisted crossing the tracks in spite of all the warnings. Which was exactly the thing that had attracted Patrizia so much to begin with.

*This was simply **killing under the shield of the laws and regulations**,* and that was the best, the greatest satisfaction of all for the slender blonde-haired Patrizia De Napoli. *If only they could imagine it, if only they knew the truth*! But they didn't and weren't going to discover it ever, if she just kept attentively behaving in the same way.

Patrizia had always enjoyed playing with scale model trains and scale railroads, *which was kind of odd anyway*. On the other hand, if the woman hadn't become a train engineer she probably would have worked in a hospital, who knows? There were people in hospitals who wanted to kill patients while disguised as - or just acting like - nurses or doctors. These killers could easily murder a few patients or the people entrusted to their care, after all. But there could be some inquiries, some suspicions arising from too many deaths occurring within the same wards or within a single building, anyway. It was much better to be cautious, not to attract unwanted attention and to go on playing her hidden role of a 'serial killer under cover', as she usually called herself in a playful way. So, she was undetected and acted without anyone's knowledge, by means of the easy, unbeatable excuse of her job and the strict procedures connected to it daily.

When the opportunity appeared, when the chance to kill someone occurred, at that moment the young woman had to be completely in command of herself, as it would have been too easy to speed the train up, to go faster so that she could get to the new victim-to-be on the tracks and hit him as soon as possible. But she simply couldn't follow her deepest desires, she was well aware of that. In fact, if Patrizia had just done so, the odometer that was automatically set on board would record her change in speed, and she would need to explain why she went faster when she was supposed to have slowed the train down as soon as she noticed someone on the tracks.

The reality was that there had never been a reason for her to act carelessly, so she never had to have an excuse for such a hypothetical, thoughtless act. What she had to do was simply proceed normally, going on and on inexorably - exactly as if she were a computer-based sawing machine that was approaching a dry tree trunk, or a seagoing ship that was slipping into the soft whitish waves of the ocean - towards her next victim by driving at the usual, required speed for that area, then moving forward, yard by yard, until the inevitable happened, and she was finally satisfied. *Very Deeply satisfied*! That way, the woman could claim she had followed the usual regulations to a tee without breaking the speed restrictions. She could say that the event was unexpected and no one could have ever evaded it because of the speed required by the railway company, and the unpredictable behavior of the victim - who had suddenly stepped onto the tracks - and all the rest.

The situation had to be entirely blamed on the person who had proved to be careless or just wanted to kill himself over some personal matter. The death had to be unrelated in any way to Patrizia's own actions, being simply a consequence of the railway circulation, *happening by chance*, so that no one was ever able to think she was responsible in the end. Of course, she was allowed to lie, to say she hadn't noticed the man/woman/child on tracks on time to change her speed or come to a stop, because of other duties she was appointed to, or because of a sudden move the unfortunate person made. Maybe also because of the bad visual angle.

Actually, every time something like that had occurred, the train-driver had really seen everything, even if she was unable to look at directly, by simply imagining in her mind the face of the person, his agony and the pain he was going to suffer as soon as the train hit and killed him. The woman saw all of that in her head, every time such a deathly event took place, but she couldn't tell it anyone, of course. She told no one that she had seen the target on time, that she could have evaded the collision, as her reflexes were really very good. Nor could she explain to other people how happy she felt inside as the body of the corpse-to-be was hit, every single time. Certainly, Patrizia kept all those sensations to herself, hidden in secrecy.

There were only two people who could tell the truth to the policemen or the judges about what happened when a collision killed someone on tracks: these were the train-driver himself and the poor victim. But she would never betray her real intentions or reveal the way things had really happened, while the victim simply was unable to because that person was already dead… Of course, if that unfortunate individual had been allowed to speak, to express his point of view, things would have been reported very differently - but that was not an option given to the dead men. By sneering at that knowledge, the tricky Patrizia focused on the route that the train was travelling at present.

After all, her job was just like the one a soldier or any hangman was requested to do: killing whenever they were ordered to do so. The reality was that she just did it a little differently: unseen and unnoticed. But the young woman, too, was ordered to do what she did, as she responded to the *cruel voice* inside her and the bloody passions that agitated her mind, and she did exactly what those voices told her to do, certainly…

*****

That morning Patrizia had to start work at 7:10 AM. When the young woman finally arrived at the train station, it was starting to snow. While she was going along the platform she gave a look at the overcast sky that wrapped all the railway station in its oppressive hold. A winter mist lay in the distance, keeping hidden all the surroundings of the town of Lucca. There was not much to see nor do before reaching the train she had been assigned to for that day, so she simply got to the café inside those premises and ordered a coffee and a slice of a cake to eat. Slowly, Patrizia savored the contents of the white cup and soon became satiated thanks to the sweet food she liked so much. He did the same every day, whenever she had to depart from that station, which occurred at least three times a week, as the other mornings she left from Pisa on the way back to this town.

While sitting at the worn-out wooden table, which had a long edge just in the middle of it, Patrizia noticed an older colleague of hers that was entering through the main door. She greeted the bald newcomer with a faint smile, but no one spoke. It was too early to have a chat and too late, at the same time, as neither of them had much time before reaching their train-sets of the day.

Andrew was his name and he was a ill-reputed train driver, as a matter of fact. Some said he had even purposely damaged the trains or the coaches themselves that he was aboard while on duty - in order to slow down the locomotive and get overtime by causing further damage along his routes. Additionally, others said that he was a thief, who stole parts from the train's machinery - but nobody had ever had any evidence about those supposed illegal actions so far or, if anybody had discovered something, he had never told it to anyone. Some people also said that his chief, the superior ranking officer, knew about Andrew's actions but didn't say anything because he was either bribed by him every month, or simply because he didn't care, as his wage was the same at the end of the month anyway, whether or not he was a good supervisor. In the end, unsurprisingly *they all were members of the same great family, sure thing - there was no uncertainty about that, of course*!

After a glimpse of the time at her watch, the young woman stood up and went to the counter. "My usual breakfast," she told the server.

"As usual, the usual one…" the bearded waiter at the other side of the counter replied in a funny tone. "You're going to die of boredom someday my dear, do you know that?"

She smiled in return. She then paid the amount requested, went outside and headed for the place where she would find the train assigned to her today. As she reached the locomotive, before getting on, she took note of its appearance and its vivid colors. Then she thought of the overall structure of the train. The *Minuetto* she was going to board any minute now was produced by a French company in 2004: 119,049 pounds overall. It was designed to tow passenger-train cars at top speeds of up to 80 miles per hour. Either diesel or electric, it had a special feature compared to other trains in that the seats were not all the same Moreover it looked a bit older than the common Coradia™ modular train system, even though some people thought it portrayed itself as a further development of the Coradia™ family. And yes, in some features they looked alike: the front was almost similar, but the sides were not, certainly. They were in use throughout Italy, both by the national railways and private operators, and were 170 feet long. Made up of two railcars, with a central coach, the three parts were united without any interruption and could add up to three different trains creating a single one. Endowed with a hydro-mechanical drive unit and a hydrodynamic braking system, the first deliveries had proved to be a bit problematic because of some software malfunctions and a few mechanical troubles found with those engines.

A multiple-unit train-set like this one had the same power and traction components as a locomotive, but instead of the components being concentrated in one car-body, they could also be spread out on each car that made up the set. In many cases these cars were only able to propel themselves when they were part of the set. For example, one might have one car with the traction motors, and another car would be the only engine for head end power generation; or another one might have a car with the transformer, and another car with the traction motors. So, it wasn't necessary for every single car in such a set to be motorized. In most cases, these trains could only be driven/controlled from dedicated cab cars. However, in a few of them, every car was equipped with a driving console and other controls necessary to operate the train, therefore every car could be used as a cab car whether it was motorized or not, if on the end of the train, certainly.

Undoubtedly, it was a popular trend in European regional train traffic that locomotive-driven traditional trains were currently being replaced by modern diesel or electric powered Diesel Multiple Unit or Electric Multiple Unit trains - that is, trains without a separate locomotive. Typically, the one Patrizia presently drove had three coaches fixed together, with either diesel or electric traction and with a varying proportion of low floor space. The common hybrid diesel locomotive was an incredible display of power and ingenuity, in its way: it combined some great mechanical technology, including a huge, 12-cylinder, two-stroke diesel engine, with some heavy duty electric motors and generators, throwing in a little bit of computer technology.

She turned on the engine, then let the motor heat up a bit, closed the door and left the station at the scheduled time. Well, *three minutes later*, as a matter of fact…

Almost every system and the controls were exactly the same on such train-sets, and just a few were in different places from one another. That made things simple and easy to grasp, which was a relief and meant that she had to only be careful and conscientious about stopping on the mark, completing station duties, running (almost) on time and generally doing everything properly. All that let her think mostly about other personal matters, along the route. This was a short rail journey, about an hour overall, with some unremarkable scenery. Actually, tourists who were lovers of great landscapes and unusual areas headed into the northernmost or southernmost peculiar zones to board a few little trains that went across the valleys and climbed into the hills. On those routes they could have a pleasant look at the typical Tuscan landscape with greenish fields and peaceful sights. On the other hand, along the train line she worked for at present, throughout the years the series of small villages in the valley bottom had turned into a built up area: there were several houses and warehouses, many of them in need of repair. With only a few stops and not a lot of artistic monuments or ancient palaces in-between, that route wasn't something that could turn a tourist's temporary interest into a long-lasting love and passion for the place, certainly.

As the train arrived at the next station and stopped, a young couple got off. The husband seemed very happy to get out and stretch his long legs - and only two other elder persons got on board. Then another individual, graying and a bit slow, probably a tourist standing on the other side of the platform, reached the doorway in a hurry in order not to miss the ride. He should have been waiting for this train on the other track, but most likely it was because - as it frequently happened - the station information screens had told him differently, therefore misleading him. It happened more frequently than you could imagine, *not that she might care at all anyway*…There were not many people aboard today, probably some passengers had a few compartments only to themselves, Patrizia thought. Then, she started driving again and the train pulled out of the station. They weren't late yet, but the woman was sure they would certainly be just before arriving at Pisa. Ultimately the final delay would be 9 to 10 minutes as usual, of course.

The last weeks had been uneventful, anyway. But she didn't give up - some interesting things were going to happen, sooner or later, and she would be right here, on the train, at the right moment in order to enjoy the next accident and possibly to be the real cause of it. The real *hidden cause*, clearly.

At a certain point, past the usual flat location where most of the suicides had occurred previously, she saw a sudden movement out of corner of her eye. Then a slender figure appeared, approaching the fence, going over it and then jumping onto the tracks. *That could only mean that...*

'*Great, after so long...!* **Finally**!' the train driver thought to herself, couldn't wait for the upcoming event.

When it finally happened, it was already snowing, so the terrain around was part white and part green. '***Blood on snow**! Did you ever imagine that one day you would see such a scene on that soft cover, the white landscape dotted in red? What an extraordinary thing to see!'* That was the first thought that came to the train driver's mind. 'This is going to become something worth remembering, indeed!' she said to herself passionately.

She wasn't able to completely see the face of the victim - she hardly ever did. Maybe today it was a young boy wrapped in a heavy jacket, even though she had noticed some long hair. As a matter of fact, it always happened that way as the speed of the train was, at the same time, both a blessing and a curse. If you wanted to do a good job, you had to drive the locomotive at a fast speed, of course within the regulations, but you couldn't look at the details of the unfortunate on tracks by doing so. On the other hand, if you slowed down the train set too early, you might allow the person to escape from there on time or to save himself, being only wounded or injured in the end. So it was very important not to miss the target while going at the right speed, certainly!

Patrizia could have evaded the collision, maybe, if she had just managed to stop the train's course a few seconds before, if she only had tried. But she hadn't done it, as she didn't want to, of course.

The woman hadn't seen the unfortunate person on tracks on time, the train-driver repeated to herself in her mind- that was what she was going to declare to the authorities during the inquiry that had to take place soon, as it had occurred all the other times: *that was a very dangerous point, the curved tracks didn't allow for quick decisions or different moves, it had been an unexpected accident*, and so on, certainly. Patrizia smirked as she reminded herself of all the other occasions she had already said the same things under similar circumstances. She had counted 10 victims so far, a good score for her.

But the woman knew she had to pay attention to her actions, as there were many lawyers out there that could have asserted that she herself was '*asleep at the switch, not ready enough and not paying attention to what was going on around her....*' or something like that. She had been playing that dangerous game for five years so far.

There had only been a few days like this one over the course of the years when Patrizia was able to rejoice because of an accident that had ended up in a death, but patience was one of her strongest values. By patience she could go on, by patience she forced himself to work along that line, day by day, until the moment when she was finally allowed to have a hand in that business, to be the real motive of the collision and the true person responsible, even though without getting official credit for the passing of another one of his many victims. In a way, it was just the same as eating a cake on a feast day, to drink some old expensive liquor over the course of a holiday or savor a traditional main course at diner in a famous restaurant in town. *You had to wait for the right moment in order to taste the things you liked most*, and those were not available all the times nor could you afford them whenever you wanted to, of course.

She would have liked to do better, *to watch more and more killings*, to be able to cause a lot of other deaths, but she simply wasn't allowed to. You know, you can't have everything as you please, but what you get at times is enough to satisfy your senses, to appease your deep wish for bloodshed and small disasters, actually. That was what Patrizia had devoted himself to, and patience was an important, necessary element of her peculiar way of living, *and her way of killing, certainly.*

After all, she had divorced herself from the common morality of mankind long ago, and she had studied thoroughly all the deceptions and the tricky arts she could, in order to better accomplish her evil purposes without highlighting herself or her actions. She never wanted to be noticed, never needed to raise her head to lord-it-over the rest of her colleagues, nor give herself away. This was the way a coward like her usually acted, even though a coward didn't usually kill so many people, she told herself, having a subtle laugh at all of that…

As a matter of fact, Patrizia was sure that she wasn't going to be tired of playing such a game any time soon, and she hoped to have a very long, pleasant career, that would be the cause of cruel death for so many others on those tracks, certainly.

As the accident had just happened, the woman remained cool and reminded herself of all the procedures she had to follow. She just didn't want to be criticized for having done something different from what the regulations required. She had to appear completely precise and law-abiding, as close to perfect as possible.

The woman repeated to herself the instructions that were going to be the four main priorities for a train-driver in such a case according to the Rule Book - *or at least what she had to prove she had done afterwards, at least in the eyes of the authorities*, of course. Those 4 steps were: the passage of trains had to be stopped on each obstructed line; the headquarter had to be informed and the emergency services were to be summoned; it was compulsory to wear protection where required and, finally, to ensure the passengers were safe. She did exactly as indicated, reported the accident, and then waited for assistance. But her voice on the radio didn't betray her look of pleasure, her great sensations and the deep satisfaction she felt inside because of such a bloody scene that covered the track directly behind her train.

The event was going to disrupt service on the train line for several hours, she was certain of it. Having jumped off and looked at all that mess in awe, Patrizia was well aware that she had only a few minutes before the first response team arrived on the scene, so she had to savor that moment, taste the whole bloody thing at her best as soon as she could, certainly. She wanted to be impressed with the scene, every single time, but after so many killings and dead men such a feeling had become partly difficult to acquire. Anyway, the train-driver didn't lose heart, as any new occurrence could prove to be more interesting, crueler and bloodier than the ones before - so you could never know for sure, frankly.

The corpse, or what was left of it, had several head injuries, multiple facial fractures, an open chest, collapsed lungs, rib fractures, cuts in the skin and soft tissue and there was a lot of blood coming from the brain, as far as she was able to see and evaluate from the spot she was in.

The simple sight of the bodily fluid that delivered necessary substances such as nutrients and oxygen to the human cells and transported waste products away from those same cells, all dispersed on the ground and lost forever, made her shudder. Certainly she was excited and pleased about what she had done, again. But the train-driver was able to enjoy such moments only for a very short time, she was well aware of it all. A four-person crew for a 'possible physical intervention' at a residential address near the scene in response to the train-driver's emergency call arrived 15 minutes later. Patrizia watched them accessing the scene by cutting through the backyard fence.

Upon a first exam, the captain on the scene immediately called for an additional ambulance, then 2 fire engines. Then they approached Patrizia in order to have her opinion about all that and have a brief chat - and after that they simply waited for the policemen to come.

Recovery workers found that no deaths or injuries had occurred among the passengers aboard because of the abrupt stop, not even in the first car, and that was a very good thing, certainly.

"Did you notice anything useful?" the slender graying policeman in charge of operations that had arrived on the scene asked the young woman.

"No, sir," the train-driver impudently lied.

"We need to wait for the judge to come to begin the official investigation. So, please fill in this form and remain on board."

"Yes, sir". About the rest, she gave the officer only very vague answers. Of course, you had to possess a good memory when you had to face such police investigations, as you'd better not contradict yourself, obviously. *Repetition, repetition, repetition*, that was the key to that all, as she usually told herself, of course.

"Okay, we'll contact you if we need additional information from you. Please refer to your local line overseer for further dispositions."

"I'm at your disposal…" Patrizia said. Nobody around could see the big, wide smile she had on her face while she was walking away to get on board again…

Those pleasant images of death would have to remain impressed on her mind for a very long period, while waiting for another accident like this to happen next. This experience was exactly what she would wish for herself, again and again, the sooner the better.

*****

The sky was overcast again and the scenery looked a bit unpleasant, slightly misty along the way, just like her mood that morning. An entire month had already passed since that last accident and things had kept going on as usual, calm and peaceful, for trains along that line. This was a good situation for everyone, but not for Patrizia, certainly…

That day they had had some problems before departing, as there was an old disabled passenger that wanted to get on board the train but no one was able to find a colleague to assist her for a long time. You never know where the people you need at work really are when it's coffee break - but they were also missing at several other times as well, of course. So the delay had taken about 13 minutes so far.

Eventually the journey was finally going well. The woman had already seen two regional trains coming down the other track, then a long uneventful time had followed until Patrizia had driven his locomotive to a curved passage leading to another turn.

After a few stops, the train was finally reaching the point where the maximum amount of suicides had occurred over the course of the last years. At a certain moment, it seemed to her she had *a glimpse of some faces she knew well*. They were the pale shapes of the dead that she had killed through her actions, or were they not...? She was almost convinced she had seen them in a line along the tracks, out of the corner of her eye, but it had lasted only a brief moment anyway, given the misty morning. Perhaps having too much sugar in her coffee cup at breakfast was playing tricks on her mind, she thought... Or, maybe, all that was clearly a sign, an indication that she needed some action - another killing to be perpetrated as soon as possible. But she knew that it didn't depend only upon her desires. It was up to the circumstances, mainly. She had just to be lucky, as a matter of fact.

Probably she had just imagined all that, but she didn't have the time to think about it, as at the next turn she saw that large blue MPV from a famous French car-maker in the middle of the train-tracks, just five miles from there. It was an old model, but it didn't move - maybe the driver was ill, or had fainted, maybe there were also some passengers aboard, she was clearly unable to tell from her position. Well, **what an incredible opportunity ahead for her**, *a pretty rare thing*, a chance not to be missed at any cost! That MPV seated at least seven passengers, which meant that hopefully there were going to be more than just one murder today!

It would be a head-on collision! Probably, a multiple killing, more than one dead-man at a time, if she was very lucky, as Patrizia had never accomplished such a great feat so far…but she was going to exactly that very soon. The train-driver was just savoring the moment when she would hit the car, the disaster that was going to befall the people in the vehicle, and time was running by fast, it was just a matter of a very short time by then…

Patrizia knew that she had to use all of her resources to the best advantage at present, as she was contracted to operate the emergency air brake two seconds before impact, which would be too late of course. Or even better – maybe as late as possible, in order to obtain the best, most powerful force at the moment of collision. While her actions had to be reputed, at the same time, as if she had acted in the best way possible before the investigating team's eyes and her superiors', of course…

'*How strange…*' a lonely thought crossed Patrizia's mind at a certain point just before the impact. '*The vehicle seems to be empty, I don't see any driver inside and…*'

The train and the vehicle collided just a second afterwards and the noises produced by the event resounded across the whole valley. As a matter of fact, there was a real explosion involved, much more incredible and unexpected than anyone would have presupposed.

No explosion was meant to happen, actually, nor was there supposed to be a destruction of the train itself along with the other means of transportation being on track – *at least not according to Patrizia's predictions.* But the explosion occurred, anyway, and the consequences were unbelievable in the end. It was just if the train had hit a bomb, or better a vehicle full of bombs, and the result was the complete destruction of that part of both tracks. The derailment of the coaches following the locomotive, and the envelopment of the deeply damaged and pierced metallic train set with a flurry of flames soon devoured everything, leaving the scene with devastation.

The incredibly fast increase in volume and release of energy in such an extreme manner generated high temperatures and emitted gases. For sure, some low explosives were the cause of all that and the deflagration started the process that almost burned the locomotive into cinders, finally.

It was truly a remarkable tragedy, a horrible disaster that Patrizia would have been glad, eager to look at and savor, probably, but not be a victim of. The fact was that the train-driver died almost immediately when the explosion took place. And she didn't even notice everything that occurred following the initial collision…

*****

From his point of view, lost in the countryside just two miles away from the point of impact, the short 30-year-old Martino looked attentively at the whole scene by means of his binoculars and relished every single bit of the disaster that took place on tracks in the distance. The hood of the brownish jogging jacket that covered his head concealed his slightly receding hairline, but his deep blue eyes were like two cold gems that pierced through the morning mist that covered part of the greenish plain encircling the railroad.

That was the fourth strike he had scored so far, all of the previous ones made exactly by using the same method: that is, filling an abandoned/stolen huge vehicle with many bombs connected to his new e-phone, placing it exactly in the middle of the railroad tracks, just on the point where an insidious *at-grade intersection* was, and then waiting for the right time. When the locomotive was close, he held in his hands the machinery and electrically initiated the explosion. And then the show was served!

His technique had proved to be really terrible but effective. There had been more than forty fatalities so far during the course of his bloody activities: four locomotives destroyed, more than six coaches eviscerated, long stretches of tracks on four lines were now unavailable for service. By now, his capability as 'the serial killer of trainsets', as the newspapers commonly called him, was pretty well known across the whole country, even though his latest killing had occurred just one year ago. The media had been saying that he had probably retired or had died. **What a great mistake**! He had to show them he was alive and ready to cause another big disaster, certainly, and he had to do so as soon as possible!

In his mind Martino savored the blood on the tracks, the surprised expression on the train driver's face, the turmoil on board along with the suffering of the many passengers and all that. How ironic that when he was younger, also Martino had liked so much the scale model railroads and was eager to simulate some small scale collisions while playing in the garden. When he had grown up, the man had lost no time before staging some disasters in a bigger scale. The 1:1 scale, the real one with real humans involved and real victims, was his preferred one, of course…

The man well reminded himself of that old quote by H.G. Wells that went this way: *'There is nothing in machinery, there is nothing in embankments and railways and iron bridges and engineering devices to oblige them to be ugly. Ugliness is the measure of imperfection'*. He knew that Wells was quite right. According to Martino's mind **only disasters and blood** were the true perfection, and those were the remarkable things he appreciated most of all.

Now he had only to stay calm for a few months while thinking how to make his next blow even bigger and better, projecting and devising everything at his best, and then finally acting, as he was used to do.

That was going to happen - just one or two months from now, if everything went well…and Martino couldn't wait for that pleasing day to come, of course.

THE END

Jeff C. Stevenson's
Shopping List

Natural Balance Fat Cats Adult Cat Food
Halo Top Sea Salt Caramel Ice Cream
Amy's Pesto Tortellini Bowls
Aidells sausage
Goat Cheese

Wagner in Three Parts

Jeff C. Stevenson

Part One: The Painter and the Dancer

Decades later, Charlotte can still recall the first time she saw the soldier in 1916, and how he seemed to appear out of nowhere. One instant, she was cutting hay and the fields around her were vacant. The next moment, she turned to sneeze, and there he was.

The man was seated on some rocks with a sketchpad balanced on his knees. She watched as he gazed into the distance, then scribbled on the pad. For several seconds, she saw him repeat these movements before Delphine asked her what she was looking at.

"That man over there," Charlotte said, gesturing with her chin. Audra and Delphine turned to see.

The three 18-year-olds were breathing heavily from their efforts and were glad for the break. They had been cutting since 10 a.m.; the dew was off by then, making it easier to maneuver their scythes through the dry grass. The fields around the French village of Lille were mostly flat marshlands where an abundance of hay was grown so there were many days' work ahead for the teenage girls. Earlier that morning, they had climbed into the back of the landowner's cart and he had dropped them off in the remote area. He'd be back later that afternoon and expected to see twenty bales. He snapped the reins, leaving the girls to their labor. Making the shoulder-high piles was hard, hot and tiresome work. Each stack of cut hay first had to be crushed down, then tied tight like a wrapped parcel. Already past noon, they only had eight completed. Until Charlotte had seen the man, there had been few breaks and very little talking between the three girls.

"What's he doing, drawing?" Audra asked.

"I think so," Charlotte said. "But where'd he come from? He wasn't there a minute ago."

The three girls watched the man go through his sketching motions. Delphine quickly lost interest, grabbed one of the water jugs. They passed it around, swatted at the bugs, conferred over when to eat lunch, decided to wait until they had a dozen bales completed.

Audra said, "That should a little easier with only eight left to do." Delphine nodded her agreement. Charlotte only continued to stare at the stranger on the rocks.

"Why don't you go over there and introduce yourself?" Delphine kidded. "He's probably a soldier who'd love to meet one of the local farm girls."

Audra said, "But make it quick. We have to get back to work."

Charlotte nodded, removed the bandana from her head, wiped her face as best she could, brushed the hay strands from her shoulders, and then began her walk across the field. They really were in the middle of nowhere and hadn't seen any carriages or farmhands since they had started work that morning. There were a few trees tucked about in broad clusters; silver lime, chestnut, some red oaks, but beyond that there were only open, hilly fields. Had he ridden out by horse? But there were none nearby, nor any carts or wagons. Even if he had walked, Charlotte would have seen him make his progress to the pile of rocks on which he now sat.

Where had he come from?

When she was only a few feet away, she called out a greeting, which startled him. He turned, said something in German. She spoke again in French; he returned a comment in German, which she didn't speak. He set aside his pad, stood to greet her. He indicated that he didn't speak French. They continued to smile shyly at one another.

He looked to be maybe ten years older than Charlotte, but it wasn't his age or overall appearance that captured her attention. It was only his eyes.

His pale blue eyes seized her immediately, held her in a penetrating, almost hypnotic gaze. She didn't know all that was occurring, but she was immobilized, captured by his scrutiny. There was a seduction going on, she was certain of that; he seemed able to look inside of her. She was drawn to him physically but also by some invisible force that made her want to move closer.

She made herself blink to free herself from his spell. She was dizzy. She put her hand to her forehead. It took a moment for her head to clear, to look away, to no longer meet his piercing gaze. When she had steadied herself, she noticed how his thin brown hair flopped over the left side of his forehead. His nose was large and fairly pointed. He had an untrimmed mustache that extended beyond the corners of his mouth. On his chin, there was a horizontal dimple.

He gestured for her to join him on the flat rocks. Charlotte glanced back at the other two girls. He called out to them in German, waved broadly at them across the distance. Audra and Delphine returned the greeting.

"I can only stay for a moment," she said, settling herself down, knowing he didn't understand her. He passed his pad to her to see what he had been sketching. She slowly flipped through the pages of mostly landscapes, a few buildings. The top page was his current attempt at the landscape that was in front of them. He had sketched out the sloping hills, a cluster of trees, the grass that she and the girls still needed to harvest in the days to come. She nodded politely; his efforts showed some skill she supposed, but her only interest in the arts was dance.

He accepted the portfolio back, opened his hands to her, and said something in German. It was her turn to show what her skill was. She giggled; he could show his talent on paper, she would have to stand, move, to show him hers. She glanced back; the girls were not looking, they were hard at work. She needed to return to them. She jumped up, took a breath to steady herself, then tried to match the ballet moves she had seen in books. Her legs quivered a bit as she spun, lifted a leg; it was hard to remain balanced on the uneven field. She finished quickly before she fell and made a complete fool of herself. He applauded, smiled broadly. He stood, took her hand, bowed. Feeling flushed, elated and embarrassed, she bowed back, couldn't help feeling a thrill at his touch. She risked a glance into his eyes. They spoke to one another, saying their goodbyes. He gestured at the field in front and all around them, then back at the work she and the girls had already accomplished. She nodded: *Yes, they would return.*

She counted on her fingers to five, held her hand up to him.

"Five more days we'll be here."

He smiled, nodded again. He understood.

#

He wasn't there the next day. Charlotte was surprised how devastated she was. She hadn't slept well, kept waking to images of the solider, recalled the sensation of his hand holding hers, the power and attraction she had found in his eyes. She had laughed off Audra and Delphine's questions, saying she didn't know anything about the man since he didn't understand French and she didn't speak German.

The following day, the three girls split up into different land lots with smaller sections to cut. Whoever finished first would join the one who was closest to them until all three were reunited and the work done. Having already cut the hay, Charlotte set to pitching it into a pile. Soon, she sensed she was not alone.

The man was there, a hundred feet away, his sketchbook under one arm. Somehow, he had found her! Even from the distance, she felt the energy that radiated from him. Her heart beat hard and fast with excitement. She wanted to run to him, which was foolish, so she took a moment to slow herself down. She fought every impulse, remained rooted in place. She wiped her brow, waved to him. Relief and something like joy settled over Charlotte once he began to make his way toward her.

The communication of hand signals and gestures began, but went smoother since they already knew that neither one could understand the other's words. He mimed where the other women were, she pointed out the general direction of where they were located and that she would join them when she finished. He showed her his latest sketch. Her mouth opened in surprise and delight. It was of her, in that very field with a scarf over her head, the pitchfork in her hand. He must have been drawing her for most of the morning since it was almost complete. She looked around, trying to see where he had hidden himself. He merely shrugged mischievously. Somehow, it didn't bother her so much; she was flattered that he had thought to include her in the landscape he had drawn.

After a few minutes, he shooed her back to work, pointed in the direction where he would be. She grabbed her pitchfork with renewed vigor, worked tirelessly for the next hour. She glanced up frequently to find that he was either under the shade of a nearby tree or nowhere to be seen. It troubled her because she didn't know where he could vanish to so quickly yet she also loved the mystery of it all, the idea of him playing hide and seek with her.

When she had finished her section, Charlotte prepared to head over to help Delphine. She was anxious that she didn't see the man anywhere. Would she have to leave without saying goodbye? How would they know where or when to meet again? She called out "Hello?" a few times in case he had dozed off somewhere but when there was no response, her heart grew heavy. The hot tears cleared trails down her dirty and sweat-soaked face.

He had left her. She was alone now

# # #

On her final day in the area, she was again separated from the other girls; they were each doing a small patch on their own.

She ran to him as soon as she spotted him. He was in his German uniform, no sketchpad.

She supposed he was preparing to leave the area, wanted to say goodbye. She fell into his arms, crying hysterically, not knowing why she was having such a passionate response to the man. He returned the embrace, murmuring to her in German as she wept and spoke in French.

Once she had calmed down, she pulled away from him, wanted to look into his eyes, experience their great attraction, feel their pull one final time.

"I missed you these last few days," she said helplessly, knowing the words made no sense to him. "And I am going to miss you when you leave. I wish I could see you again."

He smiled, reached into the breast pocket of his corporal uniform, pulled out a sheet of paper. He handed it to her. She read the words, composed in badly translated French. It was his schedule, where he would be that was closest to her in the coming months: Seboncourt, Forunes, Wavrin and *Noyelles-lès-Seclin*. The nearest was only an hour away, the furthest only two. If she could find a way to meet him, he would wait in the fields near her home on those days.

She looked into his eyes, nodded happily.

He kissed her.

# # #

In January 1917, she slipped eagerly out of her house, hurried down the path until she reached the woods where they met. He was already there, but as he started toward her, she saw he was limping. Over the months, they had each made an effort to learn the basics of the others' language, so communication had improved a little. She pointed at his leg; he explained that two months earlier, he was wounded by a shell blast during a battle near Bapaume, France. His gestures and broken French set her mind at ease; he was healing well, had convalesced in Berlin, and would return to command his unit the following month.

They moved deeper into the hillside, shrouded by the trees and the deep forest. Her parents were preoccupied with their own responsibilities, her father as a butcher and her mother as a seamstress. Charlotte was usually able to make herself scarce for a couple of hours without causing them to wonder where she was.

During their rare visits, she had learned that the soldier relished walking briskly, holding her hand, and exploring the fields near her village. She sensed it was relaxing for him after the horrors of fighting; hiking seemed to ease the tensions he experienced as a leader. She enjoyed listening to him speak, had become familiar with his cadence, his energetic tones and the passion he put into the words that she rarely understood. He sounded as if he was making a speech; his hand gestures were wide and sweeping as if he was talking excitedly to dozens or hundreds of people instead of just her. In the midst of his tirades, she'd often hear the words Prussia, Austria, and Bavaria.

After several minutes of impassioned statements in German, he would pause, scrutinize her, his pale blue eyes searching for the proper response. She would shrug, give him a weak smile, but her meek reaction to his torrent of words would only upset and sometimes anger him. She desperately wanted to please him and not cause him any additional strain. She had learned that the only way to appease his sudden rage was to yield to his physical desires. When they were in their most private place, she allowed him to kiss her deeply, touch her breasts, reach between her legs. He'd force her to her knees to satisfy his aroused state. He respected her limits, but whenever they were together—only a few times that year—he would urge her to loosen her restrictions just a little more next time.

Five months later, she did.

# # #

It was a warm summer evening in June of 1917. Charlotte was already at the private place when he staggered into view. She knew immediately that he was drunk, both by the stench and his behavior. He wanted her right then, all of her. She was actually ready to give herself fully to this man who had appeared out of nowhere and had continued to do so for more than a year.

When they were through, he kissed her passionately, and then lurched off in the near darkness. By moonlight, Charlotte stumbled home through the fields, clutching her soiled clothes, weeping at the pain she had experienced yet also at the joy this solider had brought her.

# # #

Early Monday morning, March 25, 1918, Charlotte gave birth to an illegitimate son, named him Jean-Marie. A month later, German officers delivered the first of several envelopes of cash. She never saw the man with the piercing, pale-blue eyes again, but for many years, the money continued to reach her. Not enough to get rich, but enough to get by.

She was eventually able to afford dance lessons in Paris.

# # #

NOTE: This is based on a true story. When his mother, Charlotte Lobjoie, died in 1951, Jean-Marie found sketches and paintings in her attic, including one of a woman working in a hayfield with a scarf over her head and a pitchfork in her hand. It looked exactly like his mother and was signed and dated by Adolf Hitler in 1916.

<u>Part Two: The Imagination of Margarete</u>

Margarete awoke in the middle of the night, saw the faint white glow at the far end of the room. It resembled a lamp covered by a heavy cloth so the illumination was dim, dispersed. It hovered a couple feet above the ground. Margarete carefully sat up in bed so as not to disturb Ruth who slept next to her. The dormitory was crowded, beds were shared.

The glow stealthily approached, bobbing gently up and down as if it was walking toward her. Was it getting nearer? What was it? Closer, still. She was now nervous, had never seen such a thing before. It made no noise as it stepped on the wood planks, or was it floating? A ghost? She blinked several times, wanted to be certain she was awake, that her mind wasn't playing a trick on her as it did so often.

Margarete squeezed her eyes closed, counted silently to five, opened her eyes. Whatever it was, it was gone.

She exhaled gently, felt her heart slow its crazy jackhammer of anxiousness. She fell back to sleep, disappointed that it probably hadn't been anything more concrete than a leftover dream.

# # #

The following night, it was there again. It seemed larger since it was closer to her. She tried to discern its features. It was a shimmering yellow-white light, beatific in its radiance. Maybe it was a heavenly being, a messenger or an angel?

She was on the first bunk, was able to watch the figure at eye level. Around her, the other women slept; there were no sudden gasps, whisperings or indications that any of them were seeing what she was. Only snoring, murmuring, the rustle of bodies turning. What was this radiant visitor's intent? Was she really seeing the bright shape right there in front of her?

She must have Ruth confirm its appearance, needed a witness; too often what she claimed to have seen was discredited by others.

Margarete turned over in the bed, whispered to Ruth. "Wake up! There's something here!"

The narrow window slots in the ceiling and along the walls provided glimmers of silver-blue moonlight to see by. Ruth peered past Margarete into the open space in the middle of the room. "Where? I see nothing."

Margarete twisted back around. The glowing figure was gone. She carefully crept out of the bed. The cold floor scraped her feet. She tiptoed quickly past the rows of beds, careful to wake no one. Once she had checked in all directions, she hurried back to Ruth. The wooden planks that made up the bunks were rough, easy to splinter your hands on so she always remembered to settled in slowly.

"What did you see?" Ruth asked as she pulled up the blue and white check blanket. Once they were covered, Margarete said, "I'm not sure. Something white, glowing. I saw it last night, too. Tonight, it was closer. Maybe I was asleep, but I don't think I was."

"Now neither of us are!"

"Sorry."

Ruth turned over, facing the wall. Margarete plumped up her thick, misshapen pillow, stared into the barracks, wondered about what she had seen.

# # #

Once again, the morning coffee was weak. The porridge had only a few bits of fruit, the black bread was tough, and the small portion of sausage barely filled their aching stomachs. It was early, there was much yawning and shivering. Not much chatter between the women in the communal room. It was going to be another long, busy day so they were not up to expending what little energy they had.

There was the usual long line to use the basins and lavatories. Ruth, who was behind Margarete, said to her, "Next time you have a nightmare, don't wake me, all right? We get little enough sleep as it is."

"Sorry. But I really did think I saw something."

In front of Margarete, Hilda turned. "What did you see?"

"Nothing!" Ruth snapped. "Mind your own business."

"Wasn't talking to you."

"But I was talking to you," Ruth answered. Hilda was known to be a gossip, had a reputation of cornering and conjuring information to use later, always to her advantage.

"It was nothing, Hilda, just my imagination," Margarete said, always the peacemaker.

Hilda looked at her carefully, shrugged, turned away.

# # #

Outside in the great square, Margarete enjoyed her favorite part of the day, the first deep breath of fresh air. It was such a contrast to the stuffy sleeping area in the wooden barracks, which always smelled of too many women crammed into a space that seemed to grow smaller every day. She could taste salt, knew the lake was nearby, pictured it, held that image close, tucked it away in her own private photo album. She had a strong, vivid mind's eye, used it like a camera all day long.

They were all crunching across patches of filthy gravel. Margarete thought of it as sand; maybe the ocean was close by, too. The grains under her feet went soft, white, sparkling clean. She could almost hear seagulls.

"Why are *you* smiling?" Blanka asked harshly as she passed by, jostling Margarete's shoulder. "What is there to be so happy about?"

"The beach—" Margarete started to answer, then realized that no one could see the waves curling to the shore. Blanka had moved on briskly ahead of her, really wasn't looking for an answer. Like most of the women, she assumed Margarete was batty, didn't pay much attention to her.

Looking past the barriers, Margarete marveled at the beautiful alpine setting that surrounded them, the thick forest of ash trees that were always within sight yet never within reach. She took another deep breath; if the season and wind were in agreement, the sweet honey and lemon peel scent of the Linden trees would reach her.

She followed the other women as they filed passed the manicured lawns, the row after row of bright red blooming flowers. The grounds were perfectly cared for, with dozens of robust young trees, the soil around them neat, always freshly raked. To the left were several large white cages that housed peacocks, monkeys and a parrot. Whenever the women appeared, the bird would flap its wings in a flurry of activity, cawing out, "Mama! Mama!" repeatedly. Its antics always caused Margarete to giggle.

"Hurry *up*!" Ruth chided her.

Once inside the work area, Margarete settled down to sew gray socks or cobble shoes, whichever was needed for that day. The other women worked at a slow yet steady pace, but Margarete always seemed eager for the task at hand even though she detested the war and the efforts of the soldiers. The others often asked her why she worked so intently for a cause she opposed, but she would only say, "We all do our part."

For Margarete, her part was to purposely adjust the sewing machine so that the fabric for the socks was thin at the heel and toe. This caused them to quickly wear out when the soldiers marched, resulting in sore feet and blisters. Throughout the morning, Margarete would secretly set aside the leftover material she was using for the socks or the shoe pieces she was cutting. Later, in the relative privacy of the barrack's communal area, she'd piece together a doll or necklace or bracelet, little personal items she'd create and hide away. She imagined she was fashioning the crude little keepsakes for her own future, for her own children to play with one day.

# # #

At noontime, they returned to their quarters for a quick lunch, which was turnip soup. Then it was back to continue with their work assignments.

In the evening, they trudged back to their sleeping area. Fingers were sore, backs were stiff, but sleep awaited them, the best part of the day. They were exhausted so they ate quickly and greedily—soup again—then hurried to claim the best spot on the bunk. Until lights out, those who wished to would socialize with one another, but most stared mutely into space or closed their eyes to rest.

Margarete and Ruth sought one another out, slept most nights together; many of the women did. They all grew accustomed to the various sleep habits, knew who snored, who cried out at night. There was comfort in familiarity.

"You'll sleep through the night, right?" Ruth insisted as she settled into the bunk.

"Yes," Margarete said meekly. "I promise I won't wake you."

# # #

The illuminated figure reappeared but Margarete kept her promise to Ruth. The glow was bright enough that it woke her from her sleep. The figure was perhaps twenty feet in front of her, the closest it had ever been, hovering over the floor. It wasn't moving toward her or away from her; it was simply holding its place, waiting for her to awaken. There was something benign about it, which she had never felt before. It was as if it was finally revealing its purpose to her without ever saying a word.

Surprised, Margarete found herself abruptly swinging her legs over the wooden bed frame, sharply scraping her left thigh. She hissed at the pain, rubbed the scratch, felt the moistness on her hand. She wiped the blood into her thin sleeping garment. Then, in her haste to move, she banged her arm against the post and an exposed nail tore into her, the pain like a harsh grip she couldn't escape. It seemed to urge her forward.

She was hurried along, inhaled deeply, almost retched at the horrible stench in the room.

It was the reality of the situation that rushed back at her, full force, fully intent on awakening her from her imaginations. Margarete stumbled forward, faster and faster, clenched her jaw, fighting against acknowledging what was all around her.

Too many women were crowded into the space; too many were showing up each week. She remembered how it used to be, one to a bed. Soon there would be three to a bed, if a bed was even to be had. The coffee was getting weaker. Breakfast was the only real meal of the day; it got them going for the work ahead of them, but lately it had been only soup for lunch and dinner. The soup, too, was getting to be more and more watered down as the days passed. Whenever it was time to eat, Margarete used her mind's eye to picture substantial portions, robust flavors, even seconds if she requested them. She pretended to have a full stomach, one that was packed tight with food. She saw herself pushing away from a table, unable to eat another bite.

The pain in her arm gripped her tighter, yanked her forward, her feet slapping hard and loud on the floor as she passed bunk after bunk of slumbering women. Blanka called out, concerned. "Margarete? What's going on?"

The stinging ache in her arm squeezed down, urged her onward, out through the doors, into the night. The stars overhead glittered in a way she had never noticed before, a true kaleidoscope of swirling color and magnificence. She snatched the image, held it close in her heart and mind; it was a keeper for dark nights when the clouds smothered the light of the moon, hid the heavens from her. Her freezing bare feet were hurried over the sharp gravel; she tripped, was hauled up, dragged onward.

She struggled to imagine the smell of the Linden trees, the sweet honey and lemon peel scent, the beach, presenting the toys she had made to her children.

"Open your eyes!" The voice was hard. Her arm was shaken. The gates before her parted, she was shoved forward, forced to walk down a long, dark outdoor passage.

"Sabotaging your labor!" she heard a far-off voice shout at her as she prepared to wade into the ocean.

A cold metal object was placed against the back of her head.

The sand under her feet was warm, almost hot.

She heard a seagull.

She saw a shimmering yellow-white light, beatific in its radiance.

# # #

The single gunfire shot woke all of them; they were light sleepers, probably never were asleep for very long. They moved to the center of the moonlit barracks, huddled together on the low bench that stretched the length of the room. There was confusion, questions, many were crying.

Ruth had awakened alone. She called out for Margarete, asked if anyone had seen her.

Hilda showed off her warmer, thicker robe. "I don't know what she saw the other night, but I *did* see what she was doing with those socks, why she had so much fabric left over."

Everyone started calling out for Margarete.

Blanka told them what she had seen. A despondent hush settled over the women.

In the silence, Hilda headed back to her bunk. No one looked at her.

Ruth held to her chest the small collection of dolls, bracelets and necklaces Margarete had created over the years and hidden away in her pillowcase.

Outside of the window, Ruth saw something crawling up the near-dawn sky. She stepped closer. From the camp's south wall, she saw smoke was rising. She continued to gaze, unblinking, until her vision blurred with tears.

One of the three crematorium ovens was in use.

#

NOTE: This story is based on the factual conditions of life in Ravensbrück, the largest concentration camp for women in the German Reich. Outside the gates was a long, dark passage with high walls, which was known as the shooting alley. It was there that the women were shot and then placed in the crematorium. Of the 132,000 female prisoners sent to Ravensbrück between 1939 and 1945, only 15,000 survived until liberation.

Photo of Ravensbrück barracks.

<u>Part Three: Jewelry for Triplets</u>

"Unrequited love does not die; it's only beaten down to a secret place where it hides, curled and wounded; it turns bitter and mean, and those who come after pay the price for the hurt done by the one who came before."
— Elle Newmark: *The Book of Unholy Mischief*

# # #

The man with the red hands was in a hurry to deliver the package to the Isak family.

Riding his bike furiously through the small, cramped village, he created quite a sight, was impossible not to notice. He wore the faded, shabby gray uniform tunic of a soldier but from what war, no one could determine. Oddly, his shoes were teeth-white. He clicked his bell insistently as he sped past the pedestrians, sending them scurrying. "Out of my way! Coming through! Make room!" The high-pitched ring felt like sparks that stung and caused those nearest to flinch and recoil. His eyes—the most noticeable part of his face, other than his dazzling red hands—shined blue, his thick brown hair flickered about him, flames of haste.

The townspeople assumed he was wearing crimson gloves, but when he was close enough for them to see that his uncovered fingers were scarlet, they'd gasp in alarm. Children were fascinated, adults were repulsed and curious, but the man ignored them all, intent on arriving at the home of the Isak's, delivering the twine-wrapped bundle for the triplets.

Triplets, he mused as he sped past a teenage boy, mouth agape at what he saw or thought he saw. *If you only knew,* the man with the beaming cherry-red hands thought mischievously. *You have no idea who just swept past you, or my intent, my gift, my purpose.*

The bicycle—black paint nearly completely chipped off from years of use, the aluminum dented from dozens of collisions that he always rode away from—skidded to a halt in front of the Isak's home. He tossed the bike to the ground in his eagerness to knock on the door, to feel the wood beneath his knuckles.

It had been decades since he had watched her enter and leave this property, first as a young girl, later as the caregiver to her parents, then a wife, now a mother of three. He had never lost track of her in his thoughts, not even while in the midst of the unfathomable mire of conflicts he had experienced over the years.

The door opened. Immediate disappointment; it wasn't her. Instead, a maid or nanny or servant. "Something for the triplets, for their sixteenth birthday." He thrust the package forcefully at the woman. She flinched when she saw his bright pink hands, recovered quickly, assumed it was a war wound. She managed to smile uncertainly as she accepted the shoebox-size parcel wrapped in butcher paper.

"From whom?" she asked, seeing no return address, wondering why the man's hands were so inflamed.

"From a secret admirer," he said gruffly. "From long ago. Three gifts, one for each daughter." Then he grinned, his gray teeth a muddy contrast to his bright, blue eyes. The woman glanced from the box to the man's face, couldn't pull away from him or his gaze; he had ensnared her. She started to sense something about him, something she recognized.

"Do I sign for it?" she asked, blinking, breaking the bad connection between them, for he was a bad man. She shivered suddenly, as if the temperature had just changed.

"No, accepting it is as good as a signature," he replied quickly, his hands now hidden behind his back. "Go ahead, open it now. Be sure the girls unwrap their gifts right away. After all, it is their birthday, they will be excited, and they will be eager to open presents!"

Before she could reply, he turned abruptly, reclaimed his bike, peddled it into motion, waved one red hand over his shoulder in farewell, then disappeared around the corner at the bottom of the driveway.

The woman, whose name was Cecilia, waited a moment before closing the door, glad he hadn't turned back, grateful she hadn't had to look into his eyes again. She stepped back into the house, closed the door, considered locking it, resisted the impulse. She was relieved he was off the property, hoped he would soon be out of the area. Then: *How did he know it was the girls' sixteenth birthday?*

She set the package on the table, studied it for a moment, then pulled the twine loose, tore off the paper, uncovered a box no larger than a thick novel. Inside were three small square shapes about the size of four of her fingers, each giftwrapped identically. The wrapping paper had the words *Happy Birthday* printed on it in blue letters with yellow presents secured with purple ribbons. A small card was taped to the back of each gift with one of the daughter's names on it: Anna, Brigitte, Danielle.

Curious, Cecilia held one of the packages, shook it. Something rattled. She tried the second and third with the same results.

Be sure the girls unwrap their gifts right away.

The man's words returned to her, but she dismissed them. *No need to do what he says,* she told herself. *He was an odd sort...*

Before she could complete her thought, there was a thudding sound behind her as one of the girls rushed halfway down the stairs.

"Cecilia? We heard voices. Who was at the door?" Brigitte asked, three steps from touching the first floor.

Like her identical sisters, she was a slim blonde, a distinguished-looking girl, tall, well poised with perfect posture. Her thick, fair hair was swept back in a bun, leaving more of her face exposed so her beautiful, bright, curious, expressive eyes were always front and center. That's what the Isak triplets were known for, three sets of eyes you could lose yourself in.

"A man with a gift," Cecilia said, turning and handing over the three presents. "You each have one. He said to open them right away." *I didn't mean to say that,* she thought, her unease about the whole encounter increasing.

Comparing them to one another, Brigitte looked over each package. "Who was the man?"

Cecilia shrugged. "No idea. Said the gifts were from a secret admirer."

Brigitte stomped back up the stairs, announcing to her sisters that they had each received a present. Cecilia gathered up the twine, butcher paper and box, took them to the kitchen to dispose of, wanted them out of her sight.

# # #

Earrings, a necklace, and a ring.

Once unwrapped, the triplets looked over the jewelry carefully, holding the items up to the light streaming through Brigitte's bedroom window. They traded them back and forth, wondered who *EB* was; the initials appeared somewhere on each piece.

The polished crystal and amethyst necklace was for Anna; it had a double strand of beads and was 16-inches in length. Danielle's finger ring had a purple stone in the center, and the screw-back earrings given to Brigitte had a violet-colored floral design painted on the enamel.

When they had finished passing the items around, they started to giggle.

"Who would wear this?"

"Who sent us this junk?"

"What were they thinking?"

The laugher continued, then increased once the girls put on the jewelry that had been gifted to them. They marched around the room, pretended they were in high society, their tones arrogant, their jaws locked as they mocked whomever has sent them the presents.

"Oh, *darling*, what's something ugly that we can send those silly girls?"

"How about this crummy ring? I'll pry it off my boney old finger!"

"Here! Take this necklace. It tickles the space between my sagging breasts!"

"Don't forget these god-awful, ugly earrings!"

Shrieks of laughter drew the attention of Cecilia, who started to pound on the wall until they quieted. "Girls!" she called up to them. "I'm going out to get your cake, do some errands, will be back soon. You all right by yourselves? Need anything?"

Muffled whispering, snickering. "Just a minute!" Danielle hollered.

Then, one by one, they paraded down the steps, high kicking, hands gesturing wildly.

Anna dodged her shoulders back and forth, swinging and clattering the necklace; Danielle waved her ring finger dramatically in front of her like a fan; Brigitte turned her head side to side to draw attention to her earrings. They reached the first floor, gathered around Cecilia so she could inspect their jewelry. She murmured her approval, nodding to herself.

Puzzled, Anna asked, "You *like* this junk?

"Well, it's what a woman would wear, not a teenager, but it's not bad," she said.

"Worth anything?" Brigitte asked, pulling off one earring, looking at it with renewed interest.

"You'd have to get them appraised. I just did that with my grandmother's jewelry when she passed away. Some of it had a little value, most of it had *none*." Cecilia smiled. "You mother might be home before me, so be sure to show her what you've received; maybe she knows where it came from, who sent it."

"It really *is* a mystery, isn't it?" Danielle said, grimacing as she twisted the ring around her finger to remove it. It seemed to have become smaller.

After Cecilia left, the girls tromped back upstairs, each to her room.

Brigitte flopped on her bed, both earrings attached, to read the latest Nancy Drew mystery, *The Clue in the Old Album.*

Anna closed the door to her room. She planned to write in her diary, wanted privacy. She fingered the crystal beads on the necklace with one hand as she opened her journal, composing a thought in her mind.

As usual, Danielle immediately put on Frank Sinatra. Brigitte and Anna immediately yelled at her to turn it down, close her door. The door slammed. Danielle sat at her desk while Sinatra crooned, circling the ring around and around her now slightly inflamed finger joint. It didn't seem to want to come off.

Brigitte's ears were tingling a bit, felt itchy. She tried to focus on the book but couldn't stop scratching and rubbing the sides of her head. Slowly she became aware that Sinatra's voice was only a far-off, fading muffle; she could barely hear the words to "I Don't Stand a Ghost of a Chance with You."

#

Anna wasn't able to write in her diary, distracted by the necklace, which seemed to have grown heavier the longer she wore it; now it was cutting into the nape of her blouse. She reached behind to unhook it, fumbled about, couldn't engage the clasp, kept trying. She'd done this hundreds of times before; what was so difficult about it now? She quickly grew frustrated with the effort, thought she'd yank it off but didn't want to destroy the gift. She tried sliding the necklace around so the catch was in front but it seemed to be snagged on her collar, wouldn't budge.

"Ugh!" she grunted with impatience, out of breath, panting. Her hands were trembling, her breathing was labored, she couldn't get enough air into her lungs. She took a moment, forced herself to calm down. Her attempts at removing the necklace had made a mess of things; the beads were all twisted into one mass. *They had real heft now*, Anna thought, alarmed. *Could almost be a weapon...*

She hadn't even finished that thought when she watched in disbelief as the baubles rose up, then bounced back hard against her chest several times as if they were a door knocker. She screamed, stood up from the desk, arms over her breasts protecting them. Dizziness swarmed, her legs buckled under the now impossible weight of the jewelry. She fell to her knees; it was as if someone had tugged violently on the necklace, had yanked her to the ground. She collapsed onto her back, making a solid thud on the bedroom floor.

The heavy bulk on her chest immobilized her; sobbing made it even harder to breath. She called out to her sisters for help. Danielle's room was on one side, but with the music so loud, she'd never hear. Anna managed to stretch her arms behind her, reached out to weakly pound on the wall that separated her from her sister,

Brigitte. It was Brigitte who always read, always wanted the house silent. Brigitte would hear her, she'd come immediately.

Anna kept hitting the baseboard with her open palm, managed to keep it up for almost a minute until her breath gave out and then her chest and lungs collapsed under the weight of the necklace. And then her heart stopped.

# # #

Brigitte couldn't remove either earring; they felt like they were living things that had clamped on to her earlobes and were preparing to chew them off. It even hurt to touch them; they generated heat, and the burning intensified, as did the terrible itching.

In addition to the scalding pain, every sound around her was being squeezed out of existence, replaced with an awful, hollow silence. After being muffled and then quickly buried, Frank Sinatra's voice from the next room now seemed to be permanently hushed. There was only a low, distinct hum from within Brigitte's head, as if dozens of insects were eating their way into her brain, chewing up her eardrums. She had learned in science class that without a functioning inner ear, she would not only lose her hearing, she'd lose almost all of her ability for balance.

She attempted to climb off the bed, to stand, leave the room, get help. Instead, she fell at once as if she had no legs. The book she had been reading thumped hard on the back of her thighs, a painful slap. In an attempt to stop the relentless, flaring pain, she scraped at the sides of her head. Her hands came away wet, deep red with the streams of blood that were now emptying out of her ears. Like an unplugged drain, the fluids continued to flow.

Within minutes, the room went gray, then dark. And then pitch black.

All of Danielle's fingers were inflamed and puckering; it was as if the ring had infected anything she touched. Her hands were becoming twisted, unrecognizable lumps of flesh. It was happening so quickly but she couldn't help herself from twisting and pulling at the ring, believing if she could only remove it, her hands would return to normal. But it was hopeless, she needed help.

She backed abruptly away from her desk, but in her haste, caught her leg on the chair. It clattered to the floor. The needle skipped on the record but kept playing, Sinatra kept singing, *"You might discover that I'm the lover meant for you..."*

Danielle lunged for the closed bedroom door, her arms held in front of her like the freshly scrubbed hands of a surgeon. When she reached for the doorknob, her grip had all the strength of wood ash. Her fist disintegrated into itself, the finger bones parted from one another, rattled on the floor. She howled in agony. Without thinking, she grabbed with the other hand. Same result. The bones and the ring clattered to the floor, soon followed by Danielle, whose body slumped against the door.

It took almost fifteen minutes until the stubs at the end of her wrists stopped spurting blood and tissue. She flailed about on the floor, weeping and moaning as she bled out. And then she was perfectly still.

Stefanie Isak returned home before Cecilia. The door clattered closed behind her with the help of her hip. Her arms contained two bags, last minute presents for the triplet's birthday.

"I'm home!" she called out. She glanced at the note Cecilia had left. "Girls?"

No response. Usually there was a crash of doors opening and the triplets bounding down the stairs as one. *Whoever said girls were quieter than boys never raised female teenage triplets,* Stefanie thought, as she often did. She separated the gifts into three piles on the table, put away the shopping bags. From upstairs, she could hear Sinatra singing behind Danielle's closed door. "Does it always have to be so *loud*?" Stefanie said to the ceiling, glad that she had purchased headphones for Danielle, wished she'd thought of it months ago.

"Hello? Anyone? Your mother's home!" She slapped her hand on the wall repeatedly. Usually, the music would stop. It continued. What were they doing up there? All in Danielle's room, making themselves *deaf*?

Stefanie sighed, started up the stairs. On the second floor, she was surprised to see all three bedroom doors closed.

"Brigitte?" She knocked several times.

# # #

NOTE: Stefanie Isak was the life-long, unrequited love of Adolf Hitler, and while her maiden name Isak sounds Jewish, she was not. Hitler first saw her in the spring of 1905 when he was 16-years-old and she passed him during her daily stroll. Although he claimed to have fallen madly in love, he never once spoke to her. In 1908, when he heard that she was engaged, he was infuriated, was said to be suicidal. He moved to Vienna where he lived a desperate, homeless life for several years.

Stefanie Isak in 1907.

On April 29, 1945—after more than a dozen years as his secret mistress—Eva Braun married Adolf Hitler; they committed suicide less than 40 hours later. Eva's jewelry box was among the items in the bunker where their bodies were found. It contained seven items that Hitler had purchased for her, including earrings, a necklace, and a ring.

END

Other HellBound Books Titles
Available at: www.hellboundbookspublishing.com

Shopping List

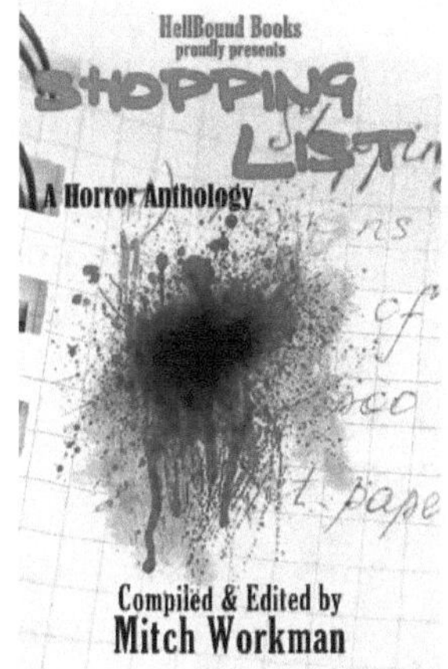

A simply superlative collection of spine-tingling horror from the very best minds in the business!

We decided upon the shopping list theme for this particular volume as an antithesis to those wildly successful writers (they know who they are) of whom it is often said *'we would read their damned shopping list if they published it!'*

Well, we have given twenty-one of the hottest authors in the independent horror scene the unique opportunity to have their own shopping lists read by you - along with their most terrifying tales of course!

Stories of gut-wrenching terror from:
Kathy Dinisi, Robert Over, Christopher O'Halloran, Eric W. Burgin, Russ Gartz, Mark Slada, Jeff Baker, Tim Miller, Nick Swain,JC Raye, Jovan Jones, Ben Stevens, David F. Gray, Brandon Cracraft, M.S. Swift, Kevin Holton, David Owain Hughes, Bertram Allan Mullin, Jeff C. Stevenson, Sebastian Crow and S.E. Rise

Demons, Devils and Denizens of Hell Vol, 2

The second volume in HellBound Books' outstanding horror anthology fair teems with tales of Hades' finest citizens – both resident and vacationing in our earthly realm… -

Compiled by the inimitable P. Mattern and featuring: Savannah Morgan, Andrew MacKay, Jaap Boekestein, James H Longmore, Stephanie Kelley, Ryan Woods, James Nichols, P. Mattern, Marcus Mattern, Gerri R Gray, and legion more…

The Big Book of Bootleg Horror 2

The second volume in HellBound Books' flagship horror anthology - this one bursting at the seams with even more fantastically dark horror from the cream of the rising stars in today's horror scene!

Featuring: Tracey A. Cross, Elizabeth Zemlicka, Shelby Thomas, Matthew Gillies, Spinster Eskie, Stephen Clements, Ken Goldman, Nathan Robinson, K.M. Campbell, Cody Grady, Sebastian Bendix, Leo X. Robertson, David Owain Hughes, Timothy McGivney, Kane Gordon, Todd Sullivan, Mike Mayak, Edward Ahern, Rose Garnett, Jaap Boekestein, Brandy Delight, Stanley B. Webb, D. Norfolk, and Thomas Gunther.

The Big Book of Bootleg Horror 3:
By Invitation Only

A very, very special edition of our anthology series - proceeds going to the awesome Alzheimer's charity *'Hilarity for Charity'*.

Only invited authors are featured - some of the biggest names in today's horror scene!

Contributing Authors:
Jack Ketchum, Michael Bray, Jeff Strand, Chad Lutzke, Eddie Generous, Lance Tuck, Wade H. Garrett, Richard Chizmar and Billy Chizmar, James H Longmore, Jaap Boekestein, Iain Rob Wright, Michael McBride, Edward Lee, David Owain Hughes, Ray Garton & Benjamin Blake

Them

Ray Sanders returns home from Florida to bury his mother.

Soon, the supernatural evidence behind his mother's demise begins to surface in the form of dreams and mysterious happenings.

During all of the madness, Sanders must face his destiny and vanquish the generations-old evil that has plagued his family since the 1800's...

In 1854, Louis Sanders, with the help of Elias Atkins, dug a well to provide water to the family farm. What they did not anticipate was the water to be infested with Odomulites - ancient sins. These malevolent beings - were trapped in our world on their way to the spirit world - formed a pact of protection with both Sanders and Atkins; the families would serve as guardians of the Odomulite nests and in return, a blind eye would be cast when the Odomulites took host bodies to inhabit and feed upon.

It was this pact, which in 2016 would propel Sanders and Julie Fontaine - a young woman with a special connection to the Spirit World - into the heart of the last active nest to rid the town of its insidious Odomulite population.

The Waning

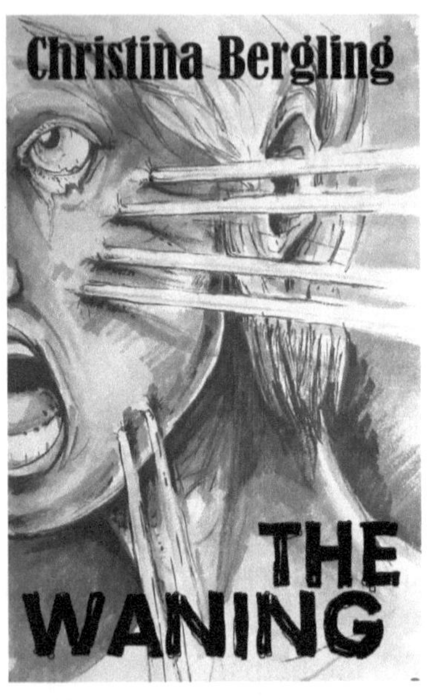

Beatrix woke up in a small metal cage, Lost in the darkness, a persistent dripping sound her only company.

She was celebrating a promotion that was the culmination of her entire ruthless, driven career; a promotion that would cement her status enough for her to take her relationship with her girlfriend out of the lesbian closet; Beatrix had finally made it.

And then she was here, disoriented and petrified in a blackness she could not define. Yet the reality of her Master may be even more terrifying than the crushing darkness and enveloping isolation. He appears as an ominous shadow in the doorway of her cell, never speaking. Instead, he teaches Beatrix the language of pain and torture, of submission and obedience, of domination and possession

With each passing day, the fight and hope in Beatrix begins to shrivel and wane. With each savage beating, her survivalist instincts rise up to overwhelm the person she was. With each dehumanizing condition, she begins to forget who she was and the life from which she was ripped.

Can Beatrix ward off the psychological breakdown of her Master? Can she resist the temptation to survive and thrive through submission? Either Beatrix will succeed at surviving and escaping the torments of her Master or her Master will succeed at breaking her completely and reforming her into his design for a human possession…

The Pleasure Hunt

After meeting the mysterious *Dark Dance* on the casual encounters website, The Pleasure Hunters Club, *Sexy Cupid* finds himself enchanted by a enigmatic seductress – *Dark Dance*.

After experiencing bizarre, nightmarish visions during their first physical liaison, *Cupid* awakes on a bench somewhere in Louisville, unable to get the mystifying creature off his mind. As he begins to search both online and through the seedy streets of the city for her, he uncovers harrowing truths about the object of his obsession, truths which fill him with both indomitable dread and inexplicable love for her.

By the time *Cupid* begins to understand the terror he faces, the shackles on his soul are already too tight as the ancient monster has her talons dug well into his flesh.

Every time he is swept away to her world of Theia - the Moon Realm - she extracts and devours yet another piece of his very essence, and despite the merciless torment of his encounters with his obsession - and the warnings of, a menacing stranger - he presses on to find her, dragging himself deeper into her darkened realm.

Cupid soon finds that he may have but one opportunity to escape the demonic *Dark Dance*, but the bewitchment she has cast upon his heart may deter him from making a stand; with his soul about to slip down the gullet of the beast, *Cupid* has to make a decision before he is forever wrapped in the wicked thaumaturge's wings of eternal damnation.

Man Eating F**ckers

The eagerly awaited sequel to Hughes' critically acclaimed *Man Eating Fks*...**

Two years on from her nightmarish descent into the woods, Storm is piecing her life back together, but trouble is forming...

A new threat is rising - one that promises to grip, shake and spin Storm's world out of control. But that's not all, as a 'friend' and sympathizer also poses a risk from the shadows, combined with a face from the past...

With the cannibals lurking in the background, waiting for an opportunity to deal white-hot vengeance, can father and daughter survive?

**** Features a bonus short story that continues the cannibalistic saga...**

Blood and Kisses

The definitive short story collecting from James H Longmore - an eclectic mix of dark horror, bizarro and Twilight-Zone style tales of the downright disturbing.

Welcome to the long awaited collection from the writer of horror novels *'Pede* and *Tenebrion*; a foreword by Richard Chizmar (co-author of *Gwendy's Button Box* and author of *A Long December*), 18 short stories, 5 flash fiction and even a poem - all skin-crawling, soul-shredding tales of terror, of the darkest things that skulk amongst the night's inky shadows, and of the everyday gone horribly awry.

Discover the alternative implication of technology becoming self-aware, enjoy the acquaintance of a charismatic new pastor who promises his flock a brand new place in which to worship his God, and spend a little time in the company of a nice young man who is inexorably caught up in his home town's terrible secret. Then there is Cupid's revelation that personally he has never experienced love, yet we discover that very emotion alive and not so well amongst the ruins of a post zombie apocalypse world, and we bear witness to a childhood innocence forever destroyed in a war-torn city.   There is more, Dear Reader, much, much more; for within these pages we have devils, demons and ghosts, lycanthropes and demi-gods, all rubbing nefarious shoulders with vilest of Hell's offspring who have slithered from the netherworld to doff their caps and wish us all the sweetest of dreams…

**A HellBound Books LLC
Publication**

www.hellboundbookspublishing.com

Printed in the United States of America

www.ingramcontent.com/pod-product-compliance
Lightning Source LLC
Chambersburg PA
CBHW050608170726
48283CB00001B/151